PRAISE FO...
GLACIE...

The Weight of Night

"There are stunning descriptions of rampaging forest fires, majestic mountain ranges and violent storms in *The Weight of Night* . . . It's in depicting nature's drama that Carbo's writing thrives."

—Marilyn Stasio, *The New York Times Book Review*

"Engrossing . . . an intricate plot complements the compelling characters."

—*Publishers Weekly*

"Carbo creates a vivid setting and strong characters, as well as a stunning mystery. Fans of page-turning suspense will find this book impossible to put down."

—*RT Book Reviews*

"Carbo extols the beauty of her setting and provides sensitive character development."

—*Booklist*

Mortal Fall

"Compulsively readable."

—*Publishers Weekly*

"If *Mortal Fall* were just a beautifully written, sharp-eyed procedural, that would be reason enough to read it. But Christine Carbo offers so much more in this fine second novel. It's a study of flawed, compelling characters and the ghosts that haunt them. It's also a fascinating look at the relationship of humans with the too-rapidly changing landscape of Glacier Park. And finally, it's the tragic story of the forces that can shatter a family. This novel works on so many levels, all of them masterfully crafted."

—William Kent Krueger, *New York Times* bestselling author

"Carbo paints a moving picture of complex, flawed people fighting to make their way in a wilderness where little is black or white, except the smoky chiaroscuro of the sweeping Montana sky."

—*Publishers Weekly*

"*Mortal Fall* is a terrific read. With a masterful hand, Christine Carbo guides her readers through an intriguing mystery full of complex relationships and smartly developed characters. Her rich descriptions immerse you in the grandeur of Glacier National Forest as this riveting story unfolds. Christine Carbo should be a part of every mystery lover's personal library."

—Allen Eskens, author of *The Guise of Another*

"Carbo brings subtlety and sensitivity to the smallest of moments."

—*Booklist*

The Wild Inside

"Stays in your mind long after you've put the book down. I'm still thinking about it. Prepare to run the gamut of emotions with this fine treat of a story. Then, in the years ahead, be on the lookout for more from this fresh new voice in the thriller genre."

—Steve Berry, *New York Times* bestselling author of the Cotton Malone series

"Grizzly bears, murder, mauling, and mayhem mix in Carbo's debut novel. Ted Systead's past and present intersect in an unexpected—and chilling—manner against the incongruously gorgeous backdrop of Glacier National Park."

—*Kirkus Reviews*

"The brutality and fragility of Glacier National Park's wilderness provides the perfect backdrop for this well-crafted, absorbing novel about the barbarities and kindnesses of the humans living on its edge. Christine Carbo is a writer to watch."

—Tawni O'Dell, *New York Times* bestselling author

"An intense and thoroughly enjoyable thrill ride. Christine Carbo's literary voice echoes with her love of nature, her knowledge of its brutality, and the wild and beautiful locale of Montana. *The Wild Inside* is a tour de force of suspense that will leave you breathlessly turning the pages late into the night."

—Linda Castillo, *New York Times* bestselling author

"Fans of Nevada Barr will love this tense, atmospheric thriller with its majestic Glacier National Park setting. *The Wild Inside* is a stunning debut!"

—Deborah Crombie, *New York Times* bestselling author

ALSO BY CHRISTINE CARBO

The Weight of Night
Mortal Fall
The Wild Inside

A
SHARP
SOLITUDE

A NOVEL OF SUSPENSE

CHRISTINE CARBO

ATRIA PAPERBACK

New York • London • Toronto • Sydney • New Delhi

ATRIA
PAPERBACK

An Imprint of Simon & Schuster, Inc.
1230 Avenue of the Americas
New York, NY 10020

First Atria Paperback edition May 2018

ATRIA PAPERBACK and colophon are trademarks of Simon & Schuster, Inc.

For information about special discounts for bulk purchases, please contact Simon & Schuster Special Sales at 1-866-506-1949 or business@simonandschuster.com.

The Simon & Schuster Speakers Bureau can bring authors to your live event. For more information, or to book an event, contact the Simon & Schuster Speakers Bureau at 1-866-248-3049 or visit our website at www.simonspeakers.com.

Manufactured in the United States of America

10 9 8 7 6 5 4 3 2 1

Library of Congress Cataloging-in-Publication Data

Names: Carbo, Christine, author.
Title: A sharp solitude : a novel of suspense / Christine Carbo.
Description: First Atria Paperback edition. | New York : Atria Books, 2018.
Identifiers: LCCN 2017055765| ISBN 9781501156335 (paperback) | ISBN 9781501156342 (ebook)
Subjects: LCSH: Glacier National Park (Mont.)—Fiction. | BISAC: FICTION / Crime. | FICTION / Suspense. | FICTION / Mystery & Detective / General. | GSAFD: Suspense fiction. | Mystery fiction.
Classification: LCC PS3603.A726 S53 2018 | DDC 813/.6—dc23
LC record available at https://lccn.loc.gov/2017055765

ISBN 978-1-5011-5633-5
ISBN 978-1-5011-5634-2 (ebook)

For Caroline and Lexie,
both 2018 graduates.
Congratulations!

Solitude is the playfield of Satan.

—VLADIMIR NABOKOV

Ali

—

Present—Thursday

I IMAGINE IT LIKE this: the two nine-year-old boys, Reeve and his friend Sam, lounge lazily on the couch watching the Cartoon Network at home in Reeve's parents' ranch-style single-story home on a hot summer day in Tallahassee, Florida. Reeve's mom and dad are both at work—his mom cutting hair at a local salon called Sasha's and his dad selling beds at the Mattress Firm. The blinds are pulled down to block the afternoon sun, and harsh spears of light stab between the slits in the darkened living room. They've eaten an entire bag of Doritos when Sam sits up straight and turns to Reeve. "Let's *do* something," he says. "These shows are *so* boring."

"Whaddya want to do?" Reeve asks.

"I don't know. Anything."

"Want to go outside?"

"Too hot," Sam groans.

Reeve pries himself away from the couch cushion and sits forward, wiping his Dorito-stained fingers on the side of his shorts. "I wish it was already my birthday," Reeve says, thinking of the day just a few weeks away, August seventh.

"Me too. You gonna have a party?"

"Probably. I think my parents got me a Nintendo."

"No way," Sam says.

"I swear."

"Yeah? Where is it?"

"I don't know."

1

"Where would they hide it?" Sam asks.

"I don't know." Reeve shrugs. "Probably in their bedroom."

A mischievous expression brightens Sam's face—one familiar to Reeve. It's one he's seen many times, the product of their age—two nine-year-old boys eager to explore. Once when they were playing by a creek, Sam found some old shark's teeth mixed up in the gravel, and after they'd plucked them all out and put them in a plastic bag they'd gotten from Sam's mom, Sam wanted to find more. He insisted they cross the creek to the other side. But Reeve knew water moccasins nested in that part of the stream where it was deep and cool from lush ferns draping over the water. "I don't think we should," Reeve said. Reeve was a cautious boy. Nobody would have ever described him as a daredevil. But Sam—he didn't mind taking risks. "See you on the other side, scaredy-cat," he had called as he took off his sneakers and fearlessly waded into the water.

"Let's look," Sam says, getting off the couch, wearing the same expression as the time he crossed the shadowy creek.

"No, my mom and dad said I can't go in their room."

"Oh, come on." He runs out of the family room, down the hallway to the master bedroom. Reeve hops off the couch and follows, worried only about the transgression of going into his parents' room for maybe a second.

The room is dim like the TV room, the stiff green curtains drawn, also to block out the August sun. The king-size bed is made with a stiff, gaudy floral-print bedspread perfectly smooth and neatly creased in all four corners.

Sam opens Reeve's parents' closet doors first and searches the floor, crouching down and shoving shoes aside to look into the corners. Then he stands and lifts his head to eye the upper shelf that he can't reach. He jumps up to see if he can get high enough to peer over the top and to the sides to spy a box big enough to hold a Nintendo.

Reeve opens drawers by the bed, but sees nothing but papers and envelopes containing Polaroid family photos, school portraits of him and his younger sister, progress reports from their elementary school, and other miscellaneous papers and special certificates. Sam comes over and torpedoes himself onto the bed, stands, and begins hopping on it. Reeve laughs and joins him—two giggling boys caught up in the giddiness of being in a forbidden place. They bounce as if it's a trampoline, the springs of the mattress squeaking, protesting with each landing, the bedspread no longer perfect.

"What about in that chest?" Sam points to the base of the bed.

"Nah, she doesn't usually put anything in there except clothes."

Sam launches himself off the mattress and lands with a thump on the floor. He flings an afghan folded across the wooden chest onto the now-rumpled bedspread, lifts the lid, and peers in. "Not in here," he says, moving its contents around with his free arm. "Just a blanket and bunch of old sweaters."

"Told ya." Reeve hops off too, his cheeks hot and flushed from the jumping. He kneels down to look under the bed, lifting the skirt. White stringy strands worn free from under the lining of the mattress box drape down like webbing made from a huge spider. Reeve blows at them, but they fall right back into place, so he moves them aside with his hand.

"Whoa," Reeve says when he spots the rifle. He's seen it only once before. He'd been out playing in the neighborhood when several other kids spotted a rattlesnake curled up in a cement drainage ditch at the end of the cul-de-sac. Word spread, and everyone in the neighborhood gathered around while his father came out to take a look. His dad told the kids and other neighbors who'd gathered to stay away from the ditch until he returned. When he did, he carried the gun, walked over with purpose, instructed all the other parents to keep their kids back, but when he looked down into the ditch, there was nothing but moss and twigs. The snake had slithered away into the brush.

"Wow!" Sam says, walking over to Reeve, who's kneeling beside the bed and holding the rifle across his thighs. The barrel is shiny smooth, its heft intimidating but stealth-like, and Reeve is excited to show Sam

that he's not always a bore. For a second, Reeve thinks he shouldn't
have pulled it out from under the bed, but it's as tempting as shark's
teeth and Sam would have grabbed it if he hadn't. "Cool," Sam says.

"I know." Reeve breathes hard with excitement, the back of his
neck slick with sweat. He's sure the gun is not loaded, and in one quick
motion, he stands and lifts the rifle to take aim at . . . at . . . he's not
sure what, maybe the chair in the corner of the room, maybe the curtains. He barely feels his finger on the trigger when a deafening boom
blasts his ears—the report so explosive and the kick so violent that he
thinks that he's just launched himself into something vast, like the sky
or outer space. And that's where he remains—tumbling through that
empty void, never really landing—for a very long time.

. . .

I also imagine the six-foot diameter spatter of reddish-brown blood
because he fired a .30-06 caliber rifle. The force of it at close range is
quite destructive and would blow a ragged hole through the victim,
typically shattering bone and tissue. There would have been spatter on
the wall, the carpet, and the bed. The bullet tore through the victim's
shoulder, blew through his heart and lodged into the wall behind them,
so there would have been a hole about the size of a pea in the plaster.

The boy—the shooter—attempted to stop the flow of blood by putting his hands over the wound, so ugly smears would stretch across
both the victim's and the shooter's clothes. He also tried to give mouth-
to-mouth resuscitation to the victim, which he'd apparently learned
about in school just months before, so his DNA could be easily collected from the victim's mouth if they'd needed it, but they didn't because the boy admitted everything.

Bloodstains as well as the spatter would also be on the bedside
table and phone because the boy called 911 and frantically said, "I've
shot my best friend. My best friend is dead. I didn't know my dad's gun
was loaded." He shouted this in a guttural panic that was recorded by
the 911 emergency service operator and would later be played over

and over by the press in the aftermath of the gun-control debates that eventually ensued across the state.

I always consider details like this since I'm trained to look at the particulars. I used to work in the bustling Newark field office until I was transferred to a resident agency, a smaller office with only one or two agents that have jurisdiction over an area, usually someplace more rural. For an agent, the best way to gain experience is to work in a variety of settings, even if it means moving across the country to the remote resident office in Kalispell, Montana.

I miss the city, but I don't mind Montana. I remember seeing the great spine of the Rockies for the first time when I drove across the eastern plains from Newark toward the Continental Divide. I'll admit I was a little freaked out at the sight of bleak fields the color of camel hair stretching into oblivion; the glimpses of old long-abandoned cabins and wood barns buckling and decomposing onto the bare ground; the rain blowing horizontally against the ribs of horses and cows; the Blackfoot Indian town of Browning settled in the high plains like an oversize, unkempt Easter basket with its turquoise, pink, and yellow ramshackle houses—as if colorful paint were all it took to lift one out of poverty. Stray dogs ran amuck, and I couldn't tell if they were neglected or if they were contented community pets wandering around and being fed by local business owners and residents. It gave me an unsettled feeling—that the new life I was stepping into was unprotected, not propped up by the busy cacophony of city life.

But when I glimpsed the Great Divide, the way the mountains heaved out of the brown prairies toward the expansive sky both warned and comforted me. I'd never seen anything like it, anything so stunning and dramatic, so separate from my sense of everyday city life. Is this why people went west, because the mountains bucking up to kiss the expansive sky made you feel as if you could have a fresh start or reach your highest dreams? Maybe, I had thought, I could grow accustomed to a place with such striking scenery, a place with buildings no higher than two stories and people with unsuspicious eyes.

It was in Montana that I met that nine-year-old shooter, Reeve Landon, when he was twenty-nine and I was twenty-eight, and he had suspicious eyes. We began dating, and when I brought up the incident, he said, "I figured you'd find out. Not because you're FBI, but because anyone googling my name *would* find out. It's not really a secret. I just don't like to bring it up every time I meet someone." Reeve then recounted to me the incident that made him one of the unlucky children whose tragedies altered Florida's gun laws in the late 1980s.

Ten months later—a year and a half after I had moved west—over coffee in a Starbucks, he told me he couldn't do it any longer, *it* referring to our blossoming relationship. He'd been thinking about it for weeks. "I'm sorry," he had said. "I just can't, Ali. I thought I could, but I'm not sure I'll ever be able to." He never said it had anything to do with what happened all those years ago, but I have a good imagination and I find myself going back to it—running my mind over and over the story like a cloth polishing silver to make it shine clearly in my mind.

The baby, though—that was a surprise. I found out I was pregnant three weeks after Reeve told me he couldn't see me any longer. We had used birth control, but it failed. I kept it from him for a time. I was at my wit's end when I found out. It felt like I was being swept away by powerful currents spinning me around and around. I even thought about ending it at first, but I was twenty-nine and had already been bitten by the bug. I'd been thinking of being a mother since my mid-twenties. I considered having the baby without ever telling him.

But then I thought about how hard it was not having a dad present in my own life. Having an absent parent can take a toll on you. I used to waste so much time fantasizing about my father's turning things around and driving up at any minute, like a prince, to rescue me. Every summer, when the other kids were heading to the Jersey Shore with their moms and dads, I desperately wanted him to show up with his smile and his dark unruly hair and say, "Hop in, chickadee. I'm all better now. Let's go to the beach." I'd wait every year on my birthday for him to arrive with a cake and presents as if I were starring in a cheesy

movie, a lonely child sitting patiently on a curb in front of her apartment building. When I didn't even get a card, my heart closed up a
little further like a dying daisy, knowing deep down that he'd never
change and that actually having him in our lives would be so much
worse, with the chronic yelling and fighting.

I decided that I could not deny the child growing inside me a
father. Reeve may have a few issues, but he's not abusive or volatile,
so I told him about the pregnancy. He was shocked, but had enough
sense not to try to talk me out of going through with it. He offered to
marry me, but the suggestion seemed pathetic—an offer he made over
greasy burgers and fries while we sat in a cheap restaurant with Kenny
Chesney playing in the background. Deep down, I knew it could never
work, even though I deeply wanted it to, so I said no thanks and we
worked out a plan. Turns out, fear can be greater than desire.

My daughter's arrival the following spring, a perfect bundle of
beauty with a tiny head of fine, dark hair, compelled us to figure out
a parenting plan on our own terms without legal assistance. I picked
her name, Emily, and we decided that when she got old enough, Reeve
would take her every other weekend, and I'd have her the rest of the
time. We also agreed that Emily would keep my surname and he'd con-
tribute what he could, when he could. I never cared about the money,
though, and so far he's been pretty consistent, sending me a check
every month. No paperwork or lawyers necessary. We never went
through the nastiness that some couples go through when their relationship collapses. It was almost like we both knew we wouldn't last,
and at the slightest provocation, we quickly assumed cordial, cooperative attitudes. Both of us probably thought we couldn't get too hurt if
we kept things businesslike.

Now we rarely speak other than to discuss Emily or her schedule or
when I see him to either drop her off or pick her up from his place. It's
possible to get over your attraction to someone; it just takes time and
the ability to move the feelings to the corner of your mind, where they
pop up only occasionally, similar to old acquaintances at the grocery

store, sometimes welcome, sometimes not. It's not ideal—coparenting never is—but Emily, who is five now, loves to spend time with her daddy and his dog, McKay.

So when I get the call from Reeve on a chilly early November day, I assume it has something to do with Emily, that he needs to reschedule his weekend with her for a work excursion, which irritates me because I know if he misses the little time he has with Emily, she'll be sad. But the second I hear his voice, I sense something is up, because he sounds a little breathless and worried.

"What's up?" I ask, sitting at my desk in my office in Kalispell. The day is cloudy and dim, so I have my desk lamp on and it's exposing every bit of dust on the black chrome-framed furniture even though I dust the damn thing all the time.

"Ali," he says after clearing his throat, "I need your help."

Help? Reeve Landon doesn't ask for help any more than I do, so I pause before saying more.

"Ali," he says again, his voice slightly rising, a trace of worry in the pitch of it, which is also unusual. "You still there?"

"I'm here. What kind of help?"

"I need you to go to my place. I need you to get McKay and take care of him for a few hours. Just until I can sort out a few things. I'd ask Wallace, but he's just left for the winter."

Now I know it's serious. Reeve rarely parts with his dog. He's worked with McKay for at least five years as part of a detection-canine program that performs conservation and biological research. Apparently there is a lot you can learn from the poop animals leave behind. It didn't take me long to understand—a few months after we began seeing each other—that the program and the dog are lifelines for Reeve. I get that. I've got a few of those myself, mainly Emily and my job.

The training is an ongoing process, Reeve has said more times than I can count, especially when he's making excuses for why he can't be there for Emily. According to Reeve, he's the only one who understands how to keep the dog on a schedule. He's taught Emily a little, but she's too young to understand much.

"Watch McKay? Why? Where are you?"

Reeve doesn't answer at first, and silence hangs between us on the line.

"Reeve," I press. "Where are you? Whose line are you using?"

"I'm at the county building, at the sheriff's office. I'm using one of their landlines. I don't know how long I'll be here."

"*How long you'll be there?* What's going on?"

"I don't know. I think they think I've done something. . . . I've already been here for four hours. They've been questioning me—making me go over the same information over and over, but mostly I've been doing a lot of sitting and waiting. They're inspecting my phone, so I had to use theirs to call to you, but look, I have to go. The officer wants me to hang up now."

"Wait," I say. "They're looking at your phone?"

"They asked to see it."

"What are they saying you've done?"

"I'm not sure," he says. "But whatever they think, it's not true."

"What's not true?"

"I don't know. That I've got something to do with whatever is up with that journalist."

"What journalist?"

He pauses, then sighs. "I'm not positive, but I think something happened to her, and whatever it is, they think I'm involved."

The sense of something icy, like a cold hand, presses against my neck and moves down my spine.

"Listen, Ali, the spare key to my cabin is under the tin can in the back." And just like that, he's gone, the line blank.

Reeve

Wednesday—The Day Before

THE HYPNOSIS CREATED by the vastness of the Montana sky and the mountains loosens its grip on me today because I am not working alone for the first time in a very long while. A reporter named Anne Marie Johnson, who's doing a story for *Sierra* magazine, is hiking with me up a dried-out creek drainage about ten miles outside Glacier National Park.

McKay, my dog, is weaving through the underbrush about twenty yards ahead of us, poking his nose into shrubbery and leaping over fallen logs. Like a metronome, his tail whips back and forth, which tells me there's scat close by, but I won't be sure which kind until we reach it. Mainly we're looking for grizzly droppings, but McKay is also trained in a dozen other species, from bats to wolverines. He can search for just about any scat made by a carnivore: black bear, grizzly bear, lynx, wolf, bobcat, coyote, and mountain lion. I'll send any sample he sniffs out to the university, where scientists will extract hormones and DNA to gather clues on the size of their population in the area, their distribution over the landscape, the areas they share, their levels of stress, indications that they're being poisoned, their mating habits and pregnancies, their lineage, their use of the resources, and many more factors.

"So you think there's some scat nearby?" Anne Marie asks me.

Anne Marie is writing a feature story on the University of Montana's detection-canine research program and has asked to tag along. I met her at the Polebridge Mercantile, a bakery/store combo that serves as a link to civilization in a township with a population of about 150. I

10

was ready to sit over coffee and answer her questions because my boss, Jeffrey O'Brien, had said, *Give her what she needs to write her story. It's good press for the program.* I figured I'd do just that, then set out on my own without her.

I don't like reporters, but she insisted on coming along so she could get a few photos and really understand how the whole process works. She promised she could handle the rugged terrain, and when I met her outside the Merc, she was wearing camouflage combat pants and a tan fleece and said she'd brought bear spray, a potent form of pepper that works on bears and other predators; a lunch; and a raincoat, in case the weather turned. She wore a Grand Canyon ball cap the color of orange clay and, most importantly, she had on real hiking boots. At least she came prepared, I thought, noticing her smile—one of those unabashed, infectious ones.

"Yeah," I say. "He's onto something. Could be black bear scat. We'll see." McKay continues to quarter back and forth through the brush, always within earshot, until he abruptly stops, his entire body stiffening except his tail, which spins rapidly in circles. "Whaddya got?" I ask him.

We walk closer, and I see he's frozen with his nose pointing at a pile that looks like dried-out batter for some bran muffins. I kneel on one knee and hold up my palm for him to wait, to settle down. He's anticipating the one thing he cares about more than anything in the world besides my daughter, Emily—a red rubber ball the size of a tennis ball, his reward for doing his job correctly. McKay licks his lips, stands erect, and quivers with excitement as I pull it from my pack and toss it for him to fetch. He leaps to go find it. It lands in a thick copse of alders with bright yellow leaves. I pull out my smartphone and begin to enter data about the sample.

"What are you recording?" Anne Marie moves closer to peer over my shoulder, and I can smell a lovely citrus scent, maybe a body wash or perfume mixed with sweat from all the climbing we've done.

"The type of animal that left the pile and how long it's been here," I answer. "In this case, a grizzly. Been here about a day. I'm also taking a GPS reading and a picture," I say, holding up my phone to snap the photo. McKay is back with his ball and shoves it at my thigh. Anne Marie backs slightly away from us. I grab the ball and throw it even farther for him, and it lands in some brush a long way out.

"He's fast," she says, laughing.

I put my phone away.

"How do you know it's a grizzly and not a black bear's scat?"

"Size, mainly. Depends on the season. In the summer, lots of berries in it. Around this time, more roots and tubers. Only a griz goes this big—scat wider than two inches in diameter—and only a griz has claws long enough to dig for roots. But it's not a perfect science," I say. "They'll know more in the lab."

She gives me that big smile again, and I can't help but notice how her eyes crinkle with mischief and a brazen joy long gone in myself. "But how does your dog find one random pile out here? In all this wilderness?" She motions to our surroundings—a drainage filled with jutting large boulders and steep hillsides choked with alder shrubs and thimbleberry and huckleberry bushes. Autumn has been rainy and gloomy so far, and this is the first sunny day in weeks. Bushes and deciduous trees have dropped gold and yellow leaves that the previous rain has papier-mâchéd to the game trails traversing the drainage.

"His sense of smell is quite good," I say—an understatement. A dog's nose is one of the most sensitive among the animal kingdom, capable of identifying cancer cells and finding illegal drugs hidden inside strong-smelling containers like gas tanks. "Most scent dogs are being trained to find evidence, drugs, bombs, or dead bodies."

When she looks down at her notepad, a piece of her dark hair falls out of one thick braid and settles in a broad-sweeping curl across her cheek. I notice a smattering of freckles across her sharp cheekbones. "Our dogs are simply trained to find the poop of certain species."

She nods, her eyes still dancing, like the information delights her. A wave of pride for McKay sweeps over me, and a joy that feels foreign spreads inside my chest. I had already explained to her that the idea came to a biologist in the late nineties after he had studied baboons and elephants in Africa and learned to extract DNA and hormones from their scat. It dawned on him that if dogs could smell ten thousand times better than humans, they could locate the samples over vast landscapes. No other wildlife sampling method can acquire so much data in such a short time without disturbing the environment.

I continue to toss the ball for McKay. I'm used to his intensity, but Anne Marie watches him closely and inches slightly away when he gets close to her legs, as if she's a little unnerved by his laser focus and his excited panting.

"Yeah," I offer, as if I'm answering a question she hasn't even posed, "he's crazed, all right. One of the more manic dogs in the program. That's what lands them in the program in the first place."

I explain to her what happened with McKay. How he's six now, but still indefatigable. As a puppy, he was given to the Humane Society because the family couldn't handle such an intense dog, one who wanted to play all the time. I picked him after the shelter called our program to alert us that he was unlikely to be adopted. He was four months old.

"Their fanaticism drives the owners crazy," I tell her. "But for us, we simply use their obsessions to our advantage. Train them to go for that goal, whatever it may be. For some, it's food or a bone. For McKay"—I wing the ball into the woods again—"it's obviously fetch. If he finds scat, he gets to play. It's that simple. A misfit in the world of pets, but perfect for science." It's not in my nature to smile, mainly because I'm alone in the woods so much, but her cheerfulness brings it out in me, and as we chat, I'm actually aware of my cheeks lifting and bulging against my will.

"Won't he slow down as he gets older?"

"Hasn't so far. But he's in great shape still."

"And you're telling me he doesn't drive you crazy?"

"No, because I wear him out on these long treks. I deplete his energy every day, unless I'm sick or injured and can't take him out. Then, yeah, it's a nightmare. Fortunately I don't get sick or injured very often."

Anne Marie studies me, only a hint of her smile still playing at the corners of her mouth. The brim of her cap shields her eyes, but I can tell she's trying to understand what kind of a person can walk the rugged Montana woods for miles almost every day of his life, poking at animal scat, with only the company of a crazy chocolate Lab.

"Sometimes," I say, "he gets so exhausted that he needs a day of rest himself." I don't tell her about the days that I try extra hard to drain his energy by taking longer, vigorous hikes right before Emily comes to visit me so that McKay will be tamer than usual around her. Nor do I tell her that being a handler is more of a lifestyle choice than a job.

I take a ziplock bag out of my pocket and put the sample in it. "Attaboy," I say to McKay. "That's it, buddy." I grab the ball and put it away, pour him some water in a foldable nylon bowl, and at first he refuses to drink in case I might still pull the ball out and throw it for him. "Drink up, buddy," I say. "Playtime's over."

He stares at me intently for a moment, then gives in and laps at the water.

I peer out at the distant slopes. The tamarack trees blaze with yellow needles, making the hillsides look from afar as if they're covered in a knitted blanket of burnt yellow and dark green. "Ready to search more?" I ask once McKay is finished drinking.

"Sure," she says, but I wonder if she's getting tired. We've already hiked about eight miles.

"You sure?" I ask.

"Positive." She sighs. "It's gorgeous out here."

I don't press her anymore because I want more samples, and she did say she could handle long-distance treks. Up ahead, there's a rocky slope at about 6,500 feet. I want to reach the summit, then circle back down. Two days ago, snow doused its top, but now the sun beats on it and its rocky serrations are bare. You never know what kind of weather you're going to get in the fall in Northwest Montana. In fact, it's impossible to live along the Continental Divide without constantly monitoring its ever-changing weather. An afternoon can easily drop from seventy degrees to forty-five with an accumulation of a few nasty clouds over the mountains.

But today there are no clouds building over the peaks. The sky and the afternoon seem to unfurl and invite us to go farther. It's delightful to see the sun, the rays strong enough at high noon to make me take off my jacket. Contentment falls upon me like an old blanket, and I feel connected to everything surrounding me. The only other time I ever feel like this is when Emily is falling asleep on my shoulder or I'm watching her descend into a giggle fit.

Anne Marie tosses her braid over her shoulder and begins to follow McKay as he leaps off into the woods again, but right as she takes her second step, she stumbles. I reach out to steady her. She flails and, just before she falls, grabs my arm at the same time I find hers, her fingernails gouging my forearm.

I manage to grab her before she goes down. "Are you all right?" I ask as she steadies herself.

"I'm fine." She looks down and inspects her legs as if she's expecting a noticeable injury, like a sprained ankle.

"Everything okay?" I double-check.

"Yeah." She looks back up at me, holding a hand up. "Just a broken nail."

I look down at my arm. One short and two longer scratches that begin to fill with blood traverse my forearm. "I can see why."

"Oh," she says when she sees the scratches and brings a hand to her mouth. "I didn't realize. . . . I'm so sorry. Here I am going on about a nail. Those scratches look like they could get infected."

"It's no big deal," I tell her. "I have ointment in my kit." I take my pack off again, pull out a rolled-up nylon pouch, and remove the tube of Neosporin. I wipe the blood with a cotton swab, apply the ointment on the scratch marks, and stick the kit back in my pack. "There," I say. "All good. You sure you're good to go on?"

"Positive," she says as I slide my pack back over my shoulders.

Ali

Present—Thursday

I STARE AT MY cell phone for a moment after Reeve hangs up. I want to call him back and tell him a few basics—mainly that unless he's under arrest, they can't hold him, and they should have informed him of that. I'm guessing they did, but most people who are questioned by cops, even if it's voluntary, feel like they can't leave until they're dismissed. Reeve can walk out at any time to go take care of McKay. But then again, I'm certain he knows this. This isn't his first rodeo. Studies show that most victims of untreated childhood trauma are practically guaranteed stints in juvie or at least some form of rehab, and Reeve followed that trajectory to a tee. Smaller events—like failing a class or getting dumped by a girlfriend or boyfriend—have sent kids spiraling out of control. Thankfully, Reeve managed to turn that all around before he ended up incarcerated as an adult.

The situation sounds serious, though. I look over at Herman, my only coworker in the Kalispell regional agency, who's sitting at his desk. A streak of light from the overheads slashes across his bald head. I call him Hollywood because he dresses to the nines, at least by Montana standards—meaning he doesn't get his suits off the rack at the local department stores like JCPenney or Herberger's—and always wears designer glasses. I get his attention and tell him that I have errands to run and might not be back in until the morning.

Herman and I have known each other for two years. He transferred to the area from the Salt Lake City field office after I had already transferred from Newark. In this business, in order to advance, you have

16

to move around—acquire a varied mix of expertise. In the smaller resident agencies, you get to work all sorts of cases: fraud, corruption, cyber scams, child pornography, interstate drug networks, terrorism, criminal networks. You get to become a jack-of-all-trades, capable of working any case, anytime, unlike the agents in the field offices, who usually specialize in only one or two areas.

Once you become multifaceted in your qualifications—a generalist—you can theoretically move anywhere in the United States. That's what Herman is shooting for. That's what I too had in mind in the beginning, but since Emily came along, I've reconsidered for her sake. Many agents used to think being sent to Montana was like being stationed in Siberia—a purgatory of sorts for difficult or embarrassing agents. But once those that liked to fish, hunt, hike, camp, and ski learned that Northwest Montana was idyllic and that, because of the Internet, there was plenty of crime to be solved no matter where you were, it became a sought-after place. *Why not live where the traffic doesn't raise your blood pressure?* I ask myself when I long for the city. Plus, I happen to like the area, not because I fish or hunt or romanticize the Wild West, but because I think it's a good place to raise Emily.

"Before you go," Herman says, "you hear about that woman up the North Fork?"

My ears perk up. "What woman?"

"Possible homicide, from what I'm hearing on the police blotter."

Word of homicide spreads quickly to all factions of law enforcement in the area, and I'm surprised I haven't heard anything until now, but I've had my head in a case involving an anti-government gun-smuggling anarchist who's been attempting to organize a group to target law enforcement personnel. Herman and I have been making headway on the case, gathering data and transcripts from other agents around Montana and Idaho who have also been tracking the guy.

"Homicide?"

"Yeah, not far from Glacier."

"Our jurisdiction?" I ask. Glacier Park is federal land, and it's always a bit tricky when there is a crime on its property how we manage it and divvy up resources. Usually it becomes a collaboration between park law enforcement, the county sheriff's office, and sometimes the Kalispell police department.

"From what I'm hearing, no. Apparently, it happened at a cabin a few miles from the park's border."

"Interesting," I say. "Perhaps I should swing by the station and see if they need our help anyway?"

"You could. Are you bored?" Herman sits back into his chair and slides his pen behind his ear. "They've already been on it all day. If they needed us, they would have already called."

"True," I say, grabbing my bag. "But I've got errands to run anyway, so I'm out of here. Let me know if anything comes up on the Smith case."

I leave the office and head north toward Columbia Falls and up the Flathead River's North Fork drainage toward the northwestern border of Glacier Park. Reeve lives near Polebridge, Montana—a place where the wildlife still greatly outnumber the people, which is part of the reason he and the rest of the full-time residents reside there—as far from crowds as they all can manage while still making a living.

But living there is also conducive to his research. Much of the land he traipses through to grab his samples is right out his back door and traversed by faint game trails from all sorts of wildlife, mostly ungulates—deer, elk, and moose—but also bears, cougars, and other predators. When I met Reeve, he was working on finding bobcat scat. Romantic, I know, but you have to understand that it's one of the things that drew me to him initially—not the scat part, but that he was a person with the slow-burn intensity of a man on a mission that very few people understand. He was concerned with nature's details for the sake of preserving nature. He could have been flying over the North Pole to gather data on snowcap levels and I'd have felt the same way, because that kind of focus—that kind of quiet commitment—was the opposite of the chaotic life I came from.

When I got to know him, I didn't get that a person could seem at one with nature only because he wasn't at one with himself. Then, of course, I've never been good at seeming "at one" with anything, either, so I figure I shouldn't cast stones.

I drive up a gravel road that runs beside the North Fork of the Flathead River, a rugged countryside of the Northern Rockies clogged with brush, deadfall, and skinny lodgepole pine trees, many of them distressed from pine bark beetle infestations. After about twenty miles of gravel road, I pull up to his cabin and am surprised to find a deputy from the county sheriff's office in his car in the drive keeping an eye on the place. He steps out when he sees me and doesn't let me pull all the way up, and I realize he wants to preserve the drive in case they need to lay plaster for tire prints. My worry over Reeve and what's happened with the woman he and Herman have mentioned rises higher.

"Excuse me, ma'am, you live here?" he says as I step out of my car.

There are perks associated with being an FBI agent, and I pull out my badge. "Agent Paige," I say. "I'm here to grab the dog."

The deputy's not stupid, though, and he looks at me with a confused expression that says, *What the hell does the FBI have to do with pets these days?*

I don't offer anything more, just begin to head to the door.

"Excuse me," he says again. "This place is off-limits, at least for now. What's this about a dog?"

"There's one in the house, and someone needs to get him out. It's that simple." I stop and turn back to him, tucking my unruly hair behind my ear. I'd like to ask him a few things, but I'm afraid if I talk to him and give him a chance to get less confused, he'll be the one asking me questions instead.

"But this place will potentially be searched soon. They're going to get a warrant. I have orders to keep anyone who wants to enter out."

I realize that means they're in the process of trying to gain probable cause to get the warrant in the first place. I think of Reeve's being questioned for hours, as he said. I try to read the deputy's badge, but I can't see it from where I'm standing. "Deputy?"

"Polly," he says.

"The dog needs to go the bathroom, Deputy Polly." I say his name correctly, although words and phrases like *polyester*, *Pollyanna*, and *Polly want a cracker* have already popped into my head. "And I don't think you'll want to have to clean that up or explain to the CS techs why the dog peed on their evidence, will you."

"I haven't heard any dog barking."

"Apparently he's a good dog." I turn and walk away, giving the drive and the entryway a wide birth so the deputy won't say anything about my creating more unwanted prints. Polyester must not want to tangle with an FBI agent, because surprisingly he doesn't follow me and stays by his car while I go find the key around back and let myself into the kitchen.

When I enter, I think McKay might bark, growl, or charge me to protect the place, but I'm wrong. He sits rigidly right inside the door before the refrigerator, staring up at the top, where a red ball perches near the back. He can't see it from where he's sitting, but he must know it's there. I shake my head in disbelief. "Okay, buddy." I kneel beside him. "How long have you been here? Staring like this?"

I pat his head, even though I remember Reeve telling me not to pat him on top of his head because it will make him lose confidence, as if I'm forcing his head toward the ground, pounding it out of him. *Pet his chest and stroke upward like this, saying, "Good boy." That instills self-assurance.*

"Hours?" I ask him, still patting his head in spite of Reeve's advice. Finally he breaks out of his trance, stands, and begins wagging his tail and trying to lick my face. He remembers me, and I feel a pang from the image of the first time Reeve walked me from the restaurant we'd met at for dinner over to his truck to "introduce"—as he called it—me to him. We'd eaten at a nice place on Flathead Lake and the air had been warm, almost tropical. I still remember how the breeze lifted my curls and caressed my neck when Reeve kissed me for the first time. When we stopped, we laughed when we noticed McKay looking up at us intently, waiting for Reeve to tell him what to do.

I look around the kitchen. It's as I remember it: rustic, with old-style appliances, tattered green throw rugs covered with brown dog hair lying at the base of the fridge and oven, the small sink filled with a few dirty dishes, including two wineglasses. My heart warms to see familiar messy, colorful crayon drawings made by Emily on the fridge. I pull out a pair of plastic booties from my pocket and put them over my feet out of habit and consideration. I'm not worried about my trace—hair or other fibers from my clothes—being found in his place. After all, my daughter comes here regularly and transfers all sorts of fibers from my home to his, but I'm hoping whatever this is doesn't get that far.

I've done an especially stellar job of keeping my personal life separate from my professional life. The only ones outside my personal life who know I have a daughter or was ever involved with someone locally is Herman and an agent named Barney Willis, the other resident agent in the Kalispell office who was here before Herman when I went through my pregnancy and took maternity leave. He transferred to the Salt Lake City office when Emily turned two.

Herman knows Emily, but isn't aware of all the details. The one time he asked about her father, I shut the conversation down quickly, and he took the hint. One of the perks of being in a remote resident office is that there aren't lots of other agents around to pry into my business, and there's no large squad of alpha males trying to shoulder me around or feeling threatened that I might get a promotion ahead of them. With Herman, there are no misogynistic jokes bubbling up behind my back like there were in Newark. Herman treats me like an equal, and mostly he respects my privacy. The other deputies and police officers in town who know me might gossip about me, about my gruffness, about my Jersey accent, but I suspect the rest of what's said is just rumor.

In the main room, I find everything the way I remember it—a statement of subdued ruggedness, of the independent loner Reeve has become or perhaps has always been. Muddy boots line up by the front-door entrance; *Field & Stream* and *Outside* magazines and some of Emily's coloring papers lay strewn across the wooden coffee table before a worn dark leather couch. An easy chair sits in the corner with a deer-and-elk-patterned blanket carelessly draped over its back. I shake my head. Reeve is the ultimate guy's guy, the irresistible hermetic male, seemingly hewn from a place like Montana—someplace vast and craggy with caves and spears—not from the narrow, soggy, crowded state of Florida. At least it seems that way on the outside.

I go to the bedroom and stand beside the bed. Twisted covers drape at the foot of it, and I think the faint smell of sweat, or maybe sex, lingers in the small room, but then I wonder if I'm only imagining it. There's something tiny and black between the pillows. I lean over and see it's a hair tie, one of the soft cloth ones. I have no idea whose it is, but I have a sinking feeling in my gut that it belongs to the woman Reeve is being questioned about. It could belong to any woman, though. Reeve is tall and handsome, and since he rocks that quiet, unassuming look of the mysterious, irresistible mountain guy who can handle himself out in the wild woods, he has a certain appeal. He has thick dark hair and a defined brawny fitness that comes from being outdoors all the time.

And he's single. Some women—psychologically healthy women—probably know enough to stay away from him, but you'd be surprised how many smart women don't trust their instincts when it comes to men who might be broken. These women believe they will be the ones to change them, make them see the light, and that in turn will restore some missing piece inside themselves. Obviously, I speak from experience. I look back at the hair tie. I know it's not Emily's. She doesn't wear the cloth scrunchies. Hers are thin, bright bands—the colors of the rainbow.

It's been over five years since I've been in Reeve's bedroom, and the memories accost me. Images of Reeve's caressing my shoulder, memories of our eating Häagen-Dazs in bed and chuckling over a silly story that I told him about getting drunk with my friends on the Jersey Shore and rearranging the letters of a business owner's sign in the middle of the night.

Then I think of Emily. My daughter, our daughter. Rage bellows up. I know better than to get so far ahead of myself, but I can't help it. I picture him sitting behind bars in jail and having to take her to see him during visitation hours. I've always known of Reeve's capacity for self-destruction, his history as a rebellious, reckless teenager. I don't want to think it, but I can't help let it slip through the cracks and leak into my mind: Could he have unconsciously found a way, short of suicide, to completely self-destruct?

I know better than to pull on such dark threads, to think such ridiculous things. *Reeve is not capable of taking someone's life*, I tell myself.

I know I shouldn't do it. If it belongs to the victim, I'm removing evidence, but I reach over anyway and grab it. I'm not sure why. If Reeve has killed a woman, then I don't want to stand in the way of justice. If they had sex in this bed, they'll most likely find plenty of evidence anyway. I just can't wrap my head around it—the murder part. The room seems like it's tilting. I feel like I'm floating in a dream world.

At times when I contemplate Emily's future and all the possible consequences from events gone right or wrong, I think my heart might rupture into a thousand pieces. I picture her earlier in the week as she dived through a blanket of gold maple leaves in our backyard, tossing them into the air and giggling as they fell onto her head and clung to her wild hair. Automatically and with years of practice long before my daughter came along, I switch my thoughts to the things I have control over, the tasks before me that need to be done. I slip the hair tie into my pocket and go back to the kitchen. *Not capable of that. At least not on purpose*—the persistent thought drips through my mind before I wipe it away. "Come on, McKay, let's go outside. Time to potty."

· · ·

Now that I've given McKay some water and let him do his business on the side of the cabin, I usher him into my car, into the back, but he immediately moves to the passenger seat. "Well-trained, my ass," I mumble to myself as I see his muddy prints all over the light-gray leather, then head over to the deputy.

He's sitting in his car, sipping coffee from a thermos. "Fine-looking hunting dog," he offers, rolling down the window, spitting a squirt of tobacco out the corner of his mouth onto the ground.

"That he is," I say.

"Where're you taking him?"

I don't answer, just look around. "So what are you thinking happened here?"

"Don't know, but if anything is messed up in there"—he lifts his chin toward the cabin—"it's on you, not me. I haven't stepped foot in there."

"Definitely on me," I say. "But all I did was find the bag of dog food and his leash, grab the mutt, and come out. I wore my booties." I pull them out of my pocket to show him. "Doesn't look like a crime scene to me, though."

"It's not. The crime scene's a few miles that way." He points south. "Some cabin where the victim stayed at a friend's."

"So what's the interest in this place?"

"Suspect," he offers.

"How so?"

"Don't know," he says. "They didn't fill me in. Obviously didn't fill you in either." He looks smug, as if he feels special that I don't know much more than him even though I'm carrying an FBI badge.

He's not really asking me anything, but I answer anyway as if he has: "Only that I should grab the dog." I continue to play the part.

"Must have something on him, though, if they want me here looking after the place."

"Must have." I smile and shrug, knowing that they're probably in the process of getting a search going. "And the friend? She's not a suspect?"

"Not sure." He shrugs.

"I'm off with the dog, then." I walk away from him and get in my car before I get the lovely chance to watch him spit again. McKay stands and bounces from seat to seat, wags his tail, and tries to lick my face some more. I tell him to settle down. He plops his butt down on the passenger seat and stares at me, panting either happily or nervously. I look at him and shake my head. *So you're still his salvation? The reason for Reeve's stability?* Statistics show that released prisoners who adopt pets have a low recidivism rate, and I can see how one can bask in the unconditional love of a pet like McKay.

But then I think of Reeve sitting in an interrogation room, and I frown and once again force away the biting thoughts. I drive us straight back to the heart of the Flathead Valley to the county building before I realize I've forgotten the damn ball.

Reeve

I SIT IN THE interrogation room, antsy and nervous. The deputies approached me when I was picking up some coffee and a pastry and asked me if I wouldn't mind following them straight to the station because they wanted to ask me some questions. I wasn't sure if they had planned to talk to me beforehand or not, and if they had, how they knew to find me at the Merc. I assumed that they'd probably stopped in to ask about me, and Fran, the owner, told them to stick around, that I routinely come in for my morning coffee anyway.

When I asked what they wanted me to come in for, they didn't tell me, just that there'd been some trouble and they needed to talk to me. When I said sure—because I wanted to be cooperative—but that I wanted to go let my dog out first, they said they'd prefer it if I could *voluntarily* come immediately to help them out. They stressed the word, saying it with a pause before and after, as if to make an unspoken point that the opposite was to be *brought* in by them if I didn't obey. Being strong-armed into changing my plans for the day didn't exactly please me.

I drove straight there as they'd requested, fear rising inside me, replacing the irritation. Clouds had rolled in again in spite of the gorgeous weather Anne Marie and I had the day before. It had rained in the night and the cold air had a nasty hook to it—a rawness that snagged my bones. I could smell stagnant woodsmoke as I went to my truck. A misty fog draped over the mountains, dissolving most of them into nothingness, as if they simply hadn't existed for billions of years.

At first I thought it had something to do with Emily. But I figured I would have heard from Ali, and if anything had happened to Ali herself, I would have been approached differently, not asked or practically forced to come into the station for questioning.

I also felt angry, even though I didn't know what they were calling me in for. I assumed it was some bullshit with the county sheriff's office that I was being dragged into for, like a poaching violation by my neighbor who likes to hunt elk. Now I wouldn't be able to take McKay for his hike, and he'd be a nightmare by midday. At the same time, the whole thing felt somehow inevitable. When you've convinced yourself that everything will eventually go to shit, you're almost eerily prepared when it does.

But I deeply resented being told what I had to do with my day as if I didn't have work to do. Because let's get this straight. I'm no stranger to crime.

The shooting incident set me off on a rocky path, and by tenth grade I had tried everything from pot to cocaine and LSD. In eleventh grade, I did two separate stints in the Leon Regional Juvenile Detention Center in Tallahassee for ten weeks for selling marijuana to other kids. When I got out, my mother hired a tutor to get me caught up, but I had to repeat my senior year. I finally got a high school diploma, then found more trouble by getting higher than a kite and shoplifting a six-pack at the local 7-Eleven. Through it all, I could never shake the feeling that if something bad happened to me, I deserved it. So when the cops asked me to come in, I didn't act surprised, probably making them suspect me all the more. "This is simply an interview—a *noncustodial* interview," they had rattled off, but they're sending mixed messages. The door to the hallway is wide-open, so that I'm aware that I can walk out anytime, and that feels comforting. But I'm sitting in a bolted-down chair at a bolted-down table, basically designed so as not to let anyone get comfortable or use the furniture as weapons. Did that mean they didn't have another room separate from the interrogation room to put me in? Or did that mean something else?

Even though I'm jumpy as shit, I force myself to sit still, my feet planted wide before me, my hands resting in my lap. Every once in a while my leg begins to bounce rapidly and uncontrollably, but then I catch it and tell myself to stop.

Finally, when the door bangs open, two detectives come in, one with a smile, one mirroring my stoniness. "How are you?" the smiling detective says.

I shrug. I want to say, *I would be better if you'd let me take care of my dog first.*

"Thanks for coming in," he says, as if I have a choice in the matter, and I know they've told me I do, but it doesn't feel that way.

"Yeah, sure." I know better than to be belligerent, but I have to suppress it. My counselor told me repeatedly that I don't do too well with authority figures—something to do with anger at my father, which by the way was understandably mutual—and I can feel my annoyance simmering, almost boiling, and I want to tell them both to fuck off.

"Aren't you wondering what this is about?" the pleasant-faced detective says while the other, more serious one with graying hair heads over to the video recorder in the corner of the room and fiddles with the buttons.

"Yes, I am. I'm hoping you'll tell me soon. I've got a dog at home that needs to be let out."

The pleasant one winces as if he feels my dog's pain, but he shrugs as if he doesn't have a lot of faith that whatever this is will go quickly. He observes my gaze with a smile as I watch the other detective press buttons. In my mind, I'm already labeling him Mr. Pleasant, and I have a flash of recognition that this is Ali's thing—to nickname everyone. I briefly consider if that's the secret to getting by in the world of law enforcement: to tag each uniform you meet as if they're simply separate pieces of luggage—one hard one, one shiny gray one, one soft-covered pink one, one paisley one—so you don't take anyone or anything too seriously. The pleasant one would be a shiny black streamlined case because he looks well put together, his hair slicked back and his uniform unwrinkled.

"You don't mind if we record this, right?" the other detective asks.

I shrug. "I'm not sure why I'm even here, but you can record if you'd like." I'm wondering if I need an attorney, but I'm not going to ask for one anyway. I know asking for one right off the bat just makes me look guilty. Also, paying for an attorney to tell me *not* to answer certain questions doesn't really make a whole lot of sense. Working in a canine research program for a Montana university doesn't involve buckets of pay.

Once I understand why I'm here, I can decide whether to answer the questions or not. Staying silent is a difficult thing for most people. For me, it's not really that hard. I spend entire days and nights without speaking a word except to McKay. Silence has become a way of life for me; it's the talking that's sometimes hard.

"Good. It's pretty much standard procedure at this point." When the serious-looking guy comes over and sits down too, Mr. Pleasant introduces them: "I'm Detective Brander and this is Detective Reynolds."

I give them a curt nod and wait for them to say more as they get comfortable in their chairs. Pleasant—Brander—opens a notebook and pulls out a pen. Reynolds just rests an elbow on the table and waits for Brander to get set. I notice that Reynolds's nose looks crooked, like it was once broken, and he has pockmarks on his cheeks. He'd have a broken zipper and frayed, worn corners.

Brander says the date, the time, and my name for the recorder. "I get that right? Reeve Landon? R-E-E-V-E?"

"Correct," I say.

"Do you know why you're here?"

I shake my head.

"For the recorder, please," Detective Reynolds says, pointing to the steady red light on the machine in the corner.

I clear my throat, fold my arms over my chest, and say, "No, I have no clue."

"Is that right?"

"Has something happened?" I ask.

Both detectives stare at me for a moment, then give each other a glance. I don't move a muscle, but it's getting more difficult as my anger rises. I can feel a twitch start in one of my tense shoulders. I feel the same sensations I used to feel when my father used to yell at me, like I'm going numb and being erased by a giant pencil. I try to keep my knee from bouncing and my breathing steady while I wait for an answer.

"Hang on." Brander holds up a pen. "We should tell you that you are free to leave at any moment, and that you are not obligated to say anything unless you want to do so, but anything you do say can and will be given as evidence. Is that clear?"

My stomach does a flip when I realize that along with the "you are free to leave" comment, I've just been cautioned, in spite of the fact that I've come of my own volition and they've told me this is only a voluntary interview. I bite my bottom lip hard. My mind begins to reel, and it's the first time in a long time I've felt the need for a swig of something strong like whiskey or a long draw of weed. I've been clean for seven years now—haven't touched a single drug since an entire year before I left Florida. I still allow myself a little alcohol—the occasional beer or a glass of wine—but rarely let it get out of hand, and can't remember the last time I was all-out drunk.

When I moved to Montana eight years ago, after many hours of therapy in Tallahassee, I left all my bad behavior behind. I was fortunate enough to have a smart counselor—a guy with a blond ponytail down to his ass who smelled like patchouli. He cared, though, and it made all the difference. I stopped the drugs, said good-bye to my mom and dad, who had divorced several years after the incident, and headed to Montana to begin a new life. I had been to Montana once before with my family as a seven-year-old to visit an uncle who lived in Kalispell and logged timber for a living. He took us to Flathead Lake and to Hungry Horse Reservoir to fish. We visited Glacier Park and the surrounding state parks. I was immediately enchanted by the mountains and knew I wanted to return.

The first year I was in the Flathead Valley as an adult, I found a job at a local restaurant, made good tips, and enrolled in the community college. I took general electives, biology, and geology and found I enjoyed them, discovered I could actually get lost in my studies and forget about the life I had left behind. After I received my associate's degree, my adviser at the college convinced me to continue on and enter the University of Montana's environmental sciences program. I did, and that's where I got involved in the dog-handling operation. "There are a thousand ways to ruin your life," my counselor in Florida told me. "But there are also a thousand ways to make it good." I figure I was lucky enough to stumble upon one of them.

"That clear?" the detective asks again.

"Yes, it is," I say.

"Let's just start from the beginning, okay?"

"Okay." I try not to laugh because it sounds ridiculous to mention a *beginning* of something when I have no clue what that something even is. "The beginning of what?"

"The beginning of your day yesterday."

Anne Marie. I have a flash of her heart-shaped face, her luminescent smile, of her biting her messy braid . . . I snap out of the memory quickly. "Yesterday?"

"Yes. We understand you were interviewed by a journalist?"

"Is she why I'm here?"

"Please just answer the question," Reynolds says.

"Yes, she's a journalist with the Sierra Club—from Missoula. She came along yesterday with me out into the field to observe what my dog and I do. What's this about?"

"Actually, please start from the very beginning," he says without answering my question. "From when you first heard from her."

He's trying to sound nice, but I don't like his tone. "Right. Okay." I tell them about what I do, about my boss's calling to tell me that a journalist from *Sierra* magazine wants to learn about my work. "He pointed her in my direction first," I say.

"Why's that?" Pleasant asks.

"Why my direction in general? Or why me first?"

"Both."

"Because there's only two of us trained so far to do this in Montana and the other is a gal, Lydia Mack, who lives past Bozeman. She's mostly collecting samples from bison around Yellowstone to study brucellosis and their stress levels, you know, since they're always being hazed back into Yellowstone or sometimes shot if they stray too far out of the park." I realize I'm probably giving more information than they want—talking more than I normally would—so I try to slow myself down and go back to the original question: Why my direction? "I'm not sure," I say. "I suppose I'm farther away from Missoula than Lydia," I offer. "About three and half hours. Maybe she wanted to take the longer trip first, or maybe she just wanted to head north first and then head south later. Anne Marie . . ." I clear my throat, a slight embarrassment washing over me that I'm on a first-name basis with her, as if they can detect what happened between us, and I can see it's not lost on them, since Pleasant sneaks a quick glance at Serious. "I mean, Ms. Johnson"—I correct myself—"intends to visit Lydia next week, as far as I know."

"And so *Ms. Johnson*"—Reynolds says it mockingly, as if to let me know he's caught the fact that I've just corrected myself—"contacted you?"

I'm beginning to wonder if I should answer any of their questions at all, but I do. "Yes, about three days after I heard from Jeff. She asked if she could come along. I told her I wasn't sure if I could have someone with me all day because I go for fairly long treks—anywhere from ten to fifteen miles a day. I told her we could meet for coffee. I thought I could meet her and answer her questions and that would be enough without her coming along. Maybe take my dog out of his kennel and let her see him by the Merc without going out into the field."

"And is that what happened?"

"No, she was adamant about coming along. About shadowing me

and actually seeing how my dog works out in the woods. I don't mean to sound rude, but if she was out of shape, you know, or unprepared, there was no way I was going to let her come along. But she came properly dressed and everything, so I agreed."

"So you deemed her fit enough?" Reynolds asks, a look in his eyes that borders on sarcastic, but I can't tell for sure. I realize they might be thinking that I've considered Anne Marie some object to be measured. I can't tell if these cops aren't very bright and are pissing me off inadvertently or if they're pouring on the attitude for a reason, trying to make me nervous. Either way, it's making me not want to cooperate.

"I only mean," I say, in an attempt to clarify, "it would have been unfair and unprofessional on my part to take someone incapable of handling the terrain along. So, yes, if you know her, she's athletic." I search their faces to see if they seem like they know her, but their expressions show nothing.

"Okay, so she looked like she could handle it. What then?" Pleasant sits back and rests his notebook in his lap.

"We got coffee. She asked me questions about the job and the program. Then she got her backpack out of her car—like I said, she came prepared. She came with me."

"And where was that?"

"Up the North Fork, the area near the Wedge and Hornet mountains. That was where I intended to collect my samples."

"What is the make and model of your truck?"

Dread darts through me again. On top of the earlier cautioning, it seems grim if they also want the make and model of my truck, but then again, I tell myself they could just be ruling me out or trying to scare me. I can't tell if I'm being paranoid or not, but the sense that I should keep my cards to myself grows stronger. My leg begins to bounce maniacally again. I feel like a caged cat with someone jabbing a sharp stick through the links at me. I'm tempted to resort to "No comment" from here on out, but I don't. "A Toyota Tundra, 2007."

"And how long were you out hiking?"

"All day. We covered a lot of territory."

"And then?"

"I took her back to her car at the Merc. Dropped her off around five thirty. It was getting dark already. I hate the time switch—losing that extra hour of light at the end of the day like that."

Brander writes a few more notes, then looks up at me and assesses me.

I sit frozen, still peeved about the way they're treating me. Stupidly and for no thought-out reason other than I do *not* like their attitudes or the sensation of being that kid again, the one trembling under the accusing glare of my father, I don't tell them about how we sat in my truck, reluctant to say good-bye. How she stared at me, her rosy cheeks freckled and her slender fingers—with natural, unpainted pale pink nails, the same ones that had dug into my flesh earlier—reaching for the door handle. How she didn't open the door and instead giggled a bit, then said, "You have any beer or food at your house? I'm starved after a hike like that."

Ali

—

Present—Thursday

AFTER I GET back to Kalispell, I go to the Flathead County sheriff's office. The town is small enough—population about 30,000—that most of the officers and workers there either know me or recognize me. I walk up to Brenda, who is usually attending the desk behind the glass in the entryway. "Hey, Smiley," I say to her. I call her that for obvious reasons, and she beams me a bright one when she greets me. My sister would tell me that I give people nicknames so I can keep them at arm's length and stay detached. She might be right, but I find it makes a few people smile as long as I don't cross any PC lines.

"What can I help you with?" she asks.

"Not much. Just checking in on that new murder case up by the park. They still have a guy in now for questioning?"

"Yes, apparently someone who lives up that way."

She nods and rings the buzzer to let me enter the county building. I walk in and head straight for the observation room. In a small town like Kalispell where the county sheriff's office, the local police department, and the FBI office are all within a mile of each other and frequently share the facility for interrogations and other resources, no one will bat an eye at me entering the observation room to check things out, especially with a homicide. I've got what I plan to say lined up anyway, though, just in case anyone asks—that obviously since the crime took place very close to the park, near its border, it's standard procedure for me to be checking into it.

When I walk in, a deputy and the detective division commander are watching. Commander Vance, whom I also know from previous cases where we've utilized the county's resources, must be observing Brander and Reynolds. She has dishwater-blond hair pulled back into a tight ponytail and her hands in her pant pockets. She looks at me and says, "Hey, Agent Paige. You've got an interest in this one?"

"Maybe." I give her my line about the proximity to Glacier and the Canadian border. Herman has already informed me that it didn't take place on federal land, but like I said, no one's going to think anything of me hanging around unless one of them figures out my connection to the guy in the interrogation room. I look at Reeve through the glass. He's sitting, feet planted apart, shoulders squared, and mouth set into a tough line. A rigidness freezes his face, telling me he's good and angry. Only his arms folded defensively across his chest and the jiggling of his right leg tell me he might be anxious as well.

Detective Reynolds leans forward, watching while Detective Brander asks Reeve a question. "Earlier," he says, "you asked if she was okay. Why did you ask us that?"

"Because you brought her up and I'm sitting in a police station, getting interviewed," Reeve says. "So I figured it might be serious."

"It is serious, but it could be a number of serious things. It doesn't necessarily have to involve her safety."

"True, but I don't picture her being involved in anything criminal, so I just asked." Reeve unfolds his arms and places both palms on the table. His knuckles are red, and I realize he's been squeezing his arms tightly into his hands, which have been shoved into the grooved fabric of his corduroy shirt. "Glad she's okay."

"We didn't say that either."

Judging by the tightness in his jaw and neck muscles, he wants to wring both of their necks, and I hope for his sake—for our daughter's sake—that he doesn't do anything stupid.

He stares coldly at them. I can feel my heartbeat pick up. *Be polite, Reeve,* I'm repeating in my head. *Don't anger them.*

"I'm confused," he finally says respectfully, and I find myself surprised at the relief I feel that he's cooperating and not being the belligerent man I know he's capable of being. An image of his losing his temper with a stranger in a bar we went to when we were first dating because the guy was being rude to me comes to my mind. Later, we had fought because I was so angry that he had failed to remember that I was a trained agent and more than able to defend myself. "Is she or isn't she okay?" he asks.

"She's not okay, Mr. Landon."

I watch the information sink in. Reeve's head draws back slightly and his brow pinches immediately in confusion. He's either surprised or simply a decent actor. I consider myself a good judge of character, but with him, sometimes I'm not so positive. "What's happened to her?" he asks.

"Why don't you tell us," Reynolds says.

"I have no idea," Reeve says.

Brander holds up his hand. "Let's slow down, Mr. Landon, we need to stick to our protocol. We need to know step by step what Anne Marie's movements were yesterday."

"I've told you," Reeve says.

"Have you told us everything?" Brander asks. "Because every little detail might help. Did she make any calls that you noticed?"

Reeve shakes his head.

"Did you meet anyone else at the Merc or on your hike?"

"Just the usual patrons were at the Merc—the owner and a few tourists I didn't recognize."

"And the hike?"

"No, no one," he says, then sits still, his mouth set in a frown. He looks taken aback by the news that Anne Marie is not okay, but I'm not sure he understands exactly how she's not okay. He confirms my impression and asks again, "What's happened to her? Is she injured?"

Neither Brander or Reynolds answers him directly, and I realize they're stringing him along. They want him to say it first—that she's dead—so that they can box him in with the fact that he knew it without them having informed him of it first. It's an outdated and somewhat hackneyed interview technique, but sometimes it works. I look at the commander, who's standing so close to the glass in the chilled room that she's throwing small clouds of fog onto it with each breath. I ask what's going on.

"Suspect says he was with the reporter during the day until sunset, when he drove her to her car at the Merc and dropped her off, which is verified by a witness at the Merc."

"And?"

"And the same witness closing up the store says she saw a woman who matches Anne Marie's description hop into a black Nissan that had been parked there all day until around five p.m. She said she saw the woman follow the Toyota Tundra north."

"And what does that prove? Wasn't she staying in a friend's cabin up that way?" I ask.

"She was, but to get to the cabin, she would need to turn south. She was slightly surprised because she'd had a conversation with the gal in the morning while she was waiting for him, and the victim had told her that she was staying at a friend's cabin down the North Fork road, even told her the friend's name, and the lady at the Merc knew her and where her cabin is—toward Columbia Falls, the opposite direction. In other words, she figured the woman would head south, not north, if she were heading home to the friend's cabin."

I bite my lower lip, wondering if she could have had something to do toward the north. There was little up that way besides meadows, streams, the North Fork and mountains and the people who built cabins amid the beauty of it all. It's not like she could have been running an errand. Still, it proved nothing to the detectives that she headed that way. She could have been wanting to find a spot to take a sunset photo for all anybody knew.

"And what does the suspect say he did after dropping her off?"

"Says he went home with his dog and fed him. Says he was alone and didn't leave his cabin all evening or night, which means he's got no alibi."

I reach into my pocket and feel the plastic bag with the scrunchie. I'm angry at myself and conflicted. I should not have tampered with evidence. *Damn it, Reeve,* I say in my head. *What have you gotten mixed up with?* "The cabin of the friend," I say. "You have an address?"

"I do." And just like that, she gives it to me—such is the trust in these parts between us and the local law. "Vivian Gould is her name."

"And she has an alibi?"

"Apparently she was traveling all night, from Seattle to here. We're in the process of getting some security footage from the two gas stations she stopped at—one to fill up and one to use the restroom and buy coffee and snacks."

"And where's she staying while her place is sealed?"

Vance tells me and I jot it down and excuse myself.

. . .

Sometimes I wonder if it's my own inability to trust that draws me to men like Reeve, men incapable of forging intimate, sustainable bonds, as if my own detachment is like a shield that makes theirs so difficult to detect. It's not just Reeve's shocking childhood story I mull over. I also have my own nagging, defining moments.

Picture this: I'm in fifth grade and I'm called to the principal's office and showed to a small room off to the side to meet with a woman I've never seen before. The principal, Mrs. Picaretti, says she just needs to chat with me about a few things. She's already sitting in the room when Mrs. Picaretti shows me in. The woman smiles when I enter, and I see immediately that she's wearing a bright red blazer and perfectly creased navy pants and that she's pretty. My younger sister is already in the room too, smiling and very chatty. When I walk closer, I notice the woman smells like flowers.

She offers me a seat, and I take it, studying her cautiously. I suspect why she's here. I have this feeling it has something to do with my dad, because he'd come over the night before and he and my mom got into a shouting match. Mom screamed for Toni and me to go to our room, and we did, but we could hear the vicious yelling continue until someone arrived, so we crept out of the room and down the hall to see a policeman standing at the doorway.

After I sit down, the lady introduces herself. She says her name is Sara Seafeldt, and I decide I like the sound of it, how it plays jump rope with my tongue. I say it a few times in a row: *Sara Seafeldt, Sara Seafeldt, Sara Seafeldt; Sara Seafeldt sells seashells by the seashore.* Toni is telling her about everything under the sun: what kind of picture she'd been drawing in class; what the school served for lunch; how our dad brought pizza one time when he came to visit; how our mom doesn't like Daddy coming to visit because "sometimes he's mean."

I glare at Toni to give her the message that she shouldn't just continue rambling, but it doesn't matter. She keeps at it while Sara Seafeldt smiles and nods at her, asking her questions like "What does your daddy do when he's mean?" and Toni replies, "He makes Mommy hurt."

"What kind of hurt?"

"You know, like crying hurt."

"So, like emotional hurt?

"Yeah, and bruises."

I tell Toni to be quiet. Toni tucks in her chin and frowns at me.

"I see." Finally Sara turns to me and asks how my day has been. I shrug but don't say anything. She asks me a series of questions about my age, what grade I'm in, if I like school, if I like being home more than I like being at school or the opposite. I give one-word or very short answers. "Ten. Fifth grade. Yes, I like school. I like being in both places," fibbing about the last.

She nods, still smiling, and asks me if I ever get to visit our daddy.

"Sometimes," I say. "But usually he visits us."

Toni is practically crawling into her lap at this point. She continues to ask questions about our parents and things in general: "Do they fight a lot in front of you? Does your mom make you breakfast? Does your dad take you places to eat when you're with him?"

Finally, when she gets up to leave, Toni gives her a big hug, encircling the lady's hips with her small, thin arms and only reluctantly letting go. Then Toni turns to me with a beaming smile. "I love Sara Seafeldt." She looks back at Ms. Seafeldt and asks, "When are you coming back?"

Ms. Seafeldt smiles, pats Toni's head, and says she'll be back to see us in another week. When she does come back a week later, Toni practically jumps into her arms while I remain in my seat in the school office.

Years later, I took higher-level psychology classes at Montclair State University in New Jersey—a feat in itself in my family since neither of my parents went to college, though my being the first to go helped us get the extra financial aid we needed. I thought I wanted to become a licensed clinical social worker just like Sara Seafeldt. One of my professors gave an entire lecture on the symptoms children display when they are in neglectful environments. *They are either too clingy or too standoffish. If they're clingy, they don't have appropriate boundaries with strangers. They say affectionate things like "I love you" too often, frequently to people they barely know. They easily hug anyone who compliments them or shows them any attention at all because they are so starved for attention themselves. They later become manipulative and dramatic just to get attention.*

I sat in the classroom, remembering Toni's clinging to the social worker, not wanting her to leave and talking about how she couldn't wait for her next visit, how she loved her. I remember secretly longing for her visits too, but I always remained aloof even when I didn't want to. Yet here I was sitting in classes to become just like Sara Seafeldt. My breathing quickened and the professor's words seemed to elongate as if he was in a tunnel, as if I were in a movie where the actor has just been told by the doctor that he has cancer and the doctor's voice fades to the edges. This was the moment I realized I would be a fraud if I was going to try to become a social worker because I would be suffering from the same emotional baggage I'd be trying to coach clients through. I'd heard the old saying that it's the psychologically damaged who become psychologists. It was then I knew I didn't have what it took to become a social worker because I was one of those children—the one who stayed detached—while Toni was the one who attached too easily, both of us on either end of the spectrum, setting ourselves up to get hurt time and time again. Both of us ultimately starved for affection. I was haunted by the question of how I could help people deal with their troubles and emotions and remain objective if I was emotionally damaged myself.

I told myself I refused to follow either pattern, Toni's or mine, because both headed to the same place. My sister's path led to giving herself up too often, too frequently, to any male who paid her any attention at all. I, in contrast, gave myself to no one—that is, until someone I deemed worthy would come along, a shiny person I thought I could trust, and then I'd jump in like a starving puppy dog.

My first two relationships ended badly because I clung too tightly, just like Toni, in the end. I told myself I'd never do that again, and I didn't for a very long time. I thought I had mastered the ability to avoid relationships altogether. My gruff, aloof attitude at work helped hone the faculty even more. But the minute Reeve Landon showed up in my life, I hopped right in. The difference with him, though, was that I never allowed myself to get clingy.

When we were together, Reeve used to make me laugh. A smile almost sneaks onto my lips when I think of how he used to look at me and sweetly say, "You're crazy, Ali. You know how I know?"

"How?" I'd ask.

"It's your hair." He'd twirl a long strand of one of my wavy chestnut curls around his forefinger and wink at me. "It gives you away." I can still remember how that wink would make me giddy.

Sometime after we first began dating, after I knew about Sam, Reeve and I were talking in his cabin and Reeve opened up to me. "Sam and I had been best friends since preschool," he said. "We used to walk to a pond about a mile and a half from our neighborhood and go fishing for brook trout. One time we didn't get back until it was late, after dark, and we both got into trouble from our parents. I had to eat dinner in my room, just like the boy in Maurice Sendak's *Where the Wild Things Are*—you know, the story about the monsters."

That was the moment I fell for him. I realized then that Sam's death marked the death of Reeve's childhood. As the days proceeded and our relationship grew, the juxtaposition of the unconquerable man before me with the vulnerable boy I knew resided in him made the giddiness I was feeling unspool into a deep, intense attachment.

But the more I felt the force of my emotions, the more afraid I became. Being at such odds was nothing new—dealing with my own father always made me want to submerse myself and simultaneously pull away to protect myself. Though it was through no fault of his own, it seemed like a bad sign that Reeve evoked in me the same unsafe emotions.

Now at times when I think of how Reeve and I became intimate so quickly, I cringe. Not because I'm disgusted by it. Quite the opposite. I'm simply embarrassed to think that I ever actually thought that such charged closeness—Reeve whispering softly in my ear, Reeve running his fingers through my hair, Reeve leaning in for that first, knee-weakening kiss—could last. That we could both be saved from the dull ache of loneliness. In the end, I stoically detached from him despite the strength of my emotions because it seemed the end of our relationship was inevitable. We both seemed to be followed by a certain darkness like a stray dog you can't convince to go away. It was as if we were always reminding each other that people never completely rid themselves of lonesomeness even in the company of a partner.

So in college, instead of getting a degree as a social worker, I switched majors and got a generic degree in criminal justice that led me absolutely nowhere in terms of a solid career and began working as a secretary for a law firm. When I heard the FBI was looking for people with only two years of work experience after college, especially females, to meet their quota, I jumped. It seemed like a good fit, especially for someone who liked the idea of being a hard-ass. That part suited me—the grueling fitness routines, the badass attitude, the extensive training on how to keep your cool when in crisis—because what I also learned in psychology was that people like me often confuse mad and sad. Those wires get crossed and you jump straight to mad because it's much easier to get fired up over something that causes you pain rather than to sit quietly in your grief, so much handier to let the heat of rage sear away the bite of sorrow.

I'm not sure why I'm having these recollections as I walk into the forensics department in the county building in downtown Kalispell, but they do whisper to me that there's no way Reeve—the boy with such deep regret over killing his best friend—could take another life. My first priority, I tell myself, is to protect Emily, and that might involve snooping around a bit in places I haven't been asked to snoop around. But as long as I don't have any direct effect on their investigation, no harm will be done.

I find the woman I want to speak to, the lead CSI, in her office. Gretchen Larson's head is down until she hears my boots scuff the carpet and looks up. Gretchen is a blond-haired, blue-eyed woman from Norway and has a slight accent to prove it. I've worked with her before, and I'm hoping she can fill me in on Anne Marie Johnson's crime scene.

"Hey," she says, standing up to greet me. "Agent Paige. What do I owe this visit to?"

"Just have a few questions about the woman in the North Fork. You worked the scene?"

"I did. Since around eight thirty this morning. I just got back and got the body off to Wilson in Missoula. Ray's still out there finishing up. That cabin on federal land?"

"Nah, just checking it out anyway since it's so close to the park's border. You know, in case your guys need a little assistance." What I'm saying is plausible. We collaborate with local police and the county sheriff quite a bit. In fact, the last case I worked with Gretchen involved the abduction of a young teen in the park, and all local agencies were utilized. But still, I'm wondering if she'll give me much.

"You've already talked to Deputy Brander?" she asks.

I sit on the edge of her desk. "I was just at the station. They're inter-viewing one guy in particular—a suspect that owns another cabin up that way and that works in the area."

"I didn't hear that. Glad they have a lead."

"What do you have so far?" I go out on a limb, but again, our agen-cy's relationship is so solid with the local force that Gretchen won't think twice about talking to me. I feel a little guilty about it, but then I think of Emily, and how they were conducting a noncustodial inter-view, not interrogating Reeve, and I figure I haven't really interfered in any major way.

"Could be a number of things: a domestic fight—a lover's rage—or something more sinister, like a burglary gone bad. She was found out-side, on her side, a bullet through her chest. Were you out at the place?"

"No," I say. "I hear the place wasn't hers. That it was a friend of hers lending her cabin for a few nights, and that's who found her this morning."

"That's correct. The woman came back early from Seattle after driving all night—around seven a.m.—and called from her phone in her cabin, where she has Wi-Fi."

"So she was shot? Do you know what kind of weapon?"

"A rifle, but we'll know more after the autopsy."

"Is that what killed her?"

"Again, we won't know that until the pathologist fills us in, whether the bullet killed her or the fall to the ground. She definitely hit her head on the way down. Not sure it matters, though. If someone intended to kill her, it shouldn't matter if the rock did it because the bullet would have eventually anyway."

"Where was she found?"

"At the base of some steps leading into the cabin. Dr. Wilson will probably be finished with the autopsy in the next day or two. If the bullet didn't kill her right away, I'm thinking the head injury might have knocked her out. The contusion is on the back of her head where I think she hit a rock on the way down. And it doesn't appear that she crawled anywhere for help, and there's only one shot to the chest." Gretchen points to the spot on herself, right near her sternum. "For her sake, I'm hoping the head trauma killed her instantly. It would be a nicer way to go than bleeding out from a shot to the chest."

"Is there any way this is suicide?"

"No, no weapon. The rifle wasn't there."

"Any sign that she was moved?"

"No. No sign of that. She was shot where she went down. The pooling's in all the right places. She was found on her side." She's referring to the blood and how it settles on a corpse. If you move a body, the areas where the lividity originally set will show.

"Any signs of struggle?"

"There's no bruising on her arms or anything, but we're hoping to find some trace on her clothes. We're processing them here. Only the body's going to Wilson. He'll check for other signs of struggle."

"Can you let me know when you and Wilson get your results?"

"Sure, but I'll get my full report to Brander," she says. "You don't want to get them from him?"

"Did you get a time of death?" I ignore her question.

"It was a little dodgy because of the temperature outside. She'd been out in forty-degree temps for hours, so it was hard for us to quantify the time, but taking the cold into consideration, we came up with anytime between eleven p.m. yesterday and three a.m. this morning. We'll find out from Wilson if she had anything to eat or not. And lab results should tell us if she had anything else in her system, like alcohol or drugs. I'm guessing she was coming in late at night and ran into someone who sealed the poor woman's fate."

"Did you get tire tracks?"

"No. Unfortunately, the road was heavily graveled and, as you know, gravel doesn't show tracks so well. Too bad the driveway doesn't turn onto a paved road, but the main North Fork road is gravel as well."

"And did you get a phone off the victim?"

"We did. Smartphone, and it has a passcode on it, but the tech should be able to get records soon. Subpoena's been sent to the provider. We've also got the laptop. It was in the cabin, also passcode protected, but hopefully the tech will be able to get into it to take a peek at her email and the like. We also found a spare key for the cabin on her key chain and a backpack with an extra long-sleeved shirt and a notebook."

"And prints?" I ask.

Gretchen leans back and pushes a blond strand behind one ear. "Not much so far. Couple of sets all over the cabin. Both smallish, so we're guessing they belong to two sets of women: the owner and the victim. In fact, we're certain several sets around the bathroom and kitchen are a match to the victim. We're not finding any that look like they belong to a man, but my print examiner is not finished examining them all yet."

"Could a man have worn gloves or wiped his prints?"

"Gloves—possibly. Wiped the place down, no. The other prints would have been smeared as well if someone had done that."

"How about trace?"

"Fibers from a fleece-type jacket, which isn't saying much in Montana. How many wear fleece around these parts?"

"Good point." I lace my hands behind my head and arch my back to stretch, as if I'm simply bored and interested only in the brainstorming of the case, but the image of Reeve's favorite fleece jacket burns brightly in my mind. "So you don't have much for Brander and Reynolds to go on?"

"There is one interesting thing. There's dog hair on the woman, but of course I heard she was last seen with a guy who uses them for research, so that would make sense. But the dog hair is definitely not in the house, so the victim never made it home before eleven p.m. on Wednesday night, or I'm certain some of it would have transferred into the cabin. There was definitely a good amount on her. Lab hair—chocolate Lab—and those shed *a lot*. So that raises the question: What did she do between the time she finished observing and interviewing the dog handler and arrived home, never to make it inside?"

"That's for Brander and Reynolds to find out," I say as nonchalantly as I can sound—almost in a singsong. "But you know—always here to help."

"You're interested in this one," Gretchen says.

"Have to admit"—I lean over toward her from where I'm perched on the corner of her desk, like I've got a secret—"this is a lot more interesting than the stuff I'm currently working on back in my office."

"The homicide cases that aren't domestic abuse typically are," Gretchen says. "Although this one could turn out to be just that. I'm guessing the detectives are checking on all her current and past boyfriends to see if any were in the area last night. Where's Agent Marcus?" She's referring to Herman. We all worked together on the last case, the kidnapping.

"Back at the office, which is where I should be too." I grab my bag. "Thanks, Gretchen," I say, and leave her to her work.

Reeve

THE SITTING AND waiting is getting unbearable. I figure at least one deputy is still watching me, but I avoid even looking at the one-way glass. I'm too stubborn for that. I stare at the table instead where someone before me has scratched *PRICKS* into the corner.

Finally the same two deputies, Pleasant and Serious, eventually come back in with coffee and offer me a cup. I take one because my throat is dry and I'm getting hungry. I've been here for at least six hours—most of it sitting alone after they've questioned me in spurts, then have told me to hang tight while they leave me alone in the quiet, cold room for long periods—but I've already made up my mind that the rest of the interrogation will be on my terms. I want to help, but clearly they're stalling, perhaps waiting to dig up some evidence that will allow them to arrest me. Their coyness irritates the hell out of me because it's obvious they aren't leveling with me, that they're just toying with me.

"Okay, let's back up a bit, shall we? Start from the beginning again."

I go through all the same details I've already covered: if Anne Marie seemed nervous or uncomfortable about anything; if she mentioned what her plans were after I dropped her off; who she was staying with. I told them she didn't seem nervous, that she didn't mention any plans, and that she said she was staying with a friend at her cabin down the road.

"Did you know where the cabin was?"

"She explained the general area by the river, and I told her I thought I knew it and that it was a nice place that her friend had."

Brander continues to jot a few notes down. I watch him play with his pen for a moment, flicking it between his fingers until he asks, "And have you ever been to the cabin?"

"No, I've never been there. I just thought I recognized the one she was describing—that I'd seen it from the road before."

"So were you there late last night or early this morning?"

"No, I was not. Like I said, I was home."

"With your dog?"

"Correct."

"And no one else?"

I shake my head. Brander stares at me for a second as if he's onto me. "For the recorder, please."

"Correct," I say again.

"Correct what? That no one else was with you? That no one can verify that you were home?"

"Correct," I repeat, in my mind referring only to the latter question. "There is no one who can verify that except for my dog," and in a way, I'm not lying. There is no person who can verify I was there except Anne Marie herself.

I'm splitting hairs, and it's tasteless of me to play such games under the circumstances, but the longer they keep me, the more irritated I become. If they don't tell me what's going on soon, I'm going to defer to the infamous two words: *no comment*. In juvie, everyone knew that if you ever got pulled in for anything, innocent or guilty, you were supposed to play the *no comment* card. Your best bet was to act like a robot stuck on repeat: *no comment, no comment, no comment*. A huge part of me hates the idea; it takes me right back to that bruised place, to that person—a junkie, a dealer, a shoplifter—who would even *need* to respond with such words, and I've worked awfully hard to separate myself from that person, to become educated, productive, and healthy.

"Why exactly do you think we've asked you here?" Brander asks.

"I don't know. Obviously it has something to do with Anne Marie, although I'm not certain what you mean when you say she's not okay."

"What do you think we mean?"

"Why don't you tell me?" I can feel my spine and shoulders tighten with anger, but also in preparation for their answer because I sense it's finally coming.

"Anne Marie is dead," Reynolds says without a hint of feeling, finally putting the words out there. Unlike Brander's, his eyes seem lifeless.

The answer stings—nicks me like a switchblade. But it's not like I wasn't prepared for it. I rub my face for a moment, then press my palms onto the table, staring at them. I take a shaky breath, then ask how.

"We can't tell you that right now."

"When did it happen?"

"Last night, after you say you dropped her off."

I take it in as I keep eye contact with Brander. He studies me. Nervousness edges up my spine. But still, I tell myself, I haven't lied. I did in fact drop her off when I said I did. And when I rethink it, maybe I *have* helped myself. I just read an article in the local news about the Montana Innocence Project, a well-intentioned group of professionals trying to exonerate wrongly accused individuals languishing in jail. The stories run through my mind: the man wrongly accused of killing his best friend who spent eighteen years in prison; another man wrongly accused of sexual assault who spent fifteen years in prison and with the advancements in DNA was later exonerated; and yet another man charged with murdering a girlfriend whose defense was conveniently never informed about the confession of a different man who had claimed to have killed her. My faith in the system is lacking, to say the least. "Am I a suspect?" I ask.

"Hmm," Reynolds says. "You seem awfully cool about the whole thing."

"Cool?" I ask. "Not sure that's the right word. Obviously, I was already aware that something had happened to her since you'd told me, so I was prepared for the possibility that she's . . ."

"Dead," he says again flatly.

"Look, I've been here all day, and I may not be the smartest guy in the room, but I'm not entirely stupid either."

Reynolds laughs and looks to Brander. "You hear that?" he says. "He's not stupid. Maybe just a little selfish considering we've just told him about a dead woman and all he cares about is whether he's a suspect or not."

I don't bother to add anything because there's no point in it. I realize Reynolds is trying to push my buttons, perhaps rattle me. Or maybe he simply just doesn't like me.

"What did you *think* happened to her?" Reynolds asks.

"I have no idea."

"What did you think it was about?"

"I've told you, I hadn't a clue. Am I under arrest or not?" I'm putting them on the spot. If I head for the door, I force their hand and they'll have to decide whether to detain me or let me go. The last thing I want is to be arrested, but I want to leave. A caged animal must get out.

Reynolds glances at Brander, but Brander keeps his stare on me. I can tell he's weighing his options before answering: let a possible killer go and have their asses on the line, or arrest me without proper evidence.

"What we've just told you is difficult for anyone to hear, even someone who doesn't know the victim all that much," Brander says nicely. "Can I get you more coffee, or even something to eat?"

"No thank you," I say, amused by their sudden politeness. "Like I said, I want to leave. I've been here all day. I'd like my phone back now, please."

"Mr. Landon," Reynolds says, his voice sharp, "we don't think you've told us everything. Just stay put. You can pick your phone up on the way out from the attendant."

I look from one to the other, itching to get out of here. I'm about to stand when Reynolds finally asks, "Did Anne Marie come to your house?"

I want to be facetious and say, *I thought you'd never ask,* but of course I don't. I wonder if there is any way they could know that she came over. If I tell them about it, I'm positive they will consider me that much guiltier, and because I didn't tell them right from the get-go, they're going to wonder why I kept it from them. But I'm no idiot: if I give them an inch, they'll take a mile and pin it on me. That's the way these guys work, and my only alibi is a chocolate Lab. I stare at them both for a moment. A cold numbness runs through me like freezing mountain water. I can feel myself going further into myself, like a piece of paper being folded into a tight origami shape.

"No comment," I say.

Ali

—

Present—Thursday

AFTER I CALL Rose, whom I actually call Shorty—an asinine little joke because she's the opposite, almost six feet. And she's strong. It's one of the things I like about her in terms of being Emily's caretaker: she gives the sense that nothing would happen under her watch. I ran a background check on her, and other than an unfortunate incident in her family involving a burglary that went wrong a few years back, she's never been in trouble for anything serious. I even went to the extent of making her sign a contract vowing that she won't talk about my or Emily's family or personal matters, and she was happy to oblige, understanding that with my profession, I don't need the community intruding in my business.

My attitude is a little on the obsessive side, but in my job, one learns one can never be too careful about things that are important. And privacy ranks high on my list for various reasons. The biggest is that in the Newark office, another agent whom I frequently butted heads with got wind of my sister and her ugly drug habits, and rumors began to take root and spread. She was twenty-three when a friend she was riding with got pulled over for reckless driving. Besides the driver, there was one other passenger besides Toni, and one of them had a plastic bag full of narcotics that they took out and hid under the seat when they realized they were getting pulled over. The cop searched the car anyway, and they ended up playing a game of He Said, She Said—it's not mine, it's hers—until the whole lot got taken in. Since they couldn't prove which one actually had possession, the driver got arrested, and the other two went free of charge. Word spread that I had something to do with that, that I pressured a local police officer not to testify that the goods were actually on my sister, even though I'll never know who they actually belonged to, nor does it matter.

Then other agents began saying that I was making it easier for her to get drugs, tipping her off on certain connections that I knew about because of my stint on the drug surveillance team. None of it was true, but the rumors got so bad that I was asked in by OPR, the Office of Professional Responsibility. I cleared up the situation, but once respect is lost among other agents, it becomes a scar that takes a long time to fade.

I ask Rose to pick Emily up from school for me, and I drive to the north end of the valley and up the North Fork road again. I want to see the cabin. I know I'm skating a bit on thin ice, hanging around and acting like I'm part of the investigation when I'm not. Someone might call me out on it, and if they do, I could get into trouble for poking around where I don't belong. I could set off a jurisdictional pissing match that could get reported to my field office in Salt Lake. I'm thinking I'd get my hand slapped by my superior, Special Agent in Charge Shackley—SAC Shackley—and they'd tell me to cease my involvement, but nothing more serious than that, so I take my chances and head to Vivian Gould's cabin, where Anne Marie was apparently staying while in town.

On the way I call Herman to check back in with him, and nothing new is up. He's still in the office, just poking around with the Smith case, and plans to leave in the next hour. I tell him I'll see him in the morning. Once I get through Columbia Falls, I drive several miles up a winding paved road that gives way to a gravel one. Eventually I see the North Fork of the Flathead River on my right and pull into a turnout area and look at the river. The water is dark and steely looking. I see no animals—no deer, ducks, geese—only a mixture of yellow-needled larches and dried-out, bark-beetle-ravaged lodgepole pine trees pressing toward the banks. I let McKay out again. He looks at me anxiously, his head cocked and his ears all boxy, as if I might pull out a ball for him to play fetch. "Sorry, dude." I hold up both my hands so he can see they're empty. "Come on," I say, and we walk down a fisherman's trail to the river, where he wades in and laps up the cold water. I let him run around a little longer, but when he comes to me and gives me his too-intense where's-my-ball? stare again, with his hind legs quivering with excitement, I walk him back up the hill to the car, make him hop back in, and pull back onto the washboard gravel road.

McKay turns in small circles on the passenger seat, scratches at the leather a few times, then settles into a curled-up wet ball of legs, paws, and a tail. My car smells like dirty wet socks, and I shake my head in disbelief that I'm carting this creature around up in the boonies.

I continue to think of Reeve as I settle into the vibrations made from the bumps and ridges in the gravel. I first met him at the Babb Bar, which is also in the boonies on the northwest side of Glacier Park. Another agent and I had been up in the area working on a case, and he'd insisted we check out the infamous Babb Bar, known for being one of the most dangerous in the state. It's located down the road from the Browning Indian reservation, which has historically been known for its high crime rate stemming from poverty. Many reservations across the United States in general have grappled for years with crime rates higher than all but a few of the nation's most violent cities. But the bar has since been converted to a restaurant and is now a fairly tame place with international visitors and twentysomething-year-old seasonal employees from Glacier stopping in for a meal since it's on the way to the park.

Reeve happened to be collecting samples for research on bobcats in the wilderness up in the same area and was inside having a bite to eat before heading back over the pass. He sat at the bar alone and gave me a small smile. I nodded my head in return, then went back over to the window where my partner was sitting. When we left after we ate, someone had slashed our tire, probably because some asshole didn't like the fact that we're FBI. While the other agent put the spare on, Reeve came out and politely asked if we needed any help. I told him no, that the only help we needed was finding the bastard who did the slashing. Reeve shrugged and said he couldn't help us in that department, went to his truck, and left.

Two weeks later, as fate would have it, I saw him in the Costco in Kalispell, where he was stocking up on supplies for his cabin. When I said I was relatively new to the area—had only been in the valley for less than a year—he said if I wanted, he'd show me the pristine North Fork area to the northwest of Glacier Park where he lived. After he explained his work to me, I understood where that mysterious look came from. I couldn't resist.

·   ·   ·

When I reach Vivian Gould's cabin, the day has turned even colder, and it feels like it might begin to snow. A bleak light diffuses across the northern mountains, and I wish I had a heavier coat with me instead of only a thin rain jacket. I tell McKay to stay, and I get out.

The white CSI van sits in the side of the drive, and I figure Ray is still inside working, as Gretchen mentioned. The cabin is larger than I expect, the color of dark chocolate with white trim. It has a nice-sized deck big enough for two pairs of chairs on either side of a white front door. Three wooden steps lead up to it. Yellow crime scene tape drapes across the outside perimeter of the property, and the outline of where the body lay earlier is chalked onto the ground near the steps. A dried pool of blood lies in its center, but spreads outside the confines of the body outline as if it has refused to conform to a designated shape, even though the taping came later. A flowerpot sits on one side and an assortment of large rocks on the other.

Gretchen said that she thought the victim hit her head on one of the rocks on her way down. Possibly the force of the blow sent her falling backward, her head crashing into the boulder. I walk over to the rocks and see one of the reasons she thinks that. A smear of blood slashes across the corner of a sharp point on one of the bigger rocks. On the pebbled ground leading to the front steps, a stain of dark, sticky blood spreads outward from where her head had been, according to the taped outline.

I stand and take in the rustling of the wind. A bitter breeze hits me and rattles the canary-yellow leaves of the aspen trees beside the cabin, blowing a few of them off their spindly branches. I get a strange sense that the wind and quaking leaves are trying to warn me, to tell me that I should simply get in my car and leave all of this alone, but I realize I'm being foolish and superstitious, which is definitely not in my nature. When Ray comes to the door, though, I startle. "Oh, sorry." He smiles at me. "Thought I heard someone drive up. You're just in time. I'm close to finishing up." He stands to the side to let me enter.

"I'll be in in a sec." I lift my phone and pull up the camera. "Just want to snap a few first."

Ray goes back in and I begin taking photos. The area inside the tape, the entire yard, is raked clean—combed for shreds of evidence. When I'm done, I go up the steps and enter. I can hear Ray shuffling around in one of the back rooms. I look past the disarray the team has left—the printing dust, the square cutouts from the large area rug, and the emptied cabinets and shelves—and notice that, unlike Reeve's place, this cabin exudes faux rustic, like some urbanite's or artisan's idea of what Wild West decor should be: an antler chandelier, plush throws, a cherry-red Aztec area rug across smooth wood-paneled flooring, a latte-colored leather couch. Even old snowshoes arranged like flowers in a large pottery vase adorn the stone hearth.

I walk through the place, calling out to Ray, "Find anything of interest?"

"Not really." He comes out so I can see him. He's holding a notepad. "I'm just finishing up with some of my labels." I go and poke my head into the bedrooms. "Both bedrooms are well kept," he says. "Suggesting that Vivian made her bed before traveling to Seattle, and the vic made her bed in what I assume is the guest room before taking off for the day."

In my mind, I say to myself, *To meet Reeve for their romantic day in the mountains.* From the looks of the bed—disturbed only by Ray or one of the other crime scene techs cutting several strips from the bedspread, sheets, and mattress—Anne Marie never made it back to hers, probably never made it back inside the cabin at all.

"We didn't bother to take samples from the master bedroom," Ray adds. "Only from the guest because it's clear the vic was staying in that room. That's where her overnight bag is."

I nod. If this had been my case, I'd be asking them to do the same, thinking a jealous mystery man might have been sleeping with Anne Marie only to find her coming home much later than expected after losing her hair tie in another man's bed. My curiosity over the cell phone records deepens, and I wonder if I can find a way to get a look at them.

Ray goes back into the bathroom, and I follow him to the door. It's heavily dusted too, and a toiletry bag filled with lotion, face wash, makeup, and deodorant sits beside the sink. I guess it belongs to Anne Marie. Voyeurism hooks into me like a barb. I've never felt it on a case before. After all, evidence is evidence. This sense of nosiness reminds me of two things: one, that the case is not actually mine, and two, that Anne Marie slept with the father of my daughter. I feel a combination of nausea and something akin to jealousy, which I'm well aware is twisted given the fact that this woman won't ever put makeup or deodorant on again.

"Not much of interest in here," he says. "Not much of interest in this cabin at all. Unless the owner is the perp, I don't think the killer stepped foot in this place, but as you can see, we've got it good and dusted and have collected as much trace as possible."

I thank him for his thoroughness and say good-bye, shutting the door behind me. When I get back in my car, I decide it's time to talk to Vivian Gould.

Reeve

WHEN I THINK of Anne Marie, my mind doesn't linger for long on the smooth, taut feel of her body, the way she softly giggled when we kissed and how I could feel the corners of her mouth turning upward in a smile when I placed my lips on hers. Nor does it stay on the image of her braid falling against my mouth as she lay on top of me, and how I desperately bit down on it.

Instead, my mind wanders back to the hike earlier in the day. Out among the exquisite beauty of mid-fall, I think of how I felt oddly cheery and connected to everything for a change, almost if I were a young kid again and could be wholly present, caught up in the joy of any given moment.

Don't get me wrong, it's not as if I don't appreciate my environment on a regular basis. Quite the opposite. I'm obviously very used to being in the woods because of my job, which demands I hike miles of wilderness nearly every day of the week, especially in the spring, summer, and fall months. In the winter, I still go, but not as far, because although I can snowshoe and ski, McKay can't cover excessive mileage in the deep snow.

The allure of its power is one of the reasons I came to Montana— me along with a whole host of people who sense that the great jutting presence of the landscape has the magnetic influence to pull your attention away from mind-numbing quotidian routines, that it can lead you back to what's real. But, for me, it's more than that. I figured the woods of the Northwest could connect me to whatever remained of my unencumbered self and would tether me securely to some hitching post of existence.

But yesterday I could have sworn I was aware of it in a different way—life's intricacies surrounding me in a more integrated manner: the high-soaring ravens, the leaves cushioning my steps, the whispy clouds in the pale blue sky, the mosaic of dark jade and coppery colors on the slopes, the breezes making the aspen leaves quiver, the shape of Anne Marie's lightly freckled cheekbones when she looked down to take her notes. All of it seemed to be part of a grand design that I was acutely conscious of and, more importantly, deeply a part of.

Because even though I'm out in the wild daily, it's rare for me to *belong*. Usually I am an observer, not a participant, as if I watch the wilderness and life happening around me from a faraway place, from another dimension. But, with Anne Marie, the details seemed to reveal all of the complexities and layers that I'd been missing out on.

I was a fool. It was an age-old spell: attraction. It had absolutely nothing to do with nature and everything to do with a sexy woman. In fact, had I really *belonged*—had I really been aware and at one with nature—I might have sensed a forewarning instead of an invitation. Perhaps I would have noticed how the slanted sunlight and the shadows lengthening across the forest floor seemed secretive. Maybe I could have read the withered fallen birch leaves plastered to the game trails like tea leaves, their rotten, pocked, and distorted shapes sending me a message. I could have noticed the frantic scuttling of the chipmunks and the pungent smell of rotting wild grasses and understood that they signaled I should tread carefully and not let my guard down, that change was in the air, that much more than winter was on the way. And what I really should have known was that I had been waiting my entire life to be punished, and that if I'd paid proper attention, I could have detected, as a horse senses a storm coming, how the reckoning had finally begun to arrive, only this time in a gorgeous disguise. The thing is, even the most self-destructive among us never really want the punishment to come on anyone else's terms. When it comes, it's not necessarily a surprise, but it's irritating and frightening as hell.

Before I make my decision about whether to walk out on the detectives, Brander brushes off my no-comment response and says, "Look, obviously we're trying to rule out people seen with Anne Marie as well as finding out as many details as we can about her day. And since you spent a large part of the day with her, we'd like to eliminate you as a suspect."

I lick my lips, nod, and wait for the rest because I sense there's more coming.

"So we'd like your permission to search your home."

I don't reply.

"We have reason to believe that she may have visited you there."

"The way I see it," I finally say, "she probably has evidence on her—fibers or something—from spending the afternoon with me: my dog's hairs and whatnot. I mean, she drove with me in my truck. And it's possible those fibers got transferred from my truck to my house by me."

"We understand that. But we can't just rule you out because you admit there might be evidence of her in your truck. We have to go down all avenues, and that includes all prospects."

"Wait a minute." Reynolds holds up a hand. "You seem to have a grasp of police procedural processes. Have you been through this before?"

I glare at him. "It's just common sense these days."

"Oh, yeah, *CSI* and all that."

"Actually, kind of." I've never watched the show in my life, but I know enough from Ali that no one leaves a room without leaving some tiny shred of evidence that they were there.

"You've thought this through. So if I'm interpreting what you said correctly, you think there might be trace of Anne Marie in your home?"

"Because she was in my truck," I say.

"I see." Reynolds looks at me. "All the more reason we need to take a look at things."

I've backed myself into a very tight corner. I know I should tell them about her coming over, but it all feels wrong. A sense of foreboding washes over me and propels me to keep my mouth shut. I picture myself behind bars and take a deep breath to quell the panic. Images of juvie detention fill my mind: the tight spaces filled with other gangly teenagers, the sharp scent of disinfectant never fully masking the smells of body odor and teenage feet, the fighting, the yelling and crying. . . . If I tell the detectives and they go to my home and find evidence that she's been there, it doesn't solve anything. I have an overwhelming sudden urge to see my daughter and my dog, as if it's my last chance to do so.

I stand, the two of them staring at me with narrowed eyes, and say what I should have said hours ago, "I'm going to let my dog out," and go to the door.

Ali

Present—Thursday

I FIND OUT FROM Rose that she's picked up Emily from school, taken her to get a baked pretzel with cheese at the mall—Emily's favorite after-school snack—and brought her home. She's happily drawing in her room, and Rose says she plans on feeding her pasta with tomato sauce out of a jar and some steamed broccoli on the side.

"Great," I say, "because I might not be home until past dinnertime."

I feel a stab of guilt that I'm not there with her, but then I do a quick count—I've been home on time four nights in a row. I picture Emily in her pale-yellow-painted room trying to draw unicorns, her latest craze. Before that, it was mermaids, and she used to ask me endlessly to draw them for her. I'm not an artist, and sometimes I get a sick feeling in the pit of my stomach when she asks me to draw something because Reeve is a good sketcher, and he used to draw whatever she wanted with ease. I would sketch something that could pass for a mermaid or a deformed squid, depending on how you looked at it, but Emily would cherish the drawing anyway, grinning and running back to her room with it, feet pitter-pattering down the carpeted hallway. I decide it's okay for me to be late.

Commander Vance mentioned that Vivian is staying in a lodge in Whitefish, which is directly to the north and nestled against the Whitefish Range.

I head to the lodge without calling Vivian, hoping to find her there. When I arrive, McKay has had enough. He is panting and whining, so I let him do his business, then give him some food from his bag, but he refuses to eat. "What do you want?" I ask, and he looks up at me and tilts his head. "Okay, Mr. High Maintenance, not hungry? What are you, then? Bored?" I put him back on the leash and walk him down to the lake. He stares at me with round cinnamon-colored eyes, his whole body quivering.

He runs over to the rocky beach, yanking me along, and picks up a stick and pushes it at me. I can practically hear Reeve's voice. *Don't ever play fetch with him unless he's worked first. Playing fetch is his reward and nothing else.* "No fetch," I say authoritatively. "I don't carry bear shit around like he does." I yank him toward me and take him back to the car and make him get in. I lock it up, head toward the lodge entrance, and ignore the whining as I stride away.

A giant Kodiak bear stands to the side of the front desk, which strikes me as funny, since we don't have Kodiaks in Montana. He's been mounted so that's he's standing straight up, over eight feet tall, with claws the size of small bananas. I find out that Vivian is on the second floor. I take the stairs up and find room 243 and knock. It takes a moment and then a woman's voice says, "Yes," from behind the door.

"Vivian?" I ask.

"Yes," she repeats.

"Agent Paige with the FBI. Could I have a word with you?"

There's a short pause, and then the sound of her pulling off the safety lock and opening the door. "Come on in," she says.

She's medium height and lithe, like a ballerina, and has long curly hair, like mine used to be before I became a mom and wearing hair down my back became a pain. At work, I could tie it back, but at home, I'd forget, and before I knew it, Emily would curl her sticky fingers in it and wind it into knots. Vivian has a thin, pale face that's splotched red around puffy eyes, from crying. I have my ID out to show her, but she simply walks back into the room, leaving the door ajar for me to follow. I figure she's already been through a lot of questioning, and I'm par for the course.

The room has a tiny kitchenette and a small sitting room with a gas fireplace in front of windows that look out over Whitefish Lake. "Nice view," I say. The sun is already low and the sky is paling over the western mountains. The lake is the color of Teflon. It looks cold and uninviting. I consider her plush cabin and her choice of this resort hotel while her cabin is off-limits and assume she must have a bit of money.

Vivian offers me a seat. I take one of the easy chairs before the fireplace while she sinks into the other. A half a cup of coffee sits on the coffee table before us, but no books or electronics are nearby, and the gas flame is not turned on. It appears as if she's just been sitting alone, doing nothing, before I came. Shock can do that, strip us of our routines, render us unable to perform the meaningless simple tasks we usually fill our time with. I take my notebook out, and Vivian doesn't look fazed—just compliant and ready for more inquiries as if she's expecting it.

I explain that I'm just going to ask her a few more questions—that I'm sure she's already been through a lot today, but that's it's helpful to talk to different people to cover all angles. She nods, and I ask her to confirm her name, her age, and where she's from. She tells me she's thirty-one and that she's from Seattle. I ask her about her job, and she says she works in the finance department of Timberhaus. When I ask if she's from Seattle originally, she tells me that she isn't, that she grew up in Kalispell, went to high school there and later to college in Spokane.

"I got an internship with Timberhaus that led to a full-time job, but I always wanted to make it back to this area, even though my family moved away some time ago, so the next best thing was buying a cabin here," she says.

"Married?" I ask her.

She shakes her head. "I had a boyfriend for six years, but we just broke up. Commitment issues." She shrugs.

I'm about to ask "Yours or his?" but realize it's not relevant, and if she answered truthfully, I wouldn't have a reply, especially as a single mom who isn't sure whether the commitment issues ultimately lay more on Reeve's shoulders or mine. "So, tell me about this particular visit and your relationship with Anne Marie. You're obviously friends—close friends?" I don't feel the need to rub the loss in her face, so I use the present tense for the sake of comfort.

"Yeah, she was my roommate in college, at Gonzaga." A mix of emotions flood onto Vivian's face for the first time since I've walked in. "We've kept in touch ever since."

"I'm sorry for your loss," I say.

She nods and swallows the surging grief back, her eyes watering, her cheeks flushing.

"Can you tell me about your plans and why Anne Marie was staying at your cabin?"

"We were talking last week—just catching up like we always do—and she told me that she planned on being in the Flathead this week because she had interviews to do up in the area, and she was interviewing someone who lived up the North Fork, close to my cabin. She was writing a piece about a dog program for someone—I think she mentioned the Sierra Club. So I offered her my place. She's visited me there before, and I said I'd been thinking about coming out for a long weekend, taking a Thursday and Friday off, and why not do it when she was in town. I love it here in the fall"—she glances vacantly out the window at the lake—"and I hadn't been out yet, so we made a plan for her to go ahead and stay on her own until I got there. There's a spare key I keep hidden and I told her where to find it—under one of the flowerpots."

"And you planned on getting there when?"

"I planned on leaving a little early from work on Wednesday and maybe stopping in Spokane to sleep and driving the rest of the way in the morning, but I ended up working late on Wednesday, and by the time I got on the road, it was already nine. I figured I'd be exhausted when I made it to Spokane, but I wasn't at all. I was wired and didn't feel like stopping, so I just drove. I guess I was excited to get to the cabin and to see Anne Marie. I wanted to have the whole day ahead of us in case we wanted to go for a hike or something."

"So you drove through the night—what, nine, ten hours from Seattle to your cabin?"

She tells me that she didn't notice the exact time, but stopped several times along the way to grab coffee, use the restroom, and whatnot. "Probably more like ten, in all," she says.

"What time did you reach your cabin?"

"I think around seven. I pulled up . . ." Vivian's face goes sheet white with the memory, and a mix of expressions pepper her face—anxiety, fear, grief. I wait for her to continue. "It was still fairly dark," she says, "but when my car lights spread across the lawn and the sides of them fanned out on the front deck and steps, I noticed something in front, like maybe Anne Marie had left a duffel bag or something outside and forgotten to take it in. I didn't want to leave the lights blaring, though, because I was aware she'd be asleep, so I turned them off quickly, thinking I'd pick up whatever it was that was left out and take it inside. But a part of me knew or sensed something was different, like it couldn't be a duffel bag. It seemed wrong for that—too big, too oddly shaped. I thought maybe a deer or another animal had been shot in the woods and then happened to walk by and died right in front of the cabin, but even that seemed way too strange. I shooed it all away, though. Right? That's what you do. Go on as usual, not thinking of such . . ."

Her voice drifts off. I register the thought. She's right. That's all one does, proceed as programmed by ourselves, by our routines—in this case, grab the bags and head to the door and check it out, not conceiving of something as abnormal as a dead body. "So you did what?"

"I turned the car off, began to get my bags out of the trunk, and then went to the cabin."

"Did Anne Marie know to expect you so early? Had you called her to let her know that you weren't going to stop in Spokane?"

"I didn't know myself until it was pretty late. I reached Spokane around two a.m. and texted her to say I was going to continue on, but I wasn't sure how far I'd go, that I'd stop somewhere if I got tired. The cell service is sketchy at the cabin. I have Wi-Fi there, but it doesn't always work so great for texts. She didn't reply, so I figured she was already asleep or wasn't getting my texts."

Two magpies with long dark tail feathers and iridescent bluish-green

wings land on the deck outside the French doors. One squawks obnox-
iously, and Vivian startles, then rubs her face with both hands as if she
needs to wake herself out of this new reality. Pesky birds, I think. Even
though it's a coincidence that they're on her deck, I've lived in Montana
long enough to know that they're known for finding the wounded, for
picking at insects or ticks on the backs of cattle or other livestock and
making the wounds worse. Since it's not officially my case, I feel sort
of like the magpie, pestering her when she's already been through it all
with the county. I wonder if Vivian has slept at all after pulling an all-
nighter and then dealing with the police all day. She still looks pallid, but
I nudge her on, knowing this is the tough part, but she's already been
over it, so she'll be okay telling it again. "And then?"

"I saw the . . ."—she pauses—"you know, I saw her. Lying crumpled
like that on the ground."

"You could see it was her?"

"Not at first. Like I said, it was dark. I had my flashlight turned on on
my phone. And her face, well, it was turned down slightly. She was on her
side, but I could see it was her—her hair, her body, her clothes. The blood."

"What did you do then?"

"It was awful, I panicked. I looked around, but it was quiet. I knelt
down and shook her, wondering if maybe she'd been drinking and
passed out or something weird like that, but I saw . . . I saw the . . . all
that blood under her, and then I screamed. I ran back to my car and
got in and tried to call for help, but then I quickly realized that my
phone didn't have service out in the car. So I had two choices: go into
the cabin and use the Wi-Fi or drive to the Merc and roust someone
up to use their phone. I ended up going in the cabin and calling 911."

"Was it locked?"

"Yes, it was, and I had to use my key."

"You keep your key on you at all times?"

"I do. On my key chain."

"And there are no extra keys besides yours and the spare Anne
Marie had?"

"No, just the two."

"Did anyone besides Anne Marie know you were coming?"

"Only a few friends in Seattle and my parents."

I tear off a sheet of paper, hand it to her, and ask her to write the names of her friends and her parents down. "Where do your parents live?" I ask.

"In Denver."

"Do you know if Anne Marie told anyone that she'd be staying with you?"

She shrugs. "I have no idea. Obviously, the guy she was interviewing knew she was staying somewhere around here. I'm not sure if she told him exactly where, and I have no idea if she told anyone else. I'm guessing Jeffrey O'Brien, the guy that runs the dog program, might have known she was coming here to do the interview, but I don't know that for sure."

"And how do you know about the guy who runs the program?"

"She's mentioned his name."

I'm thinking it's slightly odd that a reporter doing a write-up on the dog handlers would bother mentioning the name of the program director to a friend. But maybe they simply gabbed a lot. This is when it's nice to have another agent with you. If Herman had been here, I could bounce it off him after we leave or at least throw him a glance to check out his response—watch him raise an eyebrow to show he also thinks it's weird or give a one-shouldered twitch to suggest he doesn't. "So," I continue, "Anne Marie mentioned the director of the program to you?"

"Yeah, I guess." She looks down and to her side at the carpet, and I get the feeling that she's hiding something. "Just, you know, in passing."

"Did she mention the name of the dog handler up here she intended to interview?"

Vivian looks at me again, and I notice her eyes are bloodshot. She crinkles her brow, thinking. "She probably did."

"And do you recall his name?"

"No, I can't remember it."

Reeve

I GO STRAIGHT DOWN the hall to the attendant in the entrance foyer, with one of them—Reynolds or Brander—following closely behind me. I don't turn to see who it is, but I realize they're not going to let me walk through the building alone and one of them needs to escort me out. When I get to the front, I ask the woman at the desk for my cell phone. She looks past my shoulder and I finally turn to see it's Brander, the pleasanter one. Brander nods for her to give it to me. He takes out a card from his pocket. "Mr. Landon, if there's anything else you think of, please give us a call."

"I'll do that," I say, taking the card. Suddenly I feel foolish, like I've misread the situation—misinterpreted their treatment of me. Maybe I'm paranoid. I thank the woman for my phone and head for the glass doors. In the western sky, a peach color spreads behind the tree branches because the sinking sun has illuminated the cloud banks from underneath. The branches that are bare look spindly and frail. I check the time on my phone: it's 5:26 p.m.

I draw in a deep breath of autumn air. It's delicious. I want to gulp it like it's cold water, so I stand for a second and continue to take it in, my mouth open. The golden maple trees lazily drop their leaves, one or two falling silently at a time, and I have this strange longing to go scoop them up, to smell the pungent earth, as if that scent is dearer to me than anyone or anything. I stand for a moment to get my bearings, but I sense I don't have time for that—that I should hurry and get going. Once again, a strong urge to see Emily overcomes me, so I continue to my truck.

I hop in and call Ali. The phone goes to her voicemail and I leave a message for her to call me as soon as possible. I've just put my key into the ignition when a loud rap on the glass startles me, making me flinch. "Jesus," I say when I see Detective Reynolds standing beside my car. I roll down my window.

"Sorry to scare ya," he says, a lopsided grin on his face. "But just wanted to catch you before you left. We forgot to mention that we might want to chat with you again, so we'd appreciate it if you made yourself available—you know, didn't go far."

I sit still for a moment without commenting, my heart skipping a beat. There's something in the cockiness of Reynolds's face that makes me feel like I'm being stalked, like I'm trapped even in my car as I try to leave. He holds out his card. "I know you have Detective Brander's info. You should have mine too. Call us if you think of anything else, and again, please stay available."

I grab the card. It feels prickly in my hand and I want to crumple it into a small ball and toss it. "Okay, but my job demands I go to remote areas that have no cell service."

Reynolds looks like he's thinking about that, then says, "Like I said, we'd appreciate it if you made yourself available." He walks off, the sound of his boots scuffing the pavement. It's not until I hear them fade that I feel like I can begin to relax.

I sit for a moment before starting the engine, staring at the bright maple leaves falling from the trees and scattered in piles across the curbs. My heart's still hammering in my chest, and I whisper out loud, "What have you done, you fool? What's happening?"

I'm scared and pissed off. I consider going back in and asking to speak to Reynolds or Brander so that I can tell them that she came over. But an ominous feeling overtakes me. If I go in and tell them that, my life may never be the same.

I call Ali again, and this time she picks up. "Reeve," she says, "what's going on? Are you still at the county justice center?"

"I'm out in the parking lot. I just left even though they wanted me to stay longer."

"I see," she says. "How did it all go?"

I don't answer. "Where are you?" I ask her instead.

"Emily's at the house with Rose. I've got McKay. I'm on my way back to Kalispell now. I can meet you there in ten."

I agree to meet her. All I want to do right now is to see my daughter and my dog. I turn the ignition, back out, and drive to Ali's, hoping the afternoon drops away from me like the falling leaves.

Ali

WHEN I REACH my house, Reeve's truck is already in the driveway, off to the side, leaving me room to pull into the garage. McKay
has been letting loose low moans and anemic-sounding whimpers the
entire way back from Whitefish, probably from being in my car too
long and perhaps because he hasn't played fetch all day. When he spots
Reeve's truck, he starts in with an excited, full-pitched cry. I park next
to Rose, get the leash on McKay, and let him out. He strains against the
lead, smelling the ground for Reeve, heading for the front door.

Emily comes barreling out, shrieking, "Kay-Kay!" She gives him a
big hug while he wags his tail and prances with excitement around her.
Reeve follows her out and looks at me for only a second, then watches
Emily with McKay, avoiding further eye contact with me. He gives
them a moment before stepping in and commanding McKay to sit.
Once he does, Reeve kneels down and pets his chest, telling him that
he's a good boy. McKay makes funny grumbling noises and pushes his
head into Reeve affectionately, then begins sniffing Reeve's hands and
quivering with excitement.

"I don't have it," Reeve holds out his palm, then looks at me. "You
have his ball?"

"No, I forgot it. Is that a problem?"

"No. I have a spare in my pack." He motions to his truck. "He's just
going to bug everyone until he gets his fix." McKay whimpers loudly as
if to drive that sentiment home.

"Tell me about it," I say.

74

"Not me," Emily pipes in. "He doesn't bug me."

"I know, sweetie," Reeve says. "That's because he loves you more than his ball, which says a lot."

Emily grins with pride, her small pearly teeth shining in the fading light. The braids I put in her hair this morning are messy. Tendrils reach out like an electric current has charged them.

Reeve looks at me and says, "Thanks for going all the way out there to get him."

"No problem." I raise my brow and tilt my head in a we-need-to-talk gesture. "Hey, sweetie"—I turn to Emily—"would you take McKay around back?" I turn to Reeve. "If that's all right?"

"Remember, hon," he says to Emily, "work before fetch. No exceptions. I'll get his samples and his ball in a minute."

"I know, Daddy." She grabs the leash from her dad and gives us both a big smile before running around the house with McKay to the backyard.

Reeve and I step inside, and I tell Rose not to leave just yet and ask her if she can keep an eye on Emily in the backyard, since dusk is falling. Fortunately, Rose lives in an attached apartment on the side of the house that I took out a home equity line of credit to build when I was pregnant. I knew that once my maternity leave was over, I was going to need someone around at a moment's notice to take care of my daughter. With my job, I sometimes get called out in the middle of the night. Rose understands that she's pretty much always on call for me, and I pay her fairly well for it with Reeve's help.

I bring Reeve into my office and shut the door. He finds a spot against the wall and leans into it, crossing his arms. I take note of his defensive position, but have no intention of handling him with kid gloves. "What the hell is going on?"

"Ali"—he sighs and holds up a hand defensively—"I can't go into it all right now, but I'm a suspect in something that has to do with a reporter who's died."

"I've gathered that much. I saw part of your questioning."

"You did? How?"

"Easy. Just walked right in." I say this with satisfaction. "Through the one-way."

He stares at me. "And?"

"And I caught the part where you didn't admit that Anne Marie was at your place. Any particular reason for that? Because quite frankly, Reeve, I probably don't need to tell you that if they didn't have much to go on before, then you've just given it to them by not being forthright."

Reeve looks at me silently, his face rigid. Finally he says, "How do you know?"

"Know that she was at your place?"

He nods. He looks like a kid who's been caught stealing in the candy shop, and I want to kick him to snap him out of it. I roll my eyes instead. "It doesn't take a genius to figure it out. Wineglasses left unwashed." I think, *Scrunchie in your bed,* but don't say it.

"Wineglasses?" he says. "That proves nothing. I could have had any number of people over for wine."

"Then did you provide their names? Who you had over so they can verify it? So they can give you an alibi?"

"No," he says.

"Yeah, because there are no other names to provide except for hers, right?"

He doesn't answer at first, and I'm surprised at how much a hollow ache balloons inside me. It's a sobering moment because it's the first time in a while that it's hit me straight on that there's a chink in my armor when it comes to Reeve, that the story I feed myself daily—that I don't mind being single and that I haven't missed him—might have holes. I want him to say that I'm wrong, that a few friends just came over and that she was never there. I stare him down, feeling my chest rise with each angry intake of air.

Finally he says, "You're right. She was there."

It feels like a gut punch, but I recover quickly, because I'm expecting it. "Then you should have told them about it in the first place, and that makes me wonder why you didn't. Just like it's going to make *them* wonder why you didn't. Are you guilty of something, Reeve? Did something go wrong with that woman?"

"No. I can't believe you're even asking me that, Ali." His eyes are locked on mine, almost cold.

It's not comforting. People think liars have shifting eyes, and novice liars do, but accomplished deceivers do the opposite. They hold theirs still, too still, and that's the giveaway. Their stares become fixed and their calmness feels anything but reassuring. But it's not like I think Reeve is an accomplished liar. I have no reason to surmise that, other than the fact that I know he had some rough years as a youngster, and most teens who have juvie experiences know how to toss out a good story. I shake it off and plow ahead. "Are you kidding me?" I reply. "Of course I'm going to ask you that. What do you think this is? A woman has been murdered. This is serious shit. Why didn't you tell them she was with you last night?"

"I don't know. It felt wrong, like they already had me pegged." His glance slides to my desktop, and I feel like I'm at least getting part of the truth. "Like they were looking for anything to hang on me, and I didn't feel like giving it to them, okay? I didn't even know what happened to her, and they kept stringing it out, not telling me, like they were baiting me. It pissed me off."

"And you're so stupid that you can't figure out that, by lying, you just *did* give them a reason to peg it on you?"

Reeve lowers his chin like an angry, pouting child, and I see where Emily gets that look. I think of Toni with the same expression in the principal's room, annoyed at me for telling her not to talk to Sara Seafeldt, and years later, every time she got busted by my mom or me for swiping money from us for pot and eventually harder drugs.

Finally Reeve says, "I know it was stupid of me. I got nervous, okay? I didn't know what to do, and then, as the interview went on, it just got harder to come clean, especially when I wasn't even sure what kind of a game they were playing with me."

I draw a deep breath and shake my head at his utter foolishness. I've dealt with this type many times before in my job and, guilty or not, I'm incensed by the fact that I've had a child with someone senseless enough to follow the same slippery path as every other thug I've come into contact with over the years in my job. I think of my own father with his selfish lies and omissions of the truth to both my mom and to Toni and me. The times he said he couldn't get off work and couldn't make it to take us for the day, when later we'd find out he was simply drunk and high, possibly passed out. Or the times he'd show up at a school play at the very end. I'd watch him walk in and take an aisle seat, and then later he'd tell me that he was there for the whole thing.

I want to ask Reeve what all had happened, to recount the evening for me, but another part of me doesn't want to hear it. I look down at my desk, at bills I need to pay stacked neatly in a pile in a wire file tray. I can hear Emily squealing with delight out back, and my heart sinks. "At least answer this: Were you at her friend's cabin?"

"No, no, I've never set foot near that cabin."

"Have you driven to it?"

"No. She had her own car."

If he's telling the truth, I'm relieved that there will be no sign of him at the scene of the crime. I'm standing, still thinking, my hip leaning into the side of my desk. "But she was at your place?" I say again in disbelief, as if this second time around, the answer will change and all will be better.

He nods to confirm what has already been established.

"But you didn't tell them?"

"I know, Ali. I know I've backed myself into a corner. It's complicated, being like that in front of two detectives—like they're out to get you. It's hard to cooperate."

"Not for a normal person," I say, and watch his face droop with sadness to hear me say it out loud. A sting of guilt for demeaning him bolts through me, but it doesn't prevent me from slinging more his way because I'm furious, and a part of me is deeply suspicious about the fact that he did not tell them the truth. "Most people would simply tell the damn truth."

"I realize that. But we both know I'm not like most people." He gives me the unanimated, unwavering stare again. The line smacks of rehearsal—as if it's his armor, as if he's *proud* of it—and that infuriates me more. "But look, I just wanted to see Emily first and make sure things were okay with McKay. I'll be out of your hair in a minute. I'll go back and explain things to them."

"It's a little late," I say, stifling my rage, my mind racing. *Out of my hair?* I think. As if it's that easy. I want to yell at him that we have a child together and that means we'll be in each other's fucking hair for years, but I'm still clinging to the line "we both know I'm not like most people." I'm thinking about what a cop-out it is, always has been. *I can't do it,* Reeve had said to me about our relationship. *I'm just not like everyone else,* he had added later. Before, when he used to say that kind of thing, it gave me some relief because it gave me *my* out, *my* escape route. I never bothered to call him on it, but now, with Emily in the picture, I want to scream at him that I think it's one colossal justification so he can get away without growing up and taking responsibility for his actions. Instead, I force myself to calm down and remind myself that none of that matters anymore. The only thing germane is protecting Emily. "You think going back now will just make this all better?"

"If I go back and tell them everything, that I was just afraid, they'll have to understand, won't they?"

I look at my desk, on which there's a photo of Emily from a year ago with her arms wrapped around McKay. She looks like the happiest kid on the planet, even though I know she's not. She often has nightmares, complains of joint pain and bellyaches, and still throws vicious tantrums. She took longer than your average girl to potty train, and her pediatrician said that it comes with the territory of split homes. That children from parents who are separated often have psychosomatic symptoms, internalize the hurt into their bodies.

And now this unexpected curveball . . . My fury boils at the stupidity of it. I want to pick the picture up and shove it in his face, say, *See, you happy now? Getting yourself mixed up in something that can hurt this precious child?* But I realize I'm overreacting. I can't believe he's asking for my opinion, but he *is* asking, which is more than I'd have ever expected from him.

Part of me wants to advise him to go back immediately, but another part of me knows how bad it's going to look and that he might be better served by getting a lawyer and not saying another word before he digs himself in any deeper. Telling his truth, whatever that might be, to an advocate might be his best option. The less he says, the less can be used against him in court by a prosecutor. I look at him and say, "I don't know. It might, but honestly, Reeve, I think that no matter what you do from here on out, you're going to need an attorney."

"An attorney?" Reeve's face twists in anguish.

"Yes, you can do what you want, but that's what I think."

Emily bangs on the office door. "Mommy, Daddy, come outside with us," she pleads.

"Just a sec," I say, trying to sound happy, but before I even turn back to him, Reeve has opened the door and follows her back outside. There's so much more to ask him, but I'm relieved. A part of me isn't sure I want to know more than I already do, and another part of me understands I need many more details if I'm going to help him.

• • •

After a moment, Reeve has Emily bring McKay in while he goes out and fetches a backpack from his truck. He comes back in and fishes a baggie out with some extra scat he carries around and heads to the backyard to plant pieces of it behind various bushes. Then he takes McKay out and has him quarter across the yard to find it all. McKay performs his duties excitedly, and within minutes he has all the samples.

"Good boy," Reeve tells him repeatedly, and rewards him by throwing the ball for some time. Emily stands by his side shivering in the cold, watching her dad throw and asking if she can throw too. He lets her.

I go inside to see Rose off. She is moving Reeve's backpack, which he's placed beside the kitchen door, over to the side so no one trips on it, and even that infuriates me—that he'd be careless enough, like a lazy teenager, to accidentally trip one of us. She tells me that Emily's been great all afternoon, then whispers, "Is everything okay?"

"Yes, why?"

"Reeve looks . . . I don't know."

"What?"

"Well, a little stressed." She pushes her straight strawberry-blond hair behind her ears. She's dyed a few thick pink streaks into either side for fun. It doesn't surprise me that she's asking. Between Rose and Herman, I have more than my share of people interested in my and Emily's well-being.

I say that everything's okay, that I just needed to do him a favor with McKay.

"I hope the dog's not sick."

"No, nothing like that." Emily squeals again outside, and I motion to the backyard as if her joyous yelps mean all is fine. She looks at me like she's knows there's more, but doesn't push it. We've gotten to be decent friends, but she never presses me for too much personal information. In fact, no one in my small circle of friends or coworkers does. It's not my style to give personal particulars, and Rose is well aware of it. "Well, Emily is happy to see him here," she offers.

"Isn't she always?"

"Yeah, she is." Rose smiles and throws her bag over her shoulder. "I wrapped up a plate for you. It's in the fridge. Just heat it up in the microwave."

"Rose," I chide her. "I've told you."

"I know. I know. *I've hired you to take care of Emily, not of me,*" she imitates me in a low professional voice.

I laugh. "Not quite the right accent," I say. "Needs some work."

She smiles, and wiggles her fingers around the strap of her backpack to say good-bye. I watch her walk around the side to her place in the fading light, then go back into the kitchen and turn the back porch lights on. I find an extra jacket for Emily and make her put it on. I know she's seen this activity hundreds of times, but this time is a novelty, since it's in her own backyard and not out at her dad's cabin, with all the meadows and expansive wilderness surrounding them. I watch them in the diminishing light, tiny Emily with her ratty braids beside Reeve's tall frame with his broad shoulders and narrow waist. Emily looks like a little breakable doll next to him, and for a moment I see my little sister, Toni, in her. *Jesus, Ali,* I say to myself, *she's only a little girl.* Besides, she's got my grit. She won't turn out like her.

When they're finished, the sky has gone muddy dark from the low-lying clouds and no stars can be seen. We go back in with McKay, and Reeve asks if I have his dog food. From the car, I fetch the bag along with the bowl I grabbed from Reeve's kitchen floor. "Here you go," I say, handing him the food when I return.

"Thank you." He pours some dry food in the bowl and gives it to McKay beside the back door. Emily wants Reeve to pick her up and hold her, and he does, saying, "You're getting too heavy for this."

"No I'm not," she protests, nuzzling her head into his neck.

When McKay is done eating, Reeve sets Emily down, gives her a hug good-bye, tells her that he'll see her next weekend and that she should go and get ready for bed. Emily kisses his cheek and runs upstairs, ready to please her daddy. She never does what I request so quickly, but I know that I've asked for this. That the arrangement we set up—that she'd see Reeve only every other weekend—would in some ways always make him the special one, the one in demand, the one to behave around, at least for some time until she grew mature enough to recognize the inconsistencies.

I see Reeve out after he puts McKay on his leash, and when he lets McKay hop into his truck and turns to me to say good-bye, I hand him a note with an attorney's name and number I've jotted down. "Call this guy. He should be able to help you out."

"I'm not calling an attorney. That just makes me look guiltier."

"You already *are* going to look guilty," I say. "Trust me on this."

"No," he says, then shakes his head. "I mean yes, I do trust you, but I don't want to get an attorney involved. I trust you to help me." He immediately looks down at his door handle as if that was a difficult thing for him to admit.

My heart rate speeds up, and I can't tell if I'm pissed off or somehow touched by his faith in me. The temperature has dropped now that it's dark and the chill nips at my cheeks. I shuffle from one foot to the other. "Okay," I say, "I'll see what I can do, but if this gets any more out of hand, you're going to need to hang on to that name and number." I motion to the note I've just handed him.

"I will." He opens his door and hops in. He raises the flap of his center console and puts the note inside. "Thank you," he says, then backs out of the driveway and leaves.

Reeve

Wednesday—The Day Before

Aɴɴᴇ ᴍᴀʀɪᴇ ꜰᴏʟʟᴏᴡs me from the Merc to my cabin. The sun is setting in my rearview mirror and there's a pale light over the mountains in the east. Across the meadows, gold- and yellow-leaved aspen trees line up in front of swaths of green pine, their brilliant leaves shining in the glow of twilight like an elaborate layered fringe in front of the jutting mountains of the Livingston Range. The mountains seem to be leaning forward, as if each peak were aggressively pushing the other toward Canada, as if they haven't fully escaped the sense of their violent, eruptive beginnings. That duality is always present out here—the aching beauty coupled with the brutality.

I'm not sure what to think. I'm excited at the prospect of having her over, but I haven't had a woman over since Ali, and I'm nervous.

When I pull into my drive and park, I see a herd of elk at the far end of one of the meadows, their lighter backsides nearly luminescent in the gloaming. Anne Marie pulls in next to me. I get out and walk over to her car and point out the herd. She steps out and smiles.

"This is where you live? Full-time?"

"Yep. This is it."

"It's so nice out here. Do you live alone?"

"Just McKay and me."

She studies me again with the same expression she had out in the field, like she's trying to read me. For a second I think she's going to ask me, "Aren't you lonely?" But instead she says, "Are you going to let him

84

out?" She glances at my truck, where McKay is sitting like a patient human passenger, simply looking out his side window.

"In a minute." I look back out at the elk. "He might scare them off. See"—I point—"there are the bulls." Two large males with gorgeous curved antlers barely visible in the dim light bow their heads to the wild grass. "They're pretty amazing, don't you think?"

"They're wonderful." She leans across her hood. I stand awkwardly next to her, both of us looking across the golden meadow at the herd grazing, with the vivid fall foliage in the background.

Anne Marie stands up from leaning on her hood and glances up at me; we lock eyes for a moment. Her face is rosy from the rapidly cooling air. Then, with no prompting, she simply rests her head on my shoulder, as if she's known me forever, as if she's completely comfortable with me. A faint trace of her perfume still lingers in the cool air, and I feel a slackening inside me, like something's come unstuck. I hesitate for a second, then put my arm around her like I've known her for a long time too. We stand that way for a moment, taking in my home's immense surroundings, a place I never tire of. One of the cow elk lets loose a strident cry, and Anne Marie puts her fingers to her mouth, the skin on the back of her hand pale in the dusk.

I'm aware that I'm noticing every detail, just like I've done all day, as if I've been given a drug—some hallucinogen that makes every nuance pop and come to life. I almost rethink my day, wondering if someone could have put something in my coffee at the Merc or given me a substance that I was unaware of, but I know that's not the case. I try to relax and take it in—the sense that I feel very alive. It's all so exquisite—achingly beautiful, as if I've just been reborn and life has chosen to show a glimpse of its sweet underbelly to me.

Ali

Present—Thursday

AFTER REEVE LEAVES, I go in and put away the pots that Rose has cooked pasta in, washed and set on a drying mat beside the sink. When I go upstairs to check on Emily, she's in a pair of sunny yellow jammies and playing with two unicorn figurines in her bedroom. I get down on the floor beside her and brush her hair out of her face so I can see her eyes. She looks at me for a second, her eyes the color of brown M&M's, but they're not focused on me, her thoughts a million miles away in some imaginary unicorn land. She's making swishing sounds and moves the two unicorns—one glittery blue and the other pink— through the air like they're flying.

"Hey, kiddo," I say, breaking her trance.

She looks at me, this time seeing me.

"You have a good day at school?"

"Yes," she says, launching into everything that happened play-by-play, starting with her kindergarten homeroom teacher's having them trace their hands so that they can cut the shapes out and transform them into turkeys later in the week for Thanksgiving.

"*I* did that," I say, as if that activity should belong only to my generation. "Don't they come up with anything new?"

"Mommy," she scolds me.

I smile. My daughter already knows how to handle my bad attitude. "That sounds fun," I say, and let her get back to explaining the rest of her day down to every single detail, which takes another ten minutes. She's at the age where she's found her voice, and she uses it. I remind myself to enjoy her motormouth phase now because there might come a time, as a teen, when she offers very little, if anything at all. When she comes to the end of cataloguing her day for me, she says, "Mommy?"

I know that when she says "Mommy" in a questioning voice, she waits for a reply before she'll continue, so I give it to her. "Yes?"

"How come Daddy came by?"

"To say hello to you and to get McKay."

"And how come you had McKay with you?"

"Oh, I just did a favor for your daddy. He was tied up and McKay needed babysitting."

Emily thinks that's funny, throws herself back on the beige car-peted floor, and says through giggles: "Babysitting? A dog?"

"I guess you're right, smarty-pants. I should say *dog*sitting."

Emily's still laughing, and I'm tempted to tickle her, but I resist because it's bedtime, and I don't want her to get worked up when she needs to wind down. "Come on, pumpkin." I stand and hold out my hand to her. She pauses like she's thinking about something, and I brace for the question she asks at least a few times a week: *But, Mommy, why can't Daddy and McKay come live here with us?*

"Let's go get your teeth brushed," I say before it comes out, and by the time we reach the bathroom, she has let it go.

When Emily is tucked away snugly in her bed, I go to my office and sit and stare at the wall for a moment. "Damn you, Reeve," I whisper into the quiet room. I lean back and rub my face, trying to decide if I believe Reeve or not. The fact that he didn't tell the detectives about her coming over continues to nag at me. In my heart, I don't think he's capa-ble of hurting someone, but in my work, I've known far too many fam-ily members who have said the exact same thing about relatives who *have* killed someone. My experience begs me to be logical, but I think of kissing Emily good night, the small closed-lip smile on her lips as she snuggled into her pillows, and my heart tells me to follow my intuition: Reeve Landon would never intentionally hurt a living thing—unless, that is, that thing threatened to hurt someone he cared about.

Reeve

Present—Thursday

I DRIVE UP THE windy North Fork road to go home. It's pitch black with no moonlight or starlight. A wet mist shines in my headlights and the paved part of the North Fork road reminds me of glazed donuts and feels like it's purposely trying to make me lose control of my vehicle. My stomach grumbles because I haven't eaten anything since morning and I just want to get home, eat, and light a fire, but I'm not sure what to expect. I'd been entertaining the notion that perhaps the chances of the county's getting the appropriate people rounded up to drive all the way out in the evening seemed slim.

When I'm within a half mile of my cabin, I can see across the meadows that the lights are on, and I try to recall if I left them that way, but I'm sure I didn't. Ali must have left them on when she picked up McKay. But as I get closer, I see a large white van and a county sheriff vehicle parked out front. First I feel irritation at the invasion of my privacy, and then fear at what it could mean. I picture the two wineglasses I left unwashed on the counter, the plates and utensils from the lasagna left in the sink, and curse myself for being such a slob.

When I pull up, Reynolds meets me at my truck. I get out and face him. I had entertained the notion that I was taller than he was, but I can see I'm wrong. He's about the same height as me, and I stare directly into his face. Even in the dark shadows, with only the lights from the cabin and the forensic lamps lighting up the place, his face looks smug.

"Mr. Landon," he says, "nice to see you again. As you can probably

88

tell, a search warrant has been issued on your place." He passes me the document. I reach out and take it.

At first I find it hard to focus. I feel like I'm spinning with anger, and my heart is pounding too fast. The globe light from my cabin isn't reaching out far enough for me to be able to read, so I find the flashlight on my cell phone and turn it on and light up the official-looking document. I force myself to focus on the information. It lists the time frame during which the search needs to be completed—the next twenty-four hours— as well as the address, a description of my cabin, and the reason for the search: that the evidence of trace is expected to be found to provide proof that the victim was in the residence. A magistrate has signed it at the bottom and a seal of notarization is near the judge's name. I hand it back.

"You may stay on the premises," Reynolds informs me, "but we'd appreciate it if you stayed outside and didn't go in while our forensic specialists work. Besides, you won't like the process one bit."

I'm pissed, and I can feel my entire head heat up from the anger, even out in the cold night. "I don't plan to." I hop back in my car, and McKay lets loose an edgy cry.

"But again," Reynolds says, "I wouldn't go far."

I don't answer. I throw my truck in reverse and back up, practically spraying gravel with my tires. I cringe at the thought of them in my place, invading my space. I'm not sure where to go since it's late. When I pull out onto the road, I see my neighbor Ron Wallace's driveway a little way down. I make a quick decision to go to his cabin, which is only a field away from mine.

Wallace isn't around full-time, but he's been visiting for the past month for hunting season, looking for an elk to shoot. He packed up and left yesterday to go home to Oregon, empty-handed, which is un- usual for him. Usually he leaves town with the meat from a six-point already hung, quartered, bagged, and on ice for a meat processor back home. He won't mind if I go to his place and wait this one out.

Alder branches brush and scratch the side of my truck as I drive up the narrow road. When I let McKay out, he runs happily around the cabin as if he's going to find the old man. He sniffs some bushes by the side of its foundation and marks his territory by peeing on several of them. I find the spare key under a log in the wood stack. Ron had showed me where to find it one day when he asked if I'd check up on the cabin once a week, since several others had been broken into and robbed earlier in the spring. I do as he's asked and regularly take a peek, make sure nothing's broken and no pipes are leaking.

Inside, a cold chill clings to the rooms. I find the thermostat and see that he's turned it down to fifty degrees—warm enough for the pipes not to freeze, but low enough to keep from racking up an electric bill. I crank it to sixty-seven, then go into the kitchen and find a can of chili and a pot to heat it up in.

While I wait for it to cook in the cold kitchen, I take a seat at the table and calm myself by petting McKay under his ears where the fur is silky. The old yellow wallpaper is peeling from the tops of the walls, almost creating a uniform roll around the top perimeter of the kitchen, and parts of it are streaked with water stains from leaks from heavy-snow years. I entertain the thought that I should help the old man take it down and replace it next time he comes. But then I think of Ali and how serious she looked—worried—and the idea suddenly seems trivial.

I eat my chili in the cold silence. McKay settles down on the only mat on the linoleum floor, his head resting on his front paws, and stares at me with liquid-brown eyes. If I make any moves at all that appear as if I might get up, he instantly stands to attention, ready to play fetch, ready to do anything. He has not had enough exercise today, and he knows we're not in the right place, so he's more anxious than usual.

I have found some crackers in the cabinet to have with my chili, and when I bite down on one, a sharp piece of it turns upright while I chew and stabs the roof of my mouth. "Ouch," I say out loud, taken aback. McKay is immediately at my side, his tail wagging nervously. Feeling ridiculous that a shard of a cracker can cause such intense pain, even if only for a few seconds, I say, "Who'd think a piece of cracker could feel like a goddamn ice pick?"

He cocks his head, trying to make sense of my words.

When I'm done, I put my coat on, hook McKay's leash to his collar, and head out to the thick copse of trees separating our two properties. An inky darkness and the sweet smell of pine enfolds me when I enter. I don't want to turn the light on my phone on, so I stumble through the woods, tripping a few times over the uneven ground. The cold against my face makes me alert, and in spite of feeling clumsy, I'm happy for the cover. The lumpy, grassy ground, in its early iterations of freezing and unfreezing, squashes in an oddly pleasant way under my soles.

For a moment, before I get close to the meadow across from my cabin, I feel that the world is mine again, as if I'm privy to the special secret that evades so many people because they've unintentionally used concrete or a million other barriers to separate themselves from the truth: that the tall, slender trees beside me and the spongy soil beneath my boots are the lifeline to all that is real, all that sustains—all that matters.

When I get closer, though, and stand behind a pine and peer across the meadow to my own cabin, that righteous feeling quickly dissolves. The lights shine bright yellow through the small windows and little parallelograms spill out to the narrow side lawn flecked with fallen aspen leaves. They're still at it, and worry stabs me. Reynolds's vehicle and the white van sit in the same place on the drive—a little way back—and I suspect they've studied the part-gravel, part-dirt drive to find evidence of Anne Marie's tire treads. I wonder what they could still possibly be looking for besides the dishes. I wonder if they're tearing things apart like I've seen in movies, or have heard Ali mention when she's talked about messy searches that have left homes in shambles. I have to draw several deep breaths of the cool air to prevent me from marching right out of the trees and across the meadow to tell them that they need to get the hell out of my house, even though I know it would be a useless gesture.

I think again of how I have no desire to get an attorney, as Ali suggested, so the next best way to *no comment* myself out of the situation is to remove myself completely from it. I haven't been arrested, so there's no reason I need to be around these people until it all passes.

Leaning against the pine, I feel the weave of bark and the soft lichen clinging to it under my palms. Dead wet pine needles cling to the edges of my boots. I look up at the starless sky and can barely make out the tops of the trees. There's no light pollution up the North Fork drainage, and it's heavenly not to have it. But watching the intrusion into my cabin take place makes me no longer feel safe. The dark bellies of the clouds press down on me, pushing me into something small and insignificant, something expendable. When I look back over to my cabin, I see someone in a hazmat suit walk out to the van.

The ghostly alien-looking suit takes me back. Holy shit, I say to myself: a fucking hazmat suit? I hadn't expected that. For god's sake, couldn't they just go in with some gloves and grab the damn forks and wineglasses?

I feel like I'm in a bad dream and need to wake up. McKay lets out another loud whine to protest our strange venture to a place so near our home but not all the way to it, and the sound of it pierces the still night. The CSI—a woman, judging by her size and shape—jerks her head in our direction. I shush him, yank once on his leash, and hold up my palm for him to sit.

The woman continues to stare out toward us, her chin lifted, her ears probably peeled for the sound of a bear. When you hear something in the woods out in these parts, it's not a human you think about: it's a mountain lion, a bear, coyotes, wolves. After a moment, she turns to the van and opens the back door and throws in her bags, then heads back in, calling something I can't make out to someone inside.

Droplets begin to fall onto my head and my face, and I realize the heavy clouds have opened and begun to rain. I gently pull McKay toward me and quietly tell him to heel, making him hug close to my legs as we walk through the dense trees back to Ron's cabin.

· · ·

From Ron's kitchen window, I watch across the field to see the lights of the van drive by on the North Fork road and disappear into the blackness to head back to the Flathead Valley. I turn the heat back to fifty, finish cleaning up the kitchen, and make a mental note to call Ron and let him know that I stopped in and checked on everything ahead of schedule.

When McKay and I arrive back at our place, I go in cautiously, as if I'm being watched, even though I know they've left. When I enter my back door to the kitchen, I don't see anything amiss. As I figured, the glasses are gone, and so are the forks we used. The plates are still waiting to be washed in the sink. I go into the main room, and not much there is different either. Fingerprinting dust is spread in various places: on the doorknobs, on the table, on the coffee table, on the faucet in the bathroom . . .

When I go into my bedroom, I see the sheets have been taken from my bed. That pisses me off. Why the hell do they have to go and take my sheets? I'm no Suzy Homemaker; I have only one extra pair of bright-flower-patterned sheets around, and they're for Emily when she comes over. She sleeps in my bed in a pair of polka-dotted flannel pajamas she keeps at my place in the third drawer from the top of my dresser. I sleep on the pullout couch. She usually wants me to sleep with her, but I'd prefer she didn't get used to that routine, so I say no. When I talked to Ali about it, she agreed, and said she doesn't let her sleep with her very much either, unless she has a nightmare, which Ali says she's been having a lot more of lately.

It's getting late, and I'm too tired to try to clean the dust, so I get Emily's set of sheets from the closet and lay them out on the bed and try to fall asleep. I'm aware that eventually Emily will need more space— her own room, her own dresser, her own bed—but that all seems very far away right now.

McKay curls up in a ball on his dog bed near the base of my bed, and within minutes, I can hear him breathing more deeply, his feet scuffling in his sleep as if he's chasing something in his dream—maybe a rabbit, a pheasant, or a turkey, but then I think that it's most probably a red ball, and I hope he's getting it each time and that the ball doesn't elude him like so many things elude me.

Ali

___

Present—Friday

I GET EMILY READY for school. She goes to a local public elementary school and loves it, but this morning she's cranky. She refuses to eat her oatmeal, as if she has subconsciously absorbed that something puzzling is going on with someone she cares about. She argues and whines about having to put on her clothes until I lose my patience and snap at her, sending her into a pout the whole way to school.

When we arrive, I manage to get a hug and a kiss from her before she runs over to some other kids that she knows, smiling and giggling, her mood completely transformed within seconds of getting to her homeroom.

I drive to the office with a pit in my stomach. I've tried to call Reeve twice, but he's not answering, and I wonder if he's been called back in for further questioning. The search at his place would be well under way by now, possibly even done last night if they could get anyone from the crime scene unit to process it so late. I consider that Reeve might be out at his cabin, too angry to answer his phone.

When I arrive at my office, Herman is already there, busy working on the Smith case, and he lifts an eyebrow when I walk in. "Tough morning?" he asks.

"Why?"

"You're late and you look a little frazzled."

"Thanks," I say. "Good to see you too, Hollywood."

He winks at me. He knows he can say most things to me and get away with it even though I have a reputation for being somewhat difficult. When we worked a kidnapping case that took place on federal land in Glacier National Park, I took no punches from anyone and was considered a hard-ass, or in my case a bitch. I don't really care about that, but Herman knows what I'm actually like, and he certainly doesn't walk on eggshells around me.

"I've put a stack of files on the Smith case on your desk," he says. "Stuff that came from the Bozeman office yesterday while you were out."

I nod my thanks to him.

"So what were you doing? I heard you visited the county after all."

"Yeah, thought I'd swing by."

"How's their case going?"

I feel like I've been caught with my hand in the cookie jar and avoid his gaze. I pick up the files he's put on my desk. "Okay," I say. "They haven't gotten anyone yet. Just one suspect, but the case is weak if you ask me."

"Why's that?"

"Woman was last seen with the guy, but there's no motive." The means is possibly there, given that Anne Marie's cabin is about three miles from Reeve's place. If he drove with her to her place, shot her, then walked home, which would be a skip in the park for him with the distances he's used to covering, they could discount the fact that his truck had never been to the scene of the crime. As far as method, any person with a rifle could have killed Anne Marie.

"Motive is always the hardest to figure," Herman offers. He's referring to the triad of motive, method, and means. To establish probable cause, most detectives know they need to have strong evidence in all three.

I shrug, indicating that I don't have a whole lot more to give him on the subject.

Herman watches me for a second longer, studying me, and I look up at him, my brow raised in an obvious question.

"Nothing," he says back. "You stressed about something?"

"No. Do I look stressed?"

"Maybe a little."

"Gee, thanks. You're really making me feel good today."

"Sorry, never mind. I just worry about you sometimes. That's all."

"Oh my god, Herman. Please." It's true. Herman does have a nurturing side, and sometimes he pesters me about whether I'm eating right or getting enough sleep. Mainly he wants to make sure that I'm behaving, and that I'm not upsetting anyone higher up or calling attention to us. He knows I have a live wire in me always ready to cast about, and that sometimes I walk a fine line between productive and obnoxious. I blame it on my pushy Jersey side, and that line works on most people here, but I know it has a lot more to do with my childhood and the need to take control. "I'm good," I say. "Get back to work."

He laughs and goes back to his desk while I pretend to dig into the Smith case, but instead begin making a list of things I want to investigate about Anne Marie Johnson.

Reeve

Wednesday—The Day Before

SOMETIMES IN THE solitary space of my home, with the aspens beside my cabin filtering the light and casting dappled shadows onto the floor, I'm reminded briefly how it was to be a carefree youngster. How it was before it all lurched away from me in the blink of an eye—in the pull of the trigger. I have this image of me as a boy, as ebullient as Emily, bouncing through each day, intently exploring hollowed-out tree trunks in the Florida woods and trying to capture bullfrogs and lightning bugs. But then, within seconds, all the images lose their color and turn grainy and begin to break up, like an old deteriorated film that has become unwatchable. I am reminded that this was a *different* me, another person entirely. That all I can do now is shrug at the unfairness of life.

But I am not alone now. Anne Marie is walking into my cabin with me after watching the elk, and life suddenly seems fair. She looks around and asks where she can wash up. I point her to the back right. "Can't vouch for its condition," I say, "but it's through that door."

She disappears into the bathroom, and I think about what just happened while we were watching the elk. When she put her head on my shoulder, it was a spontaneous, childlike gesture and so utterly unexpected, yet almost instinctive, that it awakened a part of that boy I used to be. I felt a tenderness I reserve only for Emily. I'm not sure exactly what it is about that Anne Marie—a stranger, really—that brings out my sensitive side. Perhaps it's her unselfconsciousness.

I hang my pack and remove my boots by the door, then feed McKay. From a small wine rack on the kitchen counter, I take out a bottle of Cabernet, a Christmas gift from my boss. I also have beer in the refrigerator and a frozen lasagna, so I take it out and turn the oven on. When Anne Marie returns, her hair is wet above her ears and along her temples.

"I hope you like lasagna," I say. "Because that's all I've got."

"Sounds great to me."

I ask her if she'd like a glass of wine or a beer, and when she says wine, I ask if a Cab is fine. She says it's perfect, then walks around my cabin, taking it in. It's chilly inside, and I'm glad there's kindling and cut wood already stacked beside the woodstove so I can make a fire. She studies Emily's drawings on the fridge and when she goes into the living room, she looks at more of them on the coffee table beside the couch. "You have a child?" she asks.

"Yeah, Emily. She's five."

"Where is she?" Anne Marie plops down into one of my easy chairs and begins rubbing her feet, which I suspect are sore from hiking.

"She's with her mom." I hand her the glass of wine, then kneel down by the woodstove to make a fire.

"And where's her mom?"

"She lives in Kalispell, where Emily goes to school." I arrange the kindling into a little teepee-like structure over some wadded-up paper and strike a match, lighting the paper and blowing softly at it until it ignites the kindling. When it does, I turn to her, and add: "We're not married. Never have been."

She lifts her brow.

"I know it sounds messy, but it works well. It's good this way. I have my daughter every other weekend."

"I don't mean to sound rude, but it sounds like—well, just a little like a cop-out to me," she says.

Her bluntness surprises me at first, but then I find it refreshing. I like that she speaks her mind. I hate to admit that it reminds me of Ali. I can't help but grin.

"Why are you smiling?"

"Not sure. I can't disagree with you. It very well could be a cop-out."

"And you're proud of that?"

"Not particularly, but I know my limitations."

"Limitations?"

"Well, you know, with all my time out in the field . . ." I gesture to the mountains.

She nods, satisfied with my answer, and I'm relieved that she's going to let it go. She slumps back in the chair, resting her head against the back of it. She sighs. "That was a long hike. You're not tired?"

"I'm used to it."

"Man of the mountains." She flashes me a white smile.

"Yeah," I say. *Man of the mountains.*" I have to admit I like the way it sounds, as if I'm impervious, but then I think of my real roots, of the watery and smudged Florida sunset over the Gulf of Mexico whenever we'd go to the beach. "Well, not quite. I'm not from here. I was born in Tallahassee, not too far from the Gulf."

"I see." She closes her mouth and looks down for a second, almost as if she's shy, and I feel a slight shift of energy that I can't pinpoint, as if a single card has been removed from an elaborate card house, but nothing is collapsing yet. But then she lifts her eyes again, and they're intense and sparkling with energy, and I think I've only imagined that shift. "Man *among* the mountains, then," she offers.

"Better," I agree.

. . .

After we eat the lasagna, we continue sipping wine, and Anne Marie tells me about her own life, how she was born in Kennewick, Washington, and how she knew she wanted to become a journalist when she took photojournalism in high school and worked on the school paper. She went to college at Gonzaga University in Spokane and later moved to Missoula to work for the local newspaper there. Eventually she quit and began to freelance, mostly writing pieces about nature, but sometimes she also covers political issues.

"Political issues?" I ask. "Like what?" I've been enjoying listening to her soft voice and want to keep her talking. It's been lulling me into a sort of trance, pulling me into an even calmer space than I'm usually in after a day in the fresh air.

She shrugs. The cabin is warm now, almost too warm, and I crack a window to let in some cold air. The night is entirely silent. Anne Marie's skin is flushed, this time from the fire's heat. She looks radiant in the orange glow of the flickering flames shining through the mucky glass window of the woodstove. "Oh, just stuff, whatever's current."

"And what's current now? Besides our dog research program?"

She looks down, and again I feel that same sideways slip of energy, a slight tightening back up of the knot that had slackened when we were outside. It sends a pang through me, as if I'm losing something that I'm desperately trying to hang on to.

"Right now?" She sighs. "Well, I'm working on a piece about the NRA."

"The NRA?"

She just nods and doesn't offer anything else.

"Can't imagine there's much to dig up there. Their inner workings are kept steel-tight, from what I understand."

"That they are." She smiles.

"So is it gun control you're writing about?"

"I can't really talk about it while I'm in the research phase. Why don't I send you the piece when it comes out?"

"Fair enough," I say.

She puts her wineglass down on the coffee table. "So . . . this arrangement . . ." She leans forward to pick up the stack of Emily's drawings that I've shuffled into a neat pile on the corner of the coffee table.

"I had a feeling we'd end up back here."

"I am a journalist," she says with a wink. "Seriously, though, what went so wrong that you have to see your daughter every other weekend?"

"Honestly?" I sigh. "It's me, I suppose. I'm what went wrong."

"You?"

"Yeah, Emily's mom says I'm kind of broken, and I have to say that she's probably right."

"Broken?" She tilts her head and puts the drawings back down. "That's a strong word."

I don't say anything, but my gaze meets hers.

Anne Marie looks over to the pile of drawings again. "I like the one of the unicorn flying."

"What?" I ask at her sudden change of the subject.

She points at the picture.

"You can tell that's a unicorn from all those scribbles?"

"I can."

"I'm impressed." I lean over and pick up my glass of wine.

"Because of Sam Rickerson?"

I freeze with the glass halfway to my mouth, completely taken aback at the shift in subject again. How does she know who Sam is? I haven't heard Sam's name since I told Ali everything years ago. In my mind, I see an image of Sam's eyes going blank and rolling back in his head—a flash, and then it's gone. "What did you say?"

"Is that why you're broken?" she asks again. "Because of—"

I cut her off. "How do you know about that?" My voice sounds too low, like it's coming from far away.

"I'm a journalist."

"But . . ."

"Didn't you think I'd look you up before meeting with you?" she teases.

"I guess I didn't think about it either way." The fire cracks loudly.

"Tell me," she says, her voice different than it's been all day—less lighthearted, more pointed and forceful. Even though it catches me off guard, it's electrifying in some way because it seems as if there's a deep curiosity bubbling up in her. Her eyes are filled with passion. "How do you feel about the gun-control laws in our country?"

I put my glass down and sit up straighter. "Are you interviewing me?"

"No, no," she says, but she looks a little sheepish.

"Because I'm not interested in being interviewed. I did more interviews over the years than I care to remember. So did my parents. You can read as many articles about it as you want."

"I have read them," she says casually, holding the wineglass by her mouth. "I know that Sam's parents were enraged that the local police claimed that there was no possible way for them to press charges, that they became relentless and enlisted the support of a local congressman—a Republican, actually—to enact a law that made adults criminally liable when children were involved in accidental shootings like yours and . . ."

Her voice fades, and I'm not sure if she's simply out of details or if something in my expression makes her peter out. Or perhaps it dawns on her that I'm uncomfortable. The flickering flames cast menacing shadows around the cabin, and my chest rises and falls rapidly. I can feel my pulse behind my ears, so it's possible she's picking up on my unease.

"But no, listen." She holds up her palm in a gesture of surrender. "I'm sorry, I'm just curious. It must have been awful. Being in the spotlight like that at such a young age. Being the poster child for gun control changes in the state of Florida. Right? I mean, it was your recorded voice from the 911 call that they used to push the bill through."

I'm speechless. I hadn't anticipated this at all. Here she says she's sorry but continues on relentlessly. I stare at her, trying to figure her out, trying to make sense of the carefree woman on our hike and the incisive one before me now. Both are inquisitive, both are sexy, but one is certainly more pointed.

"It's okay," she says softly, then gives me a closed-lip smile and tilts her head charmingly. "We don't have to talk about it."

I keep looking at her, a little dazed, somewhat shocked, my eyes narrowed in confusion or perhaps distrust. I feel like a fool. Whatever sweetness and spontaneity she's brought out in me is dissipating, and now I understand why I had that uneasy feeling earlier. The knot inside me is taut, but still I'm captivated by her.

She's beautiful in the glow of the fire, her freckled skin flushed and her eyes intense with interest. She begins apologizing again for bringing it up, her voice soft and husky. She leans over and grabs the wine bottle and refills my glass in spite of the fact that I hold up my hand to indicate that I'm good. She gives me a closed-lip smile, each corner of her mouth curling up sweetly, and I begin to unwind again, but now it's different. I'm relaxed and charged at the same time. She is a reporter, I think. Perhaps this kind of pushing just comes with the territory. Ali gets like this sometimes too.

Ali

—

After declining Herman's offer for coffee from the break room, I take a moment to call Gretchen in the county crime lab. When she picks up, I mention that I'd heard she'd had a busy night of searching.

"Eh, I'm used to it," she says. "It's a bumpy drive out to the North Fork, but it was worth it. We were able to match the prints in the suspect's cabin to the prints of the victim, which explains where she was until she got to her friend's cabin sometime in the night. The guy also has several fleece jackets, standard for someone living in the woods, but the color and type of fleece found on the victim are consistent with one of the suspect's jackets."

"Doesn't prove much," I say. "Especially since we know she spent the day with him."

"True," Gretchen says. "And there are other unidentified fibers on the vic as well. Some type of black wool, which doesn't give much to go on either, since there are a lot of those types of coats around here as well."

"Was she wearing wool?" I ask.

"No, she was wearing one of those lightweight nylon jackets filled with goose down."

"So, looks like they only have the one suspect for now."

"As far as I know, but you'll have to ask them."

"I will. Just haven't had time to stop in yet today. See if they need some extra help."

"We did collect the bedsheets," Gretchen adds, and I'm grateful that she doesn't think much about my nosing around. "Reynolds wants us to see if we can determine how intimate they were."

"Hmm, yeah, it seems they're trying to establish a motive," I say. "Any other leads?"

"Not that I know of. They're all eyes on this guy—so I heard anyway—especially since he didn't admit that she was at his place that night. Kind of suspicious."

I make a mental note to remind Brander that omitting information doesn't constitute motive. It doesn't mean you've killed someone. I know Brander has recently been assigned to detective after working in patrol, and I figure he won't mind a little reminder from an FBI agent. There's no point saying this to Gretchen, so I move on to the results of Anne Marie's laptop scan.

"Nothing yet," Gretchen says. "Passcode protected, and we haven't yet cracked the code. I've got my computer guy, Ray, working on it."

I thank Gretchen, telling her to keep up the great work before we hang up.

Next I switch gears to O'Brien, whose name and office number are in the University of Montana directory. He picks up on the second ring, and I figure most of the professors and department heads don't have secretaries since the university has undergone significant budget cuts.

"Mr. O'Brien," I say, realizing that he's probably got a PhD and I've just possibly offended him by using the wrong title.

"Yes?" he says.

I introduce myself and he sighs. "Is this about Anne Marie Johnson?"

"Yes, it is."

"Is it really her?"

"Yes, I'm afraid it is."

The line goes silent for a moment, and I can't gauge his response—the worst thing about calling people. If he hadn't been two hours away, I would have preferred stopping in on him instead. "Have you not been contacted by the Flathead County sheriff's office yet?"

"No, I haven't. Why would I be?"

"No particular reason," I say. "It's just that we're trying to go down any and all avenues, talking to people who have had any contact with Anne Marie before she came to visit the Flathead, even if just by phone. Do you recall when the last time you spoke to her was?"

"Right before she went up there to meet one of my dog handlers, Reeve Landon, for a day in the field."

"Can you back up a little for me? How did you come to first have contact with Anne Marie?"

"She came to my office here at the U to ask about our program. She wanted to write an article about it for the Sierra Club magazine. She . . . she interviewed me." His voice seemed to change, falter, when he said it. I took a mental note.

"When was that?"

"A few weeks ago, I think."

"So you didn't know her before that? That was the first time you met her?"

"No, uh, no, not that I can remember"—there's a hesitation in his voice again—"although Missoula's a small town. It's possible I've met her at some function or other, but . . . but I don't think so."

I'm not sure I believe what he's saying, but then again, I might just be reading too much into it. Herman comes back in with a mug of coffee and takes a seat at his desk. I swivel away from him in my chair and lower my voice because I don't really want him knowing what I'm working on.

"So you didn't have any other contact with her besides her getting in touch with you for this article for *Sierra* on the dog program?"

"She's called before about other programs of ours. I think she's done a write-up or two about our golden eagle research efforts."

"Did she ever speak with you about anything besides work? Anything personal that would give you something to be concerned about?"

"No, no, nothing," he says, and clears his throat. "I didn't know her personally."

"Did she seem worried about interviewing Mr. Landon or about coming to the Flathead in general?"

"No, I don't think so," he says.

"Okay, Professor, thank you for your time."

I hang up and tap my pen on my desk. Herman is looking at me and says, "So what's that you're working on?"

"Not much."

"This have something to do with one of our cases?"

I shrug. "Why don't you mind your own business?"

"I can't. I'm inquisitive, and in here"—he sweeps a hand to the office—"your *bizness* is mine and mine is yours." He flashes a smile.

"Not when it's got nothing to do with you or what we're working on together," I say.

"So you're working on something personal?"

"I didn't say that either. I just have something I needed to check on." I motioned with my hand to shoo him away. "Don't you have stuff to do?"

He shrugs and goes back to the computer screen before him.

I turn to mine and pull up all social media sites for Anne Marie Johnson. On Twitter, her profile reads:

I don't like labels, but if I must: journalist, photographer, reader, nature enthusiast. "The commons" is my thing and so is #common sense! Most of all, I'm a coffee drinker and #FreshAirBreather.

I scroll through her tweets, looking at postings and repostings of political news and politically charged statements:

Lawmakers vote to remove climate information from science curriculum in Idaho.

Solar now provides twice as many jobs as the coal industry.

By 2030, all Montana glaciers could vanish. @Joe ReadyMax moved to MT to see it happen.

I scroll farther down.

3,000 times more likely to be killed by an American with a gun than a refugee.

We may live in a post-truth era, but nature does not.

Pro-life, BUT anti-refugee, anti–helping the poor, anti–modest gun control measures, anti–universal health care, pro-war and pro-death penalty. #commonsense

@POTUS If your administration really cares about protecting citizens, you should focus on gun control measures.

Anne Marie Johnson—Deleting my Facebook account means I have more time to read thoughtful essays by @O'Brien.

I go directly to Facebook and see that her page is still there, so apparently she hadn't taken it down before she died. It's the same on her Facebook page, mostly political articles on keeping public lands public, passing commonsense gun legislation, more articles on gun violence in general. When I click on the photos link, there are pictures of her hiking and biking with friends and possibly family. I recognize Vivian in one with Anne Marie and another woman who is not as pretty as either Vivian or Anne Marie but looks like she's more fun. She's taller and heftier than the other two and her head is slightly thrown back, laughing heartily at something. I move my cursor over the photo and see that her friends are tagged. The third woman is Rachel Clark, and I make a note to check her page out as well. For now, I want to focus on Anne Marie's a little longer.

I go back to her feed and load more of it. Several posts down, an entry comes up with a picture of her and a group of people outside what looks to me to be the clock tower in front of the oval-shaped lawn at the University of Montana. The caption reads: *The Golden Eagle Research Group. Honored to write a piece on it.* A link to the website

WildernessForum.com is provided, and an article composed by Anne Marie on the golden eagle studies at the University of Montana is included. I scan it and see O'Brien's name mentioned several times for heading up the research program. I click back to the group photo and study it, tapping my pen softly on some papers on my desk.

I pull up the U of M website and find O'Brien's profile picture and bio. He's got a youthful head of longish dirty-blond hair and a coy smile. I switch back to the photo and find him. He's standing in the center back row, a good two inches taller than everyone else. When I amplify it even more, I see that he has his hands on Anne Marie's shoulders, one on either side. I take a look at O'Brien's photo again, and I'm certain that it's the same person. "And he said he'd never met her," I whisper to myself.

"What's that?" Herman asks.

"Nothing," I say. "Sorry."

But then I think, Maybe he just doesn't remember. His hands on her shoulders like that would take some familiarity, though. It wouldn't be the kind of gesture you'd make with a complete stranger or even an acquaintance. It seems intimate.

I go back to Twitter and click on the article Anne Marie mentioned when she tweeted: *Deleting my Facebook account means I have more time to read thoughtful essays by @O'Brien.*

It's an essay on the privatization of land—how such practices have hurt the lower and middle class in Russia while the Russian government has allied itself with the banks to usurp all the public lands, sell them to the rich, drill for oil, mine for minerals, and develop them in general to make more money for higher-ups. The essay discusses how such practices affect the air, the water, and the animals.

I then search #common sense and #the commons. I read about the commons and see that it refers to cultural and natural resources accessible to all members of a society, including natural materials such as air, water, oceans, and a habitable earth—resources held in common, not owned privately. There are also many articles referring to "the Tragedy of the Commons," and I read the Wikipedia description of that—an economic theory about the collapse of a shared-resource system where individual users acting independently and in their own best interests cause problems for the common good of the rest of society.

I figure I'm going down a rabbit hole, and I can't see how this has anything to do with Anne Marie's death, so I move on to the phrase *common sense*, since she had a hashtag about it in her Twitter bio. I can't find much, other than several articles on gun control popping up, linking to a website that gives information about the number of deaths in the United States caused by gun violence.

#Commonsense on Twitter pulls up a bunch of tweets and links to articles discussing more gun-control issues. So the commons has nothing to do with the common sense crusade, and I'm not sure any of it matters. Clearly these are Anne Marie's personal politics, but I am curious about the gun-control articles, given Reeve's background. There are several about childhood gun accidents, including one written by Anne Marie, and when I click on it, I read that it's about a mother who was shot in a grocery store by her three-year-old daughter, who pulled a pistol out of the mother's purse while riding along in the grocery cart. I contemplate the likelihood that Anne Marie was spending time with Reeve only to interview him for the dog-handling program.

All these things are running through my head when I realize that a large presence looms beside me. Herman is standing to my left, and I had been so lost in thought, I didn't notice him walk up.

"Sorry," he says, "didn't mean to break your daydream."

"Ha, no, I'm just getting lost online," I say, exiting the screen.

"Anything interesting in the Twitter-verse?"

"Nah, it's all just noise. What's up?" I ask.

"It's about Smith. I've got some more transcripts on him from Rubatoy." Agent Rubatoy is an undercover FBI agent outside of Bozeman who received information from a government informant about our subject, Leonard Smith. Smith, who has been hosting a webcast called *Freedom Montana*, raves about being a "patriot" who wants to protect the constitutional rights of all Montanans. We have reams of information to show he is anti-government and an anarchist, which in itself is not breaking the law and entirely free speech, but the problem is, we believe he's been stockpiling weapons and buying materials for explosives, which does make him a danger to state and federal officers in general. In a conversation he had with the informant and again later with Rubatoy outside of Bozeman, Smith claimed that all he needed to do was purchase a more potent illegal firearm to help him target a few law enforcement officers.

Five months ago, Smith moved to our area and began to try to—as he put it—*organize*, so he's our problem now. So far he's continuing his webcasts, making threatening comments that aren't characteristic of your average community organizer's behavior, like how he wants to take down all local law enforcement officers, claiming that "they should be looked upon as unwanted vermin running around town" and that they "need to be shot." Later he defines *vermin* as all agents of the federal government, all judges who violate the Constitution by overturning gay marriage bans, and all police officers.

"Sure," I say, grabbing the file from him. I realize I need to put some time in working the Smith case or Herman will continue to wonder what the hell I'm up to. "Thanks." I pat the folder and look at his large liquid eyes as he lingers by my desk. He looks like he wants me to say something more. I consider telling him everything. He'd probably help me if he knew the entire story, but before I open my mouth, something tells me to keep it private, and I swallow my words.

Herman goes back to his desk and I make a note to speak to Vivian again about Anne Marie's connection to Jeffrey O'Brien. I also need to check out Rachel Clark. My intuitions might have been correct. I'll bet Anne Marie and Vivian *have* spoken more than once—"in passing"—about Jeffrey O'Brien, and that's why Vivian recalled the name so easily.

Reeve

I WAKE UP BEFORE sunrise after a restless night of sleep to the sound of elk bugling all around me. I usually enjoy lying in bed, listening to their reedy cries and hollow bellows like poignant good-morning wishes in the misty dawn, but today I'm agitated. I had tossed and turned all night, worrying that headlights might shine on my cabin in the middle of the night and a deputy would take me in for questioning again. Images of Anne Marie accosted me. Sometime after two a.m., when I had finally made the decision to just get up and start working, I finally drifted off. I wasn't under arrest, I told myself again, and I had a job to do, even if that job meant I'd be difficult to find if they had more questions.

After I let McKay out, make some coffee, and feed him when he comes back in, I eat some oatmeal, then pack my gear. I fill my CamelBak with water and throw in apples, trail mix, and beef jerky. I make sure I have everything for McKay: his doggie snacks, his leash, his ball, and his water bottle and nylon bowl. It's just another day, I tell myself. No reason to behave otherwise.

Before I leave, I see that Ali has called me twice already and has left messages for me to call her. When I do, she picks up right away. "Reeve," she says, "where are you? I've called twice."

"I'm at home. Getting ready to work."

"Work? You mean you're heading into the field?"

"Yep."

"Uh, I don't think that's such a great idea."

"Why? I'm not under arrest. No one can stop me from working. Plus, McKay can't go two days without it."

"I understand that, but under the circumstances . . . If they need to ask you more questions, you probably don't want to be difficult to find. It will make things worse. Can't you work McKay around the cabin?"

"Ali"—I ignore her question about McKay—"you told me not to tell them the truth, so what else can I say to them?"

"I didn't say that. That's not what I said at all. I meant, either way, you should get an attorney. Have you done that? Have you called the number I gave you?"

"No, I haven't. You know I can't afford an expense like that."

Ali doesn't say anything right away, which is unusual. She's rarely at a loss for words. Finally she says. "Just do me a favor, Reeve, and don't go far. For your sake, just be available and cooperative if they call you."

"I will." I tell her good-bye, then look at McKay, who's waiting on me patiently. "Time to go, buddy." He follows me to the truck, wagging his tail with excitement as he hops in and we take off for the day.

When we begin treading on one of the familiar trails, a purpose-filled anger fuels my body. Deep down, I know I'm being a little unreasonable. The detectives—they're simply trying to solve a murder, and I am the last one to be seen with Anne Marie. It makes perfect sense that I'm under the microscope, and I'm the idiot who made matters worse by not telling them that she had come over after our day together. What did I expect?

But I refuse to allow them the power to put my life on hold. I step eagerly over the uneven ground through these overgrown woods not far from a narrow creek. I'm ready to make up for the lost day in the woods, my way of giving the finger to the deputies. You can't control me, I think. Not out here.

"You're ready to work, aren't you, boy?" I ask McKay.

He lifts his head and sniffs the air, sifting through all its layers for the scents he's programmed to find. He looks at me expectantly, then runs off. I watch him bound over rocks and bushes, and feel pleased to provide what he needs most.

It takes a full day to climb to the place I want to go: an escarpment surrounded by dense trees that skirts out to a broad scree slope. When I arrive, I lean back against the textured hard rock and pull out doggie treats for McKay and a baggie of trail mix for myself. McKay settles next to me. In the dull light, the river looks like a ribbon made of pewter instead of the bright turquoise color it takes in the late spring and summer. I sit listening to the forest, to the chipmunks scurrying around to collect food for the winter and the birds that haven't flown south darting around at the tops of the pines. The layers of communication going on in the forest always amaze me; it's much more complex than we give it credit for. I think of Anne Marie—of her own complexity, which confused, irritated, and intrigued me all at the same time. A picture of her sitting by my woodstove, her wineglass glistening with the firelight as she turns it in her hands, pops into my head. A great sadness falls upon me, and suddenly I don't want to go back home at all.

I consider camping under the outcropping of rocks that form an enclosure. I can make a fire, sleep under my emergency space blanket with McKay: we'd keep each other warm. I've packed enough dog food, trail mix, and jerky to get by. I always carry my water purifier with me, so hydration is not an issue, especially this time of the year when the rain and snow in the upper elevations has been plentiful and the streams are running again. A windswept pine stands off to my side. I could string my pack containing food up into it away from the bears.

A night in the wilderness, out in the moonless dark in the frigid, skeletal depths of the austere autumn forest . . . McKay and I have done it plenty of times, but usually it's during the summer or early fall, when the late bronze sunshine lingers, shimmering across the valleys well past nine. A part of me thinks I'd like to, even in the frigid cold, and another part of me knows it's not wise. I can smell snow in the air, and sunset is only two hours away. If I'm going to beat the darkness, I need to start heading back down, but I don't move.

What I'm beginning to feel is the ugly seed of apathy, a tendency I had worked on with my counselor in Florida. Pinpointing its origins to the day I shot Sam wasn't any Freudian feat, but understanding how the reverberations of its aftermath ran through my family was trickier.

Sometimes I used to detest my counselor, Gary—the one who smelled of patchouli oil. He wore tortoiseshell glasses and constantly ran one hand through his hair to push it away from his temple even though it was tied back into a sun-streaked ponytail, which drove me kind of crazy.

When he pushed me to recall the event, I thought he was just trying to make me cry. I refused to talk about the actual moment I shot Sam—how it was with him bleeding in my arms. It was an image that accosted me every day and night for many years to come, and at moments that I couldn't predict or control. After it happened, I'd go to school and try to listen in class, or later try to play with friends, and that image would pop up out of the blue.

One time another boy, Joey, and I were playing beside his house in the shade. Ferns and lily leaves hugged the cement foundation and the dirt smelled so loamy, I could feel it in my throat. When we saw a lizard as green as the leaves dart up a long stalk, Joey quickly found a stick and tried to poke it. He got nowhere near it, only jabbing at its wake as it scurried away. In that moment, the quickness of the darting lizard and the prodding stick, all I could see was Sam, his blood everywhere, his body's final, twitchy jerks.

I never told Gary what it was like to try to give Sam CPR, his limp body in my arms, his eyes having already rolled back in his head while I gave the breaths and pumped his heart, counting to fifteen as I had been taught in school, with a maniacal, breathy voice that seemed to belong to someone else, not me.

Gary did, however, get me to talk about things that surrounded the event—like the lizard incident. When he asked how it was walking out of the house with the paramedics and the police, watching Sam being put into the ambulance, I described the stunned expressions of my parents, who had rushed home because they were my next call after 911.

I described how, within a day and a half of the incident, the press was parked on our street and on our lawn, and the phone kept ringing with calls from reporters and strangers. My mom's sister, Diana, insisted we stay at her house. Reporters captured photos of us coming out of our house to leave for my aunt's, my face blank and scared-looking, my mom's pink and splotchy from crying, and my dad's red and angry at the world, commanding me and nudging me behind him so the photographers couldn't get a clear shot, and me, confused and panicked, failing at the simple act of hiding behind his rigid torso.

My aunt lived only a subdivision or two from where we lived in Tallahassee. The grid of wide, numbered hilly streets—some with cul-de-sacs—seemed to sprawl endlessly and had provided ample space for Sam and me to ride our bikes. Aunt Diana lived not far from Sam's and my elementary school. Not far, in fact, from the hospital they took his body to, and from the Lutheran church where they would have the funeral four days later.

But everything passed by in a blur to me on the way to my aunt's in my parents' car. My mom sobbed in the front passenger seat, her head resting against the window as if her neck couldn't hold it up. My dad kept looking straight ahead, his eyes on the road. When we got to Diana's, I looked up at him, waiting for him to glance at me with his intense blue eyes or to say something, but he wouldn't, and his face contained something so great and enormous that I couldn't have begun to understand or describe it other than to say that it was scary and sad. Now, as an adult, I know his expression was anguish, but then I just knew it as the face that told me that things were never going to be the same again.

Gary forced me to try to put words to the feelings of guilt, to discuss the idea that even when you've done something horrible accidentally, people still look at you like there's something inherently wrong with you—because you *must* be a sneaky child, because you *must* be a delinquent in some way if you were in your parents' bedroom in the first place without permission . . . if you picked up something only an adult should pick up.

A week after the incident, my aunt forced my mom and me to go out for ice cream, and we rode bikes to a local creamery. At nine years old, even heavy with grief, I could perk up a bit for ice cream, partly because I still did not fully comprehend the gravity of what I had done to Sam. While we were in line, my aunt noticed some friends of hers come in—two women, one with a brace around her knee. She told my aunt that she'd twisted it while playing tennis with her son, who, she said motioning to me, was about my age. When Aunt Diana introduced us only as her sister and nephew, they looked at me curiously, as if they were trying to place me.

I felt exposed. Shy. My face flushed, and I looked down at the black-and-white-checked floor, hoping they wouldn't recognize me from the papers. My aunt changed the subject in the uncomfortable silence, telling them to enjoy their ice cream, and we sat down. When they took a table across the room, the one with the metal brace, sitting close to the edge so she could stretch her leg out, began to whisper and glance over at me, prompting the other woman to look too.

I was unable to eat my cherry-cheesecake-flavored ice cream in its sugar cone, felt it dripping down onto my hand until my aunt handed me a napkin. I'll never forget the looks, the way they held accusations: Thank god that's not my child.

The apathy, though—it's a weed I'd thought I'd rooted out long ago. But, sitting on the beveled platform of rock, I can't bring myself to care which way this goes, and it scares me. It frightens me for Emily's sake. She doesn't need a father who doesn't care, who gives up. But nipping at the heels of that always comes the darker thought: Emily might be better off without me.

I brush the thought away. It's a selfish one. I look out over the valleys below and the jutting mountains. The ridges to my left have bare rock walls that remind me of ramparts. The swaying trees and the shifting clouds above make the landscape seem to ripple and undulate, as if the mountains and valleys are breathing, conversing, and conspiring, but I know they're just insolent stone. Still, danger seems to lurk in the bleak light. Down below, I spot a black object that appears to be moving, and I wonder if it's a bear. I pull out my binoculars and look.

I should know better. I've witnessed this phenomenon hundreds of times: a dark-colored rock appearing as if it's moving when it's only an optical illusion—a trick of the light or the weakness of the human eye. I scold myself for falling for it with all my experience in the backcountry. I am not one of those who think every rustle of the leaves is a bear and every snapped twig is Bigfoot watching me.

I sit and draw the crisp air into my lungs. I can feel the timelessness out here, the sense of eternity mocking me, pointing out my futile efforts to move through it each day, all day, to gather DNA, to survive myself. It's a terrible feeling, as if the massive, unforgiving wild is snickering at my uselessness. It dawns on me that in all the thousands of miles I've walked through these mountains, I've never felt this before. Mocked. Heavy black clouds roll in above and darken the trees lurking to my side. One thing I am certain of is how my staying out here will look to Ali and to the police. After a moment, I shove my trail mix back in my pack, stand, give McKay a whistle, and head back down the mountain.

. . .

When I emerge from the woods, it's dark. I've had to hike the last thirty minutes with a flashlight, and even McKay wouldn't leave my side. "You big baby," I teased him as we went, but he continued to press his body against my legs as we walked, making me trip and lunge abruptly ahead to try to regain my footing several times. I'm happy to see the outline of the truck when we finally arrive at the entrance.

I start the engine, turn the heater on, and head home, but when we get near my cabin, from across the meadow, I notice that the lights in

Ron Wallace's cabin are on, and I wonder if I forgot to turn all of them off the night before. I drive up his dirt road to check it out. When I reach his place, I see his truck in the drive.

"You're here," I say when he comes out the door and stands on the wooden porch. He cocks his head and squints at me. "I thought you were headin' out. Thought you'd be back home in Oregon by now."

"Changed my mind. You know. Couldn't get that damn elk. Began to bother me." He chuckles as if it's no big deal, but I sense something else there, something heavy and sad in his eyes, and I wonder what would make the old man turn around, change his plans so abruptly. One eye is leaking, but it's not tears. It could be his age or the wind.

He invites me in, and I ask him if he minds if I let McKay out of the truck.

"Of course not," he says. "He need a bowl of water too?"

"No, he's had plenty, but thanks anyway. He's been fed too."

Wallace's thin, downy hair is blowing the wrong way across his side part in the chilly evening breeze, and I realize I've never seen him without a baseball cap. When he turns to go back inside, his shiny bald spot shines under the porch light.

When we're inside, he pulls a Bud Light out of the fridge and hands it to me.

"I was here last night," I say.

"I noticed. Had yourself some chili, did you?"

"I figured I could replace it before you returned."

He gives a perfunctory wave to brush the apology away. "I don't care about that. More curious about why you needed to come over so quickly right after I left." He's wearing a green-and-yellow-plaid shirt and an old leather vest over it.

"I don't usually swing by at night."

"Don't care about when you swing by or how often you check on the place. Just wondering what's up. You see someone here who didn't belong?"

"No, nothing like that." I glance up at the wallpaper, motioning to it with my chin. "We should get after that next spring when you return. Looks like crap."

"Yeah, I know." His head tilts and his eyes narrow. He's studying me, I think, and I try to decide how much to tell him. I'm wondering what he'll think of me, and then it strikes me that at least I care about what this old man with years of living under his belt thinks of me. That's something, isn't it? So I tell him. "I came over," I say, "because the county got a warrant to search my place. I didn't want to be there while they were doing that."

"What?" he asks. "A search warrant? Holy shit. That sounds serious. What on earth for?"

I don't answer.

"I heard on the news about some woman, a reporter, being found dead up this way. This have something to do with that?"

I nod, and tell him about being interrogated, skipping the part about Anne Marie coming over. I'm still feeling the need to keep my cards close, like I'm speaking to my father, and he's judging me. But I'm surprised by how easy it is to tell him about the rest of what's happened since the evening she came over.

He sits still, one bony hand pocked with liver spots resting in his lap, the other around his beer bottle on the table. The veins are pronounced, and I can't help but glance at my own hands to see how they're faring. The constant whipping from the mountain wind and the beating from high-elevation sun does a number even on thirty-six-year-old hands. I feel foolish for my moment of vanity, but he hasn't noticed. He stares at his Bud label. A silence takes over the room while he considers my situation, like a dark fog leaking in. I wonder if he is sitting there thinking that I'm responsible for killing Anne Marie Johnson. That there is a killer in his kitchen.

"I didn't do it," I whisper.

He looks up from his bottle but doesn't nod, doesn't say a thing. He swallows, and I can see his knobby Adam's apple move up, then down, his neck thin and pale but strong.

I want to repeat it: *I didn't do it.* But then I think of a short story I read in some literature course at the community college about a man who becomes undone because the town thinks he's stolen something—that he's a thief. The more he tells everyone that he didn't do it, the more they think he's guilty. And I already know I'm guilty. I've been guilty my entire life.

Finally Wallace looks down at McKay, lowers his hand, and snaps his fingers for McKay to come over. He scratches behind my dog's ears like I do and McKay leans his boxy head into his hands. He says to my dog, "I hope for your sake that things get solved quickly."

Ali

Present—Friday

On my lunch break, I grab a fish taco from a place that's decent. The food—specifically the lack of variety—is the worst part about not living out east anymore. It's hard to find good bread and quality deli meats, and sometimes I miss the endless selection of cafés, bars, and shops owned by people from just about anywhere in the world. After I eat my taco in my car in the parking lot outside the restaurant, I head over to the county building. I want to see if I can figure out what kind of headway they're making on Anne Marie's case. When I get to the incident room, Reynolds is at his desk, eating a Subway sandwich and going through files. Several deputies also have food and are staring at their monitors, sliding their mouses across pads and typing one-handedly on keyboards while eating with the other.

"Agent Paige." Reynolds puts his sandwich down and wipes his mouth with the back of his hand. "How are you?" He picks up his phone off his desk, glances at it, but doesn't do anything with it. I figure it's like a security blanket.

"I'm well," I say.

"Where's Agent Marcus?" he asks, as if I shouldn't be in here without my male counterpart, but then I think I'm being overcritical.

"Back at the office," I say. "Where's Brander? Isn't he working this one too?"

"He's out checking on all of the victim's past boyfriends. Most are in Missoula, though, but there's one up this way he's speaking to—a fellow journalist she dated. You know, that reporter who writes for the *Daily Flathead*, guy named Will Jones."

My ears perk up. "I know him," I say. Jostling Jones, I think. In fact, my connection to him isn't a pleasant one. His son, Byron, goes to Emily's school, and before I knew he was a reporter who covered the crime beat, I made a stink about the fact that his son bullied Emily on a field trip up to a place called Big Creek along the North Fork where Reeve lives, near Glacier National Park. The school offers several summer programs for kids of working parents, and Emily and Byron both were in preschool together, a sort of prelude to kindergarten. She came home from the trip to Glacier with bruises on her arms. She told me that Byron kept picking on her, and of course I take what my kindergartner tells me with a grain of salt, but when she showed me the purplish marks, I took it seriously. I'm not going to apologize for saying something about it to the teacher and to Byron's mom. I realize kids will be kids, but you don't grow up with an angry father who puts marks on your own mother's arms and not feel that a little boy's aggression should be taken seriously. And to me, it didn't look like anyone at the school was doing anything, so I said something to the principal about it.

"Not one of my favorites," I say to Reynolds. "Always seems to be poking around where he doesn't belong." Which is true, but I don't say that he's never been very favorable about me in his write-ups ever since the ordeal with Byron. When I worked the Glacier Park abduction case, Jones covered it and made sure the community got the impression that I was ineffective. In every article, he intimated the FBI was botching everything and gave Glacier Park's law enforcement credit for making any steps in the right direction. He would somehow get ahold of the most unflattering photos of both me and Herman, both of us looking like deer caught in the headlights.

Reynolds chuckles. "I like him." That bugs me, but it doesn't matter. Of course Reynolds *would* like a weasel like Jones. "But we do have to check him out," he continues. "He moved here from Missoula. Got his journalism degree at the U of M, so he must have met the victim there, because that's where she's been living since she got out of college. The others, we're checking by phone—crossing most of them off the list, since they all have alibis."

Small world, I think. I want to say out loud: What are the chances that Will Jones, the father of the boy who bullied my daughter, would have dated Anne Marie Johnson? "So . . ." I proceed casually instead, taking the gamble that they haven't yet figured out my connection to their primary suspect. The phrase sits like acid in my stomach—*primary suspect*, aka the father of my child. "Heard you got a warrant."

"Yep," he says, "the guy lied to us. She was definitely in his place—fingerprints, trace—it's all there.

"That prove anything?"

"Not alone, but it's mighty suspicious, don't you think?"

"It is." I sneak a quick peek at the stack of paperwork on his desk, wishing I could take control of the case and have access to all of it. "But he might just be a private person. Just because he was the last to be seen with her and she visited his cabin doesn't mean he killed her."

"We get that." He glances casually at his phone again. "That's why the guy's not under arrest right this moment. But my bets are on him. Because what we have to ask is: What is he hiding?"

I don't respond. The other deputies have leaned back in their chairs and are listening to our chat. My heart is beating faster than I want it to, standing among the county guys, chatting up a case that is way too close to home.

"Next step is bringing him back in to see what he has to say about it all, but we'd like to get a little more information first before bringing him back in—maybe a possible motive."

"What are you thinking?"

"Don't know yet. But there's the obvious. Guy spends the day with her. She comes over for some wine. Thinks she'll put out for him, and maybe she doesn't. He gets pissed and you can figure out the rest."

"Is there evidence that she was killed at his place? Any blood or anything?"

"No, she was definitely killed at the friend's cabin. Body wasn't moved."

"How do you explain that? Were his tire tracks at the friend's cabin?" I ask, already knowing the answer. He explains about the gravel—that they couldn't even get the owner's tracks from it. That Reeve could have driven there and they couldn't prove it, or that he even could have walked there, given his ability to cover far greater distances. "Apparently walking miles and miles is no problem for the guy," he says.

"In the middle of the night? That pissed off about not getting laid? Seriously?" I ask.

He shrugs and shoves his phone back into his pocket. "Why not? It's his area, and it's only a few miles. He knows it like the back of his hand. Might not have had condoms at his place. In fact, none were found, but we did find a pack in her overnight bag at the friend's, which suggests she wasn't on any other form of birth control. It's possible she invited him over and he followed her there. Outside the heat of the moment, maybe she has a change of heart. He gets angry and snaps and he either drives back home or walks back home, if he rode with her."

"Any footprints through the fields to prove that?"

"No, but it's grassy meadows—dried, dead wild grass this time of the year. It had been sunny that day. Warm. Footprints wouldn't have shown anyway."

I don't want to say too much, but I can't help pointing out how far-fetched it sounds. "A bit of a stretch, huh?"

"Maybe, but something's not right about the guy lying to us. What's he got to hide? And who the hell else is going to be out in the boonies at that time of the night? What seems more far-fetched is that someone else just happened to come along in the middle of the night, away from her own town, and do her in."

He has a point, but I don't acknowledge it.

"Guy has a kid too, but he didn't mention that. By the looks of the place, seems like she's only around part of the time."

My insides do a flip and my legs go weak. It's not like I wasn't expecting it, because I definitely knew what they'd discover at his place, but it still takes me by surprise, makes me realize how much I shouldn't be discussing this case. I shrug and change the subject: "Did the autopsy indicate if she was sexually assaulted?"

"No, she wasn't."

"Any sign of sexual intercourse?"

"No, but if I'm wrong about going to her place for a condom, and they used one, we wouldn't get any DNA anyway. She might have had one with her, in her pocket or something."

"Well, if she did have one on her, that blows your theory."

"Yeah, and my guess is she didn't, and they didn't sleep together. That's why I'm thinking he got irritated," Reynolds adds. "Snapped."

"Any history of violence on his part?" Immediately I want to take it back, because I know what the answer is. What I should have said was: *Any pattern of assault or abuse in his adult life?* But it's too late, Reynolds is already on it, nodding vigorously and licking his lips like he's about to catch a big fish. The pocked scars from acne he must have had when he was younger seem to grow redder, lighting up like tiny beacons.

"That's just it. Guy's spent half his teenage life in juvie. He accidentally shot another child to death when he was nine, and don't tell me that doesn't mess with a person's head for the rest of their life. We're trying to get those records unsealed so we can have a look at them, especially before we bring him back in for further questioning, but I'm telling you, the guy isn't right."

The guy isn't right. The words seem to bounce off the walls and ping around the stuffy room like a pinball. I feel that glob of acid expand in my stomach. *The guy isn't right.* Emily's daddy *isn't right.* Ali is too broken to even pick a guy that might be *right.* The bright fluorescents from overhead feel like they're showering down on me, exposing every line on my face, every emotion, every twitch of my facial muscles.

Of course, I remind myself, Reynolds doesn't know shit about people. I heard he let some lowlife suspected of running a drug operation go about six months ago because the guy fooled Reynolds in the interrogation, gave a fake alibi that his girlfriend vouched for. If he'd done his homework and checked the regional drug task force database, which catalogues known users and sellers, he'd have found that she was listed. She had several priors for selling meth. He ended up splitting town with the girlfriend and they haven't been able to locate either one of them. I can't help but think he's going to be extra cautious this time not to repeat the mistake. It's easy for investigators to get tunnel vision in general, but toss in the need to overcome a past mistake, and the chances are even higher. He's going to zero in on Reeve like McKay does on his red ball.

I'm about to respond with some comment about Reeve, suggesting that perhaps he just likes his privacy, when Brander walks in, takes his coat off, and throws it over the back of his chair.

"Hey, Agent Paige," he says, his face slightly flushed from the cold, "you find out something about this case of ours that we should know about?"

I know Brander from the Glacier campground child abduction case. He helped Herman and me track down witnesses and pull in several suspects. I liked collaborating with him; he was a hard worker and seemed to have his head on straight. Didn't seem to mind taking orders from a woman, either, which goes a long way in my book. Reynolds, on the other hand, strikes me as cocky and a little snide. He's got a perpetual smirk on his face, as if being a cop automatically makes him king of the universe. A guy with his attitude worries me, because when someone needs to preserve an ego as big as his, it becomes more important than the facts. I get the feeling that he'd have no problem throwing someone under the bus if he felt the need. In fact, rumor has it that he did indeed try to blame the dealer screwup on his last partner, who'd conveniently moved and wasn't around to defend himself. Since then, he's paired up with Brander.

"No," I say, buttoning my coat back up and heading for the door. "But it's interesting all right. Just make sure to consider all the options."

"'Consider all the options'?" Reynolds says. "What's that supposed to mean?"

"Nothing," I say. "Just, you know, we're all susceptible to tunnel vision, especially when we don't have much to go on. No witnesses, strange circumstances . . ." Brander, Reynolds, and the rest of the room are all staring at me like I'm from another planet. Reynolds's mouth hangs open, his forehead pinched in disbelief and his head pulled back like I smell bad. I shrug like it's no big deal, start heading for the door, and call over my shoulder, "Let me know if you need something. Always happy to help," trying to strike the right mix of happy-go-lucky and professional.

• • •

Since I'm at the county building, I swing by county forensics again, at the risk of bugging Gretchen, but she's not in. Ray, another crime scene team member, a tall, thin man with a bushy seventies-style mustache, is the only one in the office. He probably wasn't even born yet in the seventies, so I can't tell if he wears it to be retro or if he's simply not aware that it would behoove him to trim it a bit.

"Hey, Ray," I say. He's sitting in his office outside the lab, the door wide-open.

He smiles when he sees me and gets up from his desk. "What can I do for you today, Agent Paige?"

"Thought I'd catch up with Gretchen. She around?"

"No, she's out to lunch. With Monty," he adds, doing a little Groucho Marx thing with his heavy eyebrows.

I smile. "Ah, good for them." On a different sort of day, like when the father of my child isn't the primary suspect in a murder investigation, I'd ask more, like *Are they dating?* Monty Harris is the lead investigator for Glacier Park's police force, and he and Gretchen seem to be the last two to understand that they are actually attracted to each other. It has been obvious to the rest of us who have worked cases with them. And Ray's the kind of guy who wouldn't mind indulging in that bit of gossip, but because I don't have time for it, I move on to other, pressing things. "Just wondering if you've gotten into the vic's computer yet?"

"I have indeed," he says. "Good timing, just in the past hour. As soon as Gretchen gets back, I'll give her all I got and then we'll get a report over to the detectives."

"Anything interesting?"

"Not really. There are a lot of Word files on it, which makes sense, given that she's a journalist. I obviously haven't looked at all of them. Brander and Reynolds will have a full night of reading ahead of them. Lots of stuff."

"Let me guess: mostly pieces on the privatization of land and commonsense gun-control legislation?"

"Yes." He cocks his finger at me to say I'm spot-on. "And stuff on other research programs at universities on golden eagles, wolverines, wolves, grizzlies. You name it, she's into the wildlife, but seems her passion is the gun thing."

"How can you tell?"

"Well, it looks to me like she was writing a book. She was titling it *Shot: Violence and Profit from Guns in America*. Some sort of compilation of people who've been involved in some form of gun violence in their lives and the companies that profit from gun sales. Lots of narratives on people she's interviewed in the manuscript. Plus, it looks like she's changed the names of the people in the book. I'd have to look more closely, but at first glance, it seems like there are other files on the system that match the stories in the book with the real names of the interviewees. So if I'm correct, the detectives should be able to find out exactly who she's interviewed by matching the stories in her manuscript to the actual interviews she's got logged in her database. Could take some time, though."

"How many interviews?" I ask.

"I haven't counted them all up yet, but from what I'm seeing, looks like she's talked to all sorts of folks: those involved in accidental gun deaths, both as adults and as children. And nonaccidental shootings as well. She's even interviewed thugs in prison who have bought guns illegally to defend themselves in drug transactions or to take out the competition, to rob liquor stores . . . those sorts of things. Husbands and wives who have shot each other in crimes of passion; abused wives who have shot their husbands to protect themselves. Family members who have lost loved ones to suicide by firearm. Looks to me like it might widen the suspect pool quite a bit if one of these thugs felt threatened by what she was reporting. But you'd have to ask: Who in the heck would know she'd be out where she was and the exact time she pulled up?"

"She could have been followed," I say. "It wouldn't be that hard. Someone who knew she was staying there could have been waiting until she returned."

"I suppose. Anyway, not for me to ponder. I just give you guys the evidence." He reaches over and grabs a bag of Dove chocolate miniatures from his desk and plucks one out. He holds the bag out for me, and I grab one.

"Take two," he says. I do, which isn't usual for me. First off, I don't like chocolate, and second, when someone tells me to do something I don't feel like doing, I usually just refuse. The fact that I'm taking it anyway reminds me that I'm acting out of guilt, that I'm on shaky ground and I don't like it. I don't like it one bit. I shove the chocolate in my mouth and chew, throwing in a smile for good measure.

Reeve

Wednesday—The Day Before

"So you don't own a gun?" Anne Marie asks.

We'd moved on to other topics, but she's back at it again. It feels as if she's sniffing me out, but I'm not sure why. My body goes rigid, but I try to look relaxed, resting my left elbow on the couch.

"No, I don't."

"Even living out here?" She does a broad, dramatic sweep with her hand. "Bear, wolf, crazies like Ted Kaczynski finding their own private Montana . . . and still you don't feel the need?"

"I've got bear spray for the animals. That's enough. For anyone off their rocker, well, there's nothing I can do but leave them alone and hope they return the favor."

"That's what I thought," she says. It smacks of self-assurance, which is why I'm not being entirely truthful. I do own a rifle, but it stays locked in my equipment storage box in my truck bed and I never take it out. She's wearing a cute half-smile on her face. Not the big, sweet unencumbered grin I fell for earlier—the one that was open and spoke of fascination about life in general. Now it's like she's got a secret mission.

"Look," I say, "I don't own a gun because I simply don't want to, not because I have some big moral or political agenda. I don't care who owns guns as long as they do it responsibly, which 99 percent of the folks around here do."

She cocks her head and chews on her bottom lip as if she's thinking, as if she doesn't entirely believe me.

131

I continue: "I'm not for or against guns, if that's what you're trying to get out of me. Is this for some story of yours?"

She doesn't answer me, just takes a sip of her wine.

"I take it that's a yes."

She shrugs as if to say maybe, maybe not, like this is all some kind of a game.

"I couldn't care less about the whole political gun debate. I'm straight in the middle. I don't feel like I need a gun to protect myself or my family, but I don't judge those that do, because there are plenty of people who feel they need the security of a gun, the power to stop something ugly from happening to their loved ones." I picture Ali's Bureau-issued Glock that she wears on a shoulder holster, and the gunmetal-gray safe she keeps it locked up in when she's home. "I just think you better lock them away from your kids if you do have them around. It's that simple. And, yeah, it makes sense that you'd want to keep a gun out of the hands of someone you knew was crazy or had criminal tendencies, but that's it for me. That's as far as I go."

"That's a pretty neutral stance."

I want to ask: *What? For someone who killed his best friend when he was nine?* I shrug instead. "I suppose, but there's nothing wrong with neutral. Too many people are divided; they can't see any other perspective. It's an unwinnable debate at this point. I refuse to play the game."

"It's not a game," she says. "It's life and death. The United States is one of the most violent countries in the world. Out of the developed nations, the U.S.—with only around four percent of the world's population—has almost half of the civilian-owned guns in the world, and six times as many homicides as Canada and sixteen times as many as Germany. And you of all people should know that."

Again her reference to my past stings, but I don't say anything. My anxiety continues to coil tighter and I begin to shake my leg up and down. I see Anne Marie notice, but she pushes on. "Do you know how many children under the age of thirteen are killed every year in this country in accidents?"

"No, I don't. I don't want to know."

"Then you're just sticking your head into the sand. Over seventy to a hundred every year, and they figure those numbers are low, because people report gun deaths, not accidents. These are victims *under* thirteen I'm talking about," she stresses again, pushing her chin forward to make the point.

I want to say, *I've earned the right to stick my damn head in the sand if I want. I've chosen this Montana life for a reason—to be left alone.* The night has turned out to be entirely different from what I expected, but still she intrigues me, and I can't deny it. "Anne Marie," I say, looking into her intensely inquisitive eyes; I can see flashes from the fire reflected in them. "What's this about? I thought you wanted to know about the canine program. Why are you asking me so many questions about guns?"

"I'm just curious," she says, sighing huskily and slumping into the back of her chair. She runs her hand through the whisps of hair that aren't tied back. I'm relieved to see her sit back and relax. The tension dissipates instantly, like magic, and her sex appeal permeates the entire room, with the firelight amplifying it. "Because," she answers, "I've interviewed a number of kids who've accidentally shot someone when they were young. It hasn't worked out so well for them." A deep empathy floods her face, and I feel touched. "I'm just curious how it's affected your life," she says. "Others have gone down the wrong path. I find you interesting because you've turned things around, and, yeah, that involves the canine project. Because that's one way that you've turned things around, you know—made it through college, are doing something worthwhile now." She stares at me admiringly, a Mona Lisa smile on her face.

"I'm sure there are a lot of kids in my position who are doing something *worthwhile* now, and who decides what *worthwhile* is anyway?"

She ignores my rhetorical question unapologetically, and her confidence reminds me of Ali in the early days of our relationship. But eventually even Ali's cracks showed: her fear of getting too close, the walls she put up between me and herself as if she thought that if I saw her true self, I wouldn't like it, so she just kept me from seeing it in the first place.

"Sure there are. But you'd be surprised how many aren't living productive lives," Anne Marie continues. "How many are deeply affected by something like that for life. Their entire network of family and friends affected by one hideous pull of a trigger." She leans forward and sets her elbows on her knees, tilting her head coquettishly to the side and staring directly into my eyes. I can't tell whether she's all business or all seduction. "I'm curious how it went for you." Her eyes soften. "Can't you talk about it? Just a little?"

I haven't talked about it since I was with Ali, and I'm not sure I want to open up to this woman, who I'm guessing is looking for material; but again, she's enticing, and I find myself having a hard time saying no to someone who has so unselfconsciously laid her head on my shoulder while listening to the sorrowful calls of elk.

"What was it like, Reeve, that first year after you did it?" she whispers.

A familiar dull ache spreads through me, and my neck and face get even warmer than they already are. I feel caught, ensnared into something that I can't see my way through, wondering if I should open up and talk or protect myself like I normally do. There's something alluring and dangerous about Anne Marie—the way she's nonchalantly crossing my boundaries and drawing me in, as if she's a Greek siren, luring me in to wreck my ship on a rocky island. But then again, that's crazy thinking, and I feel foolish for considering it. I can hear Ali's voice berating me: *For god's sake, don't be such a fool, Reeve.* I tell myself that Anne Marie's just doing her job. She's curious. I'm the screwed-up one who finds it difficult to open up—getting all twisted into a tight knot because someone wants to ask me about my past.

I recall a girl I tried to see after Ali. After she'd googled me, by our third dinner date, she had the gall to ask me if maybe I had secretly *wanted* to shoot Sam—that perhaps I had some subconscious jealousy of him, some nine-year-old-boy competition brewing. But Anne Marie is not like that clueless woman. She's impassioned and driven.

The fire snaps and I feel my muscles twitch with something pent-up and edgy, a mixture of sexual attraction and anger. The room seems electrically charged, the cool air streaming in from the open window clashing with the heat from the fire. It's less tranquil than it was when we first enjoyed our meal and casually chatted about her life.

"Have you ever fired a gun since that day?" she presses on.

"No, I haven't."

"I wouldn't think so." Again, that hint of smugness comes back, drips from her words.

"You know." I match her gaze head-on.

"What?"

"Nothing. Never mind."

"Oh, come on," she says, smiling, a tease in her voice. "That's not fair; you can't do that—bring something up and then not finish it."

I look at her. She seems genuinely captivated by what I might have to add. "Okay." I take a sip of wine and gather my thoughts. "One night I was driving home with McKay. It was dark already, and I came around a bend and saw a small doe sitting in the middle of the road. I slowed down and my headlights illuminated her, but she wasn't moving."

She watches me, the smugness fading from her expression and curiosity replacing it.

"She lay there, curled in a ball as if she was just getting ready to sleep for the night, her head up looking out toward the woods, slightly dazed. She was injured, couldn't move. She tried—writhed a little—but it looked like her spine had been broken. She'd either been hit by another car or perhaps injured by a hunter, but—because she was in the road—probably hit."

Anne Marie cocks her head. "What did you do?"

"Nothing, drove onto the shoulder and around her, watched her sit in terror while I slowly went by. She stayed there like a sitting duck for the next vehicle to come along."

Anne Marie's brow furrows. I don't tell her the whole story—that Ali was actually with me, exhausted from a case she'd just finished and sleeping in the passenger seat, her head wobbling when we hit the pot-holes.

"The point is," I say, still stretching the truth, "it would have been the kindest solution. There's a responsibility that comes with living in a wild area, and sometimes that means you need a gun. So, yeah, in spite of what you might think, I *would* shoot a gun if I had one—under certain circumstances." I'm embellishing the story to make my point. I don't tell her how Ali woke when I stopped the car and watched me walk over in the shining lights. How when I came back and told her I thought it had been hit, she went over and took care of it with her own gun. I don't tell her because I don't want to turn Anne Marie off by bringing Ali's name up or, worse, by seeming weak or emasculated because I didn't shoot it.

"Okay, yeah, but that's different. That's to put an animal out of its misery. Anyone would do that."

"Not anyone," I mumble. "Not people who don't own guns."

"Still, you wouldn't shoot a gun otherwise, right?"

I don't answer her. Stubbornness overtakes me, and I have no de-sire to give her what she wants: proof that I'm some traumatized victim of a childhood gun incident, and that it's had predictable and obvious effects on me. Even though deep down I know it has, and I can tell in her self-assured, direct eyes that she knows it too.

Ali

Present—Friday

I'M BACK AT my desk, alone. Herman is out somewhere, and I'm relieved to have the office to myself. I sit back in my chair for a moment, shut my eyes, and listen to the hum of the heater. I try to process all the information I have in my mind. I know I need to work on the Smith case, but I can't let up on the Anne Marie situation.

I pull up Anne Marie's Facebook page again and find the photo of her, Vivian, and the other woman, Rachel. I scroll down. Halfway down, she's posted a video of a friend playing a guitar and singing some ballad. I know he's a friend because she's written a caption that reads: *My talented buddy, Philip Derringer, playing a song he's composed called "Dusk."* I peruse the comments and see that Vivian has added one too: *Way to go, Philip. Beautiful. So proud of you.*

When I find Philip's page, I see that there are photos of him with all three women. I decide I need to speak to both Philip and Rachel. Clearly they all know each other. For someone to kill Anne Marie Johnson in the middle of the night like that, I can't help but think she must have antagonized someone she either knew well or encountered while working as a journalist. The chances of a random act of violence out in the middle of nowhere seems highly unlikely.

I google Philip's address and telephone number and see that he's unlisted, but his Facebook site says he lives in Seattle. I try Rachel Clark, and bingo. I find that she's living right in Kalispell. She's a physical therapist working for a group called Northwest Physical Therapy, also located in downtown Kalispell. I'm about to call her when my phone buzzes and

I see that it's Rose. She informs me that she's not feeling well, that she's got the chills and is achy. I tell her to go to bed and that I'll get Emily. I look at the time on my phone. I've got one hour before school gets out.

On my way out of the building, I run into Herman at the front door. "We're like ships in the night." He smiles, and holds the glass door for me.

I grin back. "What, don't tell me you miss me?"

"But I do," he says. "Where are you off to now?"

"Rose is sick. Have to pick up Emily."

He checks his watch. "Already?"

The guy's too damn perceptive. I've already overused the errands excuse, so as I try to keep walking past him, I say, "Just want to check something out with the Smith case before I get her."

"What? Is there something new?"

"Not really, not much. I'll fill you in later." I'm digging myself in deeper. I haven't even opened the files, but at least I've shoved them in my carrier bag and can go over them at home. I figure I can come up with something productive to do on the case before returning to the office on Monday. "Gotta go." I wave over my head with my keys in my hand. Herman stands in the doorway looking at me. I can feel him watching me scurry away, wanting to ask me more questions.

· · ·

The therapy office is located in a professional area near the hospital, the valley's largest employer. It's quiet inside, and I expect it to smell like antiseptic, like a hospital or a clinic, or at least like a massage suite with therapeutic oil scents in the air, but it doesn't. Chicken soup or some other microwaved dish that someone had for lunch permeates the room. It's slightly stuffy and off-putting to smell the homey smell of soup in a clinical setting, but it's also vaguely comforting. I think I should go pick up some soup for Rose. It would be a nice gesture—me doing something for her for a change.

The woman at the reception desks tells me to wait while she goes back to ask Rachel if she can spare a few moments, and within about two minutes the tall, stalky woman I saw on Facebook comes through the door, introduces herself as Rachel Clark, and takes me back into one of the exam rooms. "Sorry," she says, pointing to a chair in the corner. "The practice isn't mine. I don't have a private office—just one I share with two other therapists."

"This is perfectly fine." I take a seat.

"How can I help you?" Rachel leans against the upholstered exam table and crosses her arms in front of her. She's wearing a white blouse rolled up at the sleeves, and her forearms look strong, the sleeves hugging them tightly. I think she'd be good at manual therapy. I'm instantly aware of a knot on the right side of my neck I've been carrying around since Wednesday when I got the call from Reeve.

"I'm here about a friend of yours. Anne Marie Johnson. I'm sure you heard what happened?"

"I did." She looks down at the floor for a second. When she looks up, her face is solemn. "Vivian called me. I was supposed to meet the two of them for drinks over the weekend, while they were both in town."

"I'm very sorry for your loss."

"What a weird thing. I just, I . . . . I don't know. I've never known anyone who's been, you know"—she holds out one palm—"killed before. Is that what *really* happened."

"I'm afraid it is."

"But by who? Why?"

"We don't know that yet, but all the information we can gather will help us find out." Again, a pang of guilt shoots through me for saying *we* as if I'm part of the investigative team. But the bottom line is that if I discover anything worthy at all, I'll certainly pass it along to Reynolds and Brander, so the way I look at it, I'm just another helping hand.

"I'm just going to ask you a few questions, that's all. Has anyone else spoken to you yet?"

"No, no one has. I wasn't sure if anyone would. I don't know anything at all. Like I said, I hadn't even seen her yet."

"How did you know Anne Marie?"

"Vivian, Anne Marie, and I were all in the same dorm in college, at Gonzaga. Anne Marie and Vivian were roommates. I was on the same floor."

"And how involved have you been in their lives since then?"

"After college, of course, we all went our own ways. Viv went to Seattle right away, and Anne Marie and I moved to Missoula. Both of us wanted to live in a mountain town, and Missoula was much cheaper than someplace like Boulder. We lived together for about half a year, but it wasn't long after that I found an opening here in the Flathead for a good-paying therapist position and moved. After I left, we'd still get together on weekends once in a while to go mountain biking, on a hike, or for a concert or something, but that got to be less and less as the years went on."

"So when was the last time you saw Anne Marie?"

She presses her lips together in concentration and looks at the ceiling. "It hasn't been that long," she says after a moment. "It was this summer. She was up this way for something . . ." She narrows her eyes, still thinking. "Yeah, that's right. It was the Backpacker's Ball for Glacier Park—that big fundraiser. I can't recall if she was reporting on it or if she just attended."

"So you got together then?"

"Yeah, she wouldn't come up this way and not drop a line. I'd do the same if I went to Missoula. It doesn't always work out for us to get together, but we at least reach out."

"What did you do this summer?"

"We met for drinks at a local pub."

"Did she stay with you?"

"No, she had a room at the Hilton Garden. We've sort of passed that stage. I have a husband now, and she'd be welcome, but our place is a matchbox. She knows that it's better to get a room somewhere."

"And Vivian's cabin? How come she wouldn't have just stayed there like she did this time?"

"As far as I understand from Vivian, this time was different because she was actually interviewing someone who also lives up near Viv's place. It was ideal—" She stops mid-sentence when she realizes how *un*ideal it actually ended up being for Anne Marie to stay up in the North Fork.

I don't let her linger on that for fear she'll start tearing up and not want to continue. "Do you recall when you saw her last if there was anything at all that she mentioned about her personal or professional life that seemed out of place or strange to you?"

She shakes her head. "No, nothing that I can think of."

"Are you sure? Nothing at all? Anything at all could be helpful—the slightest little detail that seemed different than usual. Or off. Or even if she was excited about something."

Rachel gazes at the wall, where there are pictures of human anatomy, salmon- and red-colored, sinewy muscles numbered and labeled, but she's not taking them in. "Well"—she looks back at me—"she did seem a little giddy—a little more than usual. Almost like . . . well, this sounds silly, but almost like she was crushin' on someone, but when I asked, she said there was no one."

"So how come you thought that?"

"I don't know. She kind of had this smirk like there really was. I remember telling Hal, that's my husband, that I could have sworn she was seeing someone by the way she acted, but that she wouldn't tell me who."

"And that was odd?"

"Kind of. I mean, usually we're pretty open about stuff like that with each other. Hal said that maybe she was growing up, being more careful about her relationships, which might include keeping them to herself until they became more real."

" 'Growing up'?" I ask.

"Yeah, Anne Marie, well, she's always been a little, I don't know, don't get me wrong—I love her to death. Oh my gosh, I mean . . ." Her cheeks turn bright red when she realizes the phrase she's just used. "I mean—I didn't mean," she goes on, flustered.

"I know what you meant," I say. "Please continue."

She puts her face in her hands and her rib cage shudders as she takes a deep breath. When she takes her hands away, her eyes are filled with tears. She wipes them with the sleeve of her blouse. "Where was I?"

"Anne Marie. Growing up?" I remind her.

"Yeah, she was always a little on the spontaneous side. Viv and I wondered if she'd ever settle down with anyone. She could never last more than a few months in a relationship—she'd get antsy, impatient. We called her a heartbreaker."

"Interesting. Do you think you could write down a list for me of all her past boyfriends?" I know Vivian has already done this for both me and the county, but I want to see if Rachel's list is different from Vivian's.

"Yeah, I could do that. I might miss a few, but I can recall most of them. Some were delightful, and I honestly couldn't believe she would treat them so poorly. I would have loved to date some of the guys she was with—you know, the really interesting, sexy, good-looking ones."

"Eh, we all know how those turn out." I wink, ignoring the fact that I went for one of those types myself and am now a single mom. "I'm willing to guess that Hal is a lot better than all of them combined."

She laughs. "That's actually true. I wouldn't trade him for anything. One big sexy teddy bear," she says, and I'm glad I've loosened her up, but the teddy bear thing is more personal than I want, so I shift back to serious again. "So it was your impression that she was dating someone this summer. During which month?"

"August, I think. Early August. I can't say for sure. Like I said, it was just an impression."

"Any ideas why she wouldn't have told you, other than what your husband suggested?"

"No, I don't know, except, well . . ." She looks down and I think there's something she doesn't want to say.

"Except what, Rachel?"

"Well, I don't know. I feel bad saying this, but . . ." She peters off, looks at her watch and then at the door, and I'm sure she's going to say she's got patients to see and has to go.

"Rachel, anything at all could help us find who killed Anne Marie, and we certainly take speculation into account, so nothing you say here is going to cross any lines, especially if they're just vague impressions. We're simply trying to gather a picture."

"Okay." She nods, wetting her lips. "Well, the thought crossed my mind that it could be a married man, and that's why she didn't say."

"I see. Any reason you thought that?"

"She got involved with one once before—a few years ago—and Viv and I gave her such a hard time about it that I don't think she'd ever say anything—at least to me—if she was doing that again. I probably was even harder on her about it than Vivian was."

I immediately conjure the image of O'Brien with his hands intimately grasping Anne Marie's shoulders. I know from Reeve that O'Brien is married.

"Do you remember the name of the married man from a few years ago?"

"No, she never told us his name. She was smarter than that."

"Have you heard of a man named Jeffrey O'Brien?"

"Jeffrey O'Brien? No, I can't say that I have."

I ask a few more questions, about Anne Marie's job and whether she knows what Anne Marie has been working on, but she doesn't know much other than that she's interested in land use and wildlife issues. I thank her and head to Emily's school, but right before I step out, I say, "Oh, and the photo on Facebook of the bearded fellow with the nice voice, playing the guitar . . . that a friend of yours and Anne Marie's too?"

"Yes, that's Philip Derringer. He's awesome. Nicest guy ever. Another from Gonzaga. We were all buddies." She rolls her eyes and sighs. "Another heart left in Anne Marie's wake. For a while he wouldn't hang out with any of us, but he got over it eventually, and we all became friends again. I haven't seen him in at least two years."

"What about Anne Marie?"

"Not sure, but I'm guessing not. You'd have to ask him. Viv would be more likely to know, since she's in Seattle, where he is. She probably sees him the most. He hits the music scene in Seattle a lot, and I think Viv has gone to some of his performances."

I thank her again and set out to pick up Emily before I'm late. She hates to be one of the last to be picked up.

· · ·

When I get to Emily's school, I avoid the roundabout, which is full of chatty mothers wanting to talk to teachers, attendants, and other parents through their windows, rather than grabbing their kids and getting a move on. Plus, I want to park and go in so I can surprise Emily and say hello to Claire, who works at the front desk. Claire has red hair and so many freckles that they smear together around her cheekbones like her own brand of blush. She reminds me of a childhood friend of mine whose family lived in the apartment below us. I loved her because she took my mind off everything going on at home with my mom and dad, and we'd escape into imaginary worlds for hours. I just want to make a good impression whenever I pick Emily up at school, especially since most of the moms are more acquainted with Rose than with me.

It's not that I want to call attention to myself. I'm always a bit self-conscious walking into the school in the first place, as if the other mothers are judging me, secretly whispering things: *Oh, she's that FBI lady. She's Emily's mother. I forget. I always think Rose is Emily's mother!*

Most of the other moms I meet at school often react with slightly odd expressions when they find out what I do for a living—an expression that says, *How nice, but why in the world did you have a child then?* As if female law enforcement officers are not afforded that privilege without quitting their jobs. Sometimes I get the confused, sad look that says, *But what if something happened to you on the job? Your poor child wouldn't have a mother.* I always want to ask: Would you give the same look to a father who happened to be a cop?

I don't mean to be dismissive about it, though. Of course I worry about something happening to me, leaving Emily without a mother. I'm proud of the work I do because it's important, because it's vital, but yes, I'd be lying if I didn't admit that, now that I have Emily, it frightens me much more than it used to. I've thought long and hard about what I would do if something like that were to happen, and the answer lies with Reeve. I expect him to step up. It's one more reason why I *cannot* lose Reeve to a false conviction.

I head into the building, pushing my silly insecurities away. When it comes down to it, I don't give a damn what the other mothers think of me. I just hope they stay out of my personal business.

"What a day," Claire declares in a breathy voice.

It takes me a second to enter conversational mode, but I focus and respond. "Hectic?"

"Had to send two kids home with lice this afternoon. Might want to check Emily. She should have a memo with her. We'll also be sending out emails."

"Lovely," I say.

"Yeah, tell me about it." Claire laughs. "I've been scratching my head all day, but don't worry. I don't have 'em. Mr. Josten has checked my scalp." I imagine Mr. Josten parting Claire's bright red hair to peer through his reading glasses at her pink scalp. "It's all the hats this time of the year. The kids wear the same disgusting knitted hats every day, throw them all over the playground, and then they pick up the wrong ones on their way out to recess. That's how they get transferred."

I feel like there's something crawling on my scalp now too. I resist scratching behind my ear as I thank her. That's all I need right now, I think as I head out the side door by the office to the enclosed recess area. I scan the playground. Emily's climbing on the large and colorful wooden dinosaur in the center of the play area. She's in deep concentration as she climbs each colorful rung up the dinosaur's back. I don't call out her name because I don't want to distract her and make her fall. I'm still watching her when I hear a man behind me call out, "Byron."

I freeze because I have no desire to see or speak to Byron's father, Will Jones, who is the journalist from the *Daily Flathead*. I am curious how it went when Brander asked him about Anne Marie. I'd love to ask Will Jones a few questions about her myself, but I realize I need to play it safe. Of all people, Will Jones is the last person who needs to connect the dots as to why I might be sniffing around a case that isn't officially mine. But when Emily gets to the lower rungs and I take a step toward her, I feel a tap on my shoulder. "Agent Paige," he says.

I turn and force a smile. "Will, how nice to see you."

"Nice to see you too," he says. "How's Emily?"

"She's good. How's Byron?"

"He's good. Always a handful. So are you involved on the latest, the North Fork thing?" he asks under his breath, because clearly this is not the place to discuss business.

"No," I say. "Sorry, can't help you there."

"I guess I didn't expect you would," he says coldly. "Higher-level stuff than you usually handle, huh?"

It's not really a question, and he knows it's not even an accurate statement, although since he covers the crime beat, he probably does know that we've been dealing mostly with militia and anti-government issues lately. I just ignore his dig and call to Emily, and when she sees me, she breaks into a wide grin and waves. Her curly hair springs out in all directions, her cheeks are rosy, and the gap between her two front teeth is noticeable. The sunlight is bringing out strands of a burgundy color in her hair. I go a little mushy inside, which is surprising since I'm standing next to someone who makes my blood boil. But there's something about Emily's sweet, deep concentration on the simple task of climbing a playground dinosaur that grabs me. "Excuse me, Will," I say, then go to my daughter.

Reeve

Present—Friday

WHEN I GET back to my cabin after leaving Wallace's house, I fix dinner, clean up, start a fire, and sit beside it to get warm. I could use propane, but it gets pricey because I have my own tank that I need to have filled every now and again. I try to keep the bill down by using the woodstove as much as possible. The mortgage, my truck payments, life insurance—which I'd never have if it wasn't for Emily—and the child support check I write for Ali every month eats up most of my paycheck, but I'm not complaining. I don't need much other than the basics: food, warm clothes, a place to live. I've never felt the need to keep up with the Joneses: flashy cars, the latest smartphones, granite countertops . . . I'll admit I'm a sucker for good gear for hiking and camping, though. If you're outdoors as much as I am, you notice the difference.

Of course, attorney fees don't figure into the equation. It's out of the question. I already threw the note Ali gave me with the attorney's name into my woodstove.

Now I can hear the wind whipping up and jostling the tops of the trees. It's getting to me, making me feel jittery and alone. An edginess keeps working its way up my spine, and I can't sit still. I keep getting up to look out the window, thinking I'm hearing a car driving up the drive, but I see only tall, swaying trees with their tips all leaning in the same direction as if they're engaged in some eerie choreographed dance. I know my imagination is running wild. McKay keeps lifting his head up from his paws from where he's lying to check on me, and I fig-

147

ure I must be giving off a nervy vibe. I'm tired—beyond tired—since I hardly slept the night before and spent a long day in the woods. Usually a day in the fresh air makes me sleep like a baby, but I can feel that's not going to work tonight.

After checking the window one more time and seeing only the dark, empty drive beyond my porch light and the pines still bowing with the wind, I decide to call my mom. She lives in Tallahassee, and I don't know how she's managed to stay in that city all this time. After they divorced, even my dad got out of there, moved to Gainesville, and found a job at a car dealership. My mom tends to talk a lot in order to avoid anything too serious, and I'm not sure I'm up for her chitchat, but I figure it's better than listening to the wind pick up and freaking myself out.

"Hey there, hon," she says. I hear a long, meted-out exhalation and I realize she's smoking. Last time I spoke to her, she said she had finally quit.

"Hey," I say, "you smoking again?"

She doesn't answer right away, and I take that as a yes. "Just one in the evening," she says. "No more. You happened to call right when I lit one."

I want to ask her, *Why even one?* But with my history, I have no right to preach to her. "How are things?" I ask instead.

"Good." She tells me about Ralph, a man she's been seeing for about six months now. "Went to a movie earlier. The one about the solar flares."

I can't recall the last time I paid attention to a movie, other than the ones Emily is interested in, but I say, "Yeah, yeah," as if I know exactly which one she's referring to when I really have no idea. She begins to tell me about the plot—about how the flares eventually end everything.

"Seems everything's about the world ending these days," I say.

"That's 'cause everything is going to shit."

I'm surprised to hear her say something so negative. Usually that's me, and she's the one always putting the positive spin on things. "Everything okay?" I ask.

"Oh, everything's fine." I note that she doesn't sound entirely fine, but before I can ask her, she changes the subject. "How's that precious grandchild of mine doing? Still drawing those pretty unicorns?"

"*Pretty* isn't exactly how I'd describe 'em. Fairly certain art isn't going to be her thing."

"Oh, stop," my mom says. "She's five. What do you expect? You were drawing hammerhead sharks at that age, but they certainly didn't look anything like hammerheads."

I chuckle at the thought, but consider how she seems to be holding something back. I figure it has something to do with my dad. I know he calls her occasionally, still relies on her to be the anchor like the rest of us, my younger sister and me included. I don't ask about him, though, and she doesn't bring him up. Instead, I ask about my sister, and she tells me that she's been helping Mandy out with the kids. Mandy, married with two children, lives only about five minutes from my mom. You know what they say: *A daughter's a daughter for the rest of her life; a son's a son till he takes a wife.*

"Other day she had to take Mae to the doctor for a bad cough," my mom continues. "I watched Noah." I hear her take another drag. "Talk about art; now, *he's* an artist. You should see the detail in the dinosaurs he's drawing. Drew a big T. rex for me, and I couldn't believe how accurate he got those little legs."

My mom always comes to the rescue for my sister. For me too. It sounds corny but it's true: if it weren't for my mom's stubborn strength, her belief in me, and her lighthearted but steady prodding, I probably never would have turned things around. *Reeve, are you studying? Reeve, is that support group tonight? Reeve, you have a counseling session you can't miss. Reeve, you need to go. Reeve, for god's sake, pick your head up and walk proud. Reeve, stop with the long face; things aren't that bad. Smile, hon. Shoulders back. Stand tall.* On some level, I'm still relying on her to be my compass by the very fact that I'm calling her on this night. But I don't want to tell her what's happened. It's like a haze in my head—as if my mind is a TV that has been taken over by fuzzy static. She doesn't ask me if there's anything wrong before we end our conversation, although I know her well enough to know that she probably senses it in my voice, just as I can in hers. When she says, "Call me if you need anything," and adds, "I mean it, Reeve," I realize she knows something's up.

After I hang up, it takes only a second before I notice the wind again. A branch from one of the aspen trees is banging against the glass. I go to the front window and look out on the driveway. It's too dark to see past the circle of light my porch lamp creates. I tell myself to calm down, that I'm alone, that nobody's coming to get me. I close my bloodshot eyes and feel them sting. McKay stands next to me, wondering if I'm going to let him out, so I do.

I go back in and sit in the same chair Anne Marie was in two nights ago. The fire illuminates the room in the same way, casting orange flickering light and dark shadows. Emily's pictures are still neatly stacked on the coffee table. I lean over, grab them, and shuffle through them, looking absently at each one. I stop at the one of a mermaid with bright red hair. Emily has drawn a smile with lips so big, they go outside the lines of the mermaid's face, but the mermaid doesn't actually look like she's smiling. Her lips are pulled back, baring large teeth like an angry animal. I'm studying it, wondering if she meant for it to look that way, when suddenly, outside, McKay erupts into a barking fit. I pop up out of my seat, the drawings scattering to the floor. It's not his usual let-me-in bark; it's a vociferous, bellowing tirade, one that says, *Someone or something's coming, and I'm protecting you and this place.*

I go to the front window and look outside. I can't see anyone, just McKay, stiff-legged, looking down the drive, and rearing up with a howl. I go to the kitchen, grab my canister of pepper spray and a flashlight, and step out onto the porch next to him. McKay's back is edged with a ridge of fur standing straight up. "What's out here, buddy?"

His bark turns to a snarl. I squint down the drive, trying to see through the blackness, but everything is swallowed by the dark. The wind hits my face. It still feels like snow, but there's been no moisture yet. I lean down and give McKay a big whiff. I don't smell skunk, but sometimes it takes a moment to register.

I stand up and look down the road again. I wish I had McKay's sense of smell and knew what was out there. The revelation that I feel like a sitting duck for the cops deeply annoys me—that they've been in my house, my space, and that they very well could be out there, posted, watching me. I descend the front porch steps, walk to the corner of the cabin, and shine my light out into the trees. The white light shows skinny pines bending back and forth and casting shadows. The forest looks warped, like dark shapes shifting and sliding sideways in my vision. I'm sure it's just an elk, a bear, or some other creature, but a part of me can't shake the feeling that it's the cops, that they're watching me, messing with me. "Come on," I say to McKay, who stays close by my side as we head back in. "Whatever was out there is gone now, with you throwing that kind of a fit." I open the door, follow him in, then lock it behind me.

Ali

EMILY AND I swing by the store to pick up a lice kit just to be on the safe side, and then a café that I know makes good soup, where I pick up some chicken noodle for Rose. It makes me think of my sister—how, whenever she'd get sick, I also had to stay home from school and watch her so my mom could still go to work. She had a series of jobs: at a pet store, a diner, a call-service facility, a nursing home, one of the local hospitals. Rose tries to take care of me, but there are ways in which I watch over her too. I don't bring attention to this side of me; I try hard not to succumb to it.

I have reasons for trying to suppress these instincts. When, as a kid, I admitted to Sara Seafeldt that I looked after Toni or cooked for her, she always got that overinterested do-tell look on her face—the curve of a polite smile on her lips and a small nod to go with it before she'd begin peppering me with questions about how often I'm required to look after Toni. Soon after, we'd get a dreaded visit from the Division of Youth and Family Services, now known as Child Protection and Permanency. I know the department's name was changed only because of my sister's current situation with her own daughter, Winnie—short for Wynona. She's three, and Winnie's father took Toni to court to get custody, claiming that Toni was unfit to be a mother due to her level of drug use. And he was right. Winnie was much better off with Pete.

But I can't always resist the impulse to take care of others. Traditional psychology holds that it's a way to assert control, especially when you were raised in an unstable or chaotic household. That's me to a tee.

So even though Rose is more than capable, I find myself suppressing the urge to help her out. She's even younger than Toni, and although she looks absolutely nothing like my sister, she has a silly giggle that sounds identical to Toni's. Plus, I know Rose has been through a lot. When she was sixteen, a man broke into her parents' house looking for valuables he could sell to make some drug money. It was in the middle of the week, so the burglar assumed no one was there, but Rose's older sister, Kimmie, was home sick. She walked in on him in the living room while he was unhooking the TV from the wall. She freaked out, and the guy—some nineteen-year-old named Vince, I learned when I looked up the news story, because Rose is fairly private like me at times and doesn't like to talk about the incident—fired his gun. The bullet hit her just above the hip in the abdomen, exploding her liver. She called 911, but by the time help came, it was too late.

I take a white paper bag with the soup, a roll wrapped in plastic, and a pat of butter to her doorstep. I don't want to wake her or disturb her, so I place it in the space in between the door and the screen and then text her to let her know it's there. I tell her that it might get cold, so she should just pop it in the microwave before she eats it.

Then I tackle Emily's head. First I take a comb and carefully separate her hair at the roots and check her scalp for any crawling creatures. I'm relieved when I don't see any, so I put the kit away, but make her take an early bath and wash her hair anyway. It takes me about forty-five minutes to work a comb through her thick, tangled hair. Again I'm reminded of Toni and the awful knots she used to get in her hair, how my mom would yell at her for not taking care of herself. She'd come to me crying, and I'd sit and try to work them out, but never could completely get the matted parts out. One day my dad angrily marched her into a hair salon and got her long dark locks chopped off. She wailed then too, as if she were losing an arm. Sometimes I wonder if it's the smaller wounds, like that one, that leave the deepest scars.

Since I'm already in worry mode—about Reeve, about Rose's not feeling well—I call Toni to check on her after Emily goes upstairs to play. She loves her room and all her toys, and I feel fortunate that she knows how to entertain herself, something common in only children. People are quick to point out the flaws in children that grow up with no siblings—that they can be inherently selfish because they've never had to share or deal with the constant presence of another child—but they are also often extremely self-sufficient, capable of focusing for long periods of time, and they sometimes don't develop the manipulativeness and meanness borne of defending oneself from the constant teasing and fighting that goes on between siblings.

"Hey, chickadee," I say when she answers.

"Hey, sis." Her voice sounds good, direct and sober, and I'm thankful I didn't get her on a bad night. My mood picks up considerably. "How are things?"

"They're good."

"Wonderful. How's work?"

"It's good. I've been thinking . . ." she goes on, her voice petering out like she's still considering something.

I cringe at what it might be. "About what?"

"I've been thinking of trying to get Winnie back."

"Hmm," I say. I don't add anything else because I know it will pass. She is unlikely to ever get it together enough to find an attorney and the money to take Pete back to court, nor do I want her to do that. Our mother does and is always egging her on, I'm sure. I hide my opinion from Toni, and at times I'm nervous that she'll ask me directly. Deep down, I don't think she ever will, though, because what I believe she fears the most is further exposure of her own inadequacies, her own shameful behavior—real or exaggerated in her own mind. "Have you taken advantage of your visitation times?" I ask instead.

"Of course," she says. "I miss her so much, Ali. I can't stand it." She begins to cry.

"I know you do." I hang on the line and wait for her to compose herself before saying anything more.

"When are you coming home? When are you coming back to Jersey?"

"I'm not sure." I feel the familiar stab of guilt. I have no desire to go back to Jersey, but not a day goes by that I don't feel awful for it—that I'm not out east trying to stitch it all together for her and my mother. At least they have each other, dysfunctional or not. I long ago gave up on my ability to make a difference in their lives. Another thing I learned in psychology was exactly how dangerous it is to enable the destructive behavior of the people you love. It suddenly occurs to me that maybe I'm doing the same thing with Reeve. I shake it away. "You know I have to go wherever they send me."

"Can't you put in for a transfer?" she whines, and I want the voice she had at the beginning of the conversation to return. I'm almost tempted to ask about her plans to get Winnie back, to see if it reanimates her, but I know better. "Toni," I say, "we've been over this so many times. It's not that simple. I have a daughter to think about. She's in school. She's doing well here."

Toni begins to cry harder, and I realize I shouldn't have brought up my own daughter—essentially rubbing it in. But my sister has created her own hell. I know all the elements in our lives—the addicted, abusive father; the struggling working mom; the overbearing sister—formed the gaping wounds in my sister, the burning ache that pushed her from guy to guy, party to party, drug to drug. I'm not going to make excuses for my own strong will. Somehow, against the torn backdrop of my own upbringing, my anger and bullheadedness fueled me to keep my grades up and enabled me to push myself to go to college even though I never felt like I belonged there. It was the fire that drove me to overcome the temptations that my sister fell prey to so easily. My mom and I tried to help her in the way every concerned family member tries—spending way too much money (mostly mine) to get her help that didn't stick. I guess that's part of why I was so impressed with Reeve. The help he received stuck, and he managed to stay sober against all odds.

"Ali," my sister moans. "Are you still there?"

"I'm here. I'm here. Look, are you eating well?"

"Yes."

I have no idea if I'm getting the truth or not. I ask only out of habit. "And everything's going okay at work?" Toni works at a nail salon.

"Yes, yes, everything is fine."

"Good," I say. "Okay, sis. Look, I gotta go. Gotta make Emily some dinner now."

She doesn't reply.

"Toni?"

"Yeah, I'm here. Okay. I know. You gotta go. Tell Emily her auntie loves her. Talk to you soon?"

"Absolutely," I say, but deep down I'm dreading it, because I know things will not have changed, and my sister's voice will still sound small and broken the next time.

• • •

After I make Emily dinner and let her watch *Frozen* for the thousandth time, I go into my office to look up Vivian and Rachel's musician friend in Seattle and give him a call. I figure it's a long shot that I'll get ahold of him, especially if he plays in some club on a Friday night. He doesn't answer, so I leave him a message to call me.

I'm about to go make myself some tea when my doorbell rings. I wonder if it's Rose, already feeling better and wanting to thank me for the soup, but she never rings the bell. Emily is already at the door with her hand on the knob when I get into the room. "Em," I say harshly, "you know better."

"But it's Hollywood."

"Agent Marcus," I correct her, realizing that I've created a monster with all my nicknaming. It's not completely unusual that he's here; he's certainly been over before for dinner and barbecues, but he doesn't normally show up uninvited.

"Okay, then," I say, shrugging off a twinge of uneasiness. Emily swings the front door open, and Herman is smiling down at her. He says hello and tells her he likes her mermaid jammies.

"But you're a boy," she points out.

"Doesn't mean I can't like them." He puts his hands on his hips. She giggles.

"Is everything okay?" I say when he looks up at me.

"Everything's fine."

"Can I get you some tea or coffee? I was just about to make some."

"Sure. As long as you were going to make it anyway. Tea is fine." He follows me into the kitchen, and Emily settles back in front of her movie.

"Is everything okay at work?" I fill a kettle and set it on a burner.

"Everything is fine."

I grab two mugs. "Earl Grey okay with you?"

"Sure, whatever you have."

"I have herbal tea too." I go to grab that box out of the pantry, but he stops me.

"No, no, Earl Grey is good."

Herman asks me questions about Emily and how school is going for her while I prepare the tea. He says he can't believe how much bigger she's gotten since the last time he saw her—sometime last spring. I set the mug with the tea bag already in the water before him and take a seat. "They grow like weeds," I say. "So what brings you here?"

"I just haven't had a good chance to catch up with you lately. Thought this evening was as good a time as any."

I look at him with a solid dose of skepticism.

"Okay, I'm worried about you," he says after dunking his tea bag into the hot water and blowing on the tea to cool it down.

"Worried?" I say, playing dumb.

"Ali," he says after setting his mug down, "what's going on with the county murder case?"

"The woman up the North Fork?"

He nods, pinching his lips together like he's humoring me.

"What about it?"

He tells me that Ray said I stopped in to ask about the computer files on the victim's system and wanted him to let me know that he found another gun-control piece the vic was working on called "Man Among Mountains" or "Man of Mountains." "Something like that." Herman waves a hand in the air. "Said it's an article that describes the main suspect's indirect involvement with getting Florida's gun accountability laws changed in the early nineties."

I stare at him, my head tilted toward my shoulder as if I'm trying to listen to it, as if it might whisper into my ear some good response to give him.

"So of course"—he taps his head—"I start to wonder, Why is Ali interested in all of this? And then I think I could start snooping around too, try to figure it out, or here's a novel idea: Since I work with her every day, maybe I can simply stop by and ask her."

I sense his irritation. I lick my lips. "Of course," I say. "Anytime. You know that, and . . ." I'm not actually sure what to say, so my sentence peters out.

"And?"

"And what?"

"Ali, come on, don't make me work this hard. What's up?"

"I'm just interested," I say. "Not in a big way. Just curious. I guess I'm just, I don't know, a little bored with some of these homegrown terrorism cases we've been working, these anarchists who think we're all the right hand of the devil. Just thought I could see what's going on, help them out if something comes to mind."

Herman studies me, his eyes slightly narrowed. "You're bored?"

"No, not bored. That's the wrong word." He's not having any of it and keeps his face straight, his bulky arms now crossed before his chest. "I guess just annoyed, and this is just an interesting case, that's all: Journalist gets taken out in the middle of the night out in an area where there's not a lot of people in the first place. No suspects. The owner of the cabin is a friend in transit coming to meet her. Someone had to know she was visiting—staying there. Someone had to have timed it just right. She hadn't even entered the cabin when she'd gotten there."

"She was probably followed. Or someone who knew she was staying there was waiting for her," Herman says. I'm relieved that he's taken the bait and is now in detective mode.

"Precisely. But who? They only have one suspect, and that suspect has no motive. I just don't want our colleagues zeroing in on one person and closing out other suspects in the process."

"But Ray indicated that the suspect has a history of violence. From what I hear, he hasn't been telling them the truth about his past."

"There was just one incident, supposedly. When he was nine."

"Apparently he was in and out of juvie for years." Herman pushes the bridge of his red glasses up higher on his nose with his middle finger. "It's a stretch, but Ray said Reynolds and Brander are building a modus operandi argument. That there's circumstantial evidence to suggest the victim was killed in the same way the boy's friend was killed when he was young. Rifle, shot to the chest." He holds his large hand flat on his sternum. "Close range."

I know where Brander and Reynolds are going with this. In court, you're not allowed to bring in past crimes as evidence. However, there's one exception, and that exception is modus operandi. The prosecutor asks: Do the facts or the circumstances of the two cases match up? If so, old history is fair game. "That sounds like a long shot if I ever heard one."

Herman shrugs. "Maybe, but I'm not working the case. And neither are you." The edge comes back into his voice. He gives me a serious stare. "And I think it's best that we stay out of it until they want our help."

I nod that I understand.

"Ali, I'm just saying that you need to be careful. The agency relies on us to keep good, cooperative relations with the local factions."

"Of course," I say in reproach. "I know that. That's why I'm trying to help."

"Well, it can come across the wrong way if we butt in where we're not wanted. I'm just saying what you already know: Don't piss on the relationship we've established with the locals."

I stare at the *I'd Rather Be Hiking* mug in front of me. Monty Harris from the Glacier National Park police force gave it to me, even though

I literally never hike despite having a child with a man who does it all the time. I know I should tell Herman that Reeve is the suspect we're discussing—should have already told him the day Reeve called me to fetch McKay from his place. I simply wanted to believe that none of this would amount to anything—that it would be easily put to bed. A flash of anger slashes through me. I feel my cheeks heat up. Damn, Reeve. How could you put us in this situation? I want to tell Herman everything, but I can't. My throat feels thick, slammed shut.

When I think about my family, it's not like I have everyone pegged under some boldface psych-textbook heading about classic behavioral problems that arise from families in which abuse and addiction occur. I realize it's much more complicated than that. The truth is, I'm fighting hard not to fall into some classic textbook description myself. Even as I sit here way out on the western edge of the divide, I can still see text encapsulating my personality type: *controller: can't let go; feels the need to steer situations; enables those he/she considers needing help; doesn't do well with limitations.* Sometimes I'm surprised I've lasted this long in an institution like the FBI, because it's true, I don't like to be told what to do and how to do it. In a way, coming to an RA in Montana worked out better than I thought because it provided me with a way to gain independence while still working for a strict, rule-guided organization, a way for me not to blow my own self up as I nearly did in Newark by fighting with all the wrong people. I need this job, I remind myself. I cannot afford to lose this job.

"I get it," I tell Herman.

He smiles sweetly, and I feel a pinprick of guilt for lying. I do get it, but I can't drop everything and stay away from the case. There are too many lingering questions.

"So you'll stay out of their business unless they ask?"

I nod.

"Great, then." He stands. "Thanks for the tea."

Reeve

Wednesday—The Day Before

"THE THING ABOUT guns," Anne Marie begins as she leans forward in her chair, and I watch several more strands from her braid come loose, dangling near the soft curve of her collarbone. "The thing about guns is that if you have one, you feel the need to use it, and that often leads to an accident."

"Of course people use them—just like people use their cars. You have one, you drive it. Safely most of the time, but unfortunately, every once in a while, an accident happens."

"Cars are registered, licensed, and closely monitored," she says.

I get up and add another log to the woodstove. I'm standing right next to her, and out of the blue, just like that, she slips two of her fingers inside my belt loop and gives me a pretty closed-lip smile. Her cheeks are flushed from the heat, and she shyly looks down at her own fingers in my belt loop, gives a little flirtatious tug, then lets it go. My breathing stops and I'm not sure what's happening. The gesture confuses me; it's out of context with the mood she's just set with all her questions and back in line with the way she was earlier in the day.

I want to reach out and touch her, but I don't feel as unencumbered as I did while watching the elk. Because of her questions, because she's brought up Sam, I'm anchored to a familiar heaviness I've felt my entire life. But before I have time to consider it one more moment, she starts up again.

"And these people . . . a lot of them don't own only one hunting rifle or shotgun," she continues, as if she hasn't made the gesture at all. And

161

just like that, the mood that her tiny gesture created—tender, youthful flirtation—dissipates. I furrow my brow, clear my throat, shut the stove door, and sit back down. "They own entire arsenals."

"Some people collect them," I agree.

"*Collecting* is a kind word. I guess you could call it that, but it's more than that. It's not like collecting baseball cards. It's an obsession driven by fear and paranoia."

"Not necessarily, but even if it is, so what? So what? What if it is about fear?" I ask glibly. "Is there not a lot to be paranoid about in this world of ours?"

She takes an audible breath and lets it out with a sigh that says, *You don't get it, do you?* But of course I do get it. It's not as if I haven't thought long and hard about this stuff. America is deeply divided over this issue, and mass shootings seem only to widen the rift. One side sees such tragedies as proof that things have gotten out of control with guns, and the other sees it as more evidence that we all need to be packing in order to protect ourselves and our families. Each side thinks the other is crazy and illogical. I refuse to enter the debate. With the last mass shooting in the news—one that took place in a small college just two states over—I told myself I wasn't going to read the news anymore. The woods were safer.

"What about your father?" she asks. "Does he still own a gun?"

I shut my eyes for a long moment. I'm not at all comfortable speaking about this, especially to a stranger, but something is opening up—a fissure is widening. I don't want to talk about my father, but at the same time the need to do so is bubbling up.

"Because if I had to guess—" she adds.

"I have no idea if he does or not," I say. "Quite frankly, it's none of my business."

"I take it you two aren't close?"

I shrug.

"That's understandable, given what happened."

My unease pushes me out of my seat. I walk to the window, and

McKay jumps up and follows me. I can see my reflection in the glass: disheveled hair, ruddy face, tired eyes. I can't make out that they're bloodshot, but I can feel the grit and burn of them. I can see Anne Marie in the reflection also. She's looking at me, and I figure she's simply waiting me out. She knows I won't tell her to leave.

"What's out there?" she finally says.

"Nothing."

"Then come sit back down." She moves over to the couch where I had been sitting and pats the cushion beside her. "You're making me nervous."

I rub my eyes and think of the irony in that statement. She's the one making me nervous. I turn and look at her on the couch, where light from the woodstove flickers across the planked floor and the only things separating us from the wilderness are these flimsy walls.

I don't know if my father still owns a gun. I know that he didn't get rid of it after the police returned it to him. Since under Florida law at that time Sam's parents could file no charges, the gun was not needed as evidence and was returned to my dad. He probably still has it, and I picture him taking some sort of perverse stubborn pride in still having it—the rifle used by his son. *Goddamn it,* I can hear him say. *Of course I'm not going to give it away just because there was an accident. Not like it's going to happen again. It was an accident.*

No matter that it tore apart a family's life. That Sam's parents eventually divorced after their crusade to change Florida gun laws; that I heard that Sam's dad, Larry, struggles with depression and that Sam's mom, Glenda, remarried but apparently fell prey to opioids. These bits and pieces I know from my mom, who has some way of keeping up with gossip in Tallahassee. I don't really want to know, but I can't quite tune it out, either, like a deer not being able to look away from a bright light. I imagine the loads of pain piled upon their family by what I did, by what my parents did—my dad, really—by leaving a loaded gun under the bed. I imagine how their constant grief and endless ache must have been a hundred times worse than the grief in my own family, and that is unthinkable to me. I think of how our family tragedy became a public tragedy. Years later, when my mom came to a counseling session with me (my father refused), she told me about how the newspapers referred to the deceased Tallahassee boy as a symbol, how three weeks after the funeral forty-eight people—mostly mothers—gathered to march from the local Tallahassee Civic Center to the state capitol in protest. They wore T-shirts that read *Protect your children* and carried signs that said: DON'T LET ONE PARENT'S IRRESPONSIBILITY STEAL YOUR CHILD'S LIFE.

My mom told Gary, the counselor, through choked tears, that Sam's mom was quoted on the news as saying, "This is what my baby must have been destined for—to make a difference, to save other children from reckless parents." "Like us." My mom had pointed to herself. "Reckless parents like us," she had repeated in the still room. I can't remember Gary's reply, but I fill in the blanks, thinking that he must have not had one. What could he say to something like that?

I remember her also saying through sobs that if she hadn't hidden my birthday present, none of this would have happened. I do remember Gary's reply to this one: "Even though no one is to blame, everyone is bound to feel guilty in a situation like this." And me? On top of missing my best friend, whose life I'd stolen, I felt responsible for making my mom cry, for making her feel guilty too, when I didn't think she had done anything wrong.

Ali

Present—Friday

HERMAN HAS MADE me nervous enough that after I put Emily to bed, I go to my home office and get busy trying to catch up on the Smith case that I've neglected for the past two days since Reeve's call. I pull out the folder he gave me earlier from my carrier bag and begin to go through the documents, chiding myself for taking this long to get to it.

Outside my office window, I can hear the wind coming in waves like rushing water. It rattles the branches of the maple tree in the back-yard and gives me a chill even though I'm warm and safe inside. First I go through the recorded transcripts of one of our undercover guys who is posing as a gun salesman. He's trying to lure Smith in, hinting that he has a "potent" firearm available for purchase—a Russian-made weapon with a magazine that can hold ten rounds of ammo. Attached to the transcript are a few other reports by the Bozeman office and a few local articles, including one about an NRA official who, according to evidence found by Bozeman agents, may been in contact with Smith.

I'm reading the exchange, but my mind keeps skipping to Reeve. I wonder whether I could have gotten Reeve wrong, missed some es-sential ingredient of his personality that would allow him to go off the rails, even for a moment, with a woman like Anne Marie Johnson. Sure, I know there's his childhood trauma, things left unspoken, more guilt than any one person ought to carry, and leftover anger at his fa-ther—which is never great for anyone, but Reeve had been somewhat fortunate. He had had counseling—thank goodness for his mother—

and he had self-control. He had picked himself up, moved to another state, and put himself through school. He adores Emily and of course McKay, and would never jeopardize his ability to be with them.

But could he have shot Anne Marie?

I've seen enough confessions where perpetrators have broken down, rubbed their eyes, and wept while the video camera rolled, saying that something just snapped, something changed. It wasn't them actually doing it. They were simply in a nightmare; they didn't *mean* to do it. It just happened in a single moment, and in the interrogation suite at the county, through their tears, they say regretfully that there's no taking it back. And I've spoken to enough criminals to know that almost all violence boils down to a great ball of tension, stress, and anger that has been building and gathering through a long line of past unfortunate events, abuses, and wrongdoings—tension that coils tighter and tighter inside an individual, like a compressed spring, until one day it simply unloads.

But I have this one memory of Reeve that I'll never forget. He and I are driving up the North Fork, his headlights showing the way on the dusty graveled road through tree-covered ridges. I'm exhausted from working a case involving a missing child and fall asleep while Reeve drives. I wake to find his truck parked, its engine purring idly, and see the car lights fanning out over the road. They illuminate Reeve cautiously going toward a doe huddled in the center. He stops a good ten feet from it, just close enough to get a look at it; then he walks a little from side to side, seeming unsure. Reeve holds his rifle—one I know he carries for circumstances exactly like this. Nature is not kind, and nature mixed with human contraptions, like vehicles, is even less kind. There's tension in his face and his shoulders. And something else: fear. I can see the dread in his expression, even from the distance in the headlights. It reminds me vaguely of a scene from a Mafia movie in which the boss has asked one of the newbies to prove himself, to take out someone who hasn't been loyal, and the novice is having a tough time acting on orders: pacing, sweating, and struggling with his conscience.

Reeve does a semicircle around the deer, giving it a wide berth. He looks at his rifle, but again, even from the vehicle, I can see the tremor in his hand, the entire weapon shaking. I can't see his forehead, but I imagine it beading up with sweat.

Eventually he drops the rifle by his side and comes back, his boots scuffling on the gravel road, and hops in. He sighs when he sees me awake, looking at him. "I think it's paralyzed," he says. "Unable to move. It tried, but it can't get up. It's probably either been shot or hit by a car. It should be put out of its misery, but I . . ." He shakes his head. His face looks knotted with torment.

I understand what he can't say: *I couldn't shoot it.* At the time, I just thought it was special, that it was like that with us from the start— that we could finish each other's statements for one another. Later, of course, I understood I was just deluding myself like all new couples in love who think that they are linked magically when it's actually just common sense.

I say softly to him, "I've got it." I open the truck door and step out. I hear Reeve whisper my name, but nothing more. I walk over in the glare of the lights and slowly approach the doe. I decide to just use my service weapon because it will be cleaner than firing from a rifle, even though the Bureau suggests we report all shots fired unless it's for practice.

He was right; she wasn't going anywhere. Her neck muscles strain to get up, but she can't get her front ones under her. She wiggles them for only a moment, her back ones unable to move at all. She quits straining when I come up next to her, almost as if she's surrendering, and lies still. I put my Glock next to her head, her velvety, leaf-shaped ears silvery and twitching in the headlights, and fire the shot.

I stand staring at her limp body, at the small hole oozing a trickle of blood, when Reeve comes to my side. He grabs her thin legs and drags her to the ditch on the side of the road while I put my gun back in its holster. When we return to the car, I think I see a dampness under his eyes in the dome light of the car while the door is still ajar.

It makes me think of a child—of a nine-year-old boy. Maybe because of the fear, it also makes me think of my sister in her adolescent years. Victims. That's what it makes me think of—innocent victims—and it makes me want to reach out to him and run from him at the same time. He shuts the heavy door of the truck and the interior light goes off. We drive on, over the streak of blood smeared across the gravel, not saying anything else.

No, I think now in my office: Reeve wouldn't shoot anyone or anything, really. He can't even put an injured deer out of its misery. I force myself back to the file of transcripts. My desk lamp illuminates the papers in a yellow spray of light. I go through several more pages of details, when my breath catches. I pull my head away, rub my eyes, then look again. "No way," I whisper out loud to the quiet room. In a section describing an interview with a witness, I read Anne Marie Johnson's name.

"A witness," I say to the quiet room, squinting at the report in disbelief. "Unbelievable. She's listed as a witness."

I read on, completely stunned at the coincidence of having her name in the Smith file right under our noses all this time. The report claims the FBI was initially looking at her as a suspect, as someone involved with Smith to help him purchase illegal firearms—machine guns and other unregistered firearms. But upon interviewing her, the agents quickly realized that she's only poking around where she doesn't belong—trying to get close to Smith to interview him for articles she's been writing about an array of gun-related issues. Apparently she told the Bozeman FBI that she'd been doing some investigative reporting on a connection between Smith and the NRA. Farley, one of the agents, checked her out and said she was legit, but they warned her to stay away from Smith. She had agreed to do so.

I sit listening to the wash of the wind whisk around the north corner of my house where my office sits. I'm still a little in shock that in the folder Herman has given me, there is an actual tie to the victim. I have no idea if Brander or Reynolds know about this, or if even Herman realizes this, but I'm thinking he doesn't or he would have said something to me. After all, he gave me the file. He knew I'd read it. It must have not clicked or he skimmed over the report.

I google all published articles by Anne Marie Johnson, and find only the ones I looked at earlier on the privatization of land and other wildlife studies. I make a note to talk to Ray in the morning again to see what else he's found on her computer regarding in-the-works articles on the NRA.

If she was trying to buddy up to Smith for information, then it would make sense that she hadn't actually put anything out publicly for him or anyone else to look up until she was good and ready to break her story. I tap my pen on the desk and consider the situation. Anne Marie was playing a few dangerous games in her life beyond sleeping with married men. In the morning, I need to show the file to the county guys, and I plan to do so, but first I want to talk to Vivian again.

Reeve

Present—Saturday

I WAKE TO A skiff of snow. Like powdered sugar, it coats the brown fields, my ugly lawn, and the gray and white rocks scattered about. I check the forecast and am sure it will be gone by noon, since they're predicting a high of forty-eight.

I feel like I'm on autopilot while I pack for the day. The incident last night left me with another restless night of sleep, and when I did fall briefly, I dreamed I was working. But instead of searching for wild animal scat, McKay was searching for my dad. Deep in my dream, in the way you have layers of knowledge going on simultaneously, I understood I had trained McKay with the scent from a utility jacket I still had of my father's. The woods were dark and tangled—like a distorted setting out of *The Lord of the Rings*, and I sensed he was there, but not hiding from us, just there. McKay howled fiercely with the knowledge of his presence, even though that's not the way McKay works, and I was oddly aware of that fact too. But then McKay quit. My father's presence suddenly dissipated, and several layers even deeper, I somehow understood that his vanishing—my inability to find him—represents some void inside me.

The lingering emotions from this dream leave me unsettled. I feel like I should call my mom again so that this time, I can ask how my dad's doing, but I don't. Instead I feverishly get ready for a day of research, with McKay anxiously watching my every move. I fill my larger camping pack with extra food, clip my subzero sleeping bag and my two-man tent to my pack. I grab a flashlight, two lighters, extra polypropylene long underwear, rain gear, a down jacket, an extra fleece. I'll miss Emily this weekend, but she'll be with Ali.

Before long, my pack is loaded and heavy, and stored into the back seat of my truck. I lock my place up, turning the heat down, but not so low that the pipes will freeze if there's an unexpected cold snap. The buzzing has moved to my ears, and my scalp tingles as if goose bumps are pricking every inch of it. I turn on a lamp—the one next to where Anne Marie had sat just three nights before—so that if I return when it's dark out, there'll be some light, or if I decide to stay a little longer in the woods, the lamp will make it look like someone is home.

I'm just about to lock the back door when Ali calls. I stand in my kitchen, my hip against the counter, and answer it. "Surprised you're calling this early. Everything okay?"

"Everything's fine," she says, and begins to tell me that I should make myself available, reiterating that I should get an attorney. I tell her I have to go and that she should give Emily a hug for me.

"Reeve," Ali says before we hang up. "They're getting your juvenile records unsealed. Just thought I'd give you a heads-up. You might need to talk about all of that with them. This is why I suggested an attorney."

"You know as well as I do that an attorney will tell me to discuss absolutely nothing, regardless of guilt or innocence."

The line is quiet, and I assume it's because she can't refute what I've just said. We say good-bye, and by the time I hop into the car, Ali's voice seems like a blur, with only the bit about the juvenile records repeating in my head. McKay gives a squeaky yawn-whine combo that signals his excitement to go to work and pulls me back to the journey at hand. "On our way, buddy." I rub his broad chest, throw the truck into reverse to turn it around, and head down my driveway.

Ali
—

Rose calls me first thing in the morning, thanks me for the soup, and says she's feeling better—some twenty-four-hour thing that's passed quickly. She claims she's fine watching Emily if I need to work today. I want to talk to Vivian again, so I say that it would be great if she could come by just for a bit while I take care of a few things.

When she arrives, she looks a little wan, but otherwise fine, her blue eyes bright. "Are you sure you're up for this?" I ask her.

"I feel fine. Really." She unzips her coat, opens the foyer closet, and hangs it up. "If I relapse, I'll call you. Where is the little terror?"

"Still sleeping, if you can believe it."

"Maybe she has what I had yesterday."

"Maybe. I don't think so. It's early yet." I look at my watch. It's only seven a.m., and even live-wire Emily will sleep until eight on weekends. I've spent a night tossing and turning, and was up by five thirty, angry and irritable. Damn Reeve—it's become my mantra.

"Hope not, but it won't last long either way. How's Reeve?" Rose asks.

"Reeve?"

"Yeah, he was here the other night. Seemed like something was up."

"He's good," I say, thinking about my phone call with him, urging him to stick around. I know he won't and is already out among the great, rugged wild. I want to roll my eyes, but Rose would have no clue why. I picture Reeve walking, soaking in the great sky, the ground, the mountains, and everything in between. I picture him marching

172

straight ahead through overgrown trails and climbing over boulders, trying to jump past the vast empty holes in his life, but falling deeper into them with each stride.

Rose gives me a curious look, like she's trying to figure me out. I want to say, *Why are you looking at me that way?* but I don't because I don't want the answer. She's asked me in the past why Reeve and I don't just get back together. She says it seems to her like neither one of us is completely over it. *It's in the way you look at each other*, she says. I've told her it's complicated, that she's seeing it through her young, romantic eyes.

"Anyway, I gotta run, but I'm sure Emily's fine." I change the subject back to my daughter. I want to get going. "Call me though if you don't think so." I grab my bag, throw my coat on, and head to my car.

· · ·

I was glad I called Vivian when I did, because she was planning to drive back to Seattle. She said she'd been hoping to get into her cabin to clean things up, but it was still off-limits, so she had decided to head home even though she didn't have to work on Monday. She agreed to meet me on her way out of town at a coffee shop in Kalispell.

I find her sipping on an espresso and working on her laptop. She looks up and gives me a weak smile when I walk up to her small wooden table next to a redbrick wall. "I'm just going to get some coffee," I say to her. "I'll be right back."

When I return with a cup, I sit across from her. She doesn't look much different from when I saw her in her hotel room, other than a little less shocked, but she seems tired, with dark circles under her eyes that's she covering with concealer. I can see it cracking in fine, delicate lines under her eyes, and again I think of Toni, who often wore too much makeup. I can hear my dad's slurred voice telling her, *You look like a whore with that shit on your face,* and her lowering her head, embarrassed, and my losing my temper and yelling at him: *Leave her alone, Dad. You think you know it all and you don't.*

"What can I help you with?" Vivian closes the lid on her laptop.

"I'm glad I caught you before you left. I just wanted to follow up on a few things."

"I've told you and the other officers everything I possibly can." She looks perplexed that there could possibly be more, her forehead pinched.

"I know, and we really appreciate your cooperation. You said on the phone that you don't have to work Monday?" I had since checked my notes, which confirmed that last time I visited Vivian, she mentioned that she'd taken only Thursday and Friday off.

Vivian looks slightly startled, her eyes widening for a brief moment, and I wonder what the look of surprise is about. She says, "Uh, yeah, well, I got another day off, you know, under the circumstances."

I nod. "Since we last met, I had a chance to speak to a mutual friend of yours and Anne Marie's—Rachel."

"Sure, Rachel. I called her to let her know what happened. I didn't want her to find out about it in the papers."

"She mentioned that."

"I didn't visit her, though. She wanted to come see me, but I wasn't up for it. You know, under the circumstances. I didn't want to see anyone, really."

"I understand. When we spoke last, you said that you had heard about the director of the University of Montana's canine research program from Anne Marie."

Vivian nods.

"And you recalled his name. Jeffrey O'Brien?"

"That's right."

"I need to ask—was Anne Marie involved with him romantically?"

Vivian blinks and looks down. I think I have my answer, but I want her to say it. She looks back up at me. "What makes you think that? He's married. Why would she be involved with him?"

"Why don't you tell me?"

She sighs—a good sign. It means she's surrendering to the idea that she's going to talk. She takes a sip of her coffee, then sets the cup down, but keeps her slender fingers wrapped around it. She says, "I don't know much. She met him at some fundraiser in Missoula."

"How long ago?"

"Over a year ago, at least. I'm not sure exactly when. She didn't tell me for a long time, and she made me swear not to tell anyone else when she did, not even Rachel."

"Why did she tell you and not Rachel?"

"I guess we've always been closer. You know, we were roommates in college. I guess Anne Marie felt a little judged by Rachel."

"Because she'd done this before—gotten involved with a married man?"

Vivian gives me a surprised look again, then resigns herself to it. "Yeah," she says. "She had, and we both—Rachel and I—didn't like it, and told her it was a bad idea, but I suppose Rachel must have come across harsher than me."

"So this time?"

"I still told her it was a bad idea. I told her I didn't understand why she kept putting herself in these unhealthy tangled situations that would never go anywhere. She got mad initially and said, 'How do you know it won't go anywhere? He plans to leave his wife, and I really like him.' After she was defensive, I didn't say much more. To each his own, right?" She looks sad, her eyes heavy, as if talking about it is only weighing her down more rather than relieving a burden.

"I mean," she says, "she was so pretty, smart . . . talented. I couldn't see why she needed to get involved with guys who weren't available, but then I figured some people actually probably don't *want* to commit themselves, so having a relationship with someone unavailable is the perfect solution."

What she's saying hits me on a level deeper than I would like. I shift in my seat and take a sip of my coffee. It's disappointingly weak and doesn't taste nearly as good as the heady aromas wafting through the coffee shop would suggest.

"I figure it had something to do with her father. Nice guy, but totally unavailable. Always working. Always traveling. Never home. It always begins there, right?"

"What?"

"For girls—it always begins with a shitty father."

That nicks me too. "Don't know about that," I say. "Shitty mothers wreak their havoc too. And at some point you have to take responsibility for yourself. You can't hide behind whatever your childhood dealt you. Everyone has wounds."

"I guess. I just don't understand why Anne Marie wouldn't give a nice guy a chance. Trust me, there were plenty that would have stepped up. But . . ." She shrugs to signal, *It's too late now.*

"Was there some reason you thought Jeff O'Brien wasn't a nice guy?"

"No, no." She holds up her hand. "I'm not saying that. I know hardly anything about the guy. Just that Anne Marie was hot for him—you know, that smart, scientific type who's into the wild. There were a few like that. She used to date a guy here who was engaged to someone else. I think he's married now to his fiancée at the time."

"What was his name?"

"Will. Will Jones. He's a local reporter here."

I nod. I'd have loved to be a fly on the wall when Brander and Reynolds talked to Jones's smug self. "I'm assuming you've told Detective Brander and Reynolds about all of these past boyfriends?"

"Yes, I have, in one way or another. I didn't say she actually was having an affair with O'Brien. I mean, is it really my place to say?"

"Actually, yes, it's absolutely your place to say. It could be very pertinent to finding who shot her. You should probably call them and fill them in."

"Can't you?" she asks innocently.

"I can. But it's best if they hear information like that from the witnesses so it can be documented correctly."

She nods, as if she buys my answer, although all she'd have to say to call my bluff is *Can't you document witnesses' statements correctly? Aren't you part of this official investigation?* I move on before she does: "Did Anne Marie know O'Brien's wife?"

"I think she knew of her, but hadn't ever met her. If she had, she didn't mention it."

I've seen it all in this line of work—sex dungeons in Montana backwoods homes; homeschooling where children are taught to take up arms against anyone who crosses the property line; a man who has killed an entire family who simply stopped to give him a ride because he thought they were making fun of him—so I'm rarely surprised at the boundaries people cross on a daily basis without ever thinking of the consequences. I'm not surprised by Anne Marie's recklessness, either, but I am confused about Reeve and her. I think of the hair tie I found in the bed, yet the serology and body fluid reports came back with no signs of forced sexual intercourse, and possibly no intercourse at all. Of course I can't be positive about that unless I speak to the pathologist myself or see the current report.

Reeve is the type to think of consequences, but he's more than capable of throwing them to the wind. Still, I wonder if he even knew about Anne Marie and his boss, and if he did, would he really go as far as to sleep with his boss's mistress? Would he jeopardize his job, the one thing that allows him to live in this area and do what he loves— being in the woods every day with his dog—and still be somewhat present in Emily's life, at least every other weekend, just to get laid? Of course he would; he's a guy, I think cynically. I know I'm being unfair, but I can't help it. And although Reeve thinks of consequences, he's got a self-destructive streak. He keeps it in check now, no longer doing drugs or drinking himself into oblivion as he did in Florida, but I see it come out in tiny ways, in the ways he sometimes tempts fate: staying out in the woods a little too long when he knows it's going to get dark soon, all too willingly taking an untrodden, unmapped trail that might get him lost, driving onto private property that he has no business being on. "Just to check it out, see where it leads," he'll say.

I ask Vivian a few more questions, wrap things up, and thank her. We put on our coats, and I follow her out the glass door. When we step out into the cold, she hugs herself and shivers.

"Guess you'll be glad to get out of this area."

"Yeah, I suppose," she looks sad. And something else. Stressed, I think. It's in the way her eyes dart around, taking in her surroundings. She looks anxious.

I say good-bye and begin to walk away, but then I stop and turn around. She's heading in the opposite direction, to the parking lot. I watch her go to her car, but she doesn't go to the driver's door. She walks around and hops into the passenger side.

I hurry over and catch the car just as it begins to pull out. The driver, a blond-haired man, stops the car when he sees me. I motion for him to roll down his window. He does and waits for me to say something.

He's older than she is, but somehow he manages to look young and old at the same time. His smile and the style of his hair are boyish, but there's hardness too. Crow's-feet fan out from each eye, and his skin is leathery around the edges of his face.

"Hi," I say. "And you are?"

"A friend of Vivian's."

Vivian has her head tilted forward so she can see me and is looking at me, but doesn't offer anything more.

"I didn't realize you were with anyone else here," I say to her.

"I wasn't. Tate's just helping me. I'm not in the best shape right now, as you can imagine. He's going to drive home with me."

"So you're from Seattle too?"

"I am. I came out yesterday after Vivian called me and told me about what happened. Like she said, just helping her out."

"You mind if I ask you what your last name is?"

"Austin," he says.

"Tate Austin," I say. I think it sounds slightly fake, like a stage name, so I say it. "Sounds like an actor's name."

"Yeah, people tell me that." He smiles boyishly, but there's some-

thing confident about his smile that I feel like I've seen before. I decide
that he's got to be at least ten to fifteen years older than Vivian.

"Vivian," I say, grabbing a card from my pocket. "I forgot to give
you this, just in case you think of anything important and want to give
me a call."

"You already gave me one, at the hotel. Remember?"

"Oh, that's right," I say. "My bad. Well, have a safe trip." I hold up
the card to wave, then pull out a pen to write Tate Austin's name on the
back of the card.

. . .

At my house, I tell Rose to go. "You've done enough, Shorty. Go rest
up some more. You look tired. Maybe not as recovered as you think?"

Rose claims she's fine, but doesn't argue with me. She grabs her
things, says good-bye to Emily, and slips out the door. Emily is thrilled
that I'm back before she's even done watching cartoons. She's still in
her unicorn pajamas, her potbelly sticking out and her brown ringlets
a wild mess. The house is warm and cozy, and Rose has made coffee. I
grab a cup since the one at the café wasn't very satisfying and tell Emily
she can watch for half an hour more. "Then," I say, "the TV goes off."
She nods absently, her full attention on the screen.

I go into my office and call Brander right away, leaving a message
for him to get back to me. I want to tell him about Anne Marie's connection to Smith. In the meantime, there are so many other loose threads
to follow up on first before I get Brander or Reynolds on the phone. I
want to check on O'Brien's wife, and there's something else that's bugging me: the small startle I noticed on Vivian's face when I asked her
about work on Monday. It's not lost on me that Vivian slightly resembles Anne Marie. Both of them have curly dark hair. Anne Marie's hair
is a little longer than Vivian's, although not by much, and at night it
would be easy to confuse the two women.

And who was this Tate Austin waiting for her in her car?

I pull up Timberhaus's website and look at the company page. I click on the tab that reads *Our Team*. She's in the accounting department, so I realize she's probably not high up enough on the corporate ladder to be listed. I'm right. Only the senior management team is listed. I google Vivian, which I've already done before, and go over the usual: Facebook, LinkedIn, Twitter, Instagram . . . Facebook and LinkedIn both list her as an employee of Timberhaus.

I look through my notes for the name of the friend who is a musician in Seattle. He hasn't returned my call. I know it's an hour earlier there, and if he had a nighttime gig, he probably sleeps late. I'm surprised when he answers, though—sounding chipper too. I introduce myself to him and ask him if he's heard about Anne Marie. I know the answer from Vivian, but I want to start from scratch with him.

"I have," he says sadly. "I'm kind of in shock."

"Were you two close friends?"

"On and off over the years. I knew her in college, and we stayed friends."

I don't ask about whether he was in love with her, as Rachel had indicated, at least not yet. I go through all the usual questions: "When was the last time you saw Anne Marie? . . . How did she seem? . . . How often did you speak to her or see her? . . . Is there anything at all about her that seemed strange or different from usual?" He answers with standard fare, nothing ringing any alarm bells, so I move on to the crush.

"Your mutual friend Rachel," I say. "She mentioned that you wanted to date Anne Marie at one point."

He gives a half-laugh, half-snort, and I sense some resentment or at least embarrassment in the eruption of that sound. "I guess you could call it that. That was a long time ago, though."

"How did you manage to be friends with her, given that awkward situation?"

"Wasn't hard," he mumbles, then goes quiet.

I wonder if there's more to it, but I can tell I'm not going to get much more out of him on the phone like this. "But you're closer to Vivian at this point?"

"As friends, yeah. I mean, we live in the same city. It's easy to get together, and she likes to come watch my band." I can hear the high-pitched siren of an ambulance in the background—maybe out his window or maybe he's at a coffee shop—and it reminds me of my apartment in Montclair, a twenty-minute commute to Newark, where the field office was.

"And have you chatted much with Vivian since she's been in the Flathead?"

"No, only when she called me to tell me."

"And how did you take it?"

"I was shocked. Vivian was crying, really upset, and my first priority was to calm her down and be there for her. I was supposed to see her before she left for Montana, but it didn't work out, so I was completely taken aback when she called me so upset. For me, it hit later, and I'm having trouble sleeping. It's the loss of a friend, of course, but it's also the *idea* that someone would want to harm someone in your own circle of friends. It's just freaky."

It's an honest answer, and I'm impressed with his insight. I tell him that that's normal and to be expected. "And Vivian," I say. "You were supposed to get together before she left?"

"We were supposed to get a coffee before she headed out. She was supposed to take off some time in the afternoon. I'd made a CD of my recordings for her to listen to on the long drive. My stuff hasn't made it to Spotify yet," he explains sheepishly. "Soon, though," he adds. "She canceled, though. Said she had to pack up her office."

" 'Pack up her office'?"

"Yeah, I know. I was surprised too. She sounded a little stressed. We were supposed to meet, but like I said, she called to cancel, said she needed to pack up—that she's resigning. I asked her why she hadn't mentioned it. I mean, we're good friends, and it seemed so sudden, but she got really quiet. I figured I'd stepped on her toes somehow by calling that out, but I don't know, I couldn't believe that she'd quit without telling me. Obviously she must have been putting some thought into it for some time. You don't just quit a good job like that on a whim. She had a good thing going with TH. Super stable, benefits, great pay. She'd worked herself up the ladder."

I find the information interesting. His instincts are correct. You don't just quit a job like that on a whim, and why wouldn't she tell me that same information when I questioned her? "And you had no idea she wasn't happy there?"

"None, but I'll talk to her about it when the time is right. When the grief about Anne Marie subsides a bit. But I can't see how all of this is important. I probably shouldn't be sharing Viv's personal information with you like this. I'm sorry, I didn't mean to go off subject like that. I guess I'm just still reeling a bit."

"Hey," I remind him, "I asked you. You never know what will help in the long run. By the way, do you know a guy named Tate. Tate Austin?"

"No. Never heard of him. Should I?"

"Not necessarily. He's driving her home today. Says he's a friend of hers. You know most of her friends?"

"Most of them, but there's quite a few people from work that I've never met. I don't know everyone in her life."

He doesn't seem alarmed. I thank him for his time and let him get on with his day.

Reeve

Present—Saturday

SNOW CRUNCHES UNDER my boots with each step. The air up here is cold but moist, and the snow has the consistency for making snowballs. The damp air in my lungs makes me feel out of shape, and that alone angers me—stubbornly pushes me to walk faster, to cover more ground. McKay darts back and forth just ahead of me. I've put a fluorescent orange vest on him so that hunters won't mistake him for a deer or a small bear. It's a hunter's dream, this layer of snow, and they'll be out tracking.

We've haven't found any grizzly samples yet, but we have come across all sorts of different tracks: rabbit, black bear, deer, elk, moose, and even some kind of a cat, probably lynx or small mountain lion. A cat's prints are always easy to detect because they splay outward, and since their claws are retractable, there are no visible claw points as there are in canine prints. I photographed all of them, even the white-tail tracks, just for my records. You never know when someone in the department might need extra proof that lynx or bobcat or other species reside in the North Fork area. Not long ago, the whole place was teeming with mule deer. Now you rarely see a herd, and researchers are still trying to figure out why, whether it's drought, disease, fire decimation of their favorable foliage, or an increase in predators.

The buzzing in my head has steadily quieted as I've hiked. Now that I'm out in the mountains, I can think. It's Saturday, and I haven't heard from anyone from the county. Even though they told me I shouldn't go far, they know this is my job. It demands that I go long distances out in the boonies. They can't expect me not to go to work. That's exactly what I'll tell them if they do call. But in the back of my head, I hear their voices, imagine their questions: *So why did you pack so much? Why did you take a tent and a sleeping bag? Extra food?*

"Because," I practice answering, seeing the plumes of my breath in the cool air, "we just had our first lower-elevation snow, which means the grizzlies are going to be moving higher and farther into the back-country, searching out their hibernation spots." I'm talking out loud, like a crazy person. McKay keeps glancing at me, but I continue. "And since they'll be farther back, I'll need to go more miles, take longer trips. Perfectly normal for my work this time of the year."

But as I say it, I know I'm stretching the truth. It's rare for me to camp this late in the fall, with the temperatures dropping below freezing at night. McKay peers at me again, his boxy head tilted to the side, trying to figure out if I'm giving him commands or not. "You're fine," I say in a lighthearted voice to him. "Heel up." I call him closer to my side. "Good boy."

He wags his tail, and I take my glove off, slip my hand into my pocket, and grab a dog biscuit and slip it into his mouth. "We're good."

The snow begins to melt, wet weeds and mottled leaves choking the already faint game trails. I can begin to smell the wilderness waking up as the day warms a bit—the autumn soil's musky scent. When I spent those years in juvie, the noise of the other kids yelling, jeering, and banging was an intolerable roar that I hated not being able to escape. But here it's the opposite. Anger has a way of dissipating out here, and I'm relieved to know that I can disappear into the black sea of trees against the jutting mountainsides.

That night we spent together, Anne Marie said, *You've turned things around . . . You're doing something worthwhile.* I wanted to believe her, but part of me knows I'm still hiding. The wild doesn't solve or even erase your problems, it simply helps you balance them. Helps you find a fulcrum between your inner and outer focus—like the space between the sky and the ground—so you don't drive yourself crazy. That's exactly what I thought I'd achieved over all these years, day in, day out, taking each step with McKay into the woods, but the whole situation with Anne Marie and the cops has set my seesaw out of whack—sent one side thudding heavily to the ground and back into anxiety. I continue steadily up a ridge, where thick fog shrouds the surrounding mountains and the spires of the tall trees fade into white smears. Thorny fingers of hawthorn bushes grab at my arms and legs while the November sun sits low in the sky, weakening with each passing day.

The dream I had about my father comes to me again, along with Anne Marie's questions about guns and about my relationship with him. I didn't tell her that a year after the incident, my dad decided he wanted to give me a tutorial on how to handle a gun—that after all, had I had a proper education in the first place, I wouldn't have killed Sam. Of course this was in spite of the fact that he left the gun in a reachable spot, ready and loaded. In spite of the fact that I was nine years old.

Part of this education involved taking me to a shooting range. He packed the very rifle that had killed Sam into his red Honda Prelude and made me hop in. I didn't want to go, but the last thing I was going to do was argue with my father, who since the incident had been unpredictable in his anger toward me. One minute he'd be understanding, and the next he'd fly off the handle and yell at me, tell me that I was going to turn into a no-good loser if I didn't get with it, clean my room, get better grades, help around the house.

He'd also long since quit playing hoops with me out in the driveway. Early on, we couldn't because of the reporters camped outside, but after they had moved on and things quieted down, he'd say he was too tired or had other things to do, because "damn it, lord knows how I have to do it all around here." I wasn't sure what he meant by having to do it all, because as far as I could tell, my mother seemed to be the busy one when they were both home—always bustling around the house, cooking, cleaning, doing laundry, gardening. So I didn't protest, but I was terrified. I did not want to go to the shooting range. I did not want to pick up that rifle ever again.

It was an outdoor range located in a field on the edge of town. We drove down a long straight road that wavered like water in the distance from the heat. Snakes, black racers that had been run over, lay on the hot pavement like broken fan belts. When we got there, I froze at the loud pops of gunfire. I was sitting in the passenger seat, and when my dad opened his door and started to get out, he saw that I wasn't moving. He stopped and peered over his shoulder at me. "You gettin' out?"

I stared straight ahead without answering.

"Jesus, you look like a deer in the headlights. Come out here right now."

I still didn't speak.

"Who am I?" he asked. It was a familiar question. He used it when he wanted me to do something. Usually I answered "My dad" automatically, which was the answer he wanted, but I didn't respond this time. I kept staring out the window at the car parked in front of us: some big bronze sedan from the seventies with an old bent license plate. I read the tag line on the bottom of the plate over and over. *Sunshine State. Sunshine State.*

He stepped out of the car, slammed his door, and came around to my side. "I'm your father, that's who, and I'm telling you to get out of the car."

I climbed out into the hot afternoon sun while he grabbed the rifle and the box of ammunition from the back seat. I followed him into a Quonset hut that had a counter with a man working behind it. My dad paid the man, and he smiled down at me. "Looks like he's gonna cry," he said to my dad. "A little sensitive, is he?"

My father mumbled something and said, "Come on," to me. "Quit lookin' so scared."

I walked behind him to the field where the shooters lined up. The humidity was stifling, and mosquitoes pricked at my arms. A large sign with big red lettering stood off to the side: GUN SAFETY RULES. The first rule on the list read: *Always keep the gun pointed in a safe direction. Never point it at something you don't intend to shoot.* A queasiness pinched my stomach. The second rule was: *Always keep your finger off the trigger until you are ready to shoot at your target.* The third said: *Always keep the gun unloaded until you are ready to shoot.* I wondered if my dad had ever read the third rule. But in the long run, it was the first two that plagued me for many years to come. They were so simple. So doable.

By the time we made it to the line of shooters, my heart was pumping ferociously and I was sick to my stomach. No one was shooting at the moment. "Here," my dad said, handing me a pair of bright orange, rubbery earplugs. "Put them in your ears." He told me how to hold the rifle, to point it down and away from anybody in the vicinity. He showed me the safety and demonstrated how to look through the sight and down the barrel. When the range operator yelled, "Commence firing!" my dad took aim and fired several shots. Everyone in the line began shooting again, great blasts in my ears. I couldn't distinguish my heart's pounding against my rib cage from the shots booming around me. I had trouble breathing. "You try." My dad handed it to me.

I shook my head.

"Go on, take it!" He thrust the rifle toward me, into my pounding chest. I involuntarily lifted my hands and grabbed it.

He pointed at the target, two red circles one above the other. Sweat ran down the back of my neck and my shirt. I wanted to cry, but I knew my dad would be even more disgusted with me if I did, especially out here among all these people, mostly men. I tried to take a deep breath—*Don't cry, don't cry, don't cry*, I repeated to myself—and dug the tips of my fingers into the hard, smooth wood of the rifle butt. Slowly I lifted it to take aim, my hands and arms shaking.

"Just at the top circle," he said. "Aim for the center."

The blasts of gunshots engulfed me as I tried to focus. My dad slapped at a mosquito on his neck and said, "Damn skeeters," and it seemed to happen in slow motion. I could feel my pulse behind my ears, and suddenly all I could think of was the gun violently slamming into my chin and seeing Sam's body go down in front of me. Sam's eyes:

first confusion, then terror. And the blood. Mosquitoes buzzed around my head, and along with the throbbing behind my ears and the thumping of my heart, I'd had all I could take. I dropped the gun and swatted frantically at my head, slapping the sides so hard that my palms and my scalp stung. I ran for the car. Behind me, I heard the range operator scream, "Cease fire!"

When I got to the car and turned, I saw my dad marching angrily toward me with the rifle at his side in one hand. A violent shade of purplish red consumed his face and ran all the way up to his high hairline. The range operator followed him, yelling at his back, "Don't you ever bring that kid back here, you understand? For god's sake, he could have killed someone!"

Ali

Present—Saturday

I'M WAITING TO hear back from Brander so I can fill him in on the connection between Anne Marie and the Smith case, and I'm beginning to wonder what's taking him so long. I keep getting up from my desk, looking out the window at the piles of dead leaves around the backyard that have been scattered by the wind and spread in messy rivulets in all directions. Several of the mounds look like they've begun to rot, and I picture Emily rolling in them, getting sticky-wet, pungent-smelling leaves stuck to her cheeks and hair. I know I need to get out and finish raking and bagging them. Emily's still watching cartoons, and even though she's past the time limit I gave her, I let her continue because, selfishly, I know I need time to think.

I'm on my way into the kitchen to make some tea when the door-bell rings. "I got it," I tell Emily and go right to the door. It's Herman, and I feel annoyed that he's stopping by again when a call back would suffice. I had left him a message too, because I needed to tell him about Anne Marie's appearance in the Smith file, but I could just as easily have told him about it over the phone. It makes me think he's check-ing up on me, but I realize I'm antsy and impatient, and I don't want to direct my angst toward Herman and put him in the middle. *Damn, Reeve. Look what you're doing to me.*

I politely take him to the kitchen, just as I did the night before. After all, he's my partner, and before Herman even sits down or takes his coat off, he says, "The county guys came to our office today."

189

My stomach drops. I force myself to not stop and turn, to continue toward the kitchen cabinet to grab some cups. "Why's that?"

"They wanted to talk to you. Seems there's a bit of a problem. They said they've discovered an interesting piece of information."

"About Smith?" I turn to him.

"Smith?" Herman looks at me, confused for a second, before he shakes his head and slides back to an expression of obvious displeasure. I can feel the tension, the judgment—or at least a certain amount of condemnation—coming from Herman like heat from an open oven, and the dread turns to a spark of anger. I know it's misplaced. I should be feeling fear instead, but as usual it's fury rearing up in me like an unwanted guest. I purse my lips together, cross my arms, and wait for him to say more.

He holds his hands up like he's trying to stop me from doing something. He must sense my agitation. "Ali," he says in his low voice, "they know that the suspect is . . ." He tilts his head toward the living room where Emily sits frog-legged before the TV.

"Sit down." I motion to the table. "Do you want some coffee?" I grab a cup and hold it up.

"No thank you." He takes a seat, and I pull up a chair across from him. He's sitting back rigidly, his face serious, his coat still on. He looks too big for my small round oak table.

"What else did they say?"

"That they subpoenaed his financial records and saw that he writes a check to you once a month. That you watched part of his interview and didn't mention that you knew him." His face changes from annoyance to pity, and that enrages me even more, because I hate pity. It evokes the looks of Sara Seafeldt and many other adults I encountered in my younger years—an expression that says, *Poor, poor, pitiful you. Your life is so sad.*

He brings up the fact that I also swung by the county and had an in-depth discussion with Reynolds without disclosing my connection to the suspect.

"I didn't want everyone in my business at that point," I explain. "You can understand that."

"Under different circumstances, yes, I most certainly can. Under these circumstances, no, I'm sorry, I can't. Are you kidding me? This could be your *job* on the line. You know better than this. What do you think Shackley and PR are going to say?"

I watch a busy squirrel frantically collecting supplies—nuts, pinecones, mushrooms—then scurry up the maple tree in our backyard and hop to one of the branches. I want to say, *My daughter is on the line here*, but I don't want to sound paranoid or like an alarmist. "Are you reporting me?" I ask.

"Not necessarily. I'd like to think I'm warning you, just like last night, when you also opted out of telling me the truth. What kind of a game are you playing here?"

"I'm not playing any game." I hug my arms even tighter over my chest. "Herman, listen," I say firmly, and I can see in the way he draws his head back that he notes that I'm not calling him by his nickname. "Reeve didn't do it. And I'm not saying that because he's . . ."—I snap my head in the direction of the living room just as Herman had done— "but because it just doesn't add up. It doesn't make sense, and I don't trust those bozos to do this correctly."

He shuts his eyes for a second and sighs, as if he's trying hard to gather patience for a live wire like me. It irritates me even more to be treated like a child. "I understand, but you are clearly in no position to judge his innocence."

"But I am. I know him. He wouldn't do something like that."

Again he flashes me a look of pity—a droopy-eyed, sympathetic look that says, *That's exactly why you have no place to judge.*

I get up and pace around the kitchen. I look out the window and see the squirrel coming back down the trunk. Busy fucker, I think. That's what it takes to survive—an endless vigilance. Busyness, acquisition, sustenance. And if it's not food, as it is for the animals, it's money, security, trust, love, truth, or acceptance. It never ends, the journey to find sustenance, even when you convince yourself you're seeking something different. It's really just the same effort in disguise.

I go to him, sit down again, my chair scraping on the floor. I lean toward him, jamming my elbows into the table. "Herman, you have to believe me on this."

"I get it, Ali. But are you going to jeopardize your job for this, this guy, this Reeve, who you aren't even married to, whom I've never even heard about? And even if he is so important to you, what part of conflict of interest do you not understand?"

I'm about to answer him, but the minute I open my mouth to speak, Emily comes into the kitchen and stands at Herman's side.

"Are you talking about my daddy?" she asks.

"No, honey," I fib for him, because although he knows Emily, he looks taken aback by a five-year-old's interrupting our conversation. Under different circumstances, I'd tease him for looking more spooked by her arrival than he is by the violent criminals he's usually dealing with. "Why?"

"I heard his name."

"No, I don't think so, sweetie." I feign confusion. "We're just talking about work. Go back and watch your show, okay?"

"But I heard you mention my daddy's name: *Reeve.* That's my daddy's name." She smiles at Herman, and sways shyly and playfully from side to side, her hands by her sides. A stab of guilt shoots through me for fibbing to her, basically telling her that her own senses are not to be trusted. What's worse is the silly pride on her face; her tiny chin lifting when she announces her father's name cuts me even deeper.

"Is it?" Herman smiles, still unsure how to handle the situation. "I didn't know that."

"My daddy says that he's named after a riverbank. My grandma thought she was naming him after a river, but it's actually the bank. Isn't that funny?"

"That's very funny." Herman forces a smile.

"That's what he *thinks*, anyway, but he's not sure. He said he's only

googled it, and that you can't always trust Google." She still shows rem-
nants of her toddler speech at times, and once in a while, trouble with
the r's comes out so that *river* comes across as *wiver* and *trust* sounds
like *twust.*

"Ah, your daddy's right about that," Herman says.

Emily begins to climb into my lap, but I cut the motion off by
standing up. I grab her small hand to take her back into the living
room before the TV, but she resists, pulling back. "Come on, Emily." I
clutch her wrist tightly with frustration, and she begins to scream, so
I let go immediately and tell her to be quiet. "Come on, don't you want
to watch TV?"

"I don't want to watch cartoons anymore," she says, annoyed, but at
least she's following me into the living room.

"Just a little longer. Herman and I need to discuss some work
things. And since when do you *not* want to watch cartoons?"

"No," she says, pushing her bottom lip out, glaring at me.

I want to tell her that saying no to me is not an option today, but I
don't want a tantrum. "Okay, then, why don't you go upstairs and get
dressed? Then maybe we can do something fun."

I see that resonate. Her face softens, an excitement bubbling in her
dark eyes, and I'm relieved. "Like what?"

"I don't know. We'll think of something."

"Promise?" she asks.

"Promise," I say.

She bounds up the stairs, sounding like a small elephant.

I go back into the kitchen. "Sorry about that."

"I'm sorry," Herman says. "I wasn't thinking."

"Look, Herman. The Smith file you gave me—did you read it all?"

"I skimmed it."

"Did you see Anne Marie Johnson's name?"

"What?"

"The victim's name. It's crazy, but Anne Marie Johnson, the victim,
she's in the file. Did you notice that? That's what I was referring to earlier."

He looks at me skeptically. "Go on."

I tell him about the connection between her and Smith, how she was posing as a follower of his cause for an investigative piece she was working on—that she thought there was a connection between someone high up in the NRA and our Smith. "It's in the file." I point in the direction of my office. "I can grab it for you."

"Just sit, please," Herman commands, studying me. I can see I've lost some of his trust, and it's a bad feeling, like murky water creeping up around me. My anger has faded, and fear replaces it in the form of any icy sensation in my spine. I want Herman's big warm smile back—the one that always makes me feel like I'm the best agent and coworker in the world. Now that the cat's out of the bag, the judgment in Herman's face is gone, and he simply looks sad. I see it plainly: not only have I crossed professional boundaries, but I've hurt him by not telling him about Reeve in the first place. I think of all the times he's hinted at my past, leaving sentences open-ended and asking innocent questions—*So Emily is with her dad this weekend?*—to see if I'll fill in the rest, and when I never do, he backs off. He's been a good coworker. A good friend, but I can see it now: he's questioning whether he can say the same about me.

"So"—I clear my throat—"that alone gives me—us—some reason to be checking the circumstances of her death out anyway."

"There's been no *us* here," he reminds me coolly.

I feel the sting of that. I have this sudden flare in my mind, like seeing my life unspool before me, that this is what I've always been working toward: some type of destruction. Like Reeve, somehow I'm seeking admittance into a world of sharp solitude. I picture myself jobless. I see Emily and me alone because we can no longer afford Rose, and, worse, our moving back to be near my mom and sister. I see myself hanging on to Emily like a lifeline and her rebelling, desperate to get away from a suffocating mother. Stop, I tell myself. I refocus on Herman. He's waiting for my response, but I don't say anything. I'm banking on the idea that Herman won't want to look foolish in front of his bosses for not catching the connection in the file.

Herman takes a deep breath. "Ali, obviously you found this out after you started snooping, after you put our entire department in a compromising position with the county. After you imposed a major conflict of interest."

I should apologize to him, but I don't. I shrug, but I'm hoping Brander and Reynolds don't yet know about the interviews I've done, and I feel suddenly glad that Vivian is heading back to Seattle today. "I know, but look, I'm only looking into the victim, who happens to be in the Smith file. I'm not looking into their suspect. And I haven't spoken to him lately."

"What's lately?"

I wave the question off with a flick of my hand and don't answer him. I called Reeve early this morning to tell him to stay put and be available for questioning.

"It doesn't matter anyway," he adds.

"Right, what matters is that you and I figure out how deeply she was involved in *our* case. And I've put a call in to Brander already." I look at my watch. "Now I understand why they haven't called me back yet. But, Herman, they need to know about this."

"I'll update them after I look at the file again," he says, but his expression still shows that he isn't buying this idea that we're simply going to hop onto the Smith train and let my actions dissolve into nothing. He's sitting still, chewing on his bottom lip, and I can tell he's thinking about how to proceed, when my doorbell rings.

Emily squeals some happy indiscernible sound and bounds down the stairs, yelling, "I can get it."

"Hang on there, Em!" I yell back. "Excuse me," I tell Herman, and go into the living room. Emily is patiently waiting by the door, her hand on the knob. She's dressed herself in clothes that are not coordinated at all: a polka-dotted frilly summer tank top and a brown plaid skirt. The mom in me briefly thinks that I'm going to have to get her to change before we go anywhere, and that it's going to be a fight because it will be an affront to her recent development of independence—that

is, before I see through the side window panels that it's Brander standing on my doorstep. My heart suddenly sinks as reality hits: I just could
be in over my head.

I nod to Emily, and she turns the knob with both hands and swings
the door open with great pride. She's wearing a huge grin on her face,
and I feel a stab of love so great that I'm suddenly overtaken with a
need to sweep her up in my arms and tell her that I'm sorry, that everything will be okay—that I was probably never really good enough to
do this mothering thing in the first place, but that I was going to damn
sure do everything I could to protect her now that I'd brought her into
this world.

Reeve

MY DAD DIDN'T talk to me on the ride back from the shooting range. When we got home, I remember my mom's arms around me, hugging me and telling me that everything was fine and not to worry about it. But my dad—he didn't look at me or address me for what felt like a very long time. It might have been only a day or two, but it felt like forever.

I remember my parents arguing in the kitchen that evening after dinner in hushed voices that became louder than they intended. I had just walked into the living room when I heard my mom say, "Maybe you're being too hard on him."

My dad had replied, "He needs to grow up. Look at us! We're pariahs in our own town."

My mom didn't respond. I stood by our couch, my fingers kneading into the top of one of the cushions.

"You saw the news yesterday: Sam's parents are furious that there have been no legal consequences for us. They've hired a high-profile attorney. They're working with that congressman—what's his name?"

"Bushnell," my mom answered.

"They're trying to change the law to make adults criminally liable. In the paper, it said they're *channeling*"—he said it mockingly—"their anger. They're channeling their anger by trying to make people like us *criminals* for an accident. It could have been a car crash and not a gun. Would they still be *channeling*?"

Again my mom didn't answer.

197

"What do you think about that?" my dad pressed her. "Huh?"

"I think," she said, "they've just lost their child. I think they're traumatized and upset. And other than that, I just don't know . . ."

After a moment, I could hear the back screen door slam shut. I guessed that my dad had left the kitchen. I remember hearing my mom start to weep. I remember wanting to go to her so that she could wrap her warm arms around me again and I could cry with her, but I heard my dad's voice in my head: *He needs to grow up.* I went to my room instead, where I sat on my bed and tried to read a comic book.

My dad never asked again to take me to the shooting range, but years later a friend of mine had a rifle and, soaring high as kites one day, we went into the woods where he had some tin cans lined up on a log. He began firing, the sharp charcoal smell of gunpowder choking the air.

The weed we'd been smoking all afternoon obliterated my senses, so I barely even flinched and was proud of it. When he said, "Your turn," I took the rifle, buoyed by a drug-induced lack of inhibition, and fired away, hitting only one of the cans. It was empowering. I was a new man. My father was right: I had hopped back on the horse. I should have done it long ago. I could have kissed the sky, taking control like that. I could practically hear Hendrix's "Purple Haze" playing in my head. I hooted and hollered, and through my own blurred vision, my friend looked at me with a crooked, curious smile. "You're funny, dude," I remember him saying.

A week later, he convinced me to buy the rifle from him because he needed the money for more pot. I bought it for forty bucks and kept it hidden in the run-down one-room apartment I was living in before I almost torched it because I left a bowl of soup on the burner while I passed out on the couch. I woke to flames, jerking the pot off while hot soup sizzled down my calves and sent me to the hospital with third-degree burns on my legs and hand.

In the hospital, finally sober, I realized what could have happened with my friend that afternoon in the woods—that I could easily have had another accident, this time while in an altered state of my own making. When I got out of the hospital, I decided to make a big change. I chose Montana because somehow I knew or hoped that a place so vast and unknowable would change me. I had these difficult-to-describe notions about Montana: not just beauty, but a kind of dignity in its harshness, in its starkness. I had the idea that you could live an authentic life in the mountains, a reality that isn't blurred by heat and humidity, seasons that barely change, and people who rely on gossip to find meaning. In Montana, the environment provides clear boundaries and truths: Hypothermia will kill you. A bear with its cubs should not be provoked. Unstable layers of snow might slide and create an avalanche. Getting lost in the woods without proper gear might be the end of you. Drought causes fire and fruitless crops. The leaves and pine needles change colors and drop to the ground. The lake water turns to ice, the ground freezes, and snow falls. In the warming spring, the fields turn lush and the crops grow. The mountains and the fresh air seem like possibility; each season brings new beginnings; and finally, each day holds promises under an expanding sky, not suffocating routines that smear together like a muted impressionist painting.

Now I couldn't even tell you the name of the friend I was with that afternoon, but I know his initials are *BC* because they're inscribed on the side of the stock. He was just someone I got high with for a month or two. I never saw him again, and other than hanging on to the Winchester for emergency purposes since I was heading to Montana, I never intended to fire one ever again in my life.

. . .

In the distance, a pack of wolves begins to howl, their pitch escalating as more join in. I've found a good place to camp—out in a small meadow tucked beside a great escarpment that looms black behind us. We're close to the tree line, and stunted dark pines off to the side provide a modicum of warmth, some protection from the cold. I've pitched my tent, collected kindling and the driest dead logs I could find for a fire. I made one, watching the damp logs steam and take their sweet time to get going. In the meantime, I fed McKay his dog food, and eventually, when the fire was hot enough, I cooked dinner for myself from a packet of freeze-dried stew by adding hot water I'd boiled.

Now we're sitting by the fire, McKay on a pad I've laid out for him and me on a thick log I've dragged over. It's not entirely dark yet, but close, and twilight smudges my surroundings. A band of deep-indigo sky darkens over the mountains under a lifting layer of clouds while I sit and poke at the fire and watch the wood burn and begin to morph into coals that pulsate with a glowing intensity.

McKay tilts his head at the mournful sound of the wolves and begins to whine. He moves closer to me and leans his shoulder, damp from moving through the wet underbrush all day, against my thigh. His hair prickles upright and separates, exposing the natural oils that keep him warm. It reminds me of a porcupine. "Scaredy-cat," I say to him. "You've smelled their scat a million times. No big deal."

But it is eerie, in spite of knowing they're far in the distance. Wolves won't get near us unless McKay does something stupid, like wander away from camp, but he won't. He's too well trained. Wolves and coyotes are smart enough to send a female to lure a male dog into the woods where they can surround him, but McKay is neutered and obedient. He won't budge from my side. I reach down and pat his chest. "You're a good boy." I grab the long stick I've been using to move a log that has tipped to the side into a better position on the fire.

The wind blows the smoke away from us, but every now and again it shifts, and I have to shut my eyes while I get a full blast of it in the face. That's the way I'm sitting, taking in the sound of the rustling tree branches with my eyes closed while I wait for the breeze to shift, when I hear the breaking of a twig from a footstep. I jump up immediately, opening my eyes to a face full of smoke, and look behind me. McKay growls, and I see the bright, assaulting beam of a flashlight. My heart races until I hear a familiar voice: "It's just me, you fools."

"I'm a fool?" I say after I recognize Wallace's voice. "What kind of person is out hiking up here at dark?"

McKay's tail has already begun to wag ferociously when he hears the familiar voice, and when Wallace steps into the circle of the firelight, McKay runs up to him like a long-lost friend. Wallace leans over stiffly and pets his head. "Easy, boy," he croons. "Easy. I saw your firelight up on the ridge. Wanted to see who it was all the way up here."

"Yeah, well, that's foolish. What if it wasn't me?"

"Had a feeling it was."

I shake my head. "Have a seat." I gesture to the log I've been sitting on. "Hungry?"

"Sure. What you got?"

"Nothing good. Freeze-dried stuff."

"Hmm, no fresh trout?"

"Nope. Didn't stop to fish."

"You never fish."

"Not when McKay's with me. You kidding? He'd try to fetch the fly with every cast. So you want some or not?"

"Tell you what, let's cook these up." He reaches into his pack and grabs a plastic bag containing some filleted trout.

"I can't believe you're hiking out here with the smell of fish in your pocket."

"I've got a rifle," he says.

"That won't stop a four-hundred-pound adrenaline-fueled animal from killing you. It might die later, after it bleeds internally, but by that time, you and the fish will be long gone."

"Bah," he says. "Here, cook 'em up." He hands me the bag and then rummages around his pack for some tinfoil. "You're in a lot more danger than I am, stalking grizzlies out here. What about those stories of photographers who've been mauled by the grizzlies they were trying to follow?"

"We don't stalk them, you know that."

In fact, with all the time McKay and I spend out in these woods, we've seen a grizzly only three times: twice from a distance, and one time when McKay startled one and luckily the bear took off in the opposite direction and didn't follow McKay straight back to me, which can sometimes happen with people who hike with their dogs out in the wild. There's nothing quite like being in grizzly-bear country. At its best it's surreal, an existential experience to walk among them in their territory, puncturing the human illusion that we're always in control of our world. But Wallace and I would both be fools to not admit the real danger of being in their territory during autumn when they are facing hibernation and storing up on fat reserves. At the same time, we wouldn't have it any other way. These woods would never be the same if the bears weren't living among us.

"You hear those wolves a few minutes ago?" Wallace changes the subject.

"I did."

"Pretty cool," he adds.

"They won't bother us," I say in case he's wondering, but the look on his face tells me I've insulted him by telling him what he already knows.

He wraps the fish into foil and hands them over. "Here, set these on the coals. My knees are too old to lean down after a day of hiking up here."

Wallace offers me a slug from the flask of whiskey he brought while we wait for the fish to cook. "So tell me," he says, "why are you staying all the way up here? You don't usually come up this high."

I give him my line about the grizzlies' movement to the higher northern slopes with the first snowfalls.

Wallace looks at me skeptically.

"I've camped out here plenty of times," I say, poking at some of the coals with a stick.

He gives me a dubious frown, then shrugs, like he's decided to accept it or simply drop the subject. I watch the blue flames circling the base of the tinfoil. When it's ready, we unwrap it and eat the flaky white flesh. Afterward we sit quietly, and I'm glad for the company. Eventually—maybe it's the whiskey, which I don't usually drink—but for no good reason I ask, "Ever feel like there's no place left to go, like all we have are these mountains?"

Wallace hangs his head toward his knees and laughs. His head bobs up and down a little with his chuckles. "You have no idea." His voice sounds somber.

"How's that?" I ask.

He lifts his head and stares at the fire. "It's just messy out there, that's all."

The sadness I saw on his front porch washes back onto his face. I look away, back at the pulsing of the coals and the shifting of the flames in the wind. The soles of my boots are hot, and I shift my feet farther away, the tread scraping on the dirt and gravel. "What's going on in Oregon? Why didn't you go back?"

"I told you," Wallace says, taking another sip from his flask. "Didn't get my elk. Can't go home empty-handed."

It's my turn to look at him with skepticism. "Seems to me you've gone home plenty of times in the past without getting your elk."

"Yeah, well, I'm getting old. Can't afford to do that much longer."

"What about your wife? Everything okay with her?" I've met Susan only once before when she came out with Wallace for a few weeks in the summer. She helped fix up the cabin. From what I recall, she's a painter. Watercolors. In the summer months, she prefers to paint the Oregon coast rather than the Montana mountains, so she usually stays back.

"She's fine." He stands. "All right, I'm hittin' it early tomorrow. If I don't see you, be safe out here." He then heads off to his tent, with the fire popping behind him.

"You too," I call after him.

Ali

Present—Saturday

"Mommy," emily whines, "you said we'd *do* something."

"I know, sweetie, but that's before Detective Brander showed up and asked me for help. Now I need to go to work, just for a little while. When I'm done, I promise we'll do something then. This won't take that long." I glance at Herman, hoping for a quick nod of affirmation to back me up in front of Emily, but he doesn't flinch.

"Where did Brander go?" I ask.

"He said he'd meet you at the county building in a half hour."

I point to my driveway. "Then why is his car still here?"

"He asked who lived in the apartment around back. I told him that Emily's nanny did, so he went to chat with her. I guess he figures that Rose would know the suspect."

I think this is ridiculous, and I'm irritated that's he's bothering Rose when I know she isn't feeling well and is probably in bed recovering, but I keep my mouth shut. Clearly my snooping has drawn too much attention already. Maybe I'm making things worse for Reeve.

"Mommy," Emily bleats, "you promised. You said we'd do something."

"I'm going to go back there," I announce. "If he needs me to come to the county building, then I'm going to need Rose to watch Emily," I say on my way to the door.

"But, Mommy," Emily cries. She loves Rose, but she has her mind set on going to do something with me instead.

Herman turns to her and makes a funny face to placate her. "Emily, want to go get some ice cream with me?"

She's still frowning, but once Herman's question registers, her face lights up and she licks her lips and nods. I'm thankful that she's placated, and relieved that Herman is still acting like a friend, at least for now.

. . .

"Here," I say, handing Emily a warm turtleneck and jeans I've picked out from her drawer in her bedroom. "Put these on."

"Why can't you come with us?" She's turning high-pitched again.

I force myself to take a seat on her disheveled bed to signal that we're in no hurry. "Because I have to go to work," I say softly and calmly. "Just for a little while, though."

"But you promised."

"I'll be back soon, sweetie. After you get ice cream with Herman. That sounds like fun, right? You won't even know I'm gone." I know Emily loves Herman; she's always asking me if he can come over for barbecues. She's much more social than I've ever been, and sometimes I think she's lonely spending so much time with Rose and me at home when she's not at school or with her father.

She smiles and nods enthusiastically, then pulls on the turtleneck. "I have an idea." She grins. "After we get ice cream, you, Herman, and me can all go for a picnic."

She's proud of her idea, so I refrain from telling her that it's too cold for a picnic, but I can't help but correct her grammar. "'You, Herman, and *I*,'" I say. "Come on," I encourage her, "Herman's waiting."

. . .

When I get to the county building, Brander is waiting for me inside. He tells me we're meeting with Commander Vance in her office. I'm irritated that they've involved her. I want to point out to them what a bunch of candy-asses they are. Why can't they talk to me first like professional adults without running to their commander? But I bite my tongue. I also want to ask why he felt the need to wake my nanny over this nonsense, but I don't. I know I'm the one being childish. I feel like I'm heading to the principal's office or, worse, like I'm going to see Sara Seafeldt so she can pry answers from me about my out-of-control home life and report my mom. I straighten my coat collar and pull my shoulders back.

This can't be good, I think, but brush the idea away. Commander Vance is not my boss. She can do damage to me only if she decides to call the higher-ups in Salt Lake City, which would be an aggressive, out-of-character move on her part. Besides, she and I get along just fine, and she was very pleased with the work that Herman and I did on a recent local Internet child pornography operation. Brander doesn't say a word as we approach her office door, and I smooth my hair behind my ears as I enter.

Reynolds is seated in one of the two chairs before Vance's desk, one leg crossed over the other and smiling like they've got some joke going. Vance stands up immediately when I walk in, which I appreciate. "Agent Paige." She smiles politely. "Thank you for coming, especially on a weekend."

"No problem," I say. "Happy to help."

"Have a seat." She waves to the chair next to Reynolds, who hasn't bothered to rise. I hesitate, since that leaves Brander without a chair and I'm not sure I want to sit anyway, but I figure I should be as compliant as possible. I take the seat while Brander goes over to the window and props a hip on the sill. A maple tree outside is framing Brander in gold, making him look like some college student hanging out in a professor's office. It makes me wish I was simply dealing with him, not Vance and Reynolds too.

I glance at Reynolds. The smile has faded from his face and he's got a set of cold cop eyes going. We've all developed our own version of the look over time. I remember one of my instructors in Quantico telling me: *Paige, agent eyes are* not *full of rage. Get the anger out of that face. The secret to a good glare is the* absence *of emotion!*

Reynolds is adopting that void stare, Brander is staying neutral, and Vance is going for courtesy, a small, pleasant smile still playing on her lips. "So, Agent Paige, I'm not sure if you know why we've asked you here?" Her brow lifts in question.

"I have an idea," I say, motioning with my head toward Brander. "Brander filled me in some."

"Yes." She looks at her desk for a moment and folds her hands before her. "Unfortunately, it's come to our attention that one of our suspects, Reeve Landon, apparently is the father of your child."

I sit still, not nodding, not replying.

"Is that true?"

"Yes, he's the father of my daughter."

"And, well, I was with you watching him get interrogated, and you didn't mention that you knew him. I'm curious why you didn't."

I let out a pent-up breath, keep my eyes trained on Vance, and refrain from glancing at either Brander or Reynolds. Her hair is in a tight bun, and pale, cinnamon-colored freckles dot her forehead and her cheekbones. She's still looking at me with a closed-lip smile, but her eyes pierce mine with an air of authority, like some of the SACs—special agents in charge—I've served in the past. They say loud and clear, *I've been through a lot to get to this position, and my expectations of you are high.* I want to look away, but I force myself to keep my eyes on hers. I begin with the truth: "I didn't mention that I knew him because I like to keep that part of my life private, Commander. I figured it bore no relevance on the questioning that was going on, and I didn't want to bring up my own personal stuff, or"—I shrug—"give any reason to spark gossip around the local forces before I even knew if he'd become a person of interest. I'm sure you can understand."

She doesn't nod, but I can see it register. She's a high-level female in a male-dominated profession. Of course she understands my need for privacy. In fact I know very little about her family situation, either, only that she has no kids. There's rumor that she has a female partner, but I have no idea if it's true or if they're married or what. "But," she proceeds cautiously, "you didn't just watch the interview. You've also spoken about the case to both the detectives here and to our forensics department."

It bothers me that Ray or Gretchen told them about our conversations—it feels like a betrayal, though maybe that's just my ego talking. "I was asking out of curiosity," I say. "It's an interesting case."

"Uh-huh, even more interesting because it involves the father of your child?"

"Yes, but I didn't take that part seriously. I mean, right, there's no real evidence to suggest that Mr. Landon had anything to do with it?"

"Brander and Reynolds here"—she motions to them—"they beg to differ."

"All right, well, I'm sorry for asking questions. I really just wanted to be helpful," I say as sweetly as I can muster. I can feel the heat in my cheeks and sweat begins to prickle the back of my neck. I'm hoping they haven't turned red.

"We can certainly appreciate that, and you know we always appreciate your assistance. But clearly there's a conflict of interest here, and I'm surprised that you wouldn't think better of getting involved."

"I understand that, but I figured if you found any real evidence to back your suspicion of Mr. Landon, I would fill you all in about my personal connection to him. But honestly I didn't think you would, and I don't know if anything else has emerged, but I'm still not seeing anything to suggest that you have." I can hear the edge starting to take shape in my voice, and I can feel a pulse begin to throb in my neck. I try to slow my breathing down to regain control over it.

Reynolds shifts in his seat and puffs out a quick disbelieving humph of air.

"Besides"—I lift my chin, ready to lay it on them—"the case Herman and I are working on involves the victim too."

Vance narrows her eyes and leans forward. "How so?"

I tell her about Anne Marie's connection to Smith, omitting the fact that I just found out about it, but aware that this is going to lead her to ask me why I didn't share that development with them in the first place. "I called Brander about it early this morning."

She looks at Brander.

"I didn't get back to her, what with these developments." He sounds defensive, turns to me, and says, "How long have you known this?"

I have no choice but to be honest. Saying it was the reason I was poking around from the beginning would make things even worse because it would have been equally damaging to our relationship with the county to hold back vital information about a murder victim. "I discovered it late last night when I was going through the case file."

"That's certainly an interesting piece of information," Commander Vance says, looking from Reynolds to Brander.

Brander jots down notes, but Reynolds wears a smirk that says he thinks I'm grasping at straws and that he doesn't think it will mean much in the scheme of things. I can tell he already believes they have their man.

"Yes, it is." I perk up and scoot to the edge of my seat. "Especially since it implies she's been hanging around some pretty violent types. Not to mention the gun stuff she was involved with." I turn toward Reynolds and Brander. "Have you two looked into any of the characters she interviewed for her articles?"

"Look, Agent Paige," Reynolds says, "with all due respect"—clearly a disingenuous preface based on the level of irritation in his voice—"we'll certainly look at all the elements. But right now, let's stick to what's right in front of us. Let us ask you this: Where is your ex-husband?"

"He's not my ex-husband," I say. "We have never been married."

"Excuse me. Ex-boyfriend. Where is he?"

"I don't know. Probably working."

"On a weekend? When all of this is going on? His cell phone untraceable, his cabin vacant since early this morning? That's very suspicious behavior, wouldn't you say?"

"No, not really—not for a guy who spends copious time in the woods on a regular basis. I'm sure he'll be back by this evening."

"I hope you're right," he says. "But, see"—he extends his arm dramatically to me and addresses his commander—"this is why there's a huge conflict of interest."

"You asked me a question," I say.

Vance nods and looks impatiently at Reynolds like she doesn't need his theatrics. Right then I want to smile at her, but I know that won't come across so well. "Let's back up a bit here," she says, raising a hand. "How will you be handling this Smith case going forward, given the fact that you've identified a connection between Smith and a murder victim last seen with your ex?"

"We have procedures," I say. "I'll go through the appropriate channels." I don't share what those are, since we agents rarely share anything about FBI procedures to anyone who isn't part of our organization. But I know that withholding in this moment isn't going to get me anywhere.

Vance is sitting with her thumb and forefinger framing her chin in a V shape. I can tell she's thinking. She wants to put me in my place, but she also doesn't want to push me away in case they need information from us on Smith. "Okay," she finally says, "it would be great if someone in your office could collaborate with my detectives here on these connections you claim the victim had to this Smith guy."

"Of course," I say. "That was the plan all along."

"To be clear, I think we can all agree that it would be best, because of the conflict of interest, that you recuse yourself from this case. We'll need to be in touch with someone else from your office."

"Of course," I say again, but already my mind is reeling. I see Reeve nervously pacing by the hurt deer in the shimmering headlights on the lonely gravel road. Reeve wouldn't hurt a fly, I tell myself. And then my mind hops to how I intend to find out why Vivian suddenly resigned; how close Reeve's boss, Jeffrey O'Brien, was to the victim and how jealous his wife might have been; what kind of grudge someone like Smith or Anne Marie's other interview subjects might have had against her. It's overwhelming, all these threads, and I'm almost tempted to share what I know with all three of them so they can use their resources to help me figure it all out. But I can't, because then they'll know the extent of my snooping around. I'm on thinning ice here, but Emily and her father are out there in the middle of a frozen pond, and I fully intend to bring them safely to shore.

. . .

Herman and Emily ended up at a park about two miles from the court-house. I find them in the playground, deserted of children except for Emily and one other boy in a red sweater who looks to be about her age. I see his coat tossed over to the side on the grass outside the area with the wood chips. Emily is still wearing her pink Columbia coat, and I'm glad for that because clearly the weather is cold enough that no other kids are out on the playground.

Emily and the other boy are both on a tire swing dangling from some elaborate metal contraption of ladders and railings. She and the boy are swinging back and forth and giggling, and I guess that it was gregarious Emily who approached him first, deciding she needed a friend to play with her.

There are several boulders beside the playground and Herman sits perched on one of them, watching Emily. I walk up to join him, button-ing my coat up to my neck. "Hey," I say.

Herman stays seated and gives me a stiff nod of acknowledgment. He's still angry.

"How's it going?" I ask.

"She doesn't tire, does she?"

"Nope," I say. "Maybe by tonight. The cold air will help."

"She's having fun, though. Met that boy about a half hour ago, and they've been playing ever since. She hasn't glanced over here once."

I scan the playground for the boy's mom, and Herman notices me doing that. He points to a navy-colored SUV parked beside the lot with a blond woman sitting inside, reading. "Watching from the warmth of her car," he says. "Doing more reading than watching, though. How did it go?" he asks.

"It went okay," I say, sitting down on the boulder next to his. I tell him how we discussed the conflict-of-interest part and that I told them about the Smith file and finding Anne Marie Johnson's name in it. "Vance is a professional," I say. "She's instructed Brander and Reynolds to contact you from now on for any more information on that front."

"Vance? She was there?"

"I was surprised by that too, but now I think it's a good thing. She understands my need for privacy in a male-dominated profession, and she'll keep Reynolds from stirring this into something it's not."

"What exactly are they stirring this into, Ali?"

He's definitely still angry with me, and I'm disappointed. I had hoped he'd be relieved that it was out in the open now, and that I'd met with the county. "It's a case with a lot of leads," I tell him. "And if they'd only open their eyes and quit focusing on the first person they interviewed, they'd see that there are a lot of avenues to explore."

He raises his head slightly, and I take that as some form of a nod, but then he looks down at the boulder he's sitting on and traces one finger over its uneven surface without saying a word, as if he's the parent and I'm the unruly child, and he's learned that the best way to deal with a disruptive child is to not say anything at all and remain calm.

"For example," I continue, because his silence does get to me, "Vivian Gould, the woman whose cabin the victim was shot at and who happens to bear an uncanny resemblance to the victim, quit her job but didn't mention it when spoken to."

"Spoken to by you?"

I don't answer, just forge ahead. "And Jeffrey O'Brien, Reeve's boss, also knew the victim, but denied it, and now this Smith thing. So why focus on Reeve? He's the least likely suspect of them all."

Herman turns and studies me, his forehead raised and wrinkled in concern. He's not letting it go. "You interviewed the owner of the cabin where the victim was found? And your ex's boss?"

I don't say anything.

He shakes his head in disappointment. "I should go." He stands up from the rock and brushes off his pants. A faint cloud of his after-shave wafts around me in the dank air. "Haven't even seen what you're talking about yet in the Smith transcripts, so I should look those over before they contact me. *If* they contact me, *if* they trust me now and don't think I've been colluding with you all along or won't in the future. I mean, there's only two of us, and I *am* the only other RA in the office. Kind of hard to trust me now too."

"They do," I say, but what he says prickles because I know it's true. I've compromised both of us. "It's not like that. It's fine, Herman. Everything went well with Vance. Thank you for watching Emily."

He looks sad, as if I've taken a razor blade to our relationship, and I want to repeat that I haven't done anything that irreparable, that everything will be fine with the county.

"Ali," he says, "you know you need to stay out of it from here on out, right?"

I nod.

"They're not idiots. They can solve this case without you."

"I know," I say. But in my gut, I have this deep sense that Reynolds wants to nail Reeve. My mind goes to an image of my mom, my sister, and me visiting my dad at the New Jersey State Prison in Trenton. He was dressed in an orange jumpsuit, sitting behind thick glass in a visiting booth and talking through a phone on the wall. He had been arrested for dealing heroin when I was eight. More than the visit itself, I remember most what came before that. I had begged my mom to visit him, and she finally gave in, driving us there one hot New Jersey summer day. Toni and I had on our summer dresses, and when we arrived, we waited in line outside the tall brick fortress. The heat overpowered us, making our dresses stick to our sweaty legs. A crowd was already queued up outside the door with a sign on it indicating the visiting hours.

Twenty or more women, most with children, stood braving the heat to visit their husbands, fathers, brothers, uncles. My mom looked nervous, rocking on her heels, and then when the large door opened and a prison guard stepped out, he said they were taking the first ten families in line and would come back in twenty minutes for the next ten. I counted the families in front of us and was relieved to find we were the tenth. But while the guard was admitting one family at a time, checking IDs, another women carrying a child on her hip inserted herself in front of the three of us. I looked up at Mom, waiting for her to say something, expecting for her to tell the lady that that wasn't fair, that we were there first, but she didn't. "Mom," I said, pulling on her dress, "she cut in front of us. That's not fair. We're the tenth family."

My mom stood silently, her lips pursed.

"Aren't you going to say something?" I asked her.

"It's okay, honey," she said. "It's not worth the fight."

Not worth the fight. I remember wanting to tell the woman that she couldn't do that, if my mother wouldn't speak up, but I held back because she was an adult and I was a child. *Not worth the fight,* I repeated in my head, thinking of all the times when my mom cried in the corner after my dad had hurt her in one way or another. My aunt had told my mom to call the police one time when she saw a bruise on my mom's arm. *Not worth the fight* was what she had said then too.

I promised myself I would never think that way. I for one am going to fight like hell for Reeve, for Emily, before it's too late.

"I'll talk to you later," Herman says. "I'm going to say good-bye to Emily."

"All right. Will you let her know I'm over here, and that she can keep playing for a bit?"

I watch him head over to the rope swing, his hands shoved into the pockets of his navy jacket. When he reaches the kids, they stop swinging and Herman talks to Emily, who nods her head, then looks in my direction. I wave and she smiles and waves back, then quickly performs some kind of a jump turn so she faces her new friend, pokes his shoulder, points at me, and announces, "That's my mommy, Agent Paige," I hear her loud, excited voice across the playground.

Lately she's been obsessed with names, especially Reeve's and mine—she's been trying to understand why Reeve's last name is different from ours. Some of the other kids in her class have the same last names as their dad, even if they're from split homes. When she asked me why hers wasn't Landon, I just said, "Because mine is Paige, and I'm the one whose tummy you came out of."

I smile now and wave at the blond boy, and he waves back at me; then they go back to swinging again. Herman turns, bows his head, and strides to his car without looking my way.

I sit on the boulder watching the two kids playing. The air is moister than it was earlier in the day, and I feel like I'm alone in some cold cave. I look over my shoulder toward the Stillwater River, which runs behind the park, and notice a translucent mist drifting through the trees. To the west, the sun is already lowering and leaking orange and pink stains across the horizon. Skeletal branches that have dropped their leaves reach bony fingers toward the sunset.

The regrets begin to pour in. I think about dropping the Johnson mystery, about letting all the unanswered questions lie in the hopes that Brander and Reynolds will discover them on their own, that they will follow each and every lead thoroughly. I think about what Herman said—*They're not idiots*—and I know he's right. Of course they'll follow all leads and probably get to all the same places I have gotten to on my own. But it's my daughter whose happiness is at stake—how can I sit back and just hope for the best?

Relinquishing control—I was never good at that. The notion of surrender doesn't sit well, and an edginess forces me up from the boulder I'm sitting on. My mom's words—*It's not worth the fight*—run like a ticker tape through my head. I stand beside the boulder for a moment, shoving my hands in my pockets. I kick at the wood chips, making small indentations and spraying them in all directions. I shoo the reservations away, and when my impatience gets the best of me, I walk over to Emily and say, "Hey, chickadee. Two more minutes and then we go." I lift my chin to the colored sky in the west. "It's getting late."

Reeve

Present—Sunday

DAWN BREAKS WITH the bleakest of light stealing through low-hanging clouds, casting no shadows over the frost-coated ground. I poke my head out of the tent to feel how cold it is. The breeze has ceased and the air is still. I feel the bite of it on my cheeks first, and realize it's the damp cold that's going to go to the bone all day long. In Montana, the cold and the heat are mostly dry, so this dankness is unusual, and I think this must be what it's like to live on the ocean in the north. I throw some pants over my long johns, another shirt and a jacket over my top, and get out of the tent and stretch. A thick white beard of fog trails down the closest rocky peak. The fire has burned down to a flaky white ash the color of Wallace's hair.

I got as much sleep as you'd expect lying on a hard ground with a steely-muscled sixty-pound dog on top of my sleeping bag, pinning my legs into the corner of the confined polyurethane-treated nylon tent with his sturdy shoulder and long back. I check Wallace's pup tent and see that it's empty, which I expect. I know he planned on heading out early for a hunt and would be gone before the morning light even broke.

McKay wanders over to the side of the campsite into the woods to do his business, and I follow to do the same. I'm standing there, urinating into some dried-out bear grass stalks, when I hear elk bugling close by. I zip up my pants and decide to follow the sound, picking my way through the stunted pines with their awkward growth patterns—branches twisting and turning in odd directions because of the

216

constant high-altitude winds and a need to reach for the sun in any direction they can find it. McKay stays by my side.

Within about thirty yards of the campsite, Wallace is easily visible in his hunting gear, an orange cap and vest. He's pointing his rifle at a bull bugling in clear sight. The bull is too busy calling to his mates—a harem of cows whose baying chatter I can hear farther up the ridge—to notice Wallace hunched behind a boulder, still as the rock itself. I stand quietly behind a tree observing him as he watches the great beast through his scope. I've got my hand around McKay's collar, but he's too well trained to run after anything but a ball.

Great puffs of condensation plume from the elk's wide, furred nostrils into the damp, cold air. His dark eyes are intense, not bored like they sometimes look while grazing in the fields around my cabin. He's in rut, all juiced up for mating. His bugle, guttural and glorious, bursts against the quiet morning. For an instant, I want to shape-shift, to transform into that elk. Not because Wallace is about to kill it, but because its presence is so immense, so unapologetic as he announces himself to the mountains and the mist. If I were that elk, I think, I could effortlessly glide with powerful long limbs through the fog and the bitter air into oblivion, away from trouble, away from loneliness, no booze or drugs required.

Wallace's rifle is propped on the top of the boulder, and he's going to shoot. My heart pounds. I can see his finger hooked around the trigger. The elk turns, though, his white-flanked butt now facing Wallace. He's something with his wide, massive crown of antlers lifting as he calls to his mates. I count his points and realize he's a monarch bull, which means he has an eight-point rack with long, smooth tines and an impressive whale tail, called that because of the way the last tines of his antlers split and curve to form the shape of a whale's tail. I see Wallace's body slightly relax and shift position, and I'm guessing he's waiting for the elk to rotate again so that he has a shot at his side, at his heart or other vital organs.

The bull's ears flap and its tail flicks back and forth as he turns sideways again, giving Wallace a clear shot. Wallace's finger is still poised on the trigger. I hold my breath for what seems like a long time. It will be quite the trophy elk for him. Finally he lifts his pointer, moves his hand, and lowers his rifle.

"You gonna keep standin' there trying to scare away my elk?" he calls out without looking at me, letting me know that he's aware of my presence. With explosive speed, the elk dashes off, its hoofs stomping and gouging the forest floor, his whitish tan butt bouncing through the trees like a flashing beacon. "Or you gonna say good morning?"

"I didn't scare away anything," I say. "You didn't shoot when you had the chance. *You* scared it away."

"They're so stupid when they're in rut sometimes," he grumbles as I approach him. He brushes off his pants as he stands up. "Didn't even know we were here."

Yep, that's mammals for you. I think of Anne Marie and how even as the edge bristled up our conversation, I still wanted her. "Why didn't you shoot?" I whisper to Wallace as if the elk were still there. The bull's presence lingers, his hay-like ungulate scent, like the hoofy manure smell of a horse barn, still riding on the frigid morning air.

Wallace shrugs, his rifle hanging by his side. "Come on, let's go have some coffee."

"Why didn't you shoot?" I press again.

"Too far up here. You want to haul a four-hundred-pound bull out of this area?"

"I don't. Never have wanted to haul a bull out of any place, at any time." I don't add that I'm happy enough to haul out a tiny piece of his scat in a plastic bag. "But I get you wanting more, and I thought you wanted a bull. And he was impressive."

He hangs his head, looking at the ground as he walks. His whiskers are so white, they seem translucent. I can hear his boots scuffing on the small rocks and the dried brush. "There're a lot of reasons why someone might want to be up here," he mumbles like he's bored, but I can hear a stoicism in his voice.

"I can relate," I say.

. . .

After breakfast—oatmeal packets and instant coffee—we each pack our gear and head our separate ways. Wallace plans on spending the day hunting closer to home, so that if he does come across another bull, it's not too far to quarter it and pack it out. I don't tell him what my day consists of. He already knows I'm a fanatic about my work, but right before we part ways, he looks at me and says, "So after you do your thing today, you heading home?"

I shrug. "Haven't decided that yet. I'll see how late it gets. I want to cover some major ground today." But I have decided. I have no intention of heading home. Not yet anyway. I'm not ready. I imagine the detectives looking through my youth records—seeing how I was arrested twice, the first time for selling weed after getting into a fight outside a bar with some other teenager who wouldn't pay me. The bar owner called the police to come break up our fight. I tried to run when they arrived, but the other guy had a hold of my shirt. The second time was for shoplifting beer from a convenience store while stoned out of my mind. I imagine them mulling over my past, how I shot Sam, how I have a history of uncontrollable anger.

"Because you haven't already covered this ground before?"

"Haven't covered the area I plan to go to today. Up around that ridge." I point to the northeast.

He looks up at the gray sky, to the mountain parading to the north and fading into mist. "Any farther and you'll be across the border."

"Nah, I won't make Canada. And as you can see"—I hit my pack, which I've already slumped onto my shoulders—"I've got plenty of gear."

"Okay, then." He sighs it more than says it, like he's a concerned father. "You sure you want to head farther up this time of—"

"Look, Wallace," I cut him off, perhaps a little too abruptly. "You don't need to worry about me. I know what I'm doing out here. I work this job and this dog"—I motion to McKay—"by choice."

"What about your daughter?"

I chuckle. "What? For god's sake, you sound like I'm not coming out of here."

He doesn't laugh or smile back. He looks dead serious. "Sometimes I wonder."

"What's that supposed to mean?" I ask.

"Nothing," he says. "Just be careful, then. I don't want to be reading about you in the paper."

"I don't plan to be anything but careful. And you should talk," I say, thinking about him walking around like a target with that fresh fish on him.

A long pause passes before he bends down from the waist and pets McKay on the chest where I've taught him to, even though it requires he lean over a little farther. I can hear his joints crack in the awkward stillness of our conversation, and I feel bad that I've been so insistent about it.

"It's okay," I start to say, "you can pet him—" but he stands and turns to go, simply waving one hand over his shoulder as he hikes out the way he came in.

McKay stays by my side and looks up at me to see if I'm going to follow him. "Good luck with that elk," I call out to him, but he doesn't respond, just disappears behind some trees as I watch him walk away.

Ali

Present—Sunday

Rose sits with a mug of coffee between her palms and watches me while I fix breakfast for her and Emily. I texted her earlier, asking if she was hungry, and told her that I was making pancakes from scratch, Emily's favorite, and that she should come over.

I'm drinking coffee too, and Emily is having hot chocolate. I cringe at the thought of all the sugar she'll have consumed before the morning is even over. I pour the batter into three conjoined circles to form a Mickey Mouse shape as Emily has requested. I happily do so, knowing that one day in the not-too-distant future I'll make these and she'll look at them with embarrassment and say, "Cute, Mom, but I'm a little too old for that."

After Emily eats her pancakes, which she drowned in maple syrup in spite of my instructions not to, I tell her to go upstairs and start getting dressed, guessing that by the time I make it up there, she'll simply be playing instead. But since it's Sunday, that's perfectly okay with me.

I sit down with Rose and smile. "Think she's got enough sugar for the day?"

"Oh, I don't know, maybe she needs a cinnamon roll for lunch," she says dryly, and I chuckle. "Good thing I'm not watching her today." She points at me. "This one's on you."

"I know, I know." I hold my hands up in surrender and change the subject. "So the detective from the county that was here yesterday, he came over to talk to you?"

"Yes," she says. "Odd. I wasn't expecting that."

"Sorry, I didn't have time to warn you. He'd stopped by here first, but then I had to get Emily dressed."

"Right, he said he had spoken to you first." She looks at me, searching, like she wants me to confirm that it was okay that she's talked to them in spite of the contract I'd made her sign about not discussing any of our personal matters with anyone else. Obviously, talking to authorities is not the same as gossiping, so I give her a look that indicates it's fine.

"What else did he say?"

"I was groggy because I went back to bed after I left here. You were right, I probably wasn't really over that bug." Dark smudges swell under the delicate skin of Rose's eyes, and I realize she still looks tired. "I guess they were mostly asking about Reeve."

"Yeah?"

"They wanted to know how well I know him, how often I see him, when was the last time I saw him, that kind of thing. I was kind of shocked that they were so interested in him."

"And what did you tell them?"

She gives me that searching look again, her chin tucked in and her eyes wide as she looks up from under her lids at me. "Not much. I mean, you know, I hardly see him, except now and again to trade Emily off if you need me to or if he needs me to take her in a pinch, which rarely happens. That's what I told him. And of course the last time I saw him was here the other night."

"Did he ask anything else?"

"He asked if I've noticed anything strange or out of the ordinary about him."

"And?"

"Well, it was the police," she says.

"Oh, sure." I wave a hand nonchalantly between us to put her at ease. "Actually the county, but, yeah, of course you have to tell them whatever you know."

She nods with relief. Part of me feels bad that my insistence on privacy has made her so nervous, but another part of me is glad that she's taken my requests seriously. Because I *was* serious. I have no desire for my personal life to be spread around a community in which I am one of two FBI resident agents. "And . . . ?" I encourage her to continue.

"Well, I said that Reeve is not exactly an ordinary guy, but I hadn't noticed anything off in particular. Just that . . ." She trails off, her gaze shifting to the front window. A shred of sun is peeking through the clouds and illuminating a patch of the yard and the strewn leaves that I've already told Emily we'd play in today. Well, she'll play while I rake.

"Just that what?"

"Just that he—well, both of you—seemed frazzled or upset the other night."

I shrug. The fact that she mentioned that means nothing. Anyone would be frazzled after a day of being sweated by the cops, but I'm not thrilled that they now know he came directly to my place after he left the county building.

"What do they think he's done?" she asks.

I take a sip of my coffee, deciding whether to answer that, but she's already got it figured out.

"Does it have something to do with that lady that was killed up in the North Fork?"

"Yes, it does." I set my mug back down.

"That's what I thought." She looks down at her cup like she's embarrassed for him, or actually for Emily and me.

"Did Brander tell you that?"

"He mentioned it briefly." Her eyes are large with concern.

Her look provokes a defensiveness and protectiveness in me. "Reeve's fine," I say. "Absolutely fine. There's nothing there. He just happened to be in the wrong situation. Circumstantial. The woman was doing an interview with him on his work for the U. They're just checking all bits of information at this point, that's all."

"Oh," she says. "Well, that's good." But she looks pensive and a little anxious, like she doesn't quite believe me, and I wonder if my nerves are showing or if my protest is too adamant. I stand up to deal with the dishes in the sink and the messy batter-covered bowls. "I better get these done," I say. "I need to get that kid out into the fresh air so she can run that sugar off."

Reeve

Wednesday—The Day Before

I T'S PAST MIDNIGHT. One of the cabin windows in the main room is still open, and the cool air continues to seep in, keeping the woodstove from smothering Anne Marie and me with its fierce, cloying heat. I've quit adding wood and don't plan to put in any more for the rest of the night, as it's still burning strongly. The fire and the wine have softened me—tempered Anne Marie too, because she's finally stopped asking questions. We've gone through a bottle and a half, and there is actually a lull in the conversation. I wonder if it's possible that she finally talked herself out. I stand up, grab the empty glasses and the last bottle, and say, "It's getting kind of late."

After putting the glasses and the half-drunk bottle next to the sink, which is filled with the dinner dishes, I go back to the main room and lean against the side of the couch. I wasn't sure how I wanted this night to go. I had visions of Anne Marie in my bed, of waking up cradling her warm body against mine, but after all the unexpected questions, I feel spent, a little angry, and still confused by her mixed messages and her contradictions—one minute resting her head on my shoulder or playfully, inexplicably tugging on my belt, the next minute grilling me about my past. I've come to the conclusion that she should probably just go so I can get some sleep. I have another full day with McKay out in the field in the morning.

Anne Marie says nothing for a moment, just stares at me, her head cocked, her eyes mysterious—the same seductive look that has been keeping me on edge all evening. "You're right," she says eventually. "I should go." She stands up, stretches her arms above her head, exposing the pale skin of her belly above her pants. She grabs her coat by the door and folds it over one arm.

"Well." She stares at my chest, not looking me in the eyes, as if she's suddenly shy. "Thank you for talking to me about . . ." She twitches her head to one side in lieu of saying it.

I nod. What else is there to add? I didn't really want to talk about any of it in the first place, but there's no point in reiterating that now. She stays quiet, her gaze still on my chest. She bites the corner of her bottom lip, her hand moving to the back of her neck, pulling at the wisps of hair falling out of her braid.

"I hope the day out with us in the field was helpful," I say.

"It was." She glances at McKay, who has followed us to the door. She pets the top of his head stiffly, a little robotically, and I wonder if she's still a bit unnerved by him. Some people are just not dog people. She looks up at me, meeting my eyes this time. I shouldn't judge people based on whether they like pets or not, but I do, I can't help it.

"Seriously, thank you for letting me join you," she says, gently gripping my left shoulder. I can feel the damp heat of her palm through my shirt. A jolt of energy bolts through me with her touch. God, I feel like I've been swinging back and forth between provocation and desire all evening. There's a palpable tension in the room when we lock eyes, and she says, "I'm sorry for . . . you know, for asking so many questions."

I nod that it's okay. My throat feels thick with something—loneliness, an unidentifiable aching need—and I'm not sure I want to speak.

She shrugs. "I'm just really inquisitive. I guess I've always been curious about things."

"It's what makes you a good reporter," I say, and give her a closed-lip smile.

She nods shyly, and there's the sweetness I saw in her earlier. It's what gets me. Suddenly I can't hold back. I lean down and kiss her—a long, heated kiss that starts slowly, but wells up with intensity. She pushes her pelvis into me, and I let my tongue explore the flesh of her mouth. I stop for a second so I can pull her into my bedroom. There's a small night-light on the side wall that I leave on for Emily, and I'm glad it's on because I want to see all of her.

We fall—or she pushes me, I'm not sure which—onto the bed, and she hovers on top of me. Her braid falls into my face, and I bite down on it, hungry for this human connection. The texture of her hair, it reminds me of Ali's, and I have this flash amid all the desire that I'm adrift, floating, biting on a rope in a last-ditch effort to tether myself to the human race. The sense of connection almost makes me tear up, but then Anne Marie's lips are tasting mine and I'm running my hands down her back and onto her hips. She moans softly and I start to kiss her gently on her throat when suddenly I hear an abrasive scratch down the side of the mattress.

I know exactly what it is—McKay's long front claws. It's what he does when he wants to go out—one grating scratch down the side of the mattress. Although this time, because I ignore him and go back to caressing Anne Marie, he does it again. "Go away," I mumble out the side of our kissing. But he does it again. Scratch. And again. I groan and gently move Anne Marie to my side. "I have to let him out," I whisper breathlessly. "I'm sorry. Don't move. I'll be right back."

Ali

AFTER BREAKFAST WITH Rose, Emily and I spend all afternoon raking and bagging leaves. She's in heaven, gleefully jumping into the piles and splashing the leaves up around her as if she's in a pool of water. Dry ones cling to her hair, just as I imagined, and the soggy mulch at the bottom of the pile makes her pants dirty and damp. We put them into orange lawn bags with pumpkin faces on the front that are left over from Halloween, and she proudly carries them out to the curb to display. Afterward, I make us dinner—bratwurst and potatoes—and then I do the dishes.

And because she demands it, I watch *Mulan* with her, and try to scoot out of the room to go to my office during "A Girl Worth Fighting For" because it's kind of painful to watch a kids' Disney movie when your mind is on a hundred different things. But she catches me and insists I come sit back down and watch the entire film.

When it's time to put her to bed, I read her a story, *Stellaluna*, one of Emily's favorites, about a fruit bat that is attacked by an owl and separated from her mother. I think it's one of Emily's favorites because already she's growing independent and can envision excursions to other nests without me. A part of me thinks that's a good thing, and another part of me aches when I think too much about it. I wonder if my own mother realized as the years passed how she would never get those back once we were out on our own. Of course I don't blame her. She didn't push us out. She was a single mom: she just needed to work.

228

After we close the book, I lie in Emily's darkened room with her for several minutes as she insists. When I sit up to go, she reaches out for me to stop me. "It's already been exactly five minutes," I say as if I've timed it.

She's too exhausted to question what I'm saying and accepts it—as if we had a deal and I'd honored my end of the bargain. She releases her grip on my arm. I get up, kiss her forehead, and go quietly out of her room and to my office, feeling a small slice of guilt for not staying until she fell sound asleep, for negotiating with her when there was no need to do so. Is this what life as a parent is? A series of bargains with your children until one day they begin bargaining with you to get their way. And then the haggling fades altogether because it's no longer necessary. They no longer need you at all. For them, you become like an image in the rearview mirror, appearing closer than they'll ever let you actually be again.

I slump into my chair with my feet splayed wide in front of me under the desk. The wind has subsided and it's still outside. No cars pass by on my neighborhood street, and all the world seems inky around me. I can hear the faint buzz of the gas heat being pumped into the house through the floor vents. I'm beat from working on the lawn, but I'm also anxious. I figure the meeting with the county has partly taken the wind out of my sails and partly agitated me. I consider that all of my actions to help Reeve have been a mistake, that I should have stayed out of things from the beginning, been more professional.

Deep down, I know I'm in the wrong. All day I've been trying to not think about it. Reeve is a big boy, and he doesn't need me coming to the rescue. And Emily—I can't protect her from her own father and his actions in the long run. Eventually his choices and hers will determine the type of relationship they have. And if, just if, he somehow ends up in jail, she'll have to deal with that too, just like I did. It took me a long time to realize that our parents don't necessarily have to define us. Still, like shadows, certain events from our childhood follow us everywhere we go.

. . .

The summer that Reeve shot Sam, they passed stricter stalking laws in California after an actress was shot by a man who was obsessed with her. Earlier in the year, Florida had executed Ted Bundy, and later in the year, Germans tore down the Berlin Wall. In the weeks after Sam's death, three more fatal shootings occurred across Florida, and the press got really fired up, their drumbeat prompting marches and waking up the Florida legislature to eventually pass a law that would make it illegal to leave a gun where a child could find it. Montana has no such law.

I imagine the press surrounding Reeve and his family—the barrage of phone calls and photos. After I first found out about the incident, I discovered several old pictures of Reeve on the Internet—one of him timidly smiling for the camera as a child is trained to do as he is led out of their one-story ranch-style house by his father. I imagine him, out of habit, seeing the camera and making his mouth curve upward into a stiff, fake smile because that's what kids are always taught to do in front of a camera: *Smile for the camera, honey.*

I imagine the photo being drudged up and being used against him now in court, not as evidence, but to make an impression on a jury—a way of saying, *See this boy smiling? No remorse. This boy shot his friend in cold blood and he doesn't even look sad. What makes you think he couldn't have killed Anne Marie? All it took was a shot to the chest, same as he did before.*

I sigh, then shove myself out of the chair. I go to the kitchen and make a small pot of coffee. If Reynolds and Brander can't get at the truth, then I've got my work cut out for me.

Reeve

Wednesday—The Day Before

M<small>CKAY FOLLOWS ME</small> to the door and I open it for him so he can do his thing, but then he just sits and stares at me as if I'm doing something wrong. I tell myself I'm just imagining it. McKay could not possibly be upset that I have another woman in my bedroom. He never did this when I was with Ali.

"Go on," I say.

He doesn't budge.

"I'm not going out there with you."

He still doesn't move.

"Out," I say, standing at the door, still swollen with desire for the first time in forever and here's my supposedly well-trained dog refusing to go out. The cold air hits me. I bend down, grab his collar, and try to coax him out. He digs his claws into the ground and turns his muscular body to stone, refusing to move. The wild upsurge in me begins to subside. I think of how Anne Marie's hair felt like Ali's, but not quite as soft. How her lips were wider and almost rubbery feeling in comparison. I hear her aggressive questions in my head and recall the coldness in her voice when she addressed McKay. I try to brush the thoughts away. "Are you going out or not?"

McKay still doesn't move.

"Suit yourself." I shut the door and go back in, much calmer, like I've retreated back into myself. I don't want it, but I can feel a shuttering of sorts. I'm hoping that seeing Anne Marie will ignite the craving all over again. I plan to keep McKay out in the main room this time, but when I enter the bedroom, she's sitting on the bed, talking on her phone. I'm confused. It has to be close to one a.m., but I figure she's talking to the friend who owns the cabin she's staying at.

"No, no," she's saying softly, but there's a slight edge in her voice. "I told you, I'm just at Viv's cabin."

I realize she's not talking to a friend, so she's obviously lying to someone—a boyfriend, maybe. I stand by the doorframe with McKay by my side. I suddenly feel foolish that I haven't even asked her if she's seeing someone. I didn't notice a wedding ring, but that doesn't necessarily mean anything. Anne Marie looks at me a little guiltily under hooded eyes, as if I've caught her doing something wrong. "I've got to go," she says into the phone, and hangs up.

I walk over and sit next to her, the mattress squeaking. McKay follows me back in, sitting in front of me and giving me the hairy eyeball again. I ignore him. "Your boyfriend?" I ask her.

"Not exactly," she growls, and looks down at her phone. She moves her thumb up the side like she's about to hit the off button, but before she finds it, the screen lights up again with Jeffrey O'Brien's name flashing across the screen.

She quickly hits the ignore option, then turns it off. I'm momentarily confused as to why my boss is calling her phone so late at night when I realize that he's just calling her back and that he's the one she was just talking to. It dawns on me how dense I've been. She's seeing my boss. I look at her, my mouth partially open in disbelief.

"It's over with him," she says. "I'm so tired of it anyway. He's never going to leave her." She slides her hair tie off her hair, runs her fingers through her braid to unweave it. It's long, full, and wavy like Ali's. I've wanted to see her run her fingers through that hair all night. Now she does it when I've just realized she's sleeping with my damn boss. "Just forget that," she says indifferently, then leans over to kiss me.

Panic flutters through me. I stand up, holding my palms up in a stop gesture, my longing flip-flopping into plain old fear and anger. There's no way I am risking my job by sleeping with the boss's mistress, even if I am shocked about the whole thing. I thought Jeff and Jessie were happily married.

"What?" she asks, surprised that I'm backing away from her. "I shouldn't have answered it, but he was going to keep calling if I didn't. I'm sorry. I should have just turned it off earlier. Like I said, it's pretty much over anyway. Look," she says, punching away at her phone, "I'm deleting him. There, I should have done that a while ago."

"It's fine, really. But he"—I point at the phone and shake my head— "he's my boss. You realize that, right?"

"I do," she says, shrugging.

"Come on," I say, heading for the door. I wonder if she actually thinks that my knowing about her screwing my boss would somehow add to the attraction, that I would want to play some competitive male game, willing to bash antlers with my boss over her. "Let's just call this a night," I mumble.

"But, Reeve . . ." she begins, but doesn't finish, probably because I'm already out the bedroom door.

．．．

She has no choice but to follow me. She stays in the room for a moment while I wait for her at the front door. Finally she comes out, not looking directly at me. I open the door and let the brisk air rush in. I realize I've lost something with her for good, like a beautiful bull trout slipping from my palms back into frigid waters. When we get to her car, she asks me if she can call me, just in case she has any questions for her article.

"On the canine program?" I ask.

She shakes her head sheepishly. There's a dishonesty in her eyes that bothers me, and I realize I'm upset at the way she's been using me, but it feels more like an ache—a wistfulness or a loneliness—than an actual anger. After all, I have no right—had we slept together, I'd be using her too in a way. "About the other thing," she answers.

"No," I simply say, "I don't think so."

She turns around, gets into her car, and shuts the door. She doesn't bother to roll down the window or even look at me. With the sound of her engine revving, I feel a deep frustration coupled with a strange relief that I'm returning to the normalcy of what I know—my dog and me in my uncomplicated cabin. I watch her taillights as she drives away, swallowing back a familiar taste of loneliness, the same one I felt the day my dad moved out, the same one I felt the day Ali and I split up.

Ali

Present—Monday

THE TWO-HOUR DRIVE from Kalispell to Missoula begins by winding around Flathead Lake, the largest freshwater lake west of the Mississippi in the lower forty-eight. It strikes me as funny how all locals repeat that piece of information like it's a badge of honor. A silly legend has it that a large eel-shaped monster, like the Loch Ness, inhabits the lake.

It is a gorgeous lake, though, turquoise green in parts and sparkling clear near the shoreline. Old timbers crisscross on the lake bed like giant old bones, and when the water is perfectly still, you can see them. In fact, some logs originally came from a timber mill operation in Somers from the early 1900s. The logs sank to the bottom of the lake and have been preserved for over a hundred years, and they're impressive and beautiful enough that companies are trying to remove them to sell, since they were cut at the turn of the twentieth century.

Flathead Lake is also surrounded by cherry orchards exploding in white flowery blooms in the spring, then turning yellowish orange like the color of a sunset in the fall. That's the way they are now, rows of neatly planted, fiery-leaved trees rolling down hills toward the shoreline. I'm reminded again of the power the beauty of the Northwest has in casting spells that pull you out of yourself, and some quote Reeve used to say comes to me: *To the desert go prophets and hermits.* "But I go to the mountains," he'd say.

The scenery almost makes me forget for a moment why I'm heading to Missoula, but eventually I drive through Polson at the southern tip of the lake, then several smaller towns—Ronan, St. Ignatius, Arlee—most of them located within the Confederated Salish and Kootenai Tribes of the Flathead Reservation. Unlike Browning, which is huddled in the windswept brown plains of eastern Montana, the Salish and Kootenai reside on fruitful, lush land with the impressive Mission Mountain Range jutting up to the sky and framing the east side of the large valley. As I get closer to Missoula, my mission becomes more potent.

I'm eager to interview Reeve's boss. Reeve and I talked about my meeting him when we dated, but it never worked out. Reeve always seemed to look up to him, telling me he was the perfect person to work for. "He leaves me alone, lets me get the job done, but never lets me forget the importance of what we're doing or how vital my work with McKay is." I was always busy at work or on some pressing case when he'd come to town or when Reeve needed to go to Missoula. Now I'm glad he doesn't know who I am.

When I get to Interstate 90, I take the exit ramp into Missoula and head straight to the University of Montana. Classes are in session, so it's tough for me to find parking, but after circling around a few times, I find an open visitor spot near the University Center. I navigate through bustling students and locate a directory inside the UC and find the environmental sciences department in the College of Humanities and Sciences. It's in a building called Jeannette Rankin Hall, named after a Montana suffragist, the first woman elected to the U.S. Congress.

I find the building on the north side of the oval before the clock tower. When I enter, it holds the faint fusty smell of old rotting wood mixed with the heady aroma of whiteboard markers. Even though he's the director of environmental sciences, given all the recent funding cuts, I'm expecting O'Brien's office to be a simple room in a hallway, but it's more than what I anticipate. He's actually got a bona fide office with a small reception area and an administrative assistant. She tells me that he's teaching a class but will be back in fifteen minutes and that I'm welcome to wait.

I take a seat and read some outdoor magazines until my phone vibrates. I see that it's Herman. I step out in the hallway with its shiny linoleum floor and debate whether to answer as the number flashes on my screen. He's going to want to know where I am, and I'll either have to lie or simply tell him the truth. I can hear the voice of a female professor giving a lecture drifting down the hallway from one of the rooms nearby. My conscience gets the best of me and I answer, keeping my voice low in the broad hallway. "Hollywood, what's up?"

"Where are you?"

"Why? Is something wrong?"

"No," he says, then sighs audibly. "Ali, I'm not even going to ask where you are and why you're not in the office because I really don't want to know."

I don't reply.

"But," he continues, "I'm calling you out of courtesy to let you know that I heard the county is going to issue a BOLO on Reeve."

"A BOLO?" I say. "What in the hell for?"

"They've been searching for him, checking his cabin, leaving messages, talking to any neighbors, and no one has seen him. They think he's run off, maybe to Canada."

Damn it, I want to scream in the hushed hallway. "That's ridiculous," I say. "I've told them over and over, he works in the mountains. That's where he is."

"Apparently he didn't tell them where he was going even after they asked him to stay put. They've located his truck and he hasn't been back to it in two days. Seems they have another piece of evidence pointing in his direction too."

"What kind of evidence?"

"Don't know, and quite frankly, even if I did, I wouldn't tell you. Truth is, I'm only calling you now because of that sweet daughter of yours . . . That's the only reason I'm telling you this."

"I know. Thank you," I say.

"I'm serious. I don't even want to know where the hell you are right now."

"Okay," I say. I want to feed him a lie so he doesn't worry, that I'm simply getting a haircut or staying home with Emily because she's not feeling well, but I don't. I thank him again for the information and hang up after he says, "Wherever you are, be careful."

I slide my phone in my bag and stand in the hall as students begin funneling out of classroom doors and weaving around me. Suddenly I feel old and tired amidst the vitality of the young students. I put my phone away and go back into O'Brien's office. I'm here now, I think. One thing at a time. I can't do anything about Reeve being out in the woods, but the idea of a BOLO across all the news agencies makes my stomach turn.

When Jeff O'Brien steps in, he's being trailed by two female students. He glances at me, but he's talking to and smiling at the students and heads straight into his office, the girls following. He leaves the door open, and I can see he's searching for some textbooks on his shelf. When he finds them, he plucks out two of them and gives them to the girl closest to him. She smiles sweetly, her ponytail long and sleek, swaying slightly as she moves her head while thanking him profusely. They leave, and I step in before the administrative assistant even has a chance to tell him I'm here. I don't want to waste any more time being timid or polite.

"Professor," I say, "my name is Agent Paige. I'd like to speak to you for a moment. I understand you have a break between classes now." I motion to the assistant to indicate that my information comes from her, but she's on the phone and not paying attention to us.

He glances at her, a slight annoyance flickering across his face, then says, "Sure, come on in."

I shut the door behind me without asking him if it's okay. I take a seat before his desk and get comfortable, crossing one ankle over my opposite knee. Even though smoking has been banned on campus for years, the office still holds the faint acrid smell of cigarette smoke mixed with the musty scent of neglected textbooks.

"I know we spoke on the phone, but I was in town and thought I'd stop by."

He nods. He has deep-brown eyes like Reeve's, and is equally in-scrutable.

"Can you tell me again how you know Anne Marie Johnson?"

We go through all the same information he's already given me on the phone: that he knows her only through phone conversations; she's an acquaintance, someone he's met at a professional event or two, but can't recall which ones. I pull a file out of my bag and fish out the Face-book photo I've printed, the one with his hands on her shoulders. His face turns slightly red when I show it to him, but he still doesn't let on that he knows her more intimately than he's been suggesting. He care-fully sets the photo down on his desk and slides it toward me using two pronged fingertips. Then he simply shrugs. Smart, I think. I'd do the same. He knows I can't prove anything with a pair of hands on a person's shoulders, so I use the ammo I've gathered from Vivian.

"Professor," I say, "as you can imagine, in the course of this investi-gation, we've spoken to all of Anne Marie's closest friends. You've been described by them as more than an acquaintance." I lock eyes with him and wait for a reply.

He shifts in his chair and glances at his bookshelf as if it's a window he can peer out of. Then he turns back to me and says, "I don't know what you mean. I'm not sure what you heard, but I certainly don't know any of her friends."

"Like I said, they know *of* you, Professor. Because, well, let's face it, friends talk."

He shrugs. "I can't help it if this Anne Marie woman has mentioned my name to someone."

"Let's cut the crap, shall we, Professor? You and I both know that you knew Anne Marie well. I wouldn't have come all the way here if I didn't have evidence that you weren't exactly truthful with me in our phone conversation. So I suggest you fill me in before this becomes something way bigger than you want it to become."

I see him fidget. His face looks pinched, his nostrils flared.

I wait, my eyes locked on him, until I see him calm a little and his muscles begin to relax, which I take to mean he's decided either to come clean or to kick me out, and he's pleased with the decision. But he doesn't get up and head to the door. Instead he takes a deep breath, then looks back at me and says, "All right. I knew her. I knew her pretty well. We . . ."—he twitches his head to one side as if that is a replacement for the phrase *We had an affair*—"you know, we—" He flicks his head again.

"You what, Professor?"

"We, ah, we had a relationship." Finally he's giving in.

"And did your wife know about this relationship?"

"No," he says guiltily, looking down at his hands on his desk. "That's why I didn't tell you on the phone. She can't find out."

"Let me ask you this: Where were you this past Wednesday night?"

"Here in Missoula."

"Where in Missoula?"

"I was with friends playing poker. We get together every other Wednesday and play. We stay up pretty late. I was probably there until two a.m."

I study him. He's looking at me sincerely, pathetically, hoping his wife doesn't get wind of this, but deep down, I'm wondering if she already has. "And where was your wife?"

"She was out of town. In Helena for some history tour that she wanted to do."

I pull out a piece of paper and slide it to him. "I'm going to need the names of all the guys you played poker with that evening. Names and telephone numbers, please. I'm also going to need your wife's name and contact information."

"But . . ." he says, his eyes like saucers.

"Don't worry. I don't intend to tell her your secret, but I still need to talk with her."

"But why? She'll just wonder why you're doing that. She's not stupid."

"I'm sure you can understand that we'll need to confirm what exactly your wife was up to on the night of the murder."

"I told you, she was in Helena, not the Flathead."

"I'm sure." I smile politely. I want to say to him: *Have you not considered that she's just as capable of sidestepping the truth as you are, Professor?* "And I'm just going to confirm that with her."

He continues to scramble. "Maybe I can just give you the name of someone in Helena."

"Do you have someone in mind?"

"She was going to meet a friend for the tour. Lizzie McAlister."

I jot it down. "Thank you, but I'd prefer to confirm it directly with her." I stand up and drape my bag over my shoulder to indicate I'm ready to leave. "Otherwise anything I'm told will be considered hearsay." I point to the piece of paper that he should get busy writing on while I stand and wait.

O'Brien opens his mouth as if he's going to say something, but then he shakes his head in a type of surrender, closes his mouth, and begins to write the names down for me.

· · ·

Outside O'Brien's building, the clock tower is framed by a brown hill with a white *M* shaped by cream-colored stones. A gunmetal sky drapes over the hill, which in New Jersey I would have called a mountain, but now that I'm a Montanan, I call it a hill because it has not quite got the height or the ruggedness we're used to in the Flathead Valley. The air smells of the coming winter—a cold, wet scent, as I imagine clouds or wet stones might smell. The brisk air feels good on my cheeks, but an urgency courses through me as I walk to my car.

The thought of the BOLO being issued on Reeve scares me, and I want to go straight back to find him, but my time is better spent in Missoula while I'm here, so I resist the urge. I call him instead, but it goes straight to voicemail, so I know he's either out of cell range still or he's turned his phone off. I leave him a message to call me immediately.

I sit in my car and make phone calls to the names on Jeffrey O'Brien's list. I get ahold of two of the five guys, both who say are surprised to hear from me and both whose stories about poker on Wednesday night square up. Jeffrey O'Brien was with them, and they played until at least two in the morning. It doesn't mean they're not lying or covering for him, but the chances of that are slim. They seemed genuinely surprised to get a phone call from me.

And that irritates me—not the fact that O'Brien has an alibi for the night Anne Marie Johnson was murdered, but their surprise at my call tells me that Brander and Reynolds haven't even called these men yet to investigate Jeffrey O'Brien. My suspicions about their tunnel vision loom larger than they already have for the past few days. I leave messages for the other three men to call me, then pull out of the parking lot to go find the O'Briens' house.

I find it on one of the blocks by the university. The area is quintessentially collegiate, with the maple and chestnut trees bursting with bright yellow and saffron colors, and the houses are quaint and gentrified. Fallen leaves cling to the edges of the streets and continue to drift down over parked cars lining the avenues. I pass several fraternity and sorority houses, some nicer than others.

The O'Briens' house also has a huge chestnut tree out front, and big leaves are spread uncontrollably across their small square lawn, making me feel less guilty about needing to get rid of the much smaller piles I have in my backyard. I wade noisily through the carpeted layers on the sidewalk to their front door. Maybe it's the news of the BOLO or the fact that I'm skirting work and two hours away from my office, but I feel slightly off-kilter, like I'm inside a child's kaleidoscope, the colors swirling around me. It's as if the ordinary has suddenly been twisted into something messy, colorful, and exotic, almost obscene in its showy vibrancy, like a fake cry for help.

Jessie O'Brien opens the door after I ring the bell. She's about my height—medium—with strawberry-blond hair and a slight underbite that takes away from her beauty somewhat, but not entirely because her pale and dramatic high cheekbones compensate for it. She is well dressed and that surprises me, given the state of their leaf-filled sidewalk. She has electric-green eyes that remind me of a cat's, but she smiles politely and looks at me curiously. I explain that I'd like to chat with her about an incident in the Flathead Valley, and she seems baffled. But confusion is an easy emotion to fake because all it requires is a slack stare or a knitted brow. She gives me the first, a wide-eyed surprised look, so I don't put too much stock in its authenticity, at least not yet.

When I ask to come in, she says, "Of course," and leads me to her kitchen, where we sit across an island countertop doubling as a thick butcher block. She offers me something to drink, but I decline. I glance around the kitchen. Again, in spite of the disarray of leaves outside, the kitchen is immaculate, the plants on the counter by the sink well cared for and thriving, the sink empty and clean, and the counters uncluttered and clear of all paperwork or the daily junk mail that seems to overtake mine like weeds. "I won't take too much of your time, Mrs. O'Brien," I say.

"Oh," she says, "you can call me Jessie." She sits on a stool across from me and waits for me to proceed. Her makeup looks precise and perfect. "You say there's been some kind of an incident in the Flathead?"

I get right to it because I'm not feeling very patient, partly because I shouldn't be in Missoula in the first place and partly because of what Herman told me about the BOLO. "Yes, you may have heard about it on the news. A woman has been murdered." I watch her reaction closely, but she doesn't change her wide-eyed expression of confusion, and I wonder if her forehead has been injected with Botox and wouldn't change expression anyway.

"Yes," she says. "I've heard about it on the news. Saw it in the paper and on the local news channel. What does that have to do with me?"

"The woman murdered was a journalist, and she has done some stories involving the university's environmental sciences department. Perhaps you knew her? Anne Marie Johnson?"

"Me?" She presses her palm to her chest.

"Yes, apparently she knew your husband. I thought perhaps you'd have maybe met her too. You know, at a local event or something like that."

"No, no, I've never heard of the woman." She still looks confused, but genuinely so, her pale, broad forehead still unmoving. "If I've met her before, I don't remember the name."

"Has your husband ever mentioned her?"

"Not that I recall."

"Has he ever mentioned any reporters covering their work at the university? Say, the golden eagle program or the canine research?"

"No, no, nothing. But we don't talk about his work all that much. I mean, just because, well, we've been married a long time now. It's not like we're in the stage of talking about every detail of our work lives."

"And where do you work?" I ask, taking my notepad and a pen out of my bag.

"I just retired. I worked at Community Medical Center as an X-ray tech for over twenty-five years." I calculate it in my head, thinking that if she has worked there since her early twenties, she'd be close to fifty or maybe in her early fifties now. I know from my research that her husband is younger—forty-four.

"And can I ask where you were on Wednesday evening of this past week?"

Again she presses a palm to the same spot up high on her chest, near the sharp points of each clavicle. "Me?"

"Yes. Standard procedure to ask everyone we speak to about their whereabouts on that night. It's nothing to be alarmed by, Mrs. O'Brien." I make a point to switch from her first name to her last again. A small switch, but it usually signals to the interviewee that I mean business.

"Jessie." She catches my switch and corrects me again.

"Yes, and so where were you?" I ask pleasantly, deliberately not repeating her first name.

"I was in Helena."

"Helena?"

"Yes, I was there touring the capitol. I've always wanted to know more about it. My dad used to be a Montana congressman, but I never even visited. You know, I've driven through Helena, but never had a need to stay there."

"Did you stay the night?"

"I did. I stayed at the Marriott. One of those Residence Inns."

"And is there anyone there that would be kind enough to verify that for us? Again," I say, "just standard procedure. Were you meeting someone? A friend?" O'Brien gave me the name Lizzie McAlister.

She glares at me. "Is this for real? This is crazy. I have no idea what this is all about and here you are asking me to verify where I've been?"

"Yes, that's exactly right. Is that a problem?" I ask innocently.

She pulls her head back slightly and shakes it. I've clearly frazzled her now, but I don't care. I want to see if she has a solid alibi and get on my way back to the Flathead. "No, no, it's not. I just don't understand why you're here. Why this has anything to do with me."

"We're just dotting our *i*'s and crossing our *t*'s, Mrs. O'Brien. Like I said, because your husband knew the victim, we have to verify your whereabouts on the night of her murder. That's all."

She studies me, her eyes still wide and her cheeks beginning to flush pink with anger.

I remind her of the question. "So is there anyone in Helena who can vouch for your visit there?"

"No," she says, "I can't think of anyone."

"Didn't someone meet you in Helena for the tour?"

"No."

"You didn't meet a friend?" Either her husband is lying to me or she's lying to him. "What about the tour guide, then?"

She looks down and rubs her palms on her jeans nervously. I can hear the smooth scuffing sound and wait patiently for her answer. "I . . ." she fumbles. "I didn't actually go on the tour. I stayed in my room. I wasn't feeling well."

"No?"

"No, I had a bad headache."

I sense there's more to the story, so I wait for a moment to see if she'll get even more uneasy and add something. When people lie, they usually talk more than necessary in an effort to make the lie seem real.

She looks around her kitchen agitatedly, then adds, "I just . . . I don't know. I just needed to get away. I wasn't all that interested in the tour anyway. I just wanted to get away from here." She motions to the house.

"And why is that?"

"I don't know. I guess I'm just bored. Recently retired and all. I just needed to *do* something, and the tour seemed like an interesting thing, but when I got there, I didn't feel up to it. Like I said, I had a bad headache."

"Were you supposed to meet a friend there?"

"No," she says. "I told my husband that I was meeting Lizzie, one of my friends who lives in Helena. But she's out of town. I just wanted to get away anyway."

"Why did you lie to your husband?"

"I didn't want him to worry. I've struggled with anxiety in the past, and if I told him I just needed to get out and go by myself, he'd worry."

"I see." I say this like it all makes perfect sense, but clearly her explanation sounds highly suspicious. Still, there's a deep sadness in her eyes that rings true. She looks like someone who might have needed to check into a hotel for a day or two to get away, find her bearings. "Was there anyone at the hotel, at the front desk, who could vouch for you?"

"Possibly. When I checked in, there was a young man working. He might remember me."

"Do you recall his name?"

"No, no, I don't. But I checked in on Wednesday afternoon. Around four p.m. Tall guy, maybe early twenties."

"Okay," I say after writing it down. "It should be easy enough to determine who was on shift at that time. Are you sure there was no one else who might remember you in Helena?"

She thinks about it for a moment, then shakes her head in resigna-tion. "I kept to myself. I just left the keys in the room the next morn-ing and went out the side exit. I wanted to get home after all. I—I just feel . . . I don't know. Don't you ever . . . don't you ever just . . . ?" She trails off and looks at me longingly, like I might understand, and I feel sorry for her in that moment. I'm not sure if her sadness is that of a woman who knows her husband is cheating. Or maybe she doesn't know. Could it be that since retirement she's suddenly become aware of how fleeting life can be? Is it something more menacing—like she can't figure out how to go on after ending the life of a young woman? Her story is certainly shaky. I wait silently.

"I don't know. Never mind. I'm not sure what I'm asking."

"Did you stop for gas somewhere?"

"I filled up here in Missoula. At the gas station before the entrance ramp to the highway on Orange Street."

"So not in Helena? Or on the way back from Helena?"

"No, a full tank got me there and back. I filled up in Missoula again after I returned, just yesterday."

"Do you or your husband own any guns or rifles?"

"My husband owns a shotgun, but he never uses it. His brother gave it to him for bird-hunting years ago, but he only went two or three times. Said it wasn't his thing."

"And you?"

"No, no, I have no use for a gun."

"Okay, then, Jessie." I give her that—the comfort of her first name because I'm still feeling a certain sadness for her, but that doesn't mean I believe her. "Thank you for your time. As I said, all just standard procedure." I stand up and head to her front door, and she follows me.

"Am I in trouble for something?" she asks.

I turn when I reach the door. "No," I say, "I'm sure someone at the hotel will remember you checking in."

"And if they don't?"

"We'll cross that bridge when we get to it." I smile politely.

She stares at me, still wide-eyed. I tell her good-bye and head for my car, the leaves brushing against my shoes.

"Sorry about the leaves," she calls out. "I've been meaning to rake, but just haven't gotten to it."

"I know the feeling." I give a little wave and head to my car, wondering if her alibi is going to check out, hoping for her sake it will.

• • •

Because we already have transcripts on Anne Marie, I conveniently have her address and other trivia like the fact that she rents from a landlord who lives on the same property. I find her place near the river, near the town newspaper, and I think that's convenient for a journalist. Her place is more a cottage than a house and was probably a garage at one point that got remodeled into a rental, similar to the one I remodeled for Rose. It's located behind the main tenant's house and can be accessed by the alleyway behind it. I park in a small space in the alley.

I poke around Anne Marie's place first, but the blinds are closed, so I can't peek inside. There's only one front door and it's locked, so I'm thinking the landlord locked it after Brander and Reynolds visited the place. There's a gate blocking her cottage off from the alleyway and the house in front of her. A narrow, shabby lawn with weeds and broad patches of dirt spreads between her cottage and the owner's house. Three dirt-stained chintzy lawn chairs that haven't been stored away for winter sit in the center, and two old empty bottles of Sierra Nevada Pale Ale lie in the grass next to one of the chair's legs. Dead soldiers, my dad would have called them.

Her cottage is quaint, painted in lilac with white trim, but I'm surprised at how much it looks like someplace a college student would live in, not an established professional woman. It has no gardens or other signs of permanence, like sturdy lawn chairs or a regularly watered and maintained lawn. I suppose if you have no kids and no husband and are frequently on the road, a place like this is perfect, but something about it—perhaps the little-girl paint job and the empty bottles strewn by the chairs—strikes me as immature. But I remind myself that I'm not being fair. I can't exactly judge people by the color of their house or the shape of their yard.

There are no trees, but a few lilac bushes that are losing their leaves huddle next to her fence, I presume planted to provide a modicum of privacy between her place and the one in front. I think of Rose and how she lives in my remodeled attachment, and try to imagine her still living there when she's in her thirties, when she's Anne Marie's age. I have never considered it before, but the thought doesn't seem foreign to me because I have grown quite accustomed to Rose's being in our lives, and I don't want to picture life without her. But she is young, and I'm fooling myself to think she won't be moving on at some point. And because of my dad and the shadow effect he has had on me, on my sister too, I have the all-too-familiar sense that Shakespeare was right: life is simply a stage full of characters that spend their time in the spotlight, then exit.

I walk through the gate leading to the main house, walk around front, and knock on the door. No one answers, which is no surprise, since it's a workday. From my file, I see that the owner's name is Mark Adrian, but there's no information about where he works, which isn't surprising, since there was no need for the Bozeman agents to look beyond Anne Marie and her work when they interviewed her about Smith. I don't want to waste any more time in Missoula, but I consider whether to dig deeper so I can chat with Mark, see if he knows anything. I figure I can call him later, so I close the file and get up to go, taking one last look around her place on the way back to my car.

Reeve

Present—Monday

Last night after Wallace left, I made my way around the peak and down a ridge to a lake, where I set up camp after a long day of working McKay—so vigorously that now he's exhausted and his hips look stiff to me. Suddenly I feel guilty, wondering if I'm working my dog into the ground because I can't deal with my own life.

I decide to stay by the lake for another night to give him some rest. It's a high mountain lake caught between fall and winter, with fish rising occasionally, making rings in the steely water. Soon the lake will freeze, but for now it's hanging on to its silky dark vitality. The sky has cleared of its overcast and looks brilliant. I am reminded of the day I spent with Anne Marie, her trekking behind me while I grinned like a teenage boy.

I discard the thought quickly. I force myself to concentrate on the wild, on making good choices. I'm higher up and the stakes have risen. The heat from the sun has leaked away. Leaves have deserted the berry bushes and the alders, and the needles have dropped from the tamaracks. The slightest mishaps can make all the difference this far in the backcountry, especially this time of year: a misstep into the lake water could soak one of my boots, or I could run out of food or leave something essential behind, like my lighter or flashlight.

By foot, I'm a long way from my cabin in the North Fork. It's a considerable hike from where I've parked my car—more than a day's worth—but it wouldn't be that difficult to get to me if someone took the Trail Creek Road and spent some time searching around the Mount

Hefty area near the Canadian border. I peer up at the sky and wonder if I'll eventually see helicopters flying above.

I've worked McKay for only an hour today, hiking up a game trail toward a bare ridge to the west of the lake and playing fetch with him in the opening we reached after he found some grizzly scat. I also came across several sets of fresh grizzly tracks, and I'm a little nervous about camping tonight, but I know McKay will pitch a fit if he hears anything come near us in the night, and I'm no novice camper. I've packaged my food up tightly and strung it up high in a tree away from the campsite, where a bear can't get to it. But I'm not going to lie: staying through the night alone in grizzly country can do a number on your mind if you let it. I just don't let it. I go about my day, working McKay, my bear spray dangling on my belt, being extra careful through the brushier areas, keeping an eye on the high ridges above the tree line where they sometimes like to traverse, and making a fire as soon as twilight strikes.

I wonder about Wallace and hope he's made it home safely; I have to admit that the old-timer has grown on me. I worry about his turning an ankle, falling, and breaking a hip or something, but then I think how, if I make it to his age, I will hate it if people worry about me that way. And he's not even that old. Maybe mid-seventies, and damn fit, still traipsing through these rugged mountains, battling against the passage of time and its toll on the bones.

I consider what it would be like growing old alone, imagine Emily going off to engage with the world, and I feel slightly uneasy, like I'm a parasite living off of her happiness and her vitality. I think of Ali and how it could have been with her. Just when I thought things might actually work with us, she seemed distant and argumentative, as if she was purposely pushing me away. After the first big argument we had— something silly and unmemorable—we both moved around each other differently, with trepidation, wounded animals afraid of being kicked. I tried to act like the fights weren't happening, but it affected us and the way we interacted, both of us keeping to superficial topics in our conversations for fear we'd say something wrong that would lead to conflict. And this was without even living together, without worrying about toothpaste and unchanged toilet paper rolls. The forecast was not good.

When she told me she was pregnant, I'll admit I was terrified, but a part of me softened. In spite of my fears, I took the plunge and asked her to marry me. Granted, it was a timid proposal—yeah, probably weak and lackluster, and not exactly the stuff romantic dreams are made of—but I was unsure of myself and didn't want to come across too strongly. It's not like our relationship was rolling along on four wheels, more like we were stalled with a flat. But I thought maybe we could fix it, perhaps we could be a normal, happy couple. And still, under it all, I had always carried this feeling that Ali was like a best-kept secret—this brusque woman with a hidden heart of gold was sexier than hell once you got past her defenses. Ali clearly didn't think we could be a healthy couple, so I went along with her plans, even if they sometimes made me angry—her insistence on "living quietly," as she calls it, the extent to which she'll go for privacy. She insists that we keep our family dynamics to ourselves and refrain from mentioning the fact that I'm Emily's dad beyond the schoolyard. I'm a quiet person too, so I wouldn't anyway, and I find it easy to go along with her requests for discretion, but at times she seems paranoid.

She claims it's for her job, but I sense there's more to it. In the days when we were both open with each other, she told me about the social workers from her childhood. She said that the teachers treated her and her sister differently and that sometimes the other kids made fun of them at school. I can't help but think her intense need for privacy stems from that more than anything.

But I should talk. Here I am out in the wild, finding myself reluctant to go back to reenter society. I don't plan to be gone for too long. My weekend with Emily starts on Thursday, and I fully intend to spend it with her, provided I'm not behind bars by then.

I stand from the large boulder I've been sitting on by the small, placid lake and stretch. I can't kick the sensation that I'm like a bear looking for shelter far and high against the north slopes. I want to see Emily, but I also feel an intense need to hole up, as if that will keep the past from drowning out the present. I'm about to start collecting more wood for a fire when I hear the staccato drone of a helicopter in the distance. I look up over the ridges, searching for the chopper, but don't see it.

It's supposed to be a comforting sound, an indication that the search and rescue troops are on the way, a sign that even when the world is a cruel place and hope is scarce, you're not alone, someone is coming to save you. This time, though, the patterned noise of the blades slicing through the sky, like the rapid spin cycle of a washing machine, makes my heart pound and panic rise. My scalp feels tingly. I have to remind myself to breathe.

It's the first sound of a motor I've heard in two days, and it's an affront to my finely tuned senses, the ones that have begun to hear every sound no matter how small—the flutter of a wing, the hop of a squirrel off a branch, the swish of a leaf in the fall wind. I stand still, McKay by my side, both of us gazing into the pale blue sky, and tell myself that they're not searching for me, but somehow I can't convince myself of that and am glad I've set the small tent up under the cover of several full pine trees. I decide to hold off on making the fire for a little while longer. The way my chest is pounding makes me realize that being in the woods has simply injected me with a false sense of security.

Ultimately the cops are out to find me, no matter what I've done, because somehow, someway, I must pay for the life I took all those years ago. It's an absurd thought, that the universe is out to get me— something a child hiding under a bed might conjure—yet I can't shake it. It's that alarm going off in my head, announcing to me over and over: you will get what you deserve.

Ali

Present—Tuesday

WILL JONES IS the one who ends up getting my Salt Lake City supervisors involved, tipping them off to my connection to the Johnson case.

Tuesday morning, the day after I return from Missoula, I pick up the morning paper. Staring at me from the front page on the left sidebar is Reeve and Anne Marie. The headline reads: *Be On the Lookout (BOLO) Issued on Local Man.*

Damn it. My stomach tightens. Now they've got skin in the game. They've announced to everyone that this is their man and now they're going to do everything they can to get him convicted so they don't have to admit to the public that they were barking up the wrong tree.

I read on. The article, written by Jones, goes on to say that Reeve Landon, a person of interest in the homicide of Anne Marie Johnson— at least they're not calling him a primary suspect—has been missing since his initial interview. Detective Reynolds from the county sheriff's office says that although Reeve Landon is not under arrest yet, they are actively searching for him, and would appreciate any information citizens might have on his location. The piece goes on to explain that Anne Marie Johnson was shot, and that Reeve was the last person to be seen with her after they spent the day together in the woods.

The county sheriff's deputies have repeatedly searched Landon's place near Polebridge, MT, over the last three days, but the suspect hasn't returned since he went missing Friday morning.

As I near the end of the article, I glimpse my name. I clench the sides of the paper so hard, the fingernail of my thumb turns white, and my heart beats in angry thumps.

Sources close to the investigation have also confirmed that the suspect is connected to one of Kalispell resident agency's local FBI special agents, Ali Paige. The two had previously been in a relationship and now share custody of their young daughter, Emily. Sources say that Agent Paige has not been forthcoming with the local authorities and did not immediately disclose her personal involvement with Landon when he became a person of interest in the case. Special Agent Paige has since been asked to step aside from any involvement with the case.

"Asshole!" I say out loud to my kitchen. I can feel my pulse in my temples. Reynolds. It has to be him. I'm so angry, I bite my bottom lip so hard that I draw blood. I throw the paper across the kitchen. I can hear my own breathing, and I'm surprised at how fierce I sound. I can't believe Reynolds would talk to Jones of all people—Jones, who may be cleared now, but who until recently was also a person of interest in the case.

And Will, how dare he! I wonder how he found out. Maybe he saw Reeve pick Emily up one day and recognized his face. I'm sure he went and pestered Reynolds, who couldn't resist leaking the information about me to the press. Why not? He hates me and probably hates the FBI—we're such a big operation that local departments tend to find us threatening.

I place my forehead against the heels of my hands and press hard to push back the rage. I'm in hotter water than I've ever been in before. The SLC field office will have been pinged by the article and will want to speak to me immediately. When I look up, Emily is standing in the kitchen entryway in saggy pajama bottoms, holding her fists to her eyes to rub out the sleep.

"Oh, good mornin', chickadee," I say, trying to swallow my wrath. I go kiss her, then begin to collect the papers strewn across the floor.

"Why are those on the floor?" Emily asks, going to the section closest to her, the page with her father's picture.

"Oh, they just fell. I'll get it." I rush to it, but I'm too late. She's reaching for it, saying, "Hey, that's Daddy."

I yank it out of her hand too abruptly, and kick myself for not being calmer.

"Why is Daddy in the paper?"

"Oh, just some stuff on his research."

"Can I see?"

"Aw, come on, sweetie, you've seen this photo before," I say.

"I want to see," she says in a higher pitch. She senses my reluctance. I decide it'll seem even weirder if I refuse to show her, so I fold the headline under so that only the photos are visible.

"See." I hold it out. "It's just a nice picture of Daddy, nothing you haven't seen before."

"Oh," she says, then takes her little finger and points to Anne Marie's photo. "I know her," she says.

"What?" I say.

"I know her."

"You do? How?" On top of all the rage, my heart feels like it's sinking too. Had he already introduced her to our daughter? He certainly didn't waste any time . . . or had he known her for longer than I assumed? "From your daddy?" I say pointedly.

A frown settles on her face, and she tucks her chin under. "Are you mad, Mommy?"

"No," I say, taking a breath. "So you know this woman?"

She nods.

"Through your daddy?"

She shakes her head.

"No?" I ask, but my phone is buzzing on the counter right next to us. I jump, which is uncharacteristic of me. I don't startle easily. I've

had too much training for that. We both look at it. Without even picking it up, I can see *SAC Shackley, Salt Lake City Field Office,* across the
front in bright white letters.

"Who's that?"

"Someone from work," I say.

"Aren't you going to answer?"

"No, you need breakfast and to get ready. I'll call him back in a
moment."

"When's Kaylee coming over?"

"What?"

"Kaylee," she repeats, and I remember that Kaylee's mom asked me
last week if she could drop her off early on Tuesday because she needs
to be at an early meeting for work, and was wondering if I could drive
her to school.

"Oh, that's right," I say. "She'll probably need breakfast too." I take
out some bagels, thinking I need to circle back to the photo of Anne
Marie, but right as I open the twist tie on the plastic bag, the doorbell
rings and Emily runs out of the kitchen to go let Kaylee in.

• • •

After I make Emily and Kaylee bagels and send them both upstairs
so Emily can get dressed, I sit down and close my eyes for a moment
before listening to the message. I'm nervous.

Now the whole damn community will know about my little broken family, and what's worse, I have no idea what's coming down the
pike in terms of a reprimand from Shackley. All I want to do is find
Reynolds and chew his ass out, but I'm not sure on what grounds. For
issuing the BOLO on circumstantial evidence? But Herman said they
have something more, so I can't claim that without knowing what they
have. For leaking inappropriate information to the press? He'd just turn
the tables on me.

I wonder what Reeve didn't tell me. How does Emily know Anne
Marie? I sink into a chair at my kitchen table. I don't have a leg to stand

on, and I cannot afford to lose my cool. I can't believe that I've stuck my neck out for Reeve like this and he hasn't even leveled with me. I think of the voicemail from Shackley waiting for me on my phone, picture being reported to the Office of Professional Responsibility.

I still have multiple leads to investigate and only myself to rely on. So far Reeve remains the suspect with the best opportunity to kill Anne Marie Johnson, but the suspect with the strongest motive is Jessie O'Brien. There are still unanswered questions about Vivian Gould, and there's also the rest of the Smith file. Plus, I have more phone calls to make, and I certainly can't do that if I'm worried about the local news. But first I have to find out what's waiting for me at the other end of that ominous voicemail. I take a deep breath, steady myself, and hit play.

Reeve

A STORM IS BREWING, and the sky over the ridge is turning a deep and bruised gray. I can smell the ozone and the wind has begun to pick up, rustling the bushes and the tops of the trees. Out of instinct, when I heard the chopper, I grabbed McKay and hid in a thick copse of alder brush until it left. Then, when the helicopter was out of sight, to be safe, I dismantled my tent for the time being. The helicopter is still gone now, though, and McKay and I sit on a rock a little way around the lake on its western side, protected by the thick cover of bushes still hanging on to some of their foliage.

I am caught, wondering if I should stay or not. The looming storm has forced the choppers away, but now I have the storm itself to worry about. The temperature is dropping. McKay whines every now and then and looks at me hopefully. He still seems stiff in his hips, but he wants to work, always wants to work.

I plant a sample nearby so that I can reward him with a little fetch. After he finds the scat, I take a seat on the same broad rock and throw to him. I'm careful to not cast the ball too far so I don't make him more stiff. I sit on the rock, tossing the ball, having him dart after it and return to drop it at my feet. I notice that the skin on my hands looks tanned and leathery in the ashen light, dark and radiant at the same time.

I lift my face to the building breeze, feeling unprepared for what's coming.

"Two more throws, buddy," I say. "Then we head back to the campsite. Those choppers are long gone for now."

Ali

Present—Tuesday

"AGENT PAIGE, SAC Shackley here," the message said. "I'm in Helena today to take care of some things and plan to head your way as soon as I finish up this afternoon. I'll be there by five p.m., so I expect you to make yourself available." His voice sounds calm and direct, but also sharp, tinged with anger. When he adds, "Agent Paige, don't say another word to the county sheriff," I'm certain it is anger I'm hearing.

A dipping sensation turns in my stomach, like standing on the edge of a mountain cliff. Shit. If he came all the way here, he's more than concerned. Possibly irate. I play the message over several times, trying to decide just *how* angry he sounds. Okay, I force myself to breathe calmly. I can deal with this.

I try to reassure myself that the extent of what they know comes from the article and they're simply making sure everything is on the up-and-up. I have a right to keep my life private, even if it pissed the county off, and at the point that I watched his interview, I did not know he was a prime suspect.

On the other hand, if they've gotten a direct complaint from Brander, Reynolds, or even Herman—oh god, would Herman say something to the higher-ups?—if they know I've been doing some digging on my own, that's a different story.

Five p.m., I think as I drive to the office. I've got one workday to follow up on the rest of my leads. I know I should put all of it aside before I dig myself in any deeper. It's not my case. It was never to be my case. But I've already come this far. What's the worst that could happen? I'll be reprimanded, sure. How badly, I don't know. Worst-case scenario, they tag me with an actionable offense under the inspector general. The idea turns my stomach, especially given how hard I've worked to get to this point in my career, but I can't let it affect me. Not now.

When I get to the office, I sit in my car to make some phone calls before I go in. I see Herman's car in the parking lot. I wonder if he knows that Shackley's in town.

Yesterday, on the way back from Missoula, I called the Marriott Courtyard to check on Jessie O'Brien's alibi, but the manager said that the guy working the front desk on Wednesday around the time when Jessie would have checked in wouldn't be in until Tuesday. She said she couldn't give his personal number out. Company policy. I pushed it, telling her I was working on a criminal investigation, and she finally gave it to me.

Josh Bergman is his name. I've called the guy three times, and it keeps going to voicemail. I've left messages, but I wonder if he's even gotten them—if he's a young guy, he probably doesn't even check his voicemail. I decide to call him again now before I go in.

This time Josh answers right away, and I find out that he does indeed remember Jessie. When I give him only her name, he describes her accurately: "auburn-haired, slender, maybe late forties or early fifties. Well made up," he says, then adds: "I asked her if she had a preference: if she wanted to be on the first floor or near the elevator or anything. She said the only thing she wanted was a room that was quiet. I figured she either wanted to sleep or had a lot of work to do. She asked for some water, and I gave her two bottles."

"Do you recall what time she checked in?"

"I don't remember for sure, but I can look on the system."

While I wait, his computer keys clicking away, Herman comes out the door and walks across the parking lot toward his car. When he sees me, he gives me a nod and switches directions to head my way. As he gets close, I roll down my window and hold up my finger to him and show him the phone so he knows I'm busy, then roll it back up.

He nods, standing next to my window, waiting for me to finish my call. I'm about to roll it down again and say, "This could take a little time," but I decide I can't afford to display even a smidgen of annoyance toward him. He doesn't deserve it anyway. None of this is remotely his fault.

Come on, hurry up, Josh. I tap my foot on the floorboard and give Herman a little smile. Josh finally comes back on and says, "Looks like she checked in at four fifty p.m. on Wednesday."

"And do you recall seeing her around any more after that? Like in the lobby later that evening or anything?" I already know she didn't check out, just left the keys in the room.

"Hmm," he says. "Let me think. I mean, I might have, but I can't say for sure."

"Okay, thank you." I want to press him for more information, but with Herman standing beside my car, I end the call, figuring I'll call back.

I put my phone in my bag and open my door. "What's up?" I ask.

He levels a serious look at me.

"What?"

"SAC Shackley is coming to see us later."

I look down at the pavement for a moment, then back up to meet his gaze. The cool breeze rustles my hair and nips my cheeks. "You speak to him?"

"Yes."

"What did he say?"

"Not much, just to stay put. Wants to chat with us both, but you mainly. He didn't seem to want to get into any details over the phone. Said he was busy in Helena."

"Okay," I say.

He shakes his head like he's irritated, but doesn't see the point in saying anything about it.

"Look, it's all on me, Herman. You're not responsible for any of this, and that's what I'm going to tell him, so you don't have to worry about anything."

"I'm not worried about me."

"Good, you shouldn't be."

He continues to look at me with a mixture of confusion and worry.

"All right, well, I better get moving. I've got a lot of stuff to do today before he comes." I glance at up at our shiny, dark office windows, which are on the second floor of the building. The sky above is a pale blue.

"What kind of stuff?"

When I don't say anything, he takes the hint, jiggles his keys, and turns to go. "Okay, Ali. I'll see you later."

"Wait," I say, "I'm sorry. I don't mean to be rude."

He doesn't respond, just looks at me like he's trying to be patient.

"Are you making any headway on the Smith case?"

Herman shakes his head. "Ali, you know I can't discuss that case with you anymore."

"I know, I know, I'm just wondering if you think there's any way Smith was behind whoever killed Anne Marie?"

"I'm not seeing any evidence of it yet. But I'm scanning her computer files to see if anyone else she interviewed ties back to Smith."

"Okay, thanks," I say.

He turns around and starts heading toward his car again.

"Where are you going?"

"Dentist appointment," he calls over his shoulder. "I'll be back in an hour."

"Oh," I say. "See you then."

. . .

What I should do next is enter our building, climb the stairs at the back to our offices on the second floor, go in, and sit at my desk as usual instead of quickly zeroing in on the fact that Herman said he has Anne Marie's digital files on his computer. I should contemplate how much I've damaged my relationship with Herman, wondering how to get him to trust me again. At the very least, I should sit at my desk nervously, fidgeting, chewing a pencil or biting my nails, glancing furtively at my coworker's desk before deciding to proceed with trepidation toward it to find the files. But that's not what happens.

I go in, drop my bag at my desk, and head straight for Herman's. It's a long, sleek dark desk identical to mine, utilitarian, with filing drawers that lock on the right side. I start with his files stacked neatly to the side of his computer to see if he happened to print anything out, but all I find is stuff I've already seen on the Smith case. I know he keeps his desk drawers locked, but I try to pull them open anyway to no avail. I sit down and hope he's left his computer on and that all I have to do is wiggle the mouse to bring up his last working screens, but I'm not optimistic. I'm right. He's shut down his computer, as he always does when he leaves the office. I would do the same. It's what we're trained to do.

I turn on his computer and wait for it to boot, but I know I'm not going to get far. At our office we use fobs—small security devices with built-in authentication codes that control access to our networks and data. The fob displays a randomly generated code, which changes every thirty seconds. We first have to authenticate ourselves on the fob with a PIN, then enter the current code on the device. I have no clue what Herman's PIN might be because we're always updating those as well. Conceivably Herman could have written it down somewhere, even though we're not supposed to do that, but sometimes it's difficult to remember all the new combinations of numbers and letters we're constantly coming up with, and we do work in a small office that is rarely intruded upon.

I search all the sticky notes on his desk, finding nothing. Then I rummage through his wastebasket, looking at all the notes he's tossed, but still find nothing—just some old grocery lists, a few to-do lists, some telephone numbers, restaurant receipts. I decide I'm not going to be able to access his system until he returns and boots it up himself. My best bet is to either ask him to share the files with me, which I know he won't do, especially given the fact SAC Shackley is heading our way today, or to have him boot up his computer and then move fast if he leaves the room to go to the restroom down the hall.

When I get back to my desk and sit down, the heaviness I've been avoiding descends upon me. What have I done? Even if this turns out okay, how much have I damaged my relationship with him? It's possible he'll never trust me again, which would be even worse than a reprimand from Shackley.

But I have no time for remorse. There's too much to do. I call Josh back again and tell him to contact me if he remembers anything else about Jessie O'Brien. I also ask him to check with housekeeping to see if they recall how her room looked when they cleaned it the next morning. I hold back on asking him to check the times the key card was used to get in the room because I know I'd need a subpoena for digging that deeply into the hotel registry data. He promises that he'll call me back.

For now, at least I know she did really go to Helena, but in terms of an alibi, it's still shaky. She could have left and driven to the Flathead. It would have taken her around four and a half hours to reach the cabin. Before she left, she could have mussed up the sheets, splashed a little water around the hotel bathroom sink, torn the sticker off the toilet paper if there was one, and left a few towels off the rack and an empty water bottle or two in the trash or on the counter, and it would look to housekeeping like someone had stayed the night. It's not the first time I've seen it happen in cases I've worked. But for now there's not much more I can do from my desk.

Next up on my list: Vivian Gould. Who is the guy in the car with her, and what is it about Vivian that bothers me? Is it just that she looks a little like Anne Marie? Is it too far-fetched to think that someone wanted her dead, and they happened to shoot the wrong person in the dark? She's shorter than Anne Marie—that I can easily see from the Facebook pictures—but in the middle of a moonless night, one could easily have mistaken Anne Marie for Vivian. But who would want Vivian dead, and why?

I pull up the driver's name on Google: Tate Austin. Born in Oklahoma City. Lives now in Seattle. Works for . . . bingo . . . Seattle Security Services. I recall that he seemed much older than Vivian despite his self-assured boyish smile. One of the search results is an article in the *Seattle Post-Intelligencer*'s local features section titled "Former Police Officers Open New Security Firm in Seattle." I pick up my phone and call Seattle Security Services.

A man with a chipper voice answers, and I explain that I'm an FBI agent in Montana and that I have some questions. "How can I help?" he asks.

"And you are?"

"John Lesky."

"I see from your website that you're a full-service security company. What exactly do you provide?"

"Residential, commercial, industrial."

"Just electronic systems?" I ask.

"No, we provide trained professionals—bodyguards for personal use, event protection, the like."

"And Tate Austin is your partner?"

"He's one of my bosses. He and another former police officer founded this company. I'm sorry, ma'am, but what's this about?" he asks.

"Does Mr. Austin take on clients himself?"

"Not that often, but sometimes. If he has a reason to."

"He have a girlfriend?"

"Excuse me?"

"Mr. Lesky, as I said, my name is Agent Paige. I'm with the FBI. There's been a woman murdered in Montana, and I have reason to believe that your boss was in Montana recently. Is that correct?"

"Yes, he was. For a client, but I'm not at liberty to discuss our clients."

"I see. So Vivian Gould is a client of yours?"

"I'm sorry, but as I said, I can't discuss client matters."

You pretty much just did, I think, thankful that the whole intimidating FBI thing causes people to slip. "Mr. Lesky, your boss was seen with someone involved in a murder investigation. We're going to need some cooperation; you understand? If you'd like, you can patch me through to your boss."

"Yeah, yeah." He sounds relieved. "That's a good idea. Hold on a sec."

Some elevator music begins playing when he puts me on hold until Tate Austin picks up the call. "Agent Paige," he says, "how are you?" His voice is smooth and unfazed.

"I'm doing well. I see you and Vivian have made it back to Seattle safely."

"That we did. How can I help you?"

"I'm going to just get right to it. A woman who resembles your client, Vivian Gould, was killed outside your client's cabin in the middle of the night when your client was due to come in from Seattle. Do you know anything about that?"

"I do," he says, but doesn't add anything more. That alone tells me I'm speaking to a former cop—in law enforcement, the less said, the better. This means I also won't need to explain that he can't duck behind a bunch of company privacy policies lest he be accused of obstructing an investigation.

"How do you know Ms. Gould?" I start.

"She came to us for our services."

"Before or after her friend was murdered?"

"After."

"She was frightened?"

"Yes," he says. "Wouldn't you be?"

I don't reply to that, not because he sounds snide or unhelpful, just because I don't feel the need to. I don't get the sense that he knows about me, but I could be wrong. "Mr. Austin," I say, "help us out here. We're simply trying to find who did this to your client's friend. If you have her best interests at heart, I assume you'd want that too."

"Of course," he says. "I'm happy to be of assistance as long as I don't cross any client-privilege lines."

"Fair enough," I say. "So why don't you fill me in, then." I wait for a reply. The line goes quiet for a moment, both of us waiting. I think I hear the punching of computer keys.

Finally he gives in. But first he sighs, and I almost detect a note of pity in it, which makes me nervous. "Agent Paige, I have a good relationship with the Seattle PD. Worked for them for over two decades. Sometimes they're short-staffed, you know, like thousands of other police departments. They don't have resources for all circumstances, and at times they'll refer clients my way—clients who might need a little protection that they can't justify or find the resources to make it happen on their end."

"So Vivian needs protection?"

"Yes, she does."

"And can you tell me why?"

"In her role as an accountant she recently discovered some . . . let's just say unsavory transactions going on at her former company—a big company. One that might make you run a bit scared, especially when your friend ends up murdered the day you pack up your office."

"Why didn't she tell the police in Seattle?"

"She did, but she was told that it was in her best interest to keep it quiet. Timberhaus is huge. She's pretty frightened. I can't go into all the details, but after Anne Marie Johnson turned up dead outside her place, she called the Seattle PD. They told her it was far-fetched to think someone was out to get her, especially over in Montana, but they gave her my number and told her I had the resources to protect her if that's what she wanted and was willing to pay for it. I was going to send one of my men, but since it was short notice—we were short-staffed with some big film event going on in Seattle—I just flew out myself and drove back with her. I've got a different bodyguard watching over her now, just until this case gets solved."

"And why haven't you or the Seattle PD contacted the Flathead County sheriff's department about this? Do you not think the fact that she's a whistle-blower isn't pertinent to the homicide case?"

"We have, Agent Paige. I would have assumed you'd know that, but . . ." His voice fades.

I have a bad feeling. I stay quiet.

"Well, I googled you while we were talking, out of habit, you know, and I saw that article about your connection to the case."

I close my eyes and shake my head. Damn Jones.

"Hey," he says, "I'm a cop at heart, so I get it. I get the situation you're in, and I've always liked working with the FBI. If you ever find yourself needing a job, give me a buzz. We could use a highly trained professional like yourself."

It cuts, but I was expecting it at some point. I swallow my pride and forge ahead, trying to sound official, not deflated. "Mr. Austin, is there any reason to believe that Anne Marie Johnson was killed by someone who mistook her for Vivian Gould?"

"We certainly considered the possibility of that in the beginning, but it looks as if the county firmly believes that the two cases have no bearing on each other—evidence from the autopsy that the victim has skin and blood of the primary suspect under some of her nails, and some were broken too, indicating signs of a defensive struggle with said primary suspect, whom I understand you're quite familiar with."

My heart sinks. Reeve—skin and blood? Broken nails? Not only am I shocked to hear this bit of information, but I'm disappointed to hear it from some ex-cop in Seattle. I'm thankful that he's sharing it with me, but I'm also humiliated and angry at Reeve for not telling me the full story. This is why Brander and Reynolds have been so adamant that Reeve is their man. "Thank you," I finally muster.

"You're welcome. Like I said, I get it, Agent Paige. And I'm sorry about your situation. But if you ask me, I don't think there's anyone at Timberhaus crooked enough to commit murder. But Seattle PD or I will certainly let the county know if they find something that points in that direction. I suspect our local FBI will get involved on this one as well before it's all said and done."

"I appreciate the information," I say, feeling humbled.

"You're welcome. Best of luck to you." He sounds genuine, and for a brief moment that sincerity—that willingness of one cop to help another—makes me feel less alone.

. . .

When Herman returns from the dentist, I stick it out at my desk for another hour and a half, waiting for him to use the men's room, and waiting to see if he'll leave his computer unlocked. But I'm not hopeful. We're trained to not walk away from a logged-in computer, but it's not out of the realm of possibility when you work in a small resident agency like ours. It all comes down to trust, and that's part of the problem now. If there was ever a time that Herman would leave his computer unattended, even for a short amount of time, it would not be now.

Finally, around eleven thirty, Herman stands up and stretches. I glance over and see that his screen is still on. Hope rises in me, but then fades like footsteps. He leans over at the waist, grabs his mouse, and begins clicking away. I watch as the screen goes dark. He doesn't say a word as he heads out, and I wouldn't expect him to: it's not like we fill each other in every time we need to use the bathroom.

I sit at my desk for only a second before I dart over and look in his carrier bag. There's no point in trying to get into his system, and all I can hope for is that he's printed out the documents and shoved them in his bag before he went to the dentist. It's a thick black canvas carrier bag. I open the zipper at the top and riffle through the files, all neatly labeled. Most are on transcripts from the Smith case and information passed along from Bozeman. I have many of the same files. I glance to the door. I'm out on the edge. If he returns and catches me, I'll have completely lost any remnant of trust he has for me at all. I shuffle through several files that seem to be personal. They're labeled *Bills*, *Receipts*, and *Vacation Ideas*. A pang of compassion shoots through me. Herman is collecting information for holidays.

Who would he go on vacation with? He has several local friends, but for the most part, he's a loner in this town, like I would be if I didn't have Emily. Kind of comes with the territory. It's the unpredictability of the life. It's hard to make solid plans with people when you might get a call at any time that something serious has happened. It's why I thank my lucky stars for having someone as flexible as Rose around, but even with her, I still carry my guilt for the times when I know Emily has looked up to find me and has seen only an empty seat during a school play because my phone has buzzed and I've needed to step out and take it.

Herman has family, though, and I've met his younger sister and her two children—a boy and a girl—who have come to visit him in Montana. From what I remember, they adore him and I know he loves them. I'm about to give up and zip up his bag when I see the label on the very first file: Anne Marie Johnson. In my haste, I must have skipped right over it.

I think fast. There's no time for me to photocopy the contents and get them back in his bag before he leaves. I have two options: leave them and save myself any further trouble, which is tempting given my latest discovery from Tate Austin, or take the file and hope he doesn't notice until later, after he gets home. Because that's most likely the reason Herman's made printouts in the first place, to go over them at home later. Not because he doesn't have a laptop, but because I know he simply likes to print copies in case his eyes get tired and he wants a different perspective. He's told me that many times in the past: "When all else fails, Ali, print your reports and study them the old-fashioned way. It helps bring another perspective." And he's right: looking at a piece of paper with pen in hand engages your brain differently than staring at a screen. I solved an embezzlement case in a local casino involving a spreadsheet of bookkeeping data containing multiple columns of information after I printed it out. I had been staring at the screen for hours and couldn't see the connection between the accounts payable clerk and the night manager who had been allocating funds and skimming off the top to make payments to a private account that they had set up together, until I printed out the spreadsheet. With any luck, I could grab Herman's reports now, take them to my office at home, copy them, and return them when I come back before five p.m. to be here for SAC Shackley.

I hear Herman's voice outside. He's talking to Joel, an insurance agent who works down the hall from us. I can hear Joel's voice too. It's loud, and it carries: "You still planning on taking that vacation to the Caribbean this fall?" he's asking. I make a quick decision to grab the paperwork out of the file, zip up his bag, run to my desk, and slam down into my chair just as the door opens. I don't have time to think of what I've just done. I tuck the paperwork into a manila folder and place it in my own bag. My heart is going like a jackhammer, and I'm certain my face is flushed with guilt. I shut my system down and grab my things. "I'm out of here for a bit," I say.

"Where you heading?"

"Lunch at home. I have to check on some things. Plus, Emily has an early out today. I'm picking up her and a friend of hers, Kaylee. Rose is busy; she actually has a dentist appointment too. Big day for dental hygiene." I smile, but I can hear my voice as if it's distant—high-pitched and rattling. I'm sure Herman must sense my nerves.

"What about Shackley?"

"Rose will be done with her appointment by then, and she'll watch the girls for me. I'll definitely be back before he arrives."

Herman gives me a nod, but he's eyeing me, and I can't decide if he's suspicious or not.

"See ya." I smile weakly and leave, hoping against odds that he won't look for the Anne Marie file before I return to the office and replace its contents.

Reeve

Present—Tuesday

THE HELICOPTER IS definitely gone, and it doesn't seem to be coming back. It's been driven out by banks of ugly clouds and forceful winds. I look up at the darkening clouds in the east. A snowstorm is coming, and with the drop in temperature, I wonder if it's wise for me to stay this high up at the lake. I could wake up snowed in by a foot or two. I'm reluctant to make a fire, to draw attention to my location even though I know the chopper has moved on. I'm having a hard time thinking and I've been pacing since McKay and I came back to the partial camp we set up earlier.

In the wake of the helicopter, all is eerily quiet besides the rush of the wind and the rustling bushes. There's a whooshing in my head as well. Guilt, I think: a roaring wind that fills your ears and blocks out all other thoughts. I've had moments where I've experienced self-acceptance—a quiet, gentle breeze that can go completely unnoticed unless you take a moment to be still—and that's not what I'm feeling out in these mountains today. I've been searching for it all week, and it's eluded me. It's the roar that's filling my head—a forceful, feverish howl that's infecting my brain—and even the wilderness isn't taming it. It's as if these things with Anne Marie—the time spent with her, the questions she asked, and the police suspecting me—it all came together in a perfect storm, stirring up everything murky in my soul, dredging up the things I've tried to subdue. I feel paralyzed by it.

A part of me wants to get up from the log I'm sitting on and hike straight to the county building and let whatever happens happen. But another part of me is a stubborn fighter. I've come this far after experiencing something as a child that no one should ever have to face, and I've fought to survive every step of the way. I've earned my place in these mountains, in this world, and I refuse to let some false accusations rip it all away from me. I look at the lake, at its unbroken crystal waters and the mountains perfectly rendered on its glassy surface. A breeze begins to pick up and ruffle the charcoal-colored water, smearing the reflection into pocked ripples. McKay is curled up in a ball at my feet, his body pressing against my ankle. I am reluctant to leave.

At times over the years, I've wondered what Sam would be now if I hadn't killed him—what he would be doing as an adult—but I can never get very far with the thought. There are too many avenues to go down in life. He could have been an attorney, a musician (I remember he took piano lessons), a truck driver, a construction worker, a stockbroker, a pilot, a doctor, or a scientist who helps cure cancer. Or he could have been homeless or violent or a criminal. The possibilities are endless.

I have this image of Sam's mother the morning before he comes over. She takes a small break from loading the dishwasher, just long enough to kiss his forehead and tell him to be good. She tells him that she loves him and gives his arm a quick squeeze. It's something I do with Emily now, and when I do this common thing that all parents do, it's always overlain with that image of Sam's mom doing the same . . . until the day she can't anymore because I took that ability away from her.

So trying to quiet that roar is difficult, but if there's one place that I manage to come close to subduing it, it's out in these woods. If I go back now, I might crumble, the roar might overtake me. Just another night, I think. One more night, and then we'll head back.

Ali

Present—Tuesday

I PICK UP EMILY and Kaylee from school. They're happy and overly loud. I have way too much on my mind to enjoy their giddiness stemming from their early release, but I try to hide my stress. I take them to a local coffee shop to get fruit smoothies and cookies before we go home so that I don't have to fix a snack when we get there and can go straight to work. I have to tell Emily several times in the coffee shop to quit doing pirouettes in front of the counter because she's so hyped up.

When we arrive home, Emily starts doing cartwheels off the couch, and I have to yell at her to take it outside. They whine that they want to stay in, and finally they run off to Emily's room to play, and I go to my home office. I've got less than two and a half hours before Shackley shows up when I'll need to return. I check my phone again. Herman hasn't called, and I think that's a good sign, but a part of me worries he checked his bag and has already given up on me.

I print out the reports, replace Herman's originals in my bag, then lay out all the private notes and write-ups of interviews Anne Marie has had with various people. I focus on the criminals first—people she's visited in jail. I pull out my records on the Smith file to cross-reference any names of people she's visited in jail with names we have on record as being involved with the Smith case. I'm sure Herman has done the same, and I hate to duplicate efforts, but I need to start somewhere.

It's a slow process, and I keep hearing chatter and sudden shrieks of joy from upstairs. Sometimes I hear trampling across the upstairs hallway, and I think they're playing hide-and-seek. Eventually, giggling emanates from around the corner, and I realize Emily and Kaylee are in the kitchen. I force myself away from my desk and go check on them. Emily's grabbing sugar and flour, and Kaylee is grabbing a big mixing bowl from the cabinet.

"Oh, no, no, no," I say.

"But we want to bake."

"No, Emily. Not this afternoon."

"But why?"

"Because I said so. Now put it away."

"Mommy," Emily whines.

"Emily. No," I say, harsher than I mean to, but I'm stressed, and this is the last thing I need. "Maybe go to your room and make a fort or direct one of those plays you sometimes make up for me?"

She frowns because they're not her ideas, but gives in and puts the bags of flour and sugar away. "Come on," she says to Kaylee after giving me a pouty face, and they run into the living room, jumping onto the couch.

I want to tell them no jumping on the furniture, either—that someone could get hurt—but I figure I'll pick my battles, and I'd rather have them jumping on furniture than making a mess in the kitchen. I can see it now, flour and sugar everywhere, batter smeared across the counter and on their faces and in their hair. Not going to happen today, I think. I'm just about to return to my office when Rose comes in, saying, "Knock, knock," as she enters.

"Oh, thank god."

"That bad?" she asks.

"A little on the crazy side," I say. "Very"—I mouth the word—"*hyper*."

Rose smiles like she understands.

"In fact," I say, "would you mind taking them outside?"

She grimaces. "Kind of cold out today, but I tell you what. I'll take them to my place."

"That would be great."

"Emily, Kaylee," Rose calls out. "Emily, want to show Kaylee my apartment?"

Both girls erupt in yelps of glee as if seeing Rose's apartment is like going to Disneyland, even though Emily has spent copious time in Rose's apartment.

After Rose herds them out, I return to my office and go back to checking the names of all the people, mostly men, that Anne Marie interviewed in jail. There's one woman, Frieda Lynn Marker, who's serving a life sentence for killing her husband. She blindfolded him and led him to a table with a cake for his birthday, pulled out a gun, and blew his brains out. He never even saw the cake, so lord knows why she bothered to bake it.

I see no connection to the Smith case. The others are all men in jail for a variety of reasons, from shooting girlfriends in a rage to more calculated crimes. One man gunned down a competing drug dealer in the Evergreen area in Kalispell.

It's already four fifteen, and I know I need to get back to the office early, not just to have my wits together when Shackley arrives, but also to look for an opportunity to slip the documents back into the file in Herman's bag. I don't live more than ten minutes away from the office. If I give it fifteen more minutes, I can be there around a quarter to five.

I have more names to check. I know if I look them all up now, I won't have enough time to check them out thoroughly, but I want to get through them, just to see if anything rings a bell on the Smith case before I have to deal with my supervisor. I glance at the clock again. Four thirty. I have to get going, but I have only about another three names to look up: Vince Giles Reiko, Perry Thomas Sandow, and James Roger Kurtz. I look more closely. Vince Giles Reiko rings a bell, but I'm not sure why. It's the kind of name you remember, though. "Vince Giles Reiko," I whisper out loud. "Where have I seen you before?"

I tap my pen on my desk. Are you connected to the Smith case? How do I know that name? I repeat it several times without the middle name: Vincent Reiko, Vincent Reiko. Vince. Reiko. Then it hits me. I feel like my world is slipping sideways, although I'm not sure I know exactly why; it's just that a forceful sweeping motion overcomes me. I type it in, holding my breath. My memory is confirmed: Vincent Giles Reiko. Sentenced at the age of twenty to fifty-eight years in prison for the murder of Kim Farrows, who just so happened to be home sick from school the day Reiko broke in. I don't need to look up Kim Farrows—or, as Rose called her, Kimmie. I found out about her when I first interviewed Rose, before I hired her.

My pulse picks up, and my breathing goes shallow. I still feel confused, but every sensory antenna in my body is on high alert. I hear a dog barking in the distance, a siren from far away, an airplane flying above, a noisy squirrel busy in the backyard angrily chirping at something. I feel the cool draft filter in from the window's edges behind me. In my mind, I'm also replaying Emily's voice from early in the morning—which now seems like days ago: *I know her,* she said, her petite finger straight as an arrow as she pointed at Anne Marie's photo in the paper.

From your daddy? I had asked. She had shaken her head, not because she was picking up on my irritable tone and protecting Reeve.

The conversation now takes on a different meaning. She *didn't* meet Anne Marie through her dad. My mind reels, casting everywhere to try to fit pieces together, but then my trance is broken by the loud report of a gunshot, much too close. It sounds as if it has boomed out from my backyard, right outside my window. Rose's apartment, I think. Fear explodes in my chest.

I tear away from my desk, hitting my leg on its corner, and fly out the back door. I run up the stairs to her apartment, taking the steps two at a time while I grab my service weapon from my shoulder holster. When I reach the top, I throw open Rose's door.

Emily is standing in the center, sheet white, holding a rifle in both of her hands, the weight of the rifle butt hanging toward the floor like she's going to drag it around. "Mommy!" Her face begins to crinkle in fear and fold in on itself when she sees me. She begins to wail.

Instinctually, I do a sweep of the room. Kaylee is kneeling on the couch, alive and well, her eyes large and scared. A coat closet door is open to my right, and I'm assuming that's where Emily must have found the gun. The small kitchen looks clear, and I'm wondering where Rose is when she runs out of her bedroom, sees me with my gun out, and halts in the entryway to the main room. Her hair is up in a beige towel, and it looks as though she has hastily thrown on a pair of jeans and a T-shirt because her jeans are unzipped. She must have just gotten out of the shower, which explains how I got here before her.

"Baby, you're okay." I go to Emily immediately before asking Rose what's going on, sliding my weapon back into its holster. She is scared. Her chin is shaking, and she begins to cry louder. My first priority is getting the gun out of her hands. "Let's give this to Mommy, okay?" I kneel down, trying to take the rifle out of her hands, and she's holding it so tight that I have to pry it from her. "Let go, honey."

She lets it slide from her white-knuckled fingers.

"Where did you get this?"

She looks to the gaping closet. Jackets hang innocently and snow boots and several pairs of shoes lay in piles below. She grabs for me and grips my forearm with both hands so hard that it seems almost impossible for a girl her age to have that kind of strength, that kind of desperation.

I look down at the Winchester .30-30—at the smooth Woodmarbe stock and the twenty-inch barrel. It's a lever action rifle, and on its side is the inscription of the initials *BC*. I recognize it instantly. It's Reeve's. He got it from a friend whose name he doesn't even remember. Berry or Benny Colburn or something, he guessed, but couldn't remember for sure. I feel like I'm on a merry-go-round that won't quit spinning. I look over my shoulder at Rose. "Why do you have Reeve's rifle?"

She begins to shake her head, either in confusion or denial. She looks caught, and suddenly the spinning stops and is replaced by a sensation that the ground has cracked open beneath me into a large black hole that will swallow us all. It's the same feeling I had when my dad would begin to lose his temper and my mom would get a scared mollifying look on her face. Or the day I heard he'd been arrested. Or the time Toni and I left the office after seeing Sara Seafeldt and the other kids pointing and snickering. And then again, years later, on the day I turned down Reeve's marriage proposal and I realized there are too many ways in which wounded people can't make love work. "Rose," I whisper again, "why do you have Reeve's rifle?"

"I . . . I don't . . . I was just taking a quick shower." It comes out as a whimper. "I thought the girls would be fine."

"But why do you have Reeve's rifle?"

"I—I don't know."

"You don't *know*?" I pry myself out of Emily's hands and stand up from kneeling by her to face Rose straight on. Emily tries to grab my arm, but misses and clings to my leg.

She's still crying, and I want to hug her close, to comfort her because she's scared and shocked after she's just unexpectedly fired a gun, the boom of it in her small, sensitive ears. But my training and my instinct to protect her and Kaylee from any more shots accidentally being fired hold me back momentarily. I switch the safety on Reeve's rifle. I'm overwhelmed with relief that there's only a hole somewhere in a wall or a chair and not in her, Rose, or Kaylee, but my mind is reeling, trying to fit the pieces together. I don't want to let the rifle out of my grip for obvious reasons, so I don't lean down to my daughter, who is still crying and gripping my leg. Out of instinct, out of training, I take my hand and push her away.

"Emily, stay," I command, and my heart instantly smarts with the agony of rejecting her when she is so scared, her arms outstretched, her fingers splayed, her face pinched with fear. I turn back to Rose. "Stay exactly where you are, honey," I tell Emily again without taking my eyes off Rose. "Just for a moment."

Emily freezes, still sobbing. Kaylee has also begun to wail from her perch on the sofa.

"Rose?" I'm about to repeat my question, but I see her eyes shift—

the flicker of them toward the door, a glance I've seen many times in assailants who feel caught and who intend to dash. "Don't," I say, but in that instant she bolts for the door that's still ajar and darts out, her feet bare, her towel still wrapped around her head.

"Rose," I yell as she runs out, "stop!"

"Stay here." I turn to Emily and Kaylee and say it like an agent in a serious situation, something transcending a serious-mommy voice, a deeper, stronger command she's never heard. The shock of my order stops Emily from crying, and the room goes silent except for a small whimper from Kaylee. I hate to leave the girls alone, but I can't let Rose go. "I'll only be a minute. Watch some TV."

I hurry outside, taking the rifle with me, shutting the door behind me and bounding down the stairs and across the yard. The beige towel has fallen off Rose's head and lies crumpled in the yard like an alien object among the other stray leaves.

I spot Rose down the street as I cross my lawn. She's running as fast as she can, her bare feet slapping the cold pavement. I chase after her, but I'm way behind, especially carrying the rifle. I make sure again that the safety is set, toss it gently behind some bushes on my neighbor's lawn, and run as fast as I can after her, but she has a good lead, since I took the time to tell the girls to stay put and to close the door behind me. I curse myself for not grabbing my phone off my desk when I went to check things out.

She's almost three blocks ahead now. She takes a corner. When I get to it and round it myself, I don't see her. The street is empty except for a few cars parked in driveways and more newly fallen leaves strewn about. My neighborhood has always been quiet; it's the reason I chose it. It's nothing special, an eclectic mix of houses built anywhere from the 1960s to the present: ranch-style houses mixed in with Cape Cods. Evergreens, arborvitaes, and lilac bushes shroud the sides and fronts of most of the houses on my street. I'm standing between a contemporary slant-roofed house with copious glass and a brick one-story ranch built years ago. "Rose," I yell, "where are you? Come out."

I wait to see or hear something, but it's quiet except for the wind, which has picked up. Another cold front. A dog barks in the distance, but it's not frantic enough to be protective like someone is in its yard. It sounds like the same lazy woof I heard earlier from my desk. "Rose," I call out again.

I stand still and wait, but there's no reply. "Where're you going to go with no shoes and jacket? Come out. Let's talk about this."

It's silent except for the swirl of the wind in the treetops and some normally lazy chimes from the neighboring house tolling more frantically than usual in the strengthening breeze.

"Rose," I yell, "come on! I just want to talk."

A door to the ranch-style house on my right opens, and I swing to face it. Ample bushes hide most of the front of the house. An elderly gray-haired man peers out. "Can I help you, miss?"

"Yes," I say, "you can. Can I please use your phone?"

Reeve

Present—Tuesday

THE WIND WHIPS up my hair and pelts icy cords of half-rain and half-snow into my face. *Sludging,* that's what Ali calls it, and now Emily calls it that too. One time Ali was staring out my cabin window when the rain began to turn to snow. "Sleet," I said. She insisted that it wasn't sleet. "Sleet," she said, "sounds too refined, like tiny crystallized particles of rain. These are sloppy, messy streaks of dripping white snow. You Montanans should have a better word for it."

I remember being proud to be referred to as a Montanan, because that's the way I felt, even though I'm not a native. But Ali, she clearly still saw herself as an outsider.

I've decided to stay one more night, to get some more firewood and to pitch the tent back up when we return. As we pass by the head of the lake to go collect more wood, the "sludge" is intensifying. McKay's off his game, I know, because this isn't our usual routine. We don't usually stay out this long; normally by now we'd be home in my warm cabin.

I make my way to the mouth of the creek that flows out from the lake and head a little way down for protection from the wind and sleet. McKay points his nose up into the air to detect scent. What the hell, I think, why not let him work? Truth is, he needs it.

"Go on," I say, and he bounds ahead, sniffing through the brush and disappearing into it. It doesn't take me long though to see that the riparian cover is too dense. Tangled bushes, trees, and twisted roots snake toward the streambed. Fallen trees crisscross across the forest floor. The wood will be too moist anyway; plus, I smell the kind of

283

putrid scent that could be coming from decaying fall foliage or, worse, from a dead carcass. If there's one thing I don't want to be anywhere near in the woods, it's a dead carcass in the fall when the predators are hungry and possessive.

McKay's still a little ahead of me by the streambed, so I yell for him to come back to turn and go back, but before I've even finished calling his name, he yelps and comes bounding back to me, his fluorescent vest a streak of orange, and zips past me.

"Hey," I say, immediately realizing something is wrong. Terribly wrong. But because it's in a split second, I barely have time to take a step back before a huge roar erupts from the brush. A large grizzly—maybe three to four hundred pounds of silver-haired creature—stands up on its haunches, towering above the brush. I try to take another step back as I reach for my spray, but he bounds at me in a flash. I yell loudly, trying to deter him, but he crashes toward me and swipes at my leg before I can pull the plastic safety off. He tosses me like a rag doll, and I can feel my backside crunch onto rocks and logs. I attempt again to lift my arm to spray, but the bear jumps on top of me and lets loose the loudest roar I've ever heard, a deep, throaty all-encompassing sound that feels like it alone will shatter my insides. McKay comes back and is snarling and barking.

He bites my head, a mallet boring into my scalp, and I think this is it. This is the end. His hot breath pours over me, but then he lets go. He's crushing me with his weight. From underneath, I can see only the underside of his snout and not his eyes. McKay keeps snarling and going at him from the side. The bear goes to bite my head again.

This is it. This is where he snaps my neck or punctures an artery, and I bleed out in these unsympathetic woods before the indifferent faces of these mountains. But McKay is still lunging and growling, and the bear turns and goes for him. It gives me a moment, so I pull my arm up, pull off the safety on the spray I'm still clutching, and manage to scoot myself back a few feet. I think McKay has bitten him somewhere, and I'm about to spray to get him away from McKay, who is snarling, then running away while yelping to protect himself. But when the bear sees how small McKay is in comparison to him, he turns back to face me—the larger threat—and comes for me again.

I hit the nozzle. Orange mist fogs the air, but I have no idea if I've managed to get his face. I'm worried I've only sprayed his chest, but adrenaline catapults him on top of me. I spray again, and he gets off me and retreats immediately. I pick myself up, an intense, dizzying rush filling my head. Blood drips before my eyes, and I can barely see which direction I'm heading, but I begin to back up, still holding the spray in front of me. The ground is wet and slippery. I'm not sure where McKay is; I'm too nervous to take my eyes from the direction the grizzly went.

I'm still backing up with trepidation, placing one foot at a time behind me, afraid to stumble over an exposed root, when I see a small silvery-brown blob cross into some brush ahead. I realize it's not a him, it's a her, and I think she's one angry mama, especially since I've filled the air around her and her cubs with capsaicin. Then I hear a loud thrashing again, and she appears from the dense forest and charges at me again. This time I get off a proper dose, zigzagging from high to low and covering a larger area. She halts, her large body thumping to a heavy stop, then turns and retreats into the brush again.

I stand panting, my chest heaving. I'm gulping in air. McKay lets loose another long whine, and I look down and see him by my side. He doesn't look injured, but I'll have to check him. I begin to back away again in clumsy steps from the brush, but I'm still afraid to turn my back to the bear's direction.

After a moment, I hear some breaking foliage down lower, down the drainage. I realize she doesn't appear to be coming at us anymore. I turn and begin to run back to the camp, but I can barely lift my right leg and I trip and fall to the prickly ground. I look down at it. Deep slashes traverse my thigh, tearing through the fabric and into the muscle, where she's swiped me with her long claws. Blood and some kind of white matter, maybe fasciae, bubble out. Deep cuts slash across my left forearm as well.

I continue on, hobbling forward until I get to my camp. I'm terrified she's going to come back up to the campsite, but I untie the parachute line I've used to tie up my pack with the food supplies. My hands shake so aggressively, it takes me three times as long to undo the knots, but finally I lower it from the tree. I root around in it to find my first aid kit, some scissors, and a roll of gauze, nervously looking over my shoulder and scanning the area in case she comes back.

I'm not sure I want to stay here to dress my wounds at all. Adrenaline is coursing through me and all I want to do is hightail it back down and out of these woods. But I force myself to think. If I start bushwhacking down straightaway, I have no vantage point. At least if she returns here, I'm out in a clearing and I'll have a better shot. I try not to think of how the gusting wind might blow the spray straight to the side, but I realize I can compensate for that a little by adjusting my aim slightly.

I cut away the fabric of my Carhartt from the upper leg and clean the wound the best I can, but it's bleeding profusely. I tie the leftover fabric above the gashes to apply pressure and to hopefully work as a tourniquet, then pour the tiny bottle of rubbing alcohol I have over it. The long, deep gashes are still bleeding, but I apply the gauze anyway, circling it around and around until the entire roll is used.

With still-shaking hands, I wipe my head next with some gauze pads from the kit and apply pressure to those too, but I have only a few left. I use what's remaining on my arm. I remember using some of them on the scratches Anne Marie gave me. They seem so tiny, so inconsequential, compared to these. *Anne Marie.* The vision of her comes back to me and seems to burn in the puncture wounds on my scalp, as if she is the cause of an entire chain of events culminating in a grizzly attack. But then I think of Sam, and that memory burns deeper. Flashes of shooting him, of his life leaving his body, come back to me as I try to dress my wounds, and I realize that Sam's death, not Anne Marie's, is the beginning of everything—the Big Bang setting off the whole chain of events in my life.

The wind begins to scream as it edges around the ridges and funnels into the canyon where the lake is. The sludge is all snow now and blows sideways. It's beginning to collect into a thin film on the ground, the logs, and the colorful rocks by the lake. More blood has begun to stream down my face and into my eyes. I wipe it with another shirt I have in my pack. On some level, I've asked for this nastiness. I've been scared, but mostly I've been stubborn. Who do I think I am, traipsing around out in these mountains in the fall, acting like I'm doing my job when ultimately I'm just running from the police, running from myself?

I check McKay next, running my hands over his entire body, looking for wounds. He's perfectly fine and uninjured, but he's trembling too, and he keeps trying to lick the blood on my leg. "You lucky bastard." I push him away from my leg and manage a half-grin at him, but the pull of my own smile on my torn flesh stings enough to take my breath away. "How did you come out of this unscathed?" I ask him anyway.

He tilts his head, trying to read me, his whole body still shaking like mine, either from the trauma of the bear experience or the cold, or both. The temperature has dropped by at least fifteen to twenty degrees.

"We have to go down these mountains," I say. "We can't stay here. I need to get to a hospital to get stitches." I know McKay has no idea what I'm saying, but his large liquid eyes look up at me like I'm crazy.

"I know," I say. "But we have to."

Ali

Present—Tuesday

AT FIRST, WHEN I went into the old man's house, I wasn't sure I wanted to call 911 without fully understanding what was going on, before I could admit something so awful and impossible to myself. But now if there's one thing I'm certain of, it's that Rose is guilty. Guilty of what exactly, I don't know. Whether she's an accomplice or Anne Marie's killer is the question, but the answer isn't something I can find out on my own. That had been my first impulse, of course, but I'm already in deep with Shackley, and I realize it would be worse if it looks like I am somehow covering for her.

I leave the old man, Mr. Desoto, and thank him for letting me use his phone. On my way back, I intend to pick up Reeve's rifle, which I hastily hid in the bushes outside. But first, I stand on the sidewalk outside Mr. Desoto's house and look around. The neighborhood is quiet except for the wind chimes.

"Rose," I whisper, "what in the hell have you done?"

I take a few steps when I hear a kid's voice, loud and excited from across the street. "Mom, Mom, there's someone in my tree house."

I swing around. I hear a screen door slam behind him. I can't see the boy because he's yelling from a backyard, but it sounds close. I dash across the street to the house across from me, where I think I heard his voice, and go around back. A tree house stands on long wooden stilts in the back corner of the yard next to an apple tree. The day is fading fast, and a pale sky and spindly branches frame the rickety-looking wooden contraption—a tiny square hut. Rotten, pocked

288

red apples skirt out from the tree next to it over the dead, matted grass.

"Hey," the mom says to me as she comes out the back door. I've already set one foot on the first rung of the ladder leading up to it. I look over my shoulder at them. "What's going on?" The boy—maybe eight or nine—stands to her side, lagging behind for protection.

"There was someone in your tree house?" I ask him.

He nods.

"A woman?"

He nods again.

"Did she leave?"

He shakes his head.

"Stay there," I tell them both, then climb the narrow wooden ladder. I have my gun ready as I approach a three-foot plank outside the child-sized door. "Rose," I say, "are you in there?"

If she is, she doesn't answer.

I'm fully aware that if I enter a small space with my back and head bent over, she will have the advantage and could easily hit me with something or even push me back. I could go back down and stand at the base to guard the place and wait for backup. But I have to know if she's even inside. She could have come down right after the boy yelled and ran to his mom. I was here quickly, though, and would have seen her if she did because she would have had to navigate the narrow ladder.

I have to go in. It's Rose. It's just Rose. She wouldn't hurt me. "Rose," I say firmly, "I'm going to come in. I've got my gun out, so please, okay, please don't do anything stupid."

Silence again. I hear the boy whisper something to his mom from across the lawn. I crouch down rather than bending over so that my head is up and waddle like a duck up to the small entrance. I swing open the faded wooden-planked door. It makes a loud creak, and I sit on my haunches, waiting, my elbow cocked with my gun poised. I scooch a little closer into the entryway and peek in. Twilight is just beginning, and pale slivers make their way in from the open door and the open slits between the wood planks. My eyes take a moment to adjust, but I see her. She sits in the corner, her arms wrapped tightly around her knees. She looks cold and childish, even though I know how tall she is.

"Rose," I say, "why won't you answer me?"

She still doesn't respond. I scoot the rest of the way in and kneel in front of the small door. "Okay," I say, "you're scared."

"I'm not scared," she says. It comes out more as a mumble, but I catch it. She clears her throat as if this were the first time she's spoken all day, even though we were chatting and joking around about the girls less than an hour ago.

"Then what's this about?"

She shakes her head in little vacillations, indicating that she has no desire to talk to me.

"This has something to do with Anne Marie Johnson?"

She stares at the wooden planks before her, her arms still hugging her legs. Her hair is still wet and hangs in clumped-up strands around her face. Dirt smudges mark her pale toes. The dankness and the dying wood give off a fusty smell. She doesn't shake her head, so I take it as a yes, that it does have something to do with Anne Marie. "Look," I say, "this is silly. You're sitting in some kid's tree house, and you're clearly freezing. Let's go home and get you some warm clothes."

"You don't understand," she says. "You think you're so smart, but you don't understand shit." Her voice comes out like a snarl, and again it reminds me of Toni when she told me the same thing when I tried to help her. It hits me like a flash of light that it might not be only Rose's laugh that reminds me of my sister. There might be other things: deep, scary things like the ability to lie and steal and throw other people under the bus to get your way.

"Okay, what don't I understand?"

"Nothing." She sounds petulant, like a teenager talking to her mother. But there's more than peevishness in her voice. There's a cold, hard bite to it that reminds me of criminals I've arrested in the past. This is insane, I think. It's just Rose. I've known Rose for four years. She takes care of my little girl so I can be on call most days of the week.

"Rose," I say, my voice sounding more hurt than I want it to. I want to sound cool and collected, but I can hear the strain of it through the thickening of my throat. "What's this about?"

She looks up from the plank floor and stares at me. Her eyes gleam like black angry slits in a white papery cutout of a face in the dim light. Her lips part, and I think for a second that maybe she's going to answer, but then I hear a screen door open—the same one I heard earlier—and voices from across the lawn. I recognize one of them: Herman. He's saying, "I'd like for both of you to go back inside and stay there, please." I presume to the mom and her son. Footsteps shuffle across the grass and through fallen leaves and dead apples, then stop below us.

"Agent Paige," Herman shouts up, using my last name as we would on any scene outside the personal space of our office.

"I'm here," I yell back.

"Are you in danger?"

"No," I yell down, keeping my eyes on Rose. "Can you give me a minute?" *It's just Rose. It's just Rose,* I repeat in my head. But I can't deny it: she ran. Plus, there's something deeply disturbing about the anger in her eyes. I can feel them burning in the small dank space as if they're flames emanating outward, their fervor reaching me and singeing my skin. For the first time in four years, I sense that I have deeply misjudged the person whom I've hired to care for my daughter. The thought snatches my breath away.

"I'm coming up," Herman yells from below. "The county's here too."

"Don't bother," Rose calls out in a firm, loud voice, almost as if she's bored. She puts one hand down on the plank to push herself up. "I'm coming down."

"Paige?" Herman questions the move.

"Yes, it's fine." I shuffle to the side, keeping my gun cocked before me and letting her pass. "Rose is . . ." I say, then pause and rethink my word choice. I know I need to start somewhere. "The subject," I call out loud and clear with my authority voice, "is unarmed and is voluntarily coming out of the tree-house door and down the ladder. I'll be watching from up here. She knows better than to run again."

Reeve

Present—Tuesday

As THE PALE light settles behind the jagged edges of the darkening mountains, I root around in my pile of wood I've collected for a fire because I remember a long pole-shaped piece that I'd thought would make a good walking stick when I'd collected it. My head, forearm, and thigh are bleeding heavily and the blood is soaking through the layers of bandages I've applied. It oozes down my exposed right leg in red rivulets. I look around at my camping gear and know I won't make it out if I try to carry it all on my back while limping. I decide to leave some of it behind to lighten my load, but I know I'll need my sleeping bag and tent because there's a chance we won't make it out if the storm makes it unbearable to proceed or if my leg gives out completely. I figure we're at least fourteen miles from my truck through rugged terrain.

"Come on, McKay," I say as I bend over to pick up the walking stick, ignoring the pain in my chest and back. The bear didn't bite me or scratch me there, but I think I've broken a rib or two and hurt my back when she flung me onto the ground. McKay comes over, whining, sniffing my leg for the tenth time, and trying to lick the wounds through the bandages. "No," I command, and he stops and looks up at me and points his nose up into the air again, trying to read it for signs of danger. I stand, straining to hear through the wind and the brush for any indication that she's returning, but I think she wants to get her cubs away from us just as much as we want to get away from her. But still, I've heard all the horror stories: the grizzly that came back for a second and third round until he was good and sure that the man was not a threat, and the grizzlies that stalked photographers whom they deemed threatening because, after all, the photographers were stalking them first.

Bushwhacking down the mountain is difficult. In an effort to stay clear of the grizzly's path, I've veered in the opposite direction and have managed to get myself mixed up on a steep slope that is thick with tamped-down alder branches from previous years of wind and snow. They've grown sideways against the ground, the roots from the shrubs sprouting out horizontally in parts and covering the forest floor. They're challenging to hobble across, and with the snow, they're slick and treacherous. McKay whines his disapproval. He's worried. Very worried. He sticks next to my leg like glue, making it even more arduous to walk. "You big baby," I say, "it's over now. She's gone."

But I don't know that for certain. I *think* she's gone, that she's going to stay clear of us, that she was just as scared of us as we were of her. "It wasn't her fault; she was protecting her cubs," I say to McKay, but more for myself. "They're programmed to charge if they're caught off guard. It's instinctual," I continue in a breathy voice that sounds alien to me. "It's going to be okay," I tell my dog as soothingly as I can muster.

Suddenly every part of me simply wants to get down the mountain, to my truck and to the hospital. The will to survive beats strongly with each throb of my head. I take another step, trying to steady my stick on solid ground, but I can't find purchase and slip on one of the slick roots. I crash down to my side, my rib cage screaming at me, and slide some thirty feet down the slope. I hear myself call out, and when I come to a stop, McKay bounds after me and practically lands on top of me. I swear from the pain, grit my teeth, and hit the ground with my fist. The agony in my leg reverberates up into my hip, and I wonder if I've done something to the joint. I stand carefully and try to walk, or limp, as I've been doing. I've lost my walking stick, and my tent has slipped out of the looped straps under my pack. I can't see it and figure it's under some brush farther up where I fell. I check for my sleeping bag and am relieved it's still attached securely to my pack. I'm in no shape to hike back up to get the tent, so I'll have to rely on a lean-to and my sleeping bag if it comes to that.

I stand up and test my leg. It's no worse than it was, so I gingerly continue down the steep slope, grabbing onto prickly bushes to keep from slipping.

When I finally reach the bottom of the first slope and feel the nasty storm ripping across the ridges and rushing through the canyon, the danger I'm in with my injuries begins to sink in. My wounded leg begins to feel numb, but I can't tell if it's from severed nerves or the rapidly dropping temperatures. The cold that began in my feet and hands has crept to my shoulders and is now burrowing into my chest like a deep well. It's numbing the pain from my broken ribs, but I know it's a bad sign. Each breath I take is an effort and I've been spitting blood onto the collecting snow. I need to find a place to stop and make a fire, and I begin cursing myself for not staying put where I already had a camp set up just because I was afraid she'd come back. If my injuries take me now, it won't matter if I'm a few miles down from that desolate tarn or not.

So, I think, this is what it comes down to. You make a horrible mistake when you're a kid, make a mess of your life, try like hell to get it back in order until finally you end up in the same place: dead, a casualty. Sam was a casualty of human folly, and now I would become a casualty of nature's indifference.

The branches of the alders wrap wetly around me, jabbing and stinging my injuries. Wetness has long ago seeped into my one good pant leg and through the bandaging I've applied. Through sweat and blood-filled eyes, I peer through the spindly twigs up at the great rocky ridges to the north tilting toward plateaus below. Night is falling around them and they appear like giant tidal waves about to crash upon me. I have this image of them crumbling, of dirt and rock rolling down in great waves like a lava flow. Then I picture the ground opening beneath me and swallowing me while I try to hold on to the thin, slippery tines of the alders.

A pit forms in my stomach as I imagine what Ali will have to tell Emily when I don't return home. I can see clearly now how my childhood disaster has always separated me from normal life. Suddenly it's obvious how I've used nature to keep that veneer in place. But I've been beyond foolish. Being solitary isn't all it's cracked up to be. Some people say there's a difference between solitude and loneliness—that solitude implies health and inner peace, a worthy aspiration. But now I realize that kind of solitude is possible only if you're connected to others in the first place. If you've already cut yourself off from everyone around you, then solitude will be your destruction.

McKay looks up at me expectantly. "This way," I say to him. I begin to move again, taking one careful step at a time down the next ridgeline.

Ali

Present—Tuesday

AFTER ROSE CAME down from the tree house, Herman cuffed her and escorted her to Brander and Reynolds, who were already on the scene. Before I gave my statement, I went to check on the girls. They were frightened, huddled on the couch right where I had told them to stay. I brought them to our house and dazedly made them toast and macaroni and cheese, then held them close to me while they ate until Kaylee's mom arrived to pick them both up. I had called and asked if she could return the favor and take Emily home with her. Still shaken up from firing the rifle, Emily was clingy and wanted to stick with me, but I promised her everything would be all right, that she was fine and it was just an accident. She looked at me with her dark eyes, glassy and frightened, and I saw Reeve in them for a moment, but it quickly passed, and she became brave and said she was fine going with Kaylee, that it would be fun to have a sleepover on a school night. I helped her pack an overnight bag, kissed her good-bye, and told her I'd see her after school the next day. I had a feeling tonight was going to be a long one.

Thirty minutes later, Herman, Shackley, and I are in the observation room with Commander Vance watching Brander and Reynolds try to talk to Rose. It's not working. She sits with her arms across her chest, giving them the silent treatment. They are trying to wait it out, but her petulance practically radiates through the small room, through the one-way, and into the observation room. I brought her socks, shoes, and a sweat shirt from her apartment when I came, and when I reached in the coat closet for a jacket, I remembered what Gretchen told me about the wool fibers, so I put her black wool coat in a plastic bag and brought another one for her instead. I gave the bag with the coat to Brander.

Rose is wearing the clothes I brought, and her hair has dried in dark, lank streaks down the sides of her face. Her cheekbones are pale and sharp. She looks like an entirely different woman to me, and I have to remind myself, This is Rose. Rose! There must be a better explanation than the one I've been mulling over.

After Reynolds took Rose to the county building, and after I got Emily and Kaylee taken care of, Shackley had pulled me aside and told me that, given the circumstances, we could hold off on our meeting about my misconduct for a bit. In the meantime, he planned to stick around and observe. "Don't mind me," he had said, then took a seat in the corner, making everyone nervous with his commanding presence.

In an interview, we want the truth, not a confession, not an admission. The truth. But to get the truth is sometimes very tricky. There's a certain method and rationale to interviewing, and through the Bureau, all of us agents have taken courses on it. I'll admit, I'm not very good at it. I'm too impatient, too direct, and anger too easily. But Reynolds—maybe I'm biased—he appears to be even worse than me. I think back to watching him with Reeve, how he could take a law-enforcement-weary guy like Reeve and make him so uncomfortable that he refuses to tell the whole story. That's the opposite of what we're supposed to do.

Our job is to convince the subject that confiding in us is in his or her own self-interest, so we do that by finding an angle or an in. We try to find out what resonates by watching their body language and avoid coming on too strong, the way Reynolds did with Reeve, because the last thing you want is for the subject to close down. If someone is brought in for embezzlement, you might say, *I know you're having tough times; you wouldn't be the first person to borrow money.* Of course, it's not borrowing, it's stealing. But you're seeing if you can get them to soften with a little empathy. Herman's good at it, because with Herman, everyone feels like they've found a long-lost protective uncle. With me, people feel like they've just met an accusatory stranger.

Reynolds is telling Rose that since she's the one in possession of a weapon used to kill Anne Marie Johnson, she's obstructing justice if she doesn't talk, and that she needs to talk soon. The ballistics expert has come into the crime lab and confirmed that the slug they found in Anne Marie Johnson has land and groove impressions that show it originated from Reeve's rifle. I turn to Vance and say, "This isn't working. That's my nanny in there. I've known her for four years. Let me go in."

"Absolutely not," Brander says. "Are you kidding? That's a major conflict of interest." He ignores his own chain of command and turns to Shackley, which grates on me, because I'm thinking the only reason he'd look to Shackley for his take over his own commander is because he's male. I see Shackley shake his head and give a single heavy blink to signal that it's not a good idea. Vance catches Shackley's headshake and agrees. "I don't think that's a wise idea," she says to me. "Even if you were to get something out of her, it would get torn to shreds in court because of your connection to her. I can hear it now—the defense suggesting you planted the weapon in the nanny's apartment to protect your kid's father or, worse, yourself."

Shackley's my supervisor, and given my position, I should stay quiet. I should care that he doesn't think it's a good idea, but I don't. My whole world feels like it's unraveling, that on that cold gray day when Reeve called me, a piece of yarn was plucked free and now it just keeps unspooling. "That's crazy," I respond to Vance's comment. "Rose is the last person I'd ever frame; she's a lifeline for me." The room goes quiet, with all eyes on me. I'm not sure if they're considering the idea that maybe I did frame my own nanny, or if they're looking at me because I've just gotten personal in front of a group of people who barely know me.

Rose is still sulking in front of Reynolds, and I feel a shot of anger. I turn back and face them. "If I framed Rose, why would she be refusing to speak? She'd be surprised, in shock, but she's not. She clearly knew it was there. She ran and hid, for god's sake."

No one responds, and I feel like an idiot, but I don't care. I've said my piece.

Finally, after about ten more minutes of painful silence and useless prodding by Reynolds, he scoots his chair back from the table and stands. "We're getting nowhere," he says to Rose. "I guess you'll just have to spend the night in jail." He collects his cell phone and his file and heads for the door.

Finally Rose speaks. "Wait."

Reynolds turns to look at her.

"I'll talk, but not to you."

He stands there waiting for more.

"I'll talk to the black guy," she says.

"Agent Marcus?"

"Yeah, I'll talk to him."

In the observation room, I turn to look at Herman. He doesn't look fazed, just continues sitting, one hand on top of a leg, the other draping over the table he's sitting beside. Rose knows Herman just as Emily does because he's been over for barbecues and other dinners over the years. She enjoys his company—probably finds comfort in his presence like I do, like Emily does. And it hits me—she's no dummy. She's making sure things are on her terms. How could I have missed it? My daughter's nanny is much more calculating than I ever expected.

"Okay," Reynolds says to her, "I'll see if he's available."

And just like that, Reynolds returns to the observation room and grabs Brander, and the two go out in the hallway to speak privately. I go to Herman immediately, pull up a chair, and scoot in so close to him I can smell his aftershave, something lemony that I've smelled a million times in our office, but up close, it's strange, like I'm invading his space. I don't care, though. "Herman," I whisper, ignoring Shackley's watchful eyes in the corner, "if they let you go in, please let me communicate with you. I know Rose, and I'll know when she's telling the truth and when she's lying."

Herman stares at me blankly, his face a statue's. It suggests that he's entirely unimpressed with me and anything I have to say at this point, but I know it takes work to freeze his features like that, effort borne of anger and disappointment in me.

"Come on, Herman," I press on. "Just keep your phone handy. I *know* her."

"Ali." He looks me dead in the eye. "You obviously *don't* know her like you think you do."

He's right and it stings. He's furious, I tell myself, that's why he's saying this. That's all. But he's also right. If my theory is correct, I don't know this woman at all, and I cannot let myself go there. There's no time for self-analysis or self-pity. There's only time to find the truth.

Earlier, after I first arrived to give my statements to Brander and Reynolds, I sat down with Herman and admitted everything: that I'd taken his file, that I'd been researching all of the names of people Anne Marie Johnson had interviewed in prison, cross-checking for people who might have something to do with the Smith case, and that when I saw the name Vince Giles Reiko, I'd recognized it.

"You what?" he had said, pulling his head back in disgust. "You stole the file from me?"

I had looked at him without moving a muscle. "I'm sorry," I had said, but even I could hear that it had sounded pathetic, a single drip of water on parched, cracked soil.

"I can't believe you'd do that, after you've specifically been asked to stay off the case."

"I know, Herman, but it's just too close to home."

"That's precisely *why* you've been ordered to stay out of it."

"But it had gotten out of hand with this BOLO and Reeve holing up in the woods. I had to do something. Herman, listen to me. I know in my heart that Reeve did not kill Anne Marie Johnson."

Herman had taken it in, staring at me with disbelief, like a spouse on the receiving end of an infidelity confession.

I felt horrible and wanted to melt into the floor when looking at his hurtful stare. I knew things would never be the same between us, but the sense that things would never be the same in any part of my life anyway hung in the air around me—and still does—so I had pushed on. "I know. I know you're disgusted with me. I might be too if the roles were reversed, but what if you felt like you were backed into a wall? What if you felt like you *had* to do something for your family, for your sister, for your niece or nephew?"

Herman's eyes had flashed at me, and I could see I had struck a chord.

"Please," I had continued, "you want to know what I'm thinking, right?"

He had sat for a moment before answering, as if he was considering if he did want to hear what I had to say or not, even rubbing his chin and narrowing his eyes. Finally he had given a single nod, and I had felt myself let out a pent-up breath. I laid it out for him: I told him I was certain Anne Marie Johnson had interviewed Rose about the incident with Vince Reiko, that Emily had even seen her, and that if my suspicions were correct, Vince Reiko had given Anne Marie Johnson information that Rose didn't want her to have.

I had already told this to Reynolds and Brander and asked them to have someone visit Reiko at the state prison. I had told them all that Emily had recognized Anne Marie's picture in the paper, said she knew her, but not through Reeve. I had told them that I thought perhaps Anne Marie came to visit Rose when she was watching Emily. I theorized that Rose eventually agreed to talk to her, and found out that Anne Marie had been interviewing the man who had shot her adopted sister. "I think you need to talk to Reiko," I had pleaded with them all, but mainly with Brander and Vance. "He'll have answers."

"Why should we believe your theories, Agent Paige?" Brander had asked. A simple question that said it all. I had blown any respect I'd earned in this community of law enforcement professionals.

"Look," I had pushed on, "Emily confirmed for me that she met Anne Marie through Rose."

"You know as well as I do that five-year-olds don't make reliable witnesses."

"I know, I know, but come on. Rose ran. She freaked and she ran. That's not the behavior of someone innocent." As I spoke, I realized my words were implicating Reeve too, so I rushed to add: "Plus, the rifle was in her possession."

"I already interviewed her about Reiko," he had said. "The day I came to your house."

"You did?"

"Yes, we already knew from the victim's cell phone records that she had made contact with your nanny."

So they had been more thorough than I'd given them credit for. "But if Rose didn't have anything to hide, why didn't she tell me all of that? Especially after you questioned her? She specifically told me that you asked her only about Reeve."

Brander had agreed it was strange. He had promised to read the notes again and to talk to Vince Reiko while Reynolds continued to interrogate Rose.

Now, sitting by Herman, the scent of fresh citrus from his after-shave surrounding us, I'm comforted that he'll get a shot at interrogating her. "Fine," I say to Herman, "you're right. I don't know her like I think I do, and yes, that scares the shit out of me, to think that . . ." I peter out. I can't finish because I'll choke up: *to think that I've let a possible murderer take care of my daughter for the past several years is unimaginable.* I look down at the tan industrial-grade carpet in the observation room instead. "But you'll listen to me, right? You'll check my texts?"

Herman doesn't answer, just stares at me, unblinking.

Finally Brander and Reynolds reenter the room. "Agent Marcus," Brander says. "If you're up for it, the subject would like to see you."

. . .

A half an hour later, we all watch Herman go in and take a seat across from Rose. She's been sitting with her head down on the table as if she's resting, but I can tell she's not. Her hand is tucked in where we can't see it, but I can tell by the tiny movement of her jaw that she is biting a thumbnail. When Herman comes in, she instantly raises her head, her thumbnail still in her mouth. She looks very young, immature. She seems reassured when she sees him, dropping her hand from her face and relaxing her shoulders some.

Herman says hello to her and turns the recorder back on. "I assume you've already been asked about the recording of these exchanges, correct?"

She nods, and he pulls out a chair and takes a seat. "You've had an interesting evening."

"Yeah." She sighs. "It's been crazy. I—I don't know how it's come to this." She looks around. "I haven't done anything wrong. I just didn't want to talk to them, though. I've heard how cops can be. I wanted to talk to you. I don't have anything to hide. I just want to speak to someone I'm comfortable talking to, that's all." She speaks as if she's relieved to be able to finally tell someone something.

"That's perfectly fine, Rose," Herman says. "I don't mind at all."

"I can't believe I'm sitting here over something as silly as Reeve asking me to keep his rifle."

"The rifle belongs to Reeve?"

"Yes, it's his."

"What's Reeve's last name? For the recorder?"

"Landon," she says. "Reeve Landon. Emily's father. Anyway, he asked me to keep it."

"Why did he do that?" Herman asks.

"He wanted to get it out of his life, away from Emily. You know, with his record and all." Her eyes are wide and blue as the summer sky.

"His record?" Herman plays dumb.

"Yeah, don't you know? Hasn't she told you?"

"Told me what?"

"That he shot a kid when he was young."

"I see." He says this like it doesn't affect him one way or another, and Rose sits and stares at him, waiting for more questions. It's obvious to me where she's going with it. She's going to put this back on Reeve. After all, it is his gun. It's an easy out, and a part of me wonders if they planned this together. The thought almost forces me out of my chair, but I stay seated. "When did he give you the rifle?" Herman asks.

"About a week ago, when my car broke down. He needed me to pick up Emily and take her to dance class for him because he was going to be late in the field that day. He said he wouldn't be using his truck anyway, so he let me have it for the day, you know, while my car was in the shop."

"What day was that?"

"Tuesday. Last week. And when I returned his truck and he gave me a ride to my car at the Ford place in Whitefish, he asked if I'd do him a favor. If I'd take the gun for him, just to store it. He said the lock on the metal case of his truck that he normally kept it in was broken. He said he didn't want to sell it, and he didn't want to give it to Ali to store, since her gun cabinet wasn't big enough for a rifle."

Herman sits listening, his arms relaxed and folded across himself.

It's true, I think. She did borrow his truck on Tuesday. I remember Emily saying that Rose picked her and Reeve up in Daddy's truck and then they gave her a ride to her car after school. But it makes no sense. If he wanted to protect Emily, why would he give a gun to her babysitter?

"So," Herman says, "you've had the gun since last Tuesday?"

"No, no. That was just when he *asked* me. He couldn't give it to me then because it was back at his cabin."

Now I know she's lying. Reeve has never kept a gun in the house, ever. Not even before Emily was born. I remember when his neighbor Ron's pipes busted, and Reeve told Ron he could come over and stay until the next day when he could get them repaired. Ron had wanted to bring his hunting rifle inside with him, and Reeve wouldn't let him. *Sorry, no guns in my house ever,* he had said. *I don't even keep mine in here.* Wallace had argued with him, but Reeve was insistent. He let me bring mine in only because he knew I had to keep my service gun with me at all times, but he hated it. It was one more source of unspoken conflict between us in the long run.

She's lying about that, I text. *Trust me. Reeve has never allowed a firearm in his cabin. He always keeps it locked in the back of his truck.* Herman's back is to me, so I can't tell if he looks at my text, but I think I see a slight tilt of his head forward as he glances down at his phone.

"So when did he give it to you?"

"When he came over on Wednesday, the night after he was interviewed by the county. He came to see Ali and pick up McKay."

I think back to that night. I don't remember his leaving for any length of time. He never left my or Emily's sight long enough to even give it to her.

"How did that work?"

"Easy." Her eyes shift to the glass, and I wonder if she knows I'm there, watching her, ready to catch her in a lie. A part of me wants to believe every word she says, but the way she ran, the look on her face in that boy's tree house—it's all too strange and surreal, and her story now doesn't make sense. There's a side of Rose that I don't know about, but as much as it hurts me, it's unraveling before me, and I can't deny it.

"When he left to go home," she continues. "He texted me and asked me to come down. He got it out of that metal bin behind the cab and gave it to me. I didn't think anything of it." She puts her hand to her mouth. "If I'd known, if I'd had any clue that it was used to kill someone, I would have taken it straight to the police. I told him I'd keep it stored away until he got a gun cabinet."

I think back to that night more specifically, remembering how I walked Reeve out to his truck, his face tired and sagging, the skin around his eyes russet from rubbing them, the stubble on his face blooming after a long day at the station. I had handed him the note with an attorney's number. I think harder. The only other times Reeve was alone were when I went out to grab McKay's food and left him in the house and when he went out to fetch his backpack, which had his training scat in it for McKay. But both times, it was done in a flash. And as far as when he left, as Rose is claiming, I escorted him out. Unless, I think, he circled back later. But I would have heard his truck then or seen the lights from either Emily's room or my office, and I don't remember that. I text Herman: *I walked Reeve out to his truck to say good night. I watched him drive away. She's lying.*

"Then why did you run?" Herman asks.

"Because . . ." She shrugs and blinks several times nervously and holds her arms like she's hugging herself. She looks smaller than usual. In all the years I've known her, I've never seen her sit like this, folded in on herself like she's a victim. "Because I felt bad. I had forgotten about having it when I told the girls that I was just going to take a quick shower. I was so scared when I heard that shot and then it hit me that I had Reeve's gun in the coat closet, that I was keeping it for him. I had no idea it was loaded, that Emily would find it and fire a shot. I felt awful, and Ali, you know Ali, Herman. How she can be, you know, how crazy she can get."

This catches me by surprise. I feel it slash to my core. I have been known for being terse but not unreasonable, not a live wire. But Rose, she's trying to play it like she's truly afraid of me. She's no more afraid of me than my sister, Toni, ever was. I want to protest out loud, to tell the others in the room that she's lying, but I don't even dare steal a glance at them. My jaw is so tight, it feels like it might crack.

"She could barely keep her temper over the littlest things, you know, like when I've let Emily drink part of a soda, and she's freaked out, screaming at me and yelling at me. She's . . . she's, well, she's just so intimidating." She raises her fingers to her face and delicately sets them on her left cheekbone near her eye, intimating she's been hit before, suggesting *I've* hit her there before. I'm fuming now, a tide of sheer hate roiling up in me like a megawave. I want to pound my fist on the table, but I know if I do or say anything, I'm playing into what she is claiming. None of it is true. I've never raised my voice to Rose, even when she *has* disappointed me in how she's handled a situation with Emily. Like when she was late to pick Emily up from school. She was with some friends and lost track of time. I cut her slack because it had never happened before and she had recently turned twenty-one and was celebrating. I shake my head and swallow my anger. I chance a glance at Shackley, as if I have one colleague in the room, one confidant, and mouth the words *She's lying*.

He simply shifts his gaze from me back to the interrogation room without acknowledging my gesture. I feel completely alone.

In the room, Herman is nodding, agreeing with her. I know he's just being a good interviewer, finding common ground and egging her on, but because he's angry at me, I guess a side of him must be enjoying it. "She's a pistol all right," Herman adds.

"You don't know the half of it." She looks down at her hands, which are now laced together demurely in her lap. "One time, because I didn't get Emily in her pajamas and to bed early enough before she came home from work, she, well, she . . ." She touches her face again, and I realize she's good. Really good. Someone who can tell falsehoods like that and even know when to suggest rather than actually say it out loud. Because if she did say it out loud, if she said the words *One time she actually hit me*, it would sound ridiculous coming out of her mouth because of the very fact that it's such a bald-faced lie.

"That's such bullshit," I whisper, no longer able to contain myself. Vance, Brander, Reynolds, and Shackley all look at me, but I can't tell if they heard what I said even though it came out with venom. They all turn back to the glass without commenting. I feel like I'm trapped in a bizarre nightmare or a strange hallucination.

"She what?" Herman prods.

"She, well, she slapped me." She looks down at the table.

"Slapped you?" Herman asks.

"Yes, I know. Crazy. It's sounds crazy, but that's what she is."

"And you reported her?"

"No, are you kidding? She's an FBI agent. I'm not going to go against *that*."

"So why haven't you quit the job?"

"Because I need the money and she pays me well. Four hundred a week for hanging out with a little girl that I adore. I love Emily, so I put up with that kind of craziness. I want to protect Emily from her."

Now I can barely stay seated. Bile rises up in my throat at the mention of my daughter's name within such a heap of lies. I can't keep my leg still. It's bobbing up and down, making my heel thrum on the floor. I want to get up and go pound on the glass, but I realize how bad that will look, like I really *can't* control my temper. She's crossing lines I've never imagined, suggesting I'm abusive. In my mind I see my father smacking my mom across the face and her falling back into the kitchen table with a frantic look. I may be known for telling it like it is or for even losing my temper and swearing like a sailor on the job, but if there's one thing in this world I would never, ever do, it is hit someone unless it was in self-defense for my job. I would never be like my father. Ever.

I remember wanting badly to beat my sister up—can remember it raging up in me from the depths like fire in a dragon's belly—when she lied about her drug use to my mom right in front of me and claimed that the bottle of pills my mom had found in our bathroom belonged to me. But even then, with the fury bellowing up inside me, I knew I couldn't hit her. How dare Rose—this woman I've entrusted with my little girl—sit there primly, telling flagrant lies to Herman, to people I work with. I've taken chances, lost Herman's and perhaps Shackley's trust, but I've misplaced it in my efforts to protect my family, Emily and Reeve, and even Rose, not because I'd ever hurt them.

"If what you're saying is true," Herman says, "I'm very sorry to hear that."

If what you're saying is true.

Herman's throwing us both a bone. For me, he's getting it on tape that there's no proof of such things, and I'm thankful that he's not falling hook, line, and sinker for her nonsense, but he's also trying to empathize with her. In my anger, I've forgotten he has his phone. I text again. *The things she's claiming are blatant lies. None of it is true.* I'm aware that Reynolds and Brander, maybe even Shackley, think it very well could be, but I can't care about them right now. I have to push on. Herman has to believe me. Meanwhile Rose nods, satisfied, then looks down at her hands.

Ask her why Anne Marie Johnson visited her, I text. I still don't know for certain if he's reading them or not, but I have to do something.

"How about a polygraph?" I say to the others in the room. "Ask her if she'll take a polygraph."

"Let's see if she ends up asking for an attorney or not. If she's not lying, her attorney will tell her it's in her best interest to take one."

"Then why wait? Why not have Herman explain that to her?"

"We'll see," Reynolds says, giving me a cold stare from where he's standing next to the wall, a cue to butt out. I get the feeling he's about to say, *She shouldn't even be in here,* but given the fact that I apprehended her, he's staying quiet for now. I turn back to the glass.

Herman sets his arms on the table and leans toward her. "Rose, why did Anne Marie Johnson visit you?" He *is* reading my texts. He's not ignoring me. Relief washes over me and settles my anger slightly.

"Who?"

"You know who. Anne Marie Johnson. We have evidence that she visited you. Turns out, Anne Marie is an excellent note-taker."

Rose's face goes hard, her jaw clenching, and I can see she wasn't expecting the question from Herman, or at least not in the way it was phrased, with the absolute knowledge that Anne Marie visited her.

"Rose," Herman says, "can you answer me?"

"She called. She wanted to interview me because my family lost someone, a foster sister of mine, when I was sixteen. Said she was writing some book, interviewing victims of gun tragedies, that's all. I already told that Brander guy that."

"Yes." Herman checks his notes. "But you told him you only spoke to her on the phone. In her notes, she says she visited you."

She shrugs. "Same difference. I told her I didn't want to delve into old history. It was stupid, her wanting to talk to all these different people about gun violence. What good would that do?"

"Not much," Herman agrees, trying to walk the tightrope between being on her side and nudging her to tell the truth. "She interviewed a lot of folks. Some in prison too. And she interviewed the man who was convicted for your sister's murder, a Vince Reiko. Is that correct?"

"How should I know if she interviewed him?"

"Let me rephrase that: Is it correct that Vince Reiko is the man convicted in the killing of your sister, Kimberly Farrows?"

"Yes, that's him. And she wasn't my real sister. I mean, she was a *foster* sister."

I make a note of her tone when she says the word *foster*. There's disdain there that I've never heard from her before. I turn to Brander, who is sitting next to Commander Vance in two chairs near the glass. They look like they're simply lined up to watch a movie. Reynolds is still standing, leaning against the wall. "Have you spoken to him yet?"

"Yes, we have." He offers me no more, his face going blank.

"Good," I say. I'm dying to know more. I hope they told Herman whatever they know so he can use it in there with Rose, but I don't push my luck. "Thank you."

"Did you know Vince Reiko before he shot Kim?" Herman asks.

"No." She looks into Herman's eyes, unflinching. The stare is too set in stone, too practiced-looking, her chin held high and jutting forward. I'm positive she is lying. "Of course I'd never met him before."

"That's not what he says." Herman folds his arms casually on his chest. "That's not what he told Anne Marie Johnson."

"He's a criminal," she says. "Why would you believe him?"

"Because he's already been convicted. He doesn't gain anything by making that up. He's already confessed to the shooting of your sister, Kim—"

"Foster sister," she cuts him off, glaring at him. Again she won't even utter her name. I think back to when she wouldn't talk about the incident when I brought it up years ago. I had assumed it was too painful; now I think otherwise. I get the impression that she's not even using the girl's name because she can't stand the sound of it. Plus, if I remember correctly, when I looked up the incident, Rose's parents *had* adopted Kim.

"It seems"—Herman clears his throat—"there are things Vince didn't explain the first time around, and time in prison has sobered him a bit, made him realize that maybe the love he had for you, the fact that he'd do anything for you, is starting to wane because you never visit him anymore. You never go when you say you will."

Rose lifts her chin again in defiance, and I can see the muscles in her arms tense as she clamps them around herself. She's angry. "That's bullshit," she says. "You can't just go off of what some criminal says."

"I can see why you'd be upset by that," Herman says. "And no-body—except Vince, that is—is accusing you of anything, but you should know that he says he has proof that you and he had a relationship before he shot your sister for you."

Rose's eyes shift, and she squirms in her chair. I can see that she's getting nervous now.

I text, *Tell her that he's in the room next door*, even though he's not.

I see Herman glance at his phone, and Rose fidgets. She knows he's getting texts and it's making her nervous. "In fact, while you were giving Detective Reynolds the silent treatment and not speaking all of this time, we brought Mr. Reiko in from Deer Lodge so that we can take his statement."

"You can't take his word over mine," she snarls at Herman, her face uglier than I've ever seen it, and I wonder how I, a trained agent of the law, could have missed this malicious side of her. Suddenly small things Emily has said to me over the years come back: *Mommy, meanie Rose was here today. Mommy, meanie Rose made me watch TV and leave her alone.* I chalked it up to little-kid talk, to the frustrations of an adult trying to deal with a toddler. I rethink Emily's nightmares and her bedwetting—how it took twice as long as the average little girl to potty-train her—and wonder what kind of an effect the ugliness I'm suddenly witnessing has had on my daughter. I had always chalked it up to Reeve's and my separation. Have I indirectly exposed her to the abuse of some kind of a sociopath or someone with a character disorder even though I thought I was providing the exact opposite of the abuse I experienced as a child?

It occurs to me that, despite my best efforts, I have perpetuated a cycle of abuse. I once read that abused children, especially victims of sexual abuse, can unconsciously find ways to expose their own children to predators because they are inexplicably drawn to them like moths to a flame. I close my eyes and whisper to myself in my head, *Is this what you've done, Ali, to your own child?* The lump in my throat grows thicker, and I try to swallow it down. My own breathing seems loud and scratchy in the stuffy room. I try to quiet it, keeping my eyes trained on Herman and Rose.

"We're not taking his word over yours," Herman assures her. "Just covering all bases. We want to hear your perspective too. So tell me, Rose, how did you meet Vince?"

"I already told you. I never met him before."

Herman leans forward, closer to her face, and says kindly, "I really like you, Rose." He says it with heart, leaning toward her like he might reach out and place a hand on her shoulder. Of course he doesn't, but it's working, because she's leaning slightly toward him too. "You're so great with Emily, and I love Emily. I don't want to see anything happen to you because I know Emily would be devastated if anything happened to you, so please, please help me out here by telling the truth."

I see Rose's eyes begin to water, and I realize Herman is trying a theme, and that theme happens to be my daughter, and it's striking a chord.

Rose's forehead crinkles in lines of confusion, her eyes pooling with tears. "Of course. Of course. I *love* Emily," she says, and her face flushes with emotion and looks beautiful again, the evil evaporated just like that at the mention of my daughter's name. Rose does care deeply for my little girl, I think. That's a relief, but I'm still reeling. Rose may love my daughter, but she's guilty. She's not right. This I now know.

"What has he told you?" Rose asks.

"I can't tell you that, you understand. But I can tell you that he has a photo of the two of you. He showed it to Anne Marie Johnson, even gave it to her."

A faint smile curves onto Rose's mouth.

"Why is she suddenly smug?" I ask the room.

"Because," Brander answers, "we couldn't find the photo. We think she could have taken it from the bag Anne Marie was carrying into the cabin, to obliterate the proof that she knew Reiko before he broke into her family's home. She probably thinks we can't prove he has a picture because she knows she has it. Probably already burned it or flushed it down the toilet herself. But," Brander says, "even though Reiko is definitely not the brightest bulb in the package, he was smart enough to have one of the guards make him a copy."

"Does Herman know?" I ask.

"Yes, he knows."

I look back to them. Herman is saying something to her, his voice soft and soothing. "Rose, there's a copy of the photo of the two of you. I can show it to you if you'd like."

Her face goes soft again, and she instantly looks like a little girl who's afraid, who has suddenly understood that she's in trouble. "Prison," Herman says, "is a tough place, and it's going to be in your best interest to cooperate with me, because if you don't, I can't protect you, Rose." His voice is gentle, coaxing. He's playing the safe uncle or father role. "Sentences go higher, and I know you don't want that. *I* don't want what's happened to Vince Reiko to happen to you, Rose. Cooperation goes a long way in a situation like this. The only way I can help you is if you tell me what happened."

Tears are falling down her cheeks now. She's breaking, I think, under the soothing, fatherly touch of Herman's voice. Asking for Herman, someone she knows, was the worst thing she could have done. If she'd stayed in no-comment mode with Reynolds and asked for an attorney, she would have been much better off. I can see Toni doing the same, how one minute she was a raging monster, coming at me with a vase because I wouldn't give her money I'd made in tips the week before at the restaurant I worked at, and the next, breaking into tears when I spoke softly to her, saying how sorry she was, how she would never want to hurt me, admitting to every wrong she'd ever done.

I hold back on my own tears, try to keep them from coming. I hate Rose right now, but another part of me wants to hug her, to soothe her and fill the void in her that I recognize—the same hole that's in Toni, that's in me, that's in Reeve—the one I refuse to let take root and grow in Emily. But now, in spite of all my efforts, she's going to be losing her second mommy, her best friend, because if I'm sure of one thing, it's that this woman killed Anne Marie Johnson.

"Rose," Herman says so softly, I can barely hear him, "we know you didn't get the rifle from Reeve that night. You had no time alone with him. It doesn't add up."

She looks down at her hands in her lap, then draws in a shaky breath and places her face in her palms.

"Rose," Herman presses on, "how did you get the rifle?"

She lowers her hands, her face contorted with pain.

"Did you get it the day you borrowed his truck?"

She stares at him for a moment and shrugs, blithe like a teenager, but her eyes are large and frightened looking, fixed on Herman, like she understands there's no good way out of this anymore and he's her only savior.

"Rose?" Herman says, "did you take it from him?"

She finally nods.

"Can you say it, Rose? Can you say it out loud so we have the proof that you're cooperating?"

"Yes," she says, her voice firmer than I expected, but secrets are difficult to keep. That's why they're always getting shared, why gossip is rampant with human beings, because it's very tough to keep something to yourself for any period of time, even if it's something incriminating. Get the right person in the room with a criminal and you can get them to share, just from the sheer relief of the spilling of the beans, letting someone who is asking know not just that it went down but how it went down. She's been able to keep the secret about her part in her sister's murder for seven years, but she didn't do the deed. She was the Lady Macbeth of that murder. But this time, if she pulled the trigger, that's a different beast—the kind that sprouts poisonous roots through your being. I think of the dark bags under her eyes during the last week, of her saying she was sick—some twenty-four-hour bug—and I realize she wasn't sick. She just wasn't coping. She was exhausted. The difference between a sociopath and a screwed-up person who kills is that the prior can go home and still cope, still get some sleep, even get off on the act; the latter can't. Someone like Rose wouldn't be able to manage for very long after taking another person's life with her own hands.

"I got it the day I borrowed the truck," she finally says. "The key was on the key chain. I just opened it and took it. I knew he'd never even know it was missing. He never uses it. I only took it because I wanted something to scare her with. That's all. I just wanted her to know I meant business and I wanted her to give me that photo back. To tell her not to print any information that Vince might have given her."

"What kind of information might Vince have given her?"

She shakes her head and hugs herself. "I don't know."

"Rose." Herman shifts in his seat, then leans in closer to her. He doesn't want this momentum to stop, for her to clam up. "Maybe I'm just a softy, Rose, but I gotta think that you'd do anything to protect all that you have with Emily after you've already done so much for her. You're so important to her. I can understand how you would want to protect what you've created. Is that what you've done, Rose? Protected Emily?"

Flattery mixed with some faith and an out. It was a stretch, because she was most certainly not protecting Emily, but I can see in the contortions of her face that it's registering, that she's thinking it's true.

"Rose, what might Vince have told Anne Marie besides the fact that you knew him?"

Tears are running down her cheeks now. "That we dated. That I hated Kimmie," she whispers. "That something needed to be done about her."

"What needed to be done?"

Rose moves her head in little angry shakes, as if she's tired of the fact that nobody has understood her situation, even after all of this time. "She stole things, Herman. *My* things." She places her hand on her chest. It's a good sign that she's using his first name. She could have transported herself to a kitchen, a backyard, anywhere safe at this point, because all she is seeing is Herman—kind, loving Herman. The walls of the interrogation room have faded from her vision. "And later," she continues, "she'd lie to my parents about it. They'd always believe her over me. I'd find my own clothes in her room and show them to my mother, and she'd pooh-pooh it, like it was no big deal, that sisters will be sisters. But we *weren't* sisters. Not even close. She was so manipulative and no one cared."

"That's what Vince said, that he was protecting you. That he loved you. That he would have kept the secret that you put him up to it forever if you'd simply visited him in prison more, if you'd have written him back."

"Vince." She sighs. "Why can't he just move on? I don't love him. I don't care about him."

"But something needed to be done, Rose, right?"

"Right."

"What needed to be done?"

"We needed her out of our lives. Don't you understand? My parents should never have adopted her." Deep lines cross her forehead, and suddenly she looks years older than she is. Her voice is higher-pitched and more desperate, as if she's begging for something. "But they just couldn't see it, no matter what I told them."

"Rose, did you ask Vince to shoot Kimmie?" It's so low, I almost don't hear it. I lean forward, my arms around my waist, straining to hear him.

Herman sits still, waiting for more. His back is to me, but I know his wide-eyed look of empathy and know he's giving it to Rose. It says, *Tell me your secrets and you will have my sympathy, my full embrace.* It's the best tool an interviewer has—compassion. Herman's warm, liquid eyes are only one tiny step away from a sweeping hug of acceptance. Often interviewing is simply a game of patience, waiting for the other to speak, but coupled with empathy, it can seduce the darkest secrets from the tightest vaults. And once the telling begins, it has its own force, like a stream from melting snowpack gaining in momentum— water murky with the debris of ugly justifications, self-disgust, and delusion.

"She took all the attention, all the time. You don't understand how awful it was, to have this stranger come into your life because your parents think they're so damn righteous and need to help the world. She took advantage of all of us. She stole my stuff all the time and acted all innocent. People would go on and on and on about her—how beautiful and exotic she was, how brave she was to go through foster care. She was a liar and a manipulator, but no one could see it. My parents said, 'Be compassionate! Be patient with her. This girl needs our help, blah blah blah . . . '" Rose makes her voice prudish, imitating her mother: "'You'll see,' my mom told me, 'it will all work out.'" But it didn't. It just got worse. The lying, the stealing. And you know what my parents did?" She looks at Herman dumbfounded, her palm out, and Herman nods her on. "They adopted her. Can you believe that? That was their solution to the problem. 'We need to make her feel more loved, not less,' my mom said. And then the final straw: she slept with my boyfriend Michael. She slept with Michael. I finally had someone, and she took him from me. Just like that." Rose snaps her fingers.

"I can understand how incredibly frustrating that would be," Herman says to egg her on, probably before she can realize how whiny she sounds.

"It was sickening, all the never-ending attention, all the overcompensating my parents did to make themselves feel better. So self-righteous, like they'd atoned for all of their sins in life through that one act of adoption. It was completely out of control," she says, folding her arms over her chest. "So yeah, like I said, something needed to be done."

"So you asked Vince to break in when she was home sick?"

"I had to," she says. "There was no other option."

We all exhale. It's not a full confession, but he's getting close. I'm listening so intently that I don't realize tears are streaming down my cheeks. I never cry, but I'm reacting now to the shock of it all, to the idea that Rose—a girl, a young woman whom I care deeply about—was vengeful enough at the age of seventeen to orchestrate the murder of an adopted teen and to kill a journalist to cover it up years later. All this time I've been guarding myself from bad relationships with men, including the father of my child, building thick, impenetrable walls to protect me from my own voids, and in the meantime, I've been developing the most dangerous relationship possible. I wipe a tear away with the butt of my hand and steal a glance at Shackley. He stands up, his eyes trained on me, like he's been watching me the entire time and not the interview. He motions with his thumb to the door. "Come with me," he mouths.

I stand up, straighten my blazer, and follow him out.

He takes me to one of the vacant offices, sits me down, and gets me a glass of water. "How are you holding up?" he asks.

"Just fine, sir," I say.

"You look pretty shaken."

"It's been a strange day, to say the least."

"A strange week from what I hear. Listen, I'm not going to scold you now, not after you practically ended up solving this case on your own. Plus, I know this must be extremely emotional for you. Still, I have to do my job. I have to tell you that you crossed professional boundaries. You weren't honest with the local authorities, jeopardizing our standing with them and in some ways obstructing their investigation."

"I understand," I say. I don't have the energy to make any more excuses; none of it matters now. The bottom line is that I was prepared to even lose my job if it meant I could protect Emily. "I'm willing to take whatever punishment you think I deserve, sir."

He looks at me for some time, his eyes a sharp greenish blue, his nose thin, and a hard line etched between his brows above his nose. I can't read him, and I have no idea what lies ahead for me. If I lose my job, so be it. It will be a while before I can even find someone new to babysit Emily.

"Yes," Shackley says, "I have to report this to OPR, but I'll explain the special circumstances and make clear that you actually solved the crime while they had a BOLO out on your ex. This will be more of a hand-slapping than anything. Consider it a warning. But I don't expect you'll ever cross these lines again."

"No, sir," I say.

"Agent Paige," he says, "go home and get some sleep. Let them handle the rest here tonight. You're off duty."

"But I need to—" He raises a hand to stop me.

"No, it's time to leave this one to Agent Marcus and the county. We'll fill you in when it's over."

I nod, then stand reluctantly. "Please thank Agent Marcus for me; he was incredible in there." I gesture in the direction of the interview room, where I know he still sits with Rose, trying to bang out the remaining details as she confesses to everything. I walk down the hallway to the room I left my coat in and put it on. I take another hallway leading to the reception area, say good night to the woman on the night shift, and head for the large glass doors. I push one open, feeling like I'm coming down from a bad high.

The violent wind whips my hair across my face. I swipe at the strands, trying to hold them back as I march to my car. I feel like I'm sliding someplace I've never been. Maybe it's the fatigue, but my entire being feels like jelly. I still feel anger—at myself, at Rose, at my mom and my dad for not teaching Toni and me better boundaries—but I feel a rawness too.

I open the car and hop in. The upholstery is cold and so is the steering wheel. I turn the ignition and wait for the heat to kick in. A memory from the past summer comes to mind. It was July and all the windows were open. The warm air filtered in, carrying the scent of lilacs and freshly mowed grass from the neighbor's yard. Emily was bored, so I suggested we walk out to get the mail. From the box at the curb, I let her pull out the stack. She grabbed the pile of bills and junk mail. On the top of the stack lay a bright blue flyer with large block letters in white that read: *You've won a million dollars!*

Emily had been learning to read and she stopped and studied the text. She started jumping up and down. "Mommy, we've won a million dollars! Look, look. It says we've won a million dollars!" Her smile was bright and magnificent, her eyes shining with sheer joy. It broke my heart and nearly took my breath away—that kind of innocence, that kind of faith in the world. I stood for a moment on the hot pavement, wondering how to explain to her that we really hadn't won anything. That it was advertising, which is a type of lie. *The world lies to you, sweetie, the world can be a very bad place* rang in my head, although I knew I would never say those words to her. I watched the joy leak from her face and her eyebrows draw together in confusion as I chose my words carefully to explain that we hadn't really won anything at all unless we jumped through a bunch of hoops and even then, even if we did that, the chances were very, very slim that we would win the money.

My mind moves to my mother, tired and scared, unwilling to take a stand against my drunk, drugged-up father—her weakness reinforced by him and spreading inside her so that she could barely make any decisions when it came to raising the two of us. I think of my sister, of her little spirit crushed by life with a deadbeat angry dad who had all sorts of demons of his own. I think of how she learned to cope by manipulating and lying to get a substance that could fill her black hole. I think of Reeve and what happened to him. How he pays for it every day of his life.

And last, I think of me. I don't feel sorry for myself. I'm someone who makes the best of things, and I realize as I reach for the door handle on my car that I will go to Kaylee's house in the morning because it's too late now, and I will get my daughter and hug her tightly. I will get up tomorrow and cope. I will find someone—not a perfect person, but a decent person—to help me with my daughter so that I can continue to do what's important to me.

Reeve

I HEAR HIM CALLING to me, and strangely enough, I smell the salt of the ocean. I'm back in Florida with my family, staying in the small cabin we sometimes rented on Sanibel Island. It all feels expectantly familiar, like it's home, the coconut smell of Coppertone, the briny scent of barnacles on the piers, the bright red and pink of the rhododendrons outside the cabin, the black mangroves that line the island, and the feel of soft, sandy seaweed and thin shells crushed by unthinkable ocean forces under my feet and sticking to my thin, pale ankles. There's an unbearable layer of lightness—of unawareness and innocence—laced into the bright sunshine scintillating on the channel by our cabin.

My dad had said I should wait for him before I cross the narrow passage to the bay on the other side where we intend to cast our lines for bass. But I'm eager to fish the other side and the water looks calm and easily crossable. I can barely wait to feel the tug of a prize catch. I'm positive I'm going to get the first bite this time and that I'll proudly show my dad the glimmering fish on the end of my line. I wade in, feeling the refreshing Gulf water on my legs, and begin to swim. My dad has the gear and is coming down the path soon enough.

It doesn't take long before I can feel the strength of the tide pulling against me. I pump my arms, trying to make headway to the sandy shore on the other side, but I'm not moving any closer to it. If anything, the distance is widening, and I'm being pulled toward the main channel. My dad yells at me from the shore, but I can't hear what he's saying.

The water has strong tentacles that drag me against my will. Real terror rears through me for the first time in my eight years of life—the sense that reality is a dark, gaping mouth with sharp teeth that can chew you up in an instant. Salt water sloshes into my nose and mouth. I choke and spit it out. It splashes into my eyes, and I slap at my face and wipe my eyes, at the sting of it, then realize if I don't use my arms to swim, I'll be swept farther out. I frantically go back to cycling my arms through the water, fighting against the thick and powerful churning blackness surrounding me.

"Reeve," my dad calls me. "This way, this way!" I turn to see him coming for me. He swims with the tide, reaching me quickly. He pulls my life vest toward him. Relief comes like a sweeping sensation, as powerful as the tide itself. I reach for him and miss, then reach again and grab onto his arm with every ounce of strength in me. He gets ahold of my life vest and yanks me in, my small body pulling into him. "Grab around my neck," he tells me, and I do, hanging on so fiercely that I make him choke and feel him grab my arms and pull them slightly lower, away from his windpipe. I still hang on to his slippery neck with everything I've got as he swims us safely to shore and he pulls me onto the warm sand. I lay on the ground looking up at the sky, at the palm trees in the distance.

Except the ground is not warm and sandy soft. It's rock hard and cold and they are not palm trees I'm seeing as I open my eyes; they are skinny lodgepole pines, their tall spires reaching up very high against a pale blue sky. Through blurry vision, beyond the tree spires, I see mountain ridges poke into the edges of my vision. I also see my own breath puff in small plumes above me and hear a low, persistent growl. McKay. His warm body presses into my side. I also think I hear a human's voice.

I try to prop myself up on my elbow, but I can't make it happen. I'm too weak. I'm shivering even though McKay's warm hip jabs against mine. I can't even move my arms. I turn my head to look around, and as things begin to come into focus, there's something familiar about where I am, even from the vantage point of lying prone on the ground.

My pack is next to me, and I'm unsure how and when I took it off. I must have gotten my sleeping bag out and crawled into it. Part of it is pinned under McKay.

A logging road spans the far end of a snow-dusted field, and I see a dark object in the distance. A truck. My Toyota. It dawns on me that I've given up and collapsed in the dark with the poor visibility of the snowstorm only a hundred yards away from my own vehicle. Someone is near it, though, moving around it. I squint through frosted or maybe blood-hardened eyelashes to see an official-looking person in uniform, a police officer. He's looking around, peeking into my truck windows.

I try to open my mouth, to call for help, but my face feels hot and numb at the same time. Every fiber in my body aches and burns. I try to use my voice again, to yell for help, but I'm not sure if I've said anything at all. He doesn't look my way. I try to call out again, louder this time, but still, I can't hear anything. It's like being in a dream and screaming to someone, every part of me willing my voice to be heard, but on some level of consciousness, I know that that call isn't breaking into the fabric of the real world.

The officer backs away from my truck, lifts his radio to his mouth, and begins to talk into it when his eyes scan the field and fall upon me. I see him lower his radio and come slowly toward us, his head cocked in curiosity. McKay sits up, and the sleeping bag falls away from his body and lets cold air filter in. A bigger, more aggressive growl emanates from his throat.

"Whoa." The officer holds up his hand as he approaches. "It's okay, pooch."

"It's okay," I try to tell him too, but it's only a mumble, and I'm still not sure McKay hears me. I'm not sure *I've* heard me.

He takes another step to test McKay out, to see if he will react. McKay growls again.

"I can help you," he says, taking another step forward, holding his hand out for McKay to sniff. McKay isn't happy. I'm on the ground, and he's not going to let anyone near me. He begins to snarl louder.

The man backs away, pulling up his radio again to his mouth. I can't hear all that he's saying, but catch some words and phrases. "Officer Harris here . . . situation . . . North Fork . . . might need . . . services. Stand by."

"It's okay, McKay," I say, and McKay must hear me because he noses my face, licking my cheek and whimpering. I squeeze my eyes shut with the sting of his hot tongue on my cuts. The officer must have heard too because he takes a step toward me again, calling my dog's name. "McKay? Is that your name? McKay, it's okay, buddy." He crouches down so McKay isn't so threatened by him. His brow knits together with concern when he looks over McKay's head at me lying on the ground, snow covering our sleeping bag. My bandages, which I know have torn to shreds in places, feel like they're hanging loose around my head. The sleeping bag covers my legs and arms still, even though it slid down when McKay crawled out and stood up.

The man holds out his hand, and McKay stretches his neck and sniffs his fingers, then begins to wag his tail.

"Good doggie, that's it. I'm here to help." He scoots a little closer to me.

"Are you the owner of this truck?"

My vision goes from blurry to clear, then back to blurry. My body is shivering, but my head feels as if the storm from the night before is still raging inside it, the force of a blazing hot Florida sun beating against my temples. I must be getting sick because I've been shivering most of the night in spite of McKay's heat, although we *are* lying in snow. Then the bear flashes into my mind so forcefully, I flinch. It comes to me. I don't just have a fever, I've been pounded and bitten on the head by the force of a four-hundred-pound animal. I try to scurry away. "Where is she? Where is she?"

"It's okay." He holds up his palms. "It's okay. Stay still. It's going to be all right. You're safe now. Are you having any difficulty breathing?"

"My chest . . ."

He studies me, perplexed. "Your lungs? Are you short of breath?"

"No."

"Okay, good. You're going to be okay. A grizzly do this to you?"

I manage a nod.

"Here?"

"No, high. Up."

"This morning?"

"Yesterday. We hiked," I manage to say.

"Okay. Just stay here. I'm calling for help." He stands, raises his radio again, and begins to report. "Grizzly-attack victim. Victim hiked out, so I don't think there are broken femurs, but he has got puncture wounds and severe lacerations. Breathing seems okay, but he's light-headed and having trouble speaking. He's shaking, but it's cold out. He and his dog have been out in the cold for a while, but he could have a fever. He could be going into shock, and he might be on the verge of losing consciousness. There's enough space here for the helicopter." He continues to rattle off instructions on how to find us. Then he swivels back to me and crouches again. I've never been so glad to see another person.

"Can you stand?" he asks. "I want to get you to my vehicle where it's warm. Do you think if I help you, you have enough strength to get to my vehicle?"

The thought of moving terrifies me. I want to stay perfectly still so my pounding head doesn't explode anymore. I don't answer him.

"Do you know your name?"

"Reeve," I whisper.

"Do you know your name?" he repeats, and I realize he has not heard me, that my voice is fading again. "Are you Reeve Landon?" he asks.

I try to give a single nod, but I wince from the pain.

"Okay, so you're the owner of this truck?"

"Yes."

"Hello, Reeve. I'm Park Police Officer Monty Harris. The county asked me to swing by since I was out this way checking on a few things on the northwest end of Glacier Park. They wanted me to see if your truck was still here, see if you'd decided to come out on account of the storm. Guess it took more than the storm to get you out, eh?" He continues to inspect my wounds, places his palm on my forehead. "A grizzly, huh?"

"Mama," I say, but again I can't tell if anything is escaping my lips or if I'm only imagining talking. "Wasn't her fault. Protecting cubs," I mumble.

"Rarely is," Officer Harris says, and I realize he's heard me. "If they're startled, their first defense is often offense. Come on, let's get you someplace warm. Someplace drier than this." He slowly unzips my bag, lifts the flap, and inspects me. McKay noses my arm, then my leg as the officer unfolds the top flap of the bag. "Come on, McKay," he says, pulling McKay back by his collar. When he sees my limbs, more concern crosses his face, and he pauses to think.

"So you hiked down after it happened? After you bandaged yourself?"

"Yes," I say, but it sounds like a hiss, like *esss*.

"I know this is going to be painful, but I really think we should get you into the car." He gently hooks his arm underneath mine and hoists me up. A crushing pain shoots through my head and my ribs explode in agony. I cry out.

"We're good. We'll take it slow." He takes one step.

I follow. My entire body has gone stiff, and it's hard to take a step with even my good leg. My bad leg barely moves at all, but I manage to push it forward. "That's it. Let's get you warmed up. You've made it this far," he coaxes me. "We're almost there."

Ali

Present—Wednesday

THE NEXT MORNING, I wake up groggy until the reality of the night before hits me and questions come flooding back into my mind. I wonder whether Rose has confessed to killing Anne Marie, if they've arrested her, if she's gotten an attorney. I also ache for Emily, to put my arms around her, but know she was better off sleeping through the night at Kaylee's rather than having me pick her up.

After I left the county building and went home, I couldn't sleep. I called Reeve, but again his phone went to voicemail and the automated voice informed me that his mailbox was full. I paced and paced. I made myself toast, but couldn't eat it. I wasn't hungry. I felt confused, my head pounding with questions and complicated imaginings about Rose, about how the rest of the interview went, about her life and how I could have been so blind. There should have been more clues that she wasn't right, but other than a few small things—errors and moodiness any young woman might have or make—there really wasn't much that set off alarm bells. Did that make me a bad mother? And did it make me a bad agent? That I didn't detect them?

But then again, I wasn't with her as much as Emily was. The whole point of hiring Rose was so that I could work. I should have known that a background check means nothing in the scheme of things.

I couldn't sleep, but somewhere in the early morning hours, I finally drifted off. Now I go into the bathroom and look in the mirror. My eyes look colorless and swollen, and the fear and anger I feel in the pit of my stomach is temporarily overlain by a film of groggy numbness. I splash water over my face, hoping it will make me feel alive again, and when I'm drying it with a hand towel, my doorbell rings.

My heart speeds instantly, shattering the grogginess. I run into my room and grab a sweater and head down the stairs. I see Herman through the glass. He's holding two to-go cups with lids. My pulse slows down and I feel myself soften when I see he's brought me coffee. I open the door, letting the crisp air filter in and wash over me. I step to the side to let him enter.

"Americano?" He hands me the cup.

"Thank you." I want to say more. I would like to tell him how important it is to me that he's brought me a cup in the first place. What it means to me to simply see him taking the time to swing by and fill me in, but my throat thickens and I don't. I wave him to the living room and follow him in. He takes off his overcoat and begins to fold it neatly over the back of the sofa.

"Would you like for me to hang that up?" I hold out my hand, and I realize it's trembling. I pull it back in and hug myself.

"No, it's fine here. Don't bother." He takes a seat on the couch, and I sit kitty-corner to him in the easy chair.

"How are you holding up?"

"Okay."

"When did you leave? Shackley told me that he asked you to go about halfway through the interview."

"I left when she was talking about Kimmie. Justifying her actions, saying that something needed to be done about her. How much did you end up getting from her?" I look down, as if I'm embarrassed. A part of me is self-conscious. Rose has been like family—there's no denying it—and I should have known something. I shouldn't have been so trusting.

"Everything."

"Everything?" I look up. "Without an attorney present?"

Herman takes a slow sip of his coffee, then sets it on the table. "She didn't request one. It was like she wanted to unload, to pass the burden on finally. I think she thought she could handle it all, but actually kill-ing someone was harder than she thought it would be. As each day passed, she felt worse and worse."

"She flat-out admitted to shooting Anne Marie?"

"Yep. Anne Marie had called her weeks before to discuss the shoot-ing that took place in her home when she was a teenager." Herman pauses.

"And?" I want to hear the details. I need to know how it all hap-pened so I can begin to try to make sense of it, if that's possible.

"She refused to talk to her then. Said she didn't know him other than through the trial. But when Anne Marie got to town on Monday, last week, she came to see her, after she had already picked Emily up from school."

"And Reeve's rifle?"

"She took it out of the locked case in the back of the truck the day her car was in the shop, on Tuesday, the day after Anne Marie came to see her. She said she took it just in case, in order to have something to scare the journalist with in case she didn't understand."

"Understand what?"

Herman sighs. "Who knows. Whatever lies she wanted Anne Marie to buy—her rationalizations for her pact with Vince Reiko. So she brought Reeve's rifle here and hid it in her apartment. She knew he probably wouldn't even realize it was missing since he kept it at the bottom of the storage cabinet, underneath a bunch of his other sup-plies. She had planned to return it to him and actually tried, the night he was here, on Thursday, but it was locked, and she didn't have the keys this time."

Suddenly I recall how Rose leaned over Reeve's backpack where he had placed it in the kitchen next to the back door. I thought she was moving it so no one would trip over it, but now I realize she was prob-ably searching for his keys. They weren't in his pack, though. He keeps them in his pants pocket. "But how did she know where Anne Marie was staying?"

"When Anne Marie came to see her the first time, on Monday, Rose cut the interview short when she realized what was going on. Anne Marie told her she had a photo of her and Reiko together and Rose told her to leave. She said it wasn't a good time because she was taking care of Emily."

I feel a pang of deep sorrow at the mention of Emily. Was she protecting Emily or simply using her as an excuse to get rid of Anne Marie?

"So Anne Marie asked her for another meeting when she was leaving," Herman says. "And Rose began to reconsider—figured it was best if she cooperated and kept her on her good side. Rose said she could talk on Wednesday, when her car wasn't in the shop, that she could meet her somewhere. But Anne Marie said she couldn't on that day because she had plans to stay at a friend's cabin in the North Fork and spend the day out in the woods with a dog handler who works up that way."

"But how did Rose know where Vivian lived?"

Herman continues to fill me in, slowly drinking his coffee and taking his time explaining all of the details. When his cup is empty and we're done talking, he leans back as if he's exhausted too. I thank him for going through it all with me and praise him for his fantastic work in the interrogation room.

"It wasn't that hard." He waves it off. "She's young. Manipulative and calculating, yes, but immature and frightened by her own actions. She didn't think it all through very clearly. Shooting Anne Marie was impulsive—a half-baked plan. In the long run, she wasn't going to be able to live with the fact that she had killed her. She was struggling to contain it all, and once she got started, it all came pouring out. You know how it goes, Ali, we've seen this so many times before."

"I know. It's just . . . it's just so . . ." I close my eyes and feel the sting of my lids. I can't find any words because I don't exactly know what I want to say—that it's unfair, that it's so crazy, that it's unbelievable, that it hurts . . . When I open them, I look around the room as if the walls and floor hold the answers for how to deal with all of it. I look out the window at the pale blue sky above, then turn to Herman the same way, as if in his intelligent eyes, he's got better answers for me, better explanations for why Rose did such a terrible thing. An empty sadness weighs me down, as if I won't be able to move from my chair. He must see the pain in my expression because he scoots to the edge of the couch, leans toward me, and reaches over with one large hand. He places it on top of my arm resting on the armchair. The warmth of his palm goes through my sweater sleeve and radiates up my arm. That warmth—it's what Rose wanted too during the interrogation, from her parents. It's what we all want.

"Herman," I say, "I'm so sorry for all of the running around behind your back. For snooping around."

"Hey," he said, "you did help us out in the end."

"Were they onto her at all?"

"They traced Anne Marie's calls to Rose. But when Brander questioned her, she said Anne Marie just asked her about gun violence and its aftereffects in her household. Beyond that, they didn't have any further reason to suspect Rose until you called after she'd run."

"I should have noticed things much earlier. I mean, she was under my roof, Herman. All this time."

"There was no way to know. She doesn't live with you, Ali. She watches Emily when you're away. You don't keep tabs on her personal life. Why would you?"

"I should have picked up on signs, clues, that—you know, that she had issues."

"You probably didn't want to get too close to her. After all, she was your employee."

"But she was like family to us," I say. Just yesterday, Emily's world was safe. I had thought it was safe: school, home, ballet, unicorns, teacher, nanny. It's outside the circle that parents worry about—the featureless predator in the dark alley, the Peeping Tom on the corner, the child abductor at the fair. But I know from my work that so often it's the inside circle that's the most harmful. I know that, and still, I let it happen under my own roof.

I can't help but think that with Rose, it wasn't just that I was being professional. It was also that I didn't dig deep, didn't ask about her parents, her murdered sister, and her life all that much because I didn't want to let her in, let myself get too close, not because I sensed anything off about her, but because that's who I've become—someone who doesn't let people in. If I'd let Rose in—if I'd really gotten to know her, really listened to her—would I have helped prevent the death of Anne Marie? Would I now feel any less hurt than I already do?

"I better get going." Herman slaps the tops of his knees, like he's giddying himself up to get on with the day. "Still lots of work to do on this." He looks like he's going to stand, but then he pauses on the edge of his chair like he's waiting for me to say something. I know I should address how I've behaved.

"Herman," I say slowly.

He waits for me to continue.

It's not easy for me to ask, but I swallow and slowly say it: "Do you feel like you can no longer trust me? Because of the way I've been acting, because of what I've done?"

"I don't know. Your instincts were right, and I get that you were in a tough position."

He hasn't let me off the hook, I realize, and I'm not sure what else I can say to change that. I need to give him some time. "Thank you again for the coffee."

"You're welcome," he says. "Will you be speaking to Shackley again today?"

"Not that I'm aware of. He said OPR will be looking into it." I check the time and see it's still early. "I'm going to get Emily at Kaylee's and take her to school."

Herman's mouth turns down, registering sadness. "Are you going to tell her?"

"Not today. But, yes, eventually I'll have to tell her that we need to hire someone else."

Herman breaks a smile.

"What?" I ask.

"Don't know, just glad to hear you say you'll need someone else."

"Why?"

"You know why."

I manage a smile back, lean over, and give him a hug. The sting of his not trusting me eases for now. "Thank you, Herman. If they don't fire me, I'm not going anywhere. It will take more than losing my nanny for you to get me out of our office."

Reeve

AFTER A SLOW, painful walk to Officer Harris's SUV, he helped me inside and blasted the heat. As the car began to warm, I started to shake uncontrollably under the blanket he'd given me. I tried to calm the chattering of my teeth, but they wouldn't stop pounding against one another and making an awful prattling sound. I closed my eyes and gave in to the chattering and the pain that made its way back into every part of my body. "That chattering could be a good thing," the officer told me. "Means you're alive, which makes you one lucky son of a bitch."

And that's what they're all saying now in the hospital. I've been sleeping under layers of heated blankets, and when I open my eyes, I'm surrounded by crisp white walls, a large sunlit window, and a nurse with hazel eyes. I'm barely awake, but she clamps a monitor over my finger and takes my pulse. Then she takes my temperature and writes it in a chart and moves aside for a man in regular clothes who has moved next to me. He's grinning. "You are one lucky man! How are you feeling?" He waits for only a second for a reply.

I'm too tired to say anything, so I just stare at him through half-closed eyes. "Painkillers have kicked in, I see." He smiles at me again, as if he's a giddy kid. He's not, though. His hair is gray by his temples and he has fine lines around his eyes and deeper ones on his forehead. "I'll repeat this for you again later," he says, "but I'll tell you that we've got your wounds cleaned and irrigated. And for now we're letting them drain because of possible infection. We've got you on a broad-spectrum

336

antibiotic. As far as your fever, you should feel much better soon. It's already coming down. The cultures from your wounds have been sent to the lab, and we should get the results soon. In the meantime, your CT scan came back normal, and other than several broken ribs and a torn ligament and muscle in your right leg, you're quite good. Like I said, you're very fortunate." He grins again, and I think his smile is some kind of a salute to me—because I'm lucky, as he says.

"We've got a team of doctors put together," he continues. "If it's okay with you, an orthopedic surgeon will need to repair your leg, and an ENT and a plastic surgeon are going to need to take a look at your face and your left ear. We'd like to take you to surgery as soon as your fever comes down, but we'll discuss this in more detail when you're ready."

I want to reply, but my eyelids feel thick and heavy. His voice begins to fade, and I slip back toward sleep. I feel his hand pat my arm as I begin to drift off, and I want to reach out because it feels good to be touched so lightly, so caringly, but my arm feels stuck. I hear his footsteps go to the door.

"Wait," I force myself to say against the possessive slumber.

He comes back to my side.

"McKay?"

"Sorry?"

"My dog?"

"Ah yes, your lucky dog. Thank goodness you had him to keep you warm. You owe a lot to that dog."

Don't I know it, I think, more than you will ever know.

"He's still with the officer who found you. He kept him when they put you in the chopper. He said he was fine keeping him until you told us where you wanted him to go."

"Ali," I say, "Ali Paige. Can you see if she'll take him?"

"Sure." He gives me a closed-lip smile. "We'll do that." He taps my arm again, in the same fatherly, doctorly way. I imagine I smile back before he leaves, but I'm not sure.

I close my eyes and try to recapture the dream I woke up to in the freezing field, trying to picture only the part where my father reached his hands out to me, and I hugged his neck for dear life, held on to it to stay away from unfathomable dark depths beneath me.

I think of the adrenaline pouring through me in that dream, and in real life, sluicing through on the mountainside, powering me down it through the biting cold. I think of the ocean's awful strength and swimming against it, toward him, toward my father, but, more importantly, toward another human being. It seems to me that I have been climbing out of my own life all of these years in the Montana backwoods—away from the tragic event and all the loneliness and the chronic bitterness from my father that followed or, at the least, staying on the periphery of it. But now, in this deliciously warm bed, I realize I'm crawling my way back to the living, that I have the intensity of the mountain wind and the indefatigable tide within myself. I still see the doctor's silly smile and feel his tap on my arm, even though he's left the room. His words seem like proof of this blooming thought I have, that the will to endure is not just in the nature I traipse through each day; it's inside of me too.

Ali

Present—Wednesday

I'M ON MY way to pick Emily up from school when my phone buzzes. I pick it up and see that it's Monty Harris. Strange, I think. Monty Harris is with Glacier Park's police force.

"Officer Harris, what can I help you with?"

"Hello, Agent Paige. Well, if you really want to know, you can help me with a dog."

"A dog?"

"Yes. You up for watching Reeve Landon's dog?"

"McKay? You have McKay?" Oh god, why is McKay not with Reeve? I still haven't been able to reach him, so I've decided after getting Emily we would take a drive out to his place to check on things. I pull over onto the side of the road.

"Yes, chocolate Lab. Kind of obsessive. Wants me to play fetch with him nonstop."

"That's him all right. What's going on?"

"No one told you?"

"No, no. Harris, please, what's happened?" My heart begins to knock, sending pulses up my throat.

"Reeve is in the hospital. He's okay but he's pretty injured. A grizzly attack."

"What? You're kidding, right?"

"Agent Paige, you're the last person I'd kid with. I mean . . ." He corrects himself as if he realizes what he's said has been too on the money. "I mean, I wouldn't kid you about something like that. It was up in the North Fork, but he's okay. I found them this morning when I was asked by the county to check on his truck to see if he'd come out of the woods yet."

"How badly is he hurt?" I swallow. I'm nervous to hear the answer.

"He looks worse than he is. He's lucky he had the dog with him, to keep him from freezing. I haven't gotten the full report, but from what I could see, he's got some lacerations and puncture wounds. He's able to walk—or limp, I should say. He and the dog hiked out yesterday. I found him early this morning."

"This morning?"

"Yes. He's been recovering in KRMC all afternoon." Kalispell Regional Medical Center, one of the only two hospitals in the valley. "Can I bring you the dog?"

"I'm going to pick up my daughter now and we'll go straight to the hospital. Why don't you meet us there?"

"Sure thing," he says, and I wait for him to hang up first and watch my own screen go dull. I place the phone down on the console next to me and sit on the side of the road and look around. A skiff of snow covers everything, including each spindly branch on every tree, and it seems that the branches have gone bare overnight. The sky above is clear, and I think it's beautiful, but that beauty pushes the stinging shock of Rose further into my heart and settles deep into my bones. Monty's words—*you're the last person I'd kid with*—snake through my mind.

. . .

Emily and I find Reeve's room on the third floor, and I take that as a good sign that he's not in the intensive care unit. We stop at the nurses' station and ask if the person in room 318 is taking visitors, and her face breaks into a big smile, and I'm instantly relieved. "Why, yes, he's doing quite well. Are you family?"

The question surprises me for a second, but I'm not sure why it should. "Yes," I say. "This is Emily. His daughter."

"Oh." She smiles politely at Emily, then looks back at me. "He's no longer feverish, and he's been out of surgery for a bit now. You can go in."

"Surgery?"

"Oh, you don't know. Well, I guess it has been a little crazy around here. He was kind of out of it, as you can imagine, when the helicopter brought him in. We weren't sure who to contact. Anyway, yes, surgery for some orthopedic repairs to the muscles and ligaments in his leg and a bit of reconstruction around his left ear." She touches her own ear as if she wants to make sure hers is still intact. "Your daddy is one brave man." She looks down at Emily.

Emily giggles.

"Yes sirree. One brave man." The nurse shakes her head as if it's too much to think about, having a surprise encounter with a grizzly. Emily continues to beam. I'm relieved that this is turning out to be less frightening for her than I anticipated. When I told her in the parking lot at school after she'd gotten strapped up in her booster seat, she'd sat motionless, her eyes wide as she stared at me. I turned to face her from the driver's seat and explained it clearly. I must have used my work voice, because she didn't know how to read that, so she stayed blank, waiting to gauge how I felt before committing to any emotions on her end. "So," I said when she didn't break into a cry, didn't really respond at all, "we're going to visit him now, at the hospital. He might look a little scary, but there's nothing to be frightened of. He'll probably have bandages on him, and do you want to know what the really cool thing is?"

"What?"

"We get to keep McKay while your daddy recovers."

"Yay!" She broke into a smile. "Kay Kay!" But it felt forced, like she provided the response she thought I wanted even though she was still trying to process things.

I turned the car on then and drove straight to the hospital, peeking now and then at her in the mirror, staying quiet so she could have the time to think. She simply stared out her window, somber, as if she already had registered since she'd fired the gun the day before that something was different in her life, even though she didn't know what or how to describe any of it.

Now, before the nurse, I'm glad to see her giggle. We walk to room 318. The door is ajar, so I peek my head around and see that Reeve is lying with his eyes closed. A white bandage wraps around his head and left ear. There are also large bandages circling his arm and his upper thigh, which is elevated and has an ice machine pumping an ice bag around it. An IV snakes from his other arm.

We slowly step closer and I reach out and touch his shoulder, trying not to startle him. He opens his eyes, and when he sees me, he smiles instantly. A tenderness shoots through my heart, and I smile back. I don't do simple emotion all that well unless it's anger or the raw animal love I have for Emily. So I'm surprised my heart does a little cartwheel now. His eyes are calm and still and they remind me of Emily's. When I had her and they put her tiny body in my arms, she seemed so foreign, this alien I had carried around but was suddenly exposed to the light of day. Her eyes were placid and so calm. I had felt the cartwheel then—uncomplicated love mixed with the strangeness, with the newness of it all flooding through me.

Reeve then looks at Emily, still smiling. "Hey, chickadee," he says, the same thing I call her, and I wonder if he's heard me call her that, but it doesn't matter.

"Hi, Daddy," she says, her eyes large to see him so beaten up.

"Come around to this side," he says, and she walks around to the edge of the bed that has his good arm, leans over. He wraps her into a tight hug. "It's so good to see you. I've missed you so much."

"I've missed you too."

"How are you feeling?" I ask him.

"Better," he says. "Much better."

"You've had quite the time in the woods," I say. "It's really unbelievable."

"Yeah, everyone keeps saying how lucky I am." His voice sounds groggy.

"You are. Unlucky is getting accused of a crime you didn't commit. Lucky"—I wink—"is surviving a grizzly attack after you've gone out into the deep woods by yourself in the fall." I laugh.

"That's a good way to put it," he says. "Actually, even though every bone in my body hurts, I feel very fortunate." He reaches for Emily again and squeezes her.

I'm about to go sit in the only chair in the room when an older man comes and stands in the doorway. I recognize him immediately as Reeve's neighbor. "Mr. Wallace," I say. "Good to see you. Come in."

"Ali"—he steps into the room—"I haven't seen you in some time." He greets Emily too, then focuses on Reeve. I step away to allow him to move closer toward him. "I knew it," he exclaims. "I just knew it was you when I saw the red helicopter this morning. I had a bad feeling, so I waited and then called the hospital to ask. They wouldn't give out your name but admitted when I prodded that there'd been a bear attack. How are you?"

"I've been better," Reeve says.

"I came here anyway because I just knew. When I asked for you at the service desk, they gave me this room number. Oh my god, I just can't believe it. I can't believe it. What was it like?"

Reeve's eyes shift to Emily and he gives a small shrug.

Wallace registers that he doesn't want to go into details around her. "Okay," he says. "Later, I want to hear about this later."

"You're still here?" Reeve asks Wallace. His voice sounds crackly, as if he's parched, but I sense there's something in the topic I don't understand.

"Yep, still here," Wallace grumbles.

"Emily," I say, "I saw a children's area around the corner. Should we go ask the nurse if we can get you some coloring books? Maybe draw your daddy a unicorn?"

She looks to Reeve, and he nods. "Give me a kiss first." He points at his bandage near his ear.

"Yuck," she says. "Daddy, I can't kiss you there."

"How about here, then?" He points to one of the few unbruised clear areas of his face, below his right cheekbone. She leans over and kisses him, and we leave the room for a moment to give Wallace some time with Reeve.

Reeve

"So you knew it was me?"

"Yep, I knew."

"Could have been some elk hunter."

"I know it could, but I just had this feeling. You were up so high when I saw you, and you were heading higher. Foolish." He shakes his head.

I want to bring up the fish he was carrying again, but I don't have the energy to quibble. It's still bugging me, though, why he hasn't gone home to see his wife, to Oregon. "I've earned the right to know why you haven't gone back," I say. "It was the only thing on my mind hobbling out of those woods," I tease.

Wallace laughs. "You're relentless. Seriously, that's what you're thinking about while you lay here all broken up and stitched back together?"

I don't laugh or say anything. Not to be rude—I'm just too exhausted.

Wallace grabs the chair and slides it over beside me. "I didn't go back because I found out Susan was having an affair while I was gone. Yup, that's right, it can happen to old people too."

I can see the pain in his face despite the joke, and my heart twists with sorrow, and I do something so uncharacteristic of me that it shocks me a bit too: I reach out and grab Wallace's forearm and hold it. He freezes, unsure what to do, and then I see moisture gather at the corners of his eyes. I squeeze again, then slowly slide my hand away.

"We'll talk more when you're better," he says. "You don't want the sordid details now. I'll be here this winter," he adds. "I can help you, you know, while you heal."

"I'd appreciate that," I tell him, then close my eyes for a second. "I'll need it."

"I can see that." He stands and looks me over from head to toe. "Damn," he says. "It's unbelievable. You get some rest now."

When he leaves, Ali comes in and sets her hand on my arm, just like the doctor. "Ali," I say to her. "I'm sorry for everything. Sorry for dragging you into this mess."

She shushes me. "None of that matters now. You're no longer a suspect."

My eyes open all the way for the first time. "I'm not?"

"Nope. It's not public knowledge yet, but they've found the person who killed Anne Marie Johnson."

"They have? Who?"

"Sleep now," she says. "It's just one of those crazy things. I'll fill you in later. It's nothing for you to worry about right now. All you need to know is that you're completely off the hook. And"—she looks at me, and she seems a little scared, but I can't tell for sure—"if, well, if it's okay with you, when they release you from here, you'll come home with us. Okay?"

I stare at her, at her curly hair and her energetic eyes. But behind all that energy, there's a softness I haven't seen in ages. I think it's the drugs, but I can't help myself. My eyes begin to well, and I can feel a hot tear break free and roll to the bandage on my right ear. I grab her hand and hold it. I don't have anything in mind with the gesture—or anything in mind for the future. I just want to touch her. "Thank you," I say again. "Will you two stay here, just for a little while longer?"

"Of course." She smiles at me again, picks up my hand, and kisses the back of it. "Of course we will."

Ali

Present—Wednesday

I IMAGINE IT LIKE this: Rose waits outside in her car in the drive outside Vivian's cabin in the dark. She's gambled that the nosy journalist will return after spending the day with Reeve and be in the cabin by the time she arrives after dark, after I've come home from work late because Herman and I have followed a lead to Polson on the Smith case.

Rose thinks about how Anne Marie doesn't even know that Reeve Landon is the father of the little girl she babysits. Anne Marie has no clue what she's messing with. How—if she keeps digging—she could ruin Rose's life: bring attention to the law and take her away from the little girl and the job she's come to love. Or worse, land her in prison, which would rip everything normal away. She thinks, There's no way I'm going there.

She has kept her promise and visited Vince a couple of times, mainly because she realized Vince had the power to tell on her. Thus far, he'd kept his word because he adored her, and even through the trial, he had never breathed a word about her involvement with him. He had kept to the story: it was a robbery that went wrong. He was looking for goods to steal to sell for drug money, that's all. It was an easy secret to keep because that was part of the bargain. He'd get rid of Kimmie and make his girlfriend happy and get some goods to pawn off as well. Her dad had an expensive camera, a high-end television, and good golf clubs; her mom had nice jewelry, pricey artwork, quality silver, and a laptop.

Rose drives up the North Fork road after nine, after she's put Emily to bed and I've returned from Polson.

347

When she arrives at Vivian's place, it's after ten and dark. The porch light is on, but no rooms are lit inside the cabin. She wonders if Anne Marie has gone to bed. She knocks on the door to wake her up. She didn't drive all the way up the North Fork to not take care of things. She wants to speak to her, to demand that Anne Marie give her the photograph back, to warn her to quit poking around where she doesn't belong. She's borrowed Reeve's gun out of the back of his truck just in case she needs a little muscle, something to threaten her with.

She knocks several times, the rap on the door loud in the field beside the cabin and the woods out back. When all goes silent and no one comes, she turns the flashlight on and checks the side windows. She sees a travel bag with clothes spilling out of it in one of the rooms and assumes it's Anne Marie's. She checks the rest of the windows, looking for the black carrier bag Anne Marie had with her when she came to talk to her. She pulled out a notebook from it when she came to interview her and held it in her lap to take notes, then shoved it back in when she left. It would be much simpler if she could just break in and grab the bag, but she's certain the journalist has it with her. She goes back to her car. I can wait, Rose thinks, until she comes back.

She gets impatient when Anne Marie doesn't show after an hour. In fact she's angry. Maybe she's not coming back at all. Maybe she's staying somewhere else. Maybe she's with Reeve, whom she spent the day with. And that pisses Rose off even more, because there's a part of Rose that cares for Reeve because he's Emily's dad. Maybe she even likes him, or maybe she just feels sorry for him because she knows about his past, and it turns her stomach to think of the pushy journalist with him late into the evening. Rose considers driving over to Reeve's to check, but what good would that do if she sees that she's there?

No, she decides. She'll stay put. There's no other chance to see this woman. At the very least, she'll have to come back for her things, and Rose intends to get things straightened out with the annoying woman who has come out of nowhere and poked her nose in Vince Reiko's and her past. She can't leave with Anne Marie Johnson knowing her secret, knowing her past. The longer she waits, the angrier and the more stubborn she becomes.

Minutes tick by, and Rose hears an owl hooting in the side woods. She refuses to let herself think about those days when Kimmie came to live with them. About how one awful girl could enter their home and turn her life upside down. But worse than that, she doesn't want to think about how her own mother let it happen, practically encouraged it, and how her own father was too weak to stop it.

And under all of that, there's a deep prickling knowledge that she refuses to pay attention to in the deepening night, a knowledge that infuriates her more than anything else as she sits and waits. It's the understanding that, for the rest of her life, it will require a battle of sheer will to act like she is normal when, in reality, her conscience is constantly waging war in her head. She knows that she will never, ever return to whatever innocence she possessed before she had a teenage fantasy of getting rid of her sister to spite her parents and hatched a plan to embolden Vince Reiko to do something about it, and she understood that one malignant move could make her veer into an entirely different lane for the rest of her life.

She forces the thought out of her head and thinks about prison. About the two times she's visited Vince Reiko to keep up the charade that she still cared about him so he would remain loyal to her. The thought of being confined is too scary for her to handle. When she decided to stop visiting him—considering that even if he mentioned something about her to someone, it wouldn't matter anyway because no one would believe him—she had no idea that he had a photo of the two of them together. She's angry at herself that she's forgotten something so important. The stale visitation room with its skanky medicinal odor of disinfectant and the broken panel on the ceiling exposing the electric wiring above has stayed in her mind. It unsettles her that no one cared enough to fix it. It had to be ten times worse inside the actual prison quarters.

She needs that picture back, and even more, she thinks how nice it would be to shut Anne Marie Johnson up forever. She pictures Reeve's rifle and fantasizes about pulling the trigger—about how one pull could solve so many problems. And this time she'd be solving her own problems, not relying on some stupid guy. And her conscience? That's already destroyed anyway.

Before she knows it, it's going on one a.m. Rose has turned the car on a number of times to heat it up, but it's off now, and everything is quiet until she hears the sound of tires on gravel and turns to see headlights coming up the long drive. Rose stays in her car, her fists clenching. When Anne Marie drives up, she sees her turn a dark head to look at the waiting car, then pull past it and into the main parking area of the drive.

Rose steps out of her car so that Anne Marie can see her. She's holding the rifle, perhaps just for show, perhaps for more. She's not sure how this will play, but she's glad she has it as a show of strength.

"Oh, it's you," Anne Marie says. "I thought you were my friend Vivian."

Rose forces a lopsided smile through her pent-up anger.

"What are you doing here? Why do you have a gun?" Anne Marie looks scared.

"Just, you know," Rose says, "it's late out here. You never know what you're going to run into. Always good to come prepared. Plus, I thought you might want to see it, you know, for your story. Pretty sure this one here"—she cradles it in both palms, letting her hands sink and lift a little with the heft of it, not knowing Reeve well enough to know the story behind the weapon she's holding—"could be responsible for the accidental shooting of a little boy in Florida by the very guy you just spent the day in the woods with."

"Reeve?" Anne Marie asks.

"That's him."

"How do you know him?"

"It just so happens I nanny for his little girl, Emily, and when you told me about interviewing a dog handler, well, there's only one man in these parts who does that. Small world."

"Oh." Anne Marie begins to scoot a little closer toward the cabin because even she knows it's strange to run into the young woman she's just tried to question about her involvement with a previous boyfriend in jail, who shows up unannounced and carrying a rifle in the middle of the night. "And how did you know I'm staying here?" Anne Marie asks.

"You got that call from your friend when you were talking to me, remember? She gave you the address and you wrote it down on your notepad: 7900 North Fork Road."

"I see. But it's kind of late. What is it that you need?"

"I'd like for you to give me the photo that Vince gave you."

Anne Marie turns to face her straight on because she can't resist. After all, regardless of the fact that a woman is holding a rifle, she may get more information on the story she's after. And thus far in Anne Marie's life, she's been invincible, just like a fast-driving, carefree college student—the kind of person who leaves empty beer bottles on her lawn. Deep down, she doesn't believe anything bad will really ever befall her, in spite of the tragedies she writes about and reports on. "You're admitting that you do know him?"

"I didn't say that," Rose says. "I just want the photo."

"Why would I give it to you?"

"Because I'm standing here with a rifle." Rose lifts it and points it at Anne Marie. She already removed the safety when she got out of the car, just to be ready. Just in case, she told herself.

"Whoa, now." Anne Marie lifts up her hands. She has a backpack draped over one shoulder, so one of her arms doesn't lift up quite as high as the other. "Is that necessary?"

"Is it *necessary* that you come snooping around my life?" Rose snarls at her. "What makes you think any of this is *your* business?" The fury begins to spill out, the resentment at her mom, at her dad, at Kimmie, and most of all at herself for getting into something so unwise with Vince Reiko when she was a teenager. Anger at the fact that there's no turning back once you've gone down certain roads in life. "You show up acting like everyone's story is your own and that you have a right to dig up information like it belongs to you. Well, it doesn't, and I want the photo back."

Anne Marie's face looks white in the porch light and she begins to back up toward the cabin, realizing that she's not in a good situation. "Okay," she says. "Just wait out here. I'll get it. It's inside."

"No," Rose says. "I don't believe you. Where's your bag, the one you had the other day?"

"It's inside." Anne Marie takes another step backward.

And that's all it takes—just one more step. Rose pulls the trigger. Anne Marie clutches her chest immediately, her face shocked, and falls back in one swift motion. Anne Marie crumples to the ground. Rose can hear the crunch of Anne Marie's skull on one of the decorative rocks beside the porch steps.

Rose stops breathing for a second, and when she begins again, she can barely catch it because it comes too rapidly. She doesn't have time to think about what she's just done. She rushes to Anne Marie, who has been knocked unconscious, kneels down, and rummages through her backpack. She finds the notebook, opens it up, and sees some notes about Reeve and, further in, about Vince. She flips through the pages nervously, finding the photo tucked into one of the dividing manila folders in between the pages. She looks at it for only a second. It's a picture of her and Vince she'd completely forgotten about—one taken by a stranger, a fisherman passing by, she now remembers, in front of the Flathead River, a place they went to meet and hang out at. She looks so much younger in the picture, her cheeks still full of adolescence and her hair streaked naturally by the sun. She shoves it in her pocket, replaces the notebook, and runs back to her car. She throws the rifle in and drives home.

Later in her apartment behind my place, where Emily and I lie quietly in our beds, Rose doesn't get a wink of sleep. She listens to every sound in the night: the screeching tires of someone—probably invincible teenagers—out very late; the sound of cats fighting from a few houses over; dogs barking in response to the cats' yowls. She strains to hear police sirens coming in the dark, but they don't. Her thoughts spin in many directions, but she understands one thing: that although she will try to hide what she has just done so compulsively to the reporter, she will pay for it for the rest of her life. She will sneak Reeve's rifle back into the compartment in his truck the next time she gets a chance; she will visit Vince and tell him she loves him, even though she doesn't; she will try to act like nothing has happened.

No, Rose won't be able to sleep peacefully ever again, because although she is a very troubled person, she's not completely heartless. She's suddenly more acutely aware than ever before, even more than after Vince went to trial, was convicted, and went to jail for an idea that began in her own mind, that there are always consequences, that the past has the ability to lock a tight chain around you, and there's nothing to do but drag it around. And that's where she'll remain, dragging it around for a very, very long time.

Acknowledgments

Many thank-yous to the amazing team of publishing professionals at Atria, led by the revered Judith Curr. The team's hard work in seeing my novels through to publication always astounds me. I am tremendously grateful to my editor, Daniella Wexler, for her impressive editing skills; and to the Atria copy editors for catching errors and inconsistencies in the manuscript. Many thanks to David Brown for his enthusiastic help and hard work in publicity, Will Rhino for his guidance in marketing, and Chris Sergio for his fabulous design work.

My agent, Nancy Yost, always makes all the difference with her business expertise, guidance, unwavering support, and, most importantly, sense of humor. Thank you also to Sarah Younger for being so helpful.

I owe special thanks to John Cooney and Bryan Denson for all FBI-related matters and for taking the time to explain how the Bureau and its agents work. Thank you again to Frank Garner, former chief of police in Kalispell, and Commander Brandy Hinzman with the Flathead County sheriff's office for clarifying local law enforcement matters.

My appreciation is beyond words for Suzanne Siegel's friendship and all of her assistance: priceless research, reading of drafts, wise counsel, and limitless reassurance. Much gratitude to Kathy Dunnehoff, friend, plotter, author, and instructor, for all of her support and spot-on writing advice, and to the brilliant Cindy Brown, fellow mystery author, for all of her inspiration and assistance in helping to shine light on several main plot points in this book. To Janet Vandermeer, thank you for the enormous help in reading pages and for all the invaluable book-launch help.

My family is an incredible support system as I continue to find my way through the world of publishing: my husband, Jamie; my children, Mathew, Caroline, and Lexie; my parents, Robert and Jeanine Schimpff; my brothers, Cliff and Eric, and their wives, Pam and Lee Anne; my aunts, Janie Fontaine and Barbara Dulac.

I owe countless thanks to many more folks for their generous support in my journey as an author. I can't name them all, but I owe heartfelt thank-yous to Jackie Brown, Patti Spence, Ginnie Cronk, Mara Goligoski, Marian Ellison, Sarah Fajardo, and Derek and Elizabeth Vandeberg. Huge thank-yous to other supportive authors, all the extraordinary booksellers out there, book reviewers, all the amazing book clubs I've participated in, both local and afar, and of course all you wonderful readers! With each book, I continue to be overwhelmed and inspired by the encouragement I receive.

Any mention of landmarks, popular local establishments, or made-up establishments resembling actual businesses is only done to gain verisimilitude. Always, all errors, deliberate or by mistake, are wholly mine.

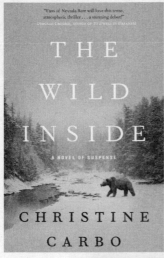
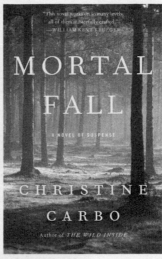
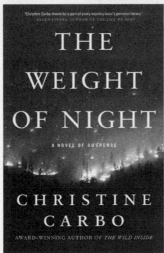